THE FIVE WOUNDS

also by KIRSTIN VALDEZ QUADE

Night at the Fiestas: Stories

THE FIVE WOUNDS

A Novel

KIRSTIN VALDEZ QUADE

W. W. NORTON & COMPANY
Independent Publishers Since 1923

This is a work of fiction. Names, characters, places, and incidents are the products of the author's imagination or are used fictitiously. Any resemblance to actual events, locales, or persons, living or dead, is entirely coincidental.

For information about permission to reproduce selections from this book, write to Permissions, W. W. Norton & Company, Inc., 500 Fifth Avenue, New York, NY 10110

For information about special discounts for bulk purchases, please contact W. W. Norton Special Sales at specialsales@wwnorton.com or 800-233-4830

Manufacturing by Lake Book Manufacturing
Production manager: Lauren Abbate

Library of Congress Cataloging-in-Publication Data

Names: Quade, Kirstin Valdez, author.
Title: The five wounds : a novel / Kirstin Valdez Quade.
Description: First edition. | New York : W. W. Norton & Company, [2021]
Identifiers: LCCN 2020030288 | ISBN 9780393242836 (hardcover) |
ISBN 9780393242843 (epub)
Subjects: LCGFT: Novels.
Classification: LCC PS3617.U25 F58 2021 | DDC 813/.6—dc23
LC record available at https://lccn.loc.gov/2020030288

W. W. Norton & Company, Inc., 500 Fifth Avenue, New York, N.Y. 10110
www.wwnorton.com

W. W. Norton & Company Ltd., 15 Carlisle Street, London W1D 3BS

1 2 3 4 5 6 7 8 9 0

For my family

Part I

SEMANA SANTA

This year Amadeo Padilla is Jesus. The hermanos have been preparing in the dirt yard behind the morada.

This is no silky-haired, rosy-cheeked, honey-eyed Jesus, no Jesus-of-the-children, Jesus-with-the-lambs. Amadeo is muscled, hair shaved close to a scalp scarred from teenage fights, roll of skin where skull meets neck.

Amadeo is building the cross out of heavy rough oak instead of pine. He's barefoot like the other hermanos, who have rolled their cuffs and sing alabados. They have washed their white pants, braided their disciplinas the old way, from the thick fibers of yucca leaves, mended rips in the black hoods they will wear to ensure their humility in this reenactment. The Hermano Mayor—Amadeo's skinny grand-tío Tíve, who surprised them all when he chose his niece's lazy son—plays the pito, and the thin piping notes rise.

Today Amadeo woke with the idea of studding the cross with nails to give it extra weight. He holds the hammer with both hands high above his head, brings it down with a crack. The boards bounce, the sound strikes off the outside wall of the morada and, across the alley, the Idle Hour Cantina.

Amadeo has broken out in a sweat. Amadeo sweats, but not usually from work. He sweats when he eats, he sweats when he drinks too much. Thirty-three years old, same as Our Lord, but Amadeo is not a man with ambition. Even his mother will tell you that, though it breaks her heart to admit it. Yolanda still cooks for him, setting a plate before him at his place at the table.

This afternoon, though, even Amadeo's tattoos seem to strain with his exertion, and he's seeing himself from outside and above. A flaming Sacred Heart beats against his left pectoral, sweat drips from the point of a bloodied dagger on his bicep, and the roses winding around his side bloom against the heat of his effort. On his back, the Guadalupana glistens brilliantly, her dress scarred with the three vertical cuts of the sellos, the secret seals of obligation. The lines, each the length of a man's hand, are raised and pink and newly healed, evidence of his initiation into the hermandad.

Though Amadeo has lived in Las Penas his whole life, today he sees the village anew: the lines are sharper, the colors purer. The weeds along the edge of the fence, the links of the fence itself, the swaying tops of the cottonwood trees—everything is in preternatural focus. The morada is lit by the sun sinking orange at his back, the line sharp between cinderblock and sky. He brings the hammer down, hitting each nail true, enjoying the oiled rotation of his joints, the fatigue in his muscles. He feels righteous and powerful, his every movement predetermined. He feels born for the role.

Then he pounds the last nail, and he's back in his body, and the hermanos are wrapping up, heading home.

———

WHEN AMADEO PULLS UP the gravel drive to the house, his daughter Angel is sitting on the steps, eight months pregnant. She lives in Española with her mom. He hasn't seen her in more than a year, but he's heard the news from his mother, who heard it from Angel.

White tank top, black bra, gold cross pointing the way to her breasts in case you happened to miss them. Belly as hard and round as an horno. The buttons of her jeans are unsnapped to make way for its fullness, and also to indicate how this happened in the first place. Her birthday is this week, falls on Good Friday. She'll be sixteen.

"Shit," Amadeo says, and yanks the parking brake. This last week was the most important week in Jesus's life. This is the week everything happened. So Amadeo's mind should be trained on sacrifice and resurrection, not his daughter's teen pregnancy.

She must not see his expression, because she gets up, smiles, and waves with both hands. The rosary swings on his rearview mirror, and Amadeo watches as, beyond it, his daughter advances on the truck, stomach outthrust. She pauses, half turns, displays her belly.

She's got a big gold purse with her, and a duffel bag, he sees, courtesy of Marlboro. Angel's hug is straight on, belly pressing into him.

"I'm fat, huh? I barely got these pants and already they're too small."

"Hey." He pats his daughter's back gingerly between her bra straps, then steps away. "What's happening?" he says. It's too casual, but he can't afford to let her think she's welcome, not during Passion Week, and with his mother away.

"Ugh. Me and Mom got in a fight, so I told her to drive me here." Her tone is light. "I didn't know where you and Gramma were. I've been here, like, two hours, starving my head off. Pregnant people need to eat. I almost broke in just to make a sandwich. Don't you guys check your phones?"

Amadeo hooks his thumbs in his pockets, looks up at the house, then back at the road. The sun is gone now, the dusk a nearly electric blue.

"A fight?" In spite of himself, Amadeo takes some pleasure in Angel's indignation at her mother. Marissa has always made him feel insufficient.

"I can't even. Whatever," she says with conviction. "What me and the baby need right now is a support system. That's what I told her."

Amadeo shakes his head. "I'm real busy," he says, like an actor portraying regret. "Now's not a good time."

Angel doesn't look hurt, just interested. "Why? You got a job or something?"

She lifts her duffel and begins to walk toward the door, swaying under the weight of luggage and belly. "My mom's not here," he calls. He's embarrassed to tell her the real reason he wants her gone, embarrassed by the fervor that being a penitente implies.

"Where'd Gramma go?" There's real worry in her voice. She holds the screen open with her hip, waiting for him to unlock the door.

"Listen, it's a busy week." He rushes this next part, his breath short. "I'm carrying the cross this year. I'm Jesus."

"Uh, okay. She'll be back soon, right?"

Yolanda took her vacation after the end of the legislative session, right before Holy Week, exactly when Amadeo needs her most. "Maybe I'll just stay out there forever," she told him lightly as she packed. "I love Vegas. The shows, the lights, the commotion."

"She didn't say when she'd be back. End of next week, probably."

Angel heaves her duffel and purse on the kitchen floor with a dramatic sigh, and only then does it occur to Amadeo that he should have carried the bags in for her. But she doesn't seem to notice. She's still talking.

"I told my mom, 'Whatever, I'm going to Gramma's, then. *She* loves me.'"

———

THAT NIGHT Angel chatters about food groups as she makes dinner—a can of chili dumped over an underdone squash and a package of frozen cheese bread—then takes over the TV. She talks to her belly. "See, baby? That heifer is going *home*. You can't be like that to your girls."

Amadeo sits at the other end of the couch, strangely nervous. He tries to remember the last time he was alone with his daughter, but can't. Two or three Christmases ago, maybe; he remembers sitting awkwardly in this same room asking Angel about her favorite subjects while Yolanda was at the grocery store or the neighbors'.

He wipes his palms along his thighs, works his tongue inside his mouth. Frozen-eyed porcelain dolls stare at Amadeo from Yolanda's corner cabinet, where they sit in their frilly dresses on shelves beside souvenir bells and shot glasses. With a sudden stitch in his gut, Amadeo thinks of Tío Tíve. What will he say about Angel being here?—the fruit of his sin, laden with sin of her own.

"So," Amadeo says. "Your mom's probably going to want you back soon, no?"

"I got to teach her she's not the only one in my life. She's got to learn to respect me."

Amadeo kneads his thigh. He can't tell her to leave. Yolanda would kill him. He just wishes his mom were here. Yolanda and Angel are pretty close; Yolanda sends the girl checks, twenty-five here, fifty there, takes her out to dinner in Española or Santa Fe, and a couple times a year the two go shopping at the outlets.

"Maybe you could come back when my mom gets home." A needle of guilt slides into his side.

Angel doesn't seem to have heard him. "I mean, the woman's all preaching to me about how I messed up and why couldn't I learn from her mistake, but what am I going to do now, huh? I mean, I *get* it: I ruined her stupid life. Fine. But if she's going to pretend she's all mature, she should actually act mature."

Amadeo should call his sister, get her to come take Angel to Albuquerque to stay with her and the girls. Saving the day—that's right up Valerie's alley. But he isn't talking to Valerie now, hasn't since Christmas.

Angel looks like her mother, the same glossy, thick hair and high color, though her features aren't as fine as Marissa's. Amadeo's genes, he supposes. Amadeo wonders if Marissa acted this young back then. Marissa was sixteen, Amadeo eighteen, but they felt old. Her parents had been angry and ashamed, but had thrown a baby shower for the young couple anyway. Amadeo had enjoyed being at the center of things: congratulated by her relatives and his, handed tamales and biscochitos on paper plates by old women who were willing to forgive everything in exchange for a church wedding. He stood to sing for them, nodding at Marissa: "This is dedicated to my baby girl." *Bendito, bendito, bendito. Los ángeles cantan y daban a Dios.* They all clapped, old ladies dabbing their eyes, Yolanda blowing kisses across the room. Amadeo had felt virtuous, responsible for his girlfriend and unborn child.

Later, of course, there was no wedding, no moving in together. Angel was born and learned to walk and talk, with no help from Amadeo. The old women shook their heads, resigned; they should have known better than to expect anything from Amadeo, from men in general. "Even the best of them aren't worth a darn," his grandmother used to say. "Except you, hijito," she'd add kindly, if she noticed Amadeo in the room. "You're worth a darn."

By the time Angel was five, he was relieved at how easily the obligation slipped from his shoulders. All it took was for him to stop answering Marissa's calls—fewer than you'd expect—and he was a free man.

As though answering a question, Angel says, "I didn't drop out of school for reals. I'm doing this whole program and I'm going to graduate and everything, so don't worry." She looks at Amadeo, expectant.

Amadeo realizes he forgot to worry, forgot even to wonder. "Good. That's good." He gets up, rubs his shorn head with both hands. "You got to have school."

She's still looking at him, demanding something: reassurance, approval. "I mean, I'm serious. I'm going to graduate." Then she's off, talking about college and success and following her dreams, echoing what she hears at the teen parenting program she attends. "Brianna, my teacher? She says I got to invest in myself if I'm going to give him a good life. You won't see me like my mom, doing the same old secretary job for ten years, just trying to snag herself an architect. I'm doing something big." She turns to her belly. "Isn't that right, hijito?"

This depresses the hell out of Amadeo. He opens a beer and guzzles half of it before he remembers who he is this week. "Fuck," he says, disgusted, and pours it down the sink.

Angel looks up at him from the couch. "You better clean up your mouth. He can hear every little thing you say."

"Fuck," says Amadeo, because it's his house, but he says it quietly, and thinks about the sound passing through his daughter's body to the child inside. He stands. "I got to go."

———

EVERY NIGHT OF LENT, the hermanos have gathered in the morada to pray the Rosary under Tío Tive's watchful eye, and every Friday they meditate on the Stations of the Cross. On their knees, heads bowed. There are nine hermanos, and, with the exception of Amadeo, they're all over seventy. Tío Tive is the oldest, eighty-seven, still going strong.

"Jesus prayed," recites Al Martinez. "Abba, Father, all things are possible to you; remove this cup from me." Amadeo likes Al. He's a chatty big guy and gets teary when he talks about this or that grand-child. Not long ago, he retired from long-haul driving, and his shoulders are rounded from a career spent leaning over a steering wheel toward a horizon.

The cinderblock walls are painted white, and a few benches face front. The only thing worth looking at is the crucifix. This Christ is not like the Christ in the church: high-gloss complexion, chaste beads of blood where crown meets temple, expression exquisite, prissy, a perfect balance of compassion and suffering and—yes, it's there—self-pity. No, this Christ on the morada wall is ancient and bloody. There is violence in the very carving: chisel marks gouge belly and thigh, leave fingers and toes stumpy. The contours of the face are rough, ribs sharp. Someone's real hair hangs limply from the statue's head.

Each night a different hermano says the Holy Mysteries, and together they intone the responses. This is Amadeo's favorite part, when all their voices merge in a rumbling low current, the same predictable rise and fall. Tonight, though, with Angel's arrival, he's edgy and distracted. Amadeo considers calling her mom to get her, but at the thought of explaining to Marissa about the procession, he rejects the idea. "You can't take care of your daughter because *why*?" He can hear her scorn.

He watches the praying men: Tío Tíve, in the diabetic shoes he gets subsidized from the VA, his lips trembling; Frankie Zocal, blue veins pulsing his lids; Shelby Morales, his gray ponytail draped over his shoulder like a girl's.

"The soldiers clothed him in a purple cloak, and plaiting a crown of thorns, they put it on him," says Al, clear and low, as if willing himself to hold a blaze of feeling in check.

Nine men is a far cry from the old days, Al explained to Amadeo a few weeks ago as they stepped into the heavy dusk. In earlier generations, membership rolls, even for an hermandad this deep in the mountains, could be in the hundreds. Back in those days, when one priest was shared among many far-flung isolated communities, the hermandads weren't just centers of worship, but mutual aid societies, political councils, community centers. They buried the dead.

"We got your tío to thank for the hermandad. He really brought it back," Al Martinez said. "Even when my dad was a kid, the tradition was dying out. There wasn't nothing left of the old morada. But Tíve bought the gas station, fixed it up, reminded us what we once had. It's the one good thing to come out of his boy's passing."

The morada isn't much to look at. Outside there's the dark skeleton of a sign on a pole, the bright plastic panels long gone, and two dead pumps. The plate-glass window has been covered in matte beige house paint left over from a long-ago job. Occasionally strangers will pull in for gas and look around, confused by the trucks parked in front, before heading straight through the village and away.

"Maybe ours isn't as nice as the moradas in Truchas and Abiquiu and Trampas," Al Martinez said. "Maybe it doesn't show up on no post-cards. Las Penas doesn't have one scrap of charm, and I say, good. They can have their sculptors and natural-food stores. Let the tourists go to Taos."

First the Rosary, then silent individual prayer. It's meant to last an hour, but you'd be surprised how long that feels, how quickly supplication and penitence and entreaty get old. Within a minute or two, knees are wincing, kneecaps grinding between concrete and bone, and by the time the Rosary is over, the legs have gone numb. Toenails ache, pressed against the floor.

Amadeo thinks of his daughter alone in the house. She could be up to anything: going through his belongings, having friends over. Entertaining boys, even.

Amadeo falters on the Apostles' Creed. He opens his eyes and looks at Tíve, and sure enough, the old man has him in his disapproving gaze. Amadeo clamps his eyes shut.

"Amen," intone the hermanos, and the Rosary is over before Amadeo even gets into it.

Silent prayer is the most difficult part. *Please, God*, Amadeo thinks, then loses the thread. His knees are pulverized. He wonders if he's doing permanent damage. Outside, evening sounds: a car passing, the squawk of a night bird, the ping of moths against the painted-over windows.

———

AMADEO'S ENTRADA—his initiation and first audience with the hermanos—took place five weeks ago, on Ash Wednesday.

"At sundown, you knock," Tíve had prepped him, when they met for lunch at Dandy's Burgers in Española. His voice was low, and Amadeo threw a glance at the family at the table next to them. They weren't paying attention, though. A boy about six or seven with ketchup on his pants was trying to eat his hamburger while his mother kept getting in his face with a napkin. Outside, Tíve's dog Honey, a rust-colored Doberman, watched them through the window, one pale eyebrow raised, her undocked ears giving her a bat-like aspect.

"Three times you knock." Tíve demonstrated on the table, scowling from under the brim of his trucker's cap.

Amadeo's mother adores her uncle. She has ideas of what a family should be, and according to these ideas, Tíve's role is lonely, lovable curmudgeon. Mostly, Amadeo suspects, Tíve wants to be left alone, and not the way old people in TV movies want to be left alone, secretly waiting for some misguided young person to come along so that they might save each other. Tíve may be old, but he has no desire to spin yarns or reminisce or impart wisdom.

"Okay." Amadeo nodded agreeably. He was hungry, but didn't want to unwrap his hamburger first. Discreetly, he popped a fry into his mouth.

His great-uncle glared. Shriveled as he was, dude could be scary. "You fast and go to Mass that day, you hear? From here on out, you need to be regular with Mass. And confession, too." Tíve handed him a brochure on the Rosary. "You know the words, right?"

"Doesn't it mean more if I make up my own prayers?" Amadeo flapped the brochure. "Aren't these just pre-memorized?" His uncle's look of disgust shamed him.

Tíve reached into the breast pocket of his flannel shirt and handed Amadeo a folded piece of notebook paper. "Learn it good," he said. "And don't go talking about it to no one. These are secrets."

Amadeo squinted at the unsteady block letters that had been copied out with a blunt pencil. It looked like a poem with many stanzas, and Amadeo had a flash of his fifth-grade language arts textbook, and a long rhyming poem about a butterfly that he'd liked to read to himself after school, whispering the words in his room, enjoying the rhythm, the inevitability of the sounds. *Sky, eye, why.* Stupid as fuck.

Midway down the page was a grease smudge, and Amadeo pictured his great-uncle frowning over the paper under the dim kitchen light, the cold remains of a sad, solitary dinner of scrambled eggs beside him.

"Hey, wait. This is in Spanish," Amadeo said.

"Oh, hell," Tíve muttered. He began unwrapping his burger, as if giving up.

Even Yolanda doesn't speak Spanish well, though she, at least, can follow along with the telenovelas she watches weekday nights on her bedroom television. "I could do a much better job with English," Amadeo offered, then, at his uncle's incredulity, corrected himself. "I mean, I'm kidding. I can definitely learn it. I did Spanish in high school."

The first part of the ritual was a call-and-response.

Novicio: Dios toca en esta misión, las puertas de cu clemencia. God knocks at this mission, on the gates of his mercy.

Hermanos: Penitencia, penitencia, si quieres tu salvación. Penance, penance, if you want salvation.

"Go on. Practice," said Tíve, and Amadeo, suddenly shy, spoke his lines. He was surprised when, in reply, his great-uncle began to sing, his voice gravelly and beautiful. At the table next to them, the little boy paused in his chewing, his cheeks full, and watched.

To enter this morada, place the right foot, praising the most sweet names of Jesus, Mary, and Joseph.

Once he crossed the threshold, Amadeo was to kneel before the old men who were to be his brothers, and ask for forgiveness.

"Then you cut me?"

"You take the oath first."

"And then?"

Tíve gave an almost imperceptible nod.

"Deep?" Amadeo whispered, keeping his voice steady.

His great-uncle shrugged. "Not too deep. Go on, do your lines."

Pardon me, my brothers, if in anything I have offended you or given scandal.

And Tíve sang in reply. *May God pardon you who are already pardoned by me.*

Amadeo's eyes filled, an abrupt sadness caught in his throat. He looked away, embarrassed.

Tío Tíve cleared his own throat. "Be ready."

There were practical reasons for the sellos—the three vertical cuts that were going to be made in his back—when he began whipping himself, the blood would flow from the wounds, so the skin wouldn't swell or bruise.

At first Amadeo had enjoyed the prospect of kneeling before the sangrador who would mark him. On the morning of Ash Wednesday, though, his courage began to fail. All day, he thought of the sellos, and his knees weakened.

He shaved for the entrada (though he didn't shower again, because he wanted to preserve the smudge of ash on his forehead, proof to his great-uncle that he'd gone to Mass), put on a new plaid shirt still stiff from the package, dress shoes, splashed cologne on his neck. Even so, he could smell the unpleasant tang of his sweat.

In the end, just before presenting himself at the morada door, Amadeo had buckled to his fear: though he'd fasted all day, he dug a bottle of vodka out of his sweater drawer, broke the seal on it, and took deep gulps.

The entrada, then, was a blur of impressions. The hermanos' song, cresting and falling like waves. The secret oath, binding him for life. And the pedernal: obsidian with a knife-sharp edge, a dangerous crescent moon. Al Martinez's big hand warm and steady on his shoulder, the man's low assurance. "They'll be shallow, son. Deep breath." Amadeo's heart like a steady, too-loud drumbeat, his sides slick with cold sweat. And, as the blade slid into the skin of his back, Amadeo's swelling sense of his own falseness.

———

Now, FINALLY, Tíve crosses himself. "All right," he says irritably. "Amen." Amadeo stands, legs needling. Around him the hermanos gather themselves. Some will talk quietly in the parking lot about this or that, trying out their rusty voices, and others will hurry to their families, kiss their wives, take their places on the couch in front of their TVs.

Angel is waiting for him at home, so Amadeo lingers. Tíve's Doberman Honey is beside herself with joy to see the men emerge, and tears around the lot, barking her head off, her long, narrow muzzle pointed to the sky. Based on this particular specimen, it's hard to believe the breed is a fierce one; Honey is relentlessly attention-seeking and ill-mannered, her expression demented and eager. Her reddish fur is dull, as if she'd once been a normal black or brown dog and had been left to fade in the sun. She pushes her head under Tíve's hand and wags her tail nub furiously.

"Buddy," says Al Martinez in the doorway, clapping a hand on Tío Tíve's skinny shoulder. Tíve flinches. "I want to show you Elena's newest—my second granddaughter!" He's already pulling his phone out of his pocket, expertly swiping at the screen. "See her?"

Tíve peers at the photo, and Amadeo also cranes to see a charmless, purple-faced infant with a frothy lace headband strapped around her wrinkled head. "Well," Tíve says.

"Oh, she's a beauty. Got her grandma's pretty mouth." Al brings the phone close to his own face, examines it blissfully, then tucks it into his pocket. He clears his throat. "Listen, buddy, Isaiah, my youngest, wants to join us. He wants to be an hermano. And since we're taking novicios"—he angles his head at Amadeo—"he'd be a great candidate. He wants to get back to his history."

"No," says Tíve. "No more novicios."

"But Tíve. He's a good boy, a manager at Lowe's. Just turned forty. We need young people. You said so yourself."

"No," says Tíve. "It's not the right time."

Anger flashes across Al's face, then disappointment. He glances again at Amadeo, seems about to say something, then says quietly, "Please, brother. Isaiah needs this. I did good with Elena, but Isaiah is bad into chiva, in and out of rehab and all that, even robbed his sister once, took the computer and TV and everything. We don't know what to do with ourselves. He's doing better now, but it'd give him comfort, give him something bigger than him. He thinks it could save him, and I do, too."

"You're not bringing that poison into the morada. Hell no." Tíve heads for his truck, his walk stooped and uneven.

"Harsh," Amadeo says, but he can't deny feeling pleased, because he *was* chosen, and not just for the hermandad, but for the most important role there is. "His son Elwin OD'd."

"I know." For a long moment, Al continues to gaze after Tíve, his expression troubled. Quietly, Al says, "In my grandpa's day, there was a Jesus who asked for nails. Best Jesus they ever had."

Amadeo swallows. "Seriously? He actually got nailed to the cross? With real nails?"

Al Martinez nods. "That's some sacrifice, huh? Think of it." He slowly turns his hand, one way and then the other, then touches the center of his palm.

"Who was he?" Amadeo has the sense that he is teetering on the edge of a great mystery. Around him, the night is huge.

Al shrugs. "I just know what my dad told me his dad told him. I just know he did it." He tosses his keys lightly and heads to his car.

Amadeo stands alone in the deserted lot. After that, a man would never be the same again. He imagines the scene, as he always imagines the olden days, in black and white: the man's steadfast expression as the nail pierces his flesh, the searing light that fills him. The gathered people fall to their knees.

———

AT SIX THIRTY in the morning on Holy Wednesday, Amadeo wakes to the gurgle and hiss of pipes in the wall near his head. He flops over in his limp bed, tries not to think about Angel. Christ's pain, he reminds himself. Think of that. Each night, Amadeo practices his expression in the bathroom mirror after he showers, water running down his forehead. He spreads his arms, makes the muscles in his face tighten and fall, tries to learn the nuances of suffering. Now, lying in bed, he tries again, but his face is stiff as tire rubber. He tries to train his mind on that long-ago man, who with a few nails, made something real.

It makes him queasy to think of Angel, queasier to think about whoever got her this way. This is not a detail that made it into the story Amadeo heard from his mother, but he doesn't need facts to picture it: some cholo dealing chiva from the window of his lowrider.

When he wakes again, Angel is looming over him, prodding his shoulder. "Dad? Can you drive me to school? You need to get up."

Amadeo murmurs something into his pillow as she shuts the door. Later, faintly, he hears her call his name again, but the sound doesn't break through the surface of his sleep.

When he wakes, it's after ten, and the house is sunny and empty. He still has two hours before Mass. Angel has left a note on the table: *Got a ride with Tío Tíve.* No signature, no *XOX*. Guilt sits heavy in his gut. He eats the cold eggs and bacon Angel has left out for him, and then, because that jumpy, awful feeling won't go away, he cracks open a beer.

Angel never used to work out, has never once joined a team or performed a proper push-up. All through elementary school she feigned menstrual cramps and carpal tunnel syndrome to get out of PE, and in middle school, thanks to sweeping cuts in public school funding, she never had to register for it at all. But because studies show that exercise during pregnancy results in lower rates of illness and obesity in infants, every afternoon Angel takes a walk. Brianna, Angel's teacher at Smart Starts!, gave them each a daily planner and a sheet of foil stars to mark their daily exercise. Angel loves her planner with its maroon plastic cover stamped to look like leather, and she loves pasting the star neatly next to each date.

The Smart Starts! curriculum is mainly an exercise in record keeping. In journals and planners and charts, the girls record not just their exercise, but also their consumption of prenatal vitamins, their day-to-day feelings. Each day they note their highlights and lowlights, Peaches and Pits. Those who have given birth record their babies' feedings and bowel movements and naps, and those who haven't record their own feedings and bowel movements and naps.

"It's about being mindful," Brianna tells the class. "It's about becoming aware of how you're actually living your life so you can make the conscious choices necessary to live the life you want." She sits on the edge of her desk, knocking the heels of her big hiking sandals against the side. Those hiking sandals are one of many things Angel likes about Brianna. Their clunkiness makes her look small and tough and somehow very feminine.

Brianna. One of the prettiest names Angel has heard. She's never had a teacher who used her first name with students, and the fact that Brianna does makes her approachable and modern and, if anything, more worthy of respect. She grew up in Oregon, she's told them, which Angel imagines as a lush green Eden filled with burbling creeks and open, loving people. Around her teacher, Angel truly is her best self: hardworking, good, nearly innocent.

At home—at her mom's house—Angel varied her walking route as much as possible. You see a lot, walking through Española, and not just the low, brown Rio Grande making its slow way out of town. Once she saw a white-clad Anglo Sikh woman with blond eyebrows pause in her telephone conversation to vomit into the gutter. "I'm back," she said when she was done, straightening her turban. Another time a man reeled around the parking lot of the Jade Star restaurant, yelling at passersby, perplexingly, "I want to get my rock salt!" Sometimes she passes addicts, slumped docile and unseeing behind this or that building, drowning in their fixes, but Angel gives them a wide berth. Once one looked up at her imploringly. "Hey," he said, defeated. Outside the public library one afternoon, she even came upon a whole dog circus run by a rescue organization and got to watch terriers in tutus leaping through rings and driving toy cars and balancing on one another's backs. It was an amazing showcase of talent—and to think that once they'd been nobodies sitting in a pound, just waiting around to be put to death.

Way out here, though, there's just dry piñon and clumpy grass and short withered cactus, occasionally rabbits or quail, and the single road curving through the hills. Strange that with all this open land stretching around her, her path should be so much more restricted than in Española. Turn right at the end of the driveway, and the cracked asphalt soon gives way to dirt and then ends completely. Turn left, and a mile or so later you're in the sad little village of Las Penas.

Most of the families out here have been on the same land for hundreds of years. Trailers and newer cinderblock structures are wedged into yards alongside crumbling adobe ruins. Some families, like the Romeros, continue to farm small plots of corn and squash and chile, irrigated by acequias, the straight green rows defiant in the face of discount Walmart food. The same few surnames: Padilla, Martinez, Trujillo, Garcia. Marriage and intermarriage like shuffling the same deck of cards.

Sometimes Angel can see what the Anglo artists see in the landscape. Here, in the fore, the young corn plants wave new-green leaves. A ground squirrel sits tall, then lowers his head to scratch with two dainty hands at a spot on his chest. Above, as though painted, the mountains rise, blue and golden.

All this beauty. Also underfunded public schools, dry winters, a falling water table, shitty job prospects. Mostly what people have now is cheap heroin. "It's genocide, and we're doing it to ourselves," Mrs. Lujan, Angel's English teacher said last year, tears in her eyes after another of her students—a junior Angel only knew by sight—had overdosed. "Please, please, please," she begged the class. "Please don't do it."

Angel was, frankly, aghast to find only her dad here, and even given her woefully low expectations of him, he has still managed to disappoint her. He couldn't even get up to take her to school? Was he really so busy being unemployed? What had Angel thought—that he'd have any interest in literally anything other than himself? It's crazy how wrapped up he is in this penitente thing. Every night he has to go pray the Rosary, he told her yesterday.

"Do you even *own* a rosary? Since when'd you start going to church?"

"You don't ask a man about his prayers," he said.

Angel held her hands up. "*O*-kay." So she spent the evening scrolling through her phone, trying to watch television. She tried calling her grandmother again, to no avail. Finally she went into her grandmother's room and lay on the pink canopy bed, pressing her face into the pillow to inhale the velvety, perfumy scent.

Today is warm for April, and Angel breaks a sweat. She thinks of her sticker and picks up her pace. Above, the clouds are as fluffy and benign as those in a picture book.

The road rises and falls gently. In a car, taken with some speed, these hillocks cause a thrilling drop in the stomach. Angel remembers being little and yelling for her dad to go *faster faster faster!* And he always would, laughing at her laughter. On foot, the hills are just challenging.

She looks at her phone again. No missed calls. She's tried her grandmother a thousand times in the last several days, and the calls always go to voicemail.

She brings up her mother's number on the screen, but doesn't press it. In the last year or so, a silence has settled between them, a silence instigated by Angel to both punish her mother and bring her closer. But it doesn't seem to be working. Angel tries to hold out, to remain incommunicado until her mother is forced to call first, but her mother always wins. The galling fact is that Angel is a kid and needs her mother more than her mother needs her.

Marissa has no right to be mad at Angel—not when Angel was almost murdered by her mother's stupid jerk boyfriend. You always hear about girls who don't report their abusers to their mothers and teachers and grandmothers, but Angel never understood that. *Her* mother, she was certain, would annihilate anyone who touched her. Of *course* Angel told her mother. With pleasure, she anticipated the scene that would follow: Marissa tossing Mike's belongings into the yard—the hardback history books he keeps wrapped in plastic and alphabetized, his tilted drafting table that takes up half the living room, his expensive, needle-tipped pencils. Her mother would charge at him—possibly with a knife—her whole little body radioactive with fury.

But when Angel explained that Mike tried to strangle her, Marissa just shook her head. "He was joking. Mike jokes around."

"No way," Angel said, hand at her throat to demonstrate. "He tried to kill me." But the truth is, now Angel *does* wonder if it had been a joke.

"Mike wouldn't do that." Marissa took Angel's face in her hands—not very gently—and tipped it this way and that to examine her neck. "There's no bruises."

"So he did a shitty job of it! Plus I don't bruise easy." Angel's eyes smarted and she hated herself, because she doesn't know how to feel. It *hadn't* hurt when Mike encircled her throat, and he hadn't even squeezed, but still her heart had thrashed with terror.

Marissa turned and began putting the clean dishes away. Her temple pulsed. "I think he was kidding around and you couldn't take a joke."

And even if this was true—it *might* be true—her mother's betrayal was so shocking that Angel didn't at first believe the conversation was over. She waited for her mother to turn back, to apologize and admit how wrong she was and to make sure that Mike never, ever touched her baby again, but Marissa was opening the freezer, taking out the jumbo shrimp for Mike's favorite coconut curry.

Angel lasted a week more at home, refusing to speak to her mother or Mike, with the disturbing sense that she had indeed blown things out of proportion.

But then yesterday she awoke gasping from a nightmare in which he was strangling her, his face nearly touching her own, and her anger was so total, so visceral, that she paced her room until morning, when she announced she was moving in with her dad and grandmother. Her mother had driven her here in silent fury, the muscle along her jaw pulsing, while Angel's heart skittered.

"No one's here," Angel said, dismayed, when her mom pulled into the empty driveway.

"So what, you want to stay or go home? I'm not waiting around for your dad to get back from wherever the fuck." Marissa's hands tightened on the steering wheel. "Didn't you call? You haven't been here in how long and you didn't even call?"

Angel heaved herself out of the car and tried knocking, leaving the car door open wide so her mother couldn't pull away. She texted both her dad and her grandmother, but no one replied. How hard was it to have one single damn thing work out in her favor?

"I'm staying." Angel retrieved her duffel from the backseat, then leaned in the passenger side, but Marissa didn't look at Angel. When she spoke again, she couldn't keep the desperate hitch from her voice. "Bye, Mom."

"Bye," Marissa said, shifting into reverse, waiting for Angel to shut the door. She hasn't even called to make sure someone eventually came home and let Angel in. For all Marissa knows, Angel could have been kidnapped that afternoon. Murdered. Her womb scooped from her belly like the seed from an avocado.

When Angel was in middle school, she and her mother used to have big weeping fights about who should vacuum or who was responsible for the clutter on the kitchen table. Sometimes, after, they would lean against each other on the couch, exhausted, her mother gently scratching Angel's head with her nails, but mostly the fights left Angel feeling alone, disturbed to see her mother so destroyed by emotion, as destroyed as Angel herself felt.

But this silence is worse. She wonders whether her mother intends to teach her a lesson or if she truly hates Angel or if she's already completely forgotten Angel's existence.

Now here she is in Las Penas, with only a duffel bag. Angel used to be a collector: Beanie Babies, plastic pigs, little pom-poms with hats and googly eyes stuck on. She liked arranging her collections on shelves, liked having the manufacturer's checklist before her, ticking off the ones she had, circling the ones she didn't. She liked the search for completeness. But just before she announced she was leaving, Angel bagged up all that stuff and shoved it in the green trash bin outside. Better to be unencumbered. Better to be light and free, so she can, if need be, jump and fight and run.

Partially she trashed it all to wound her mother, who encouraged these collections. Marissa herself collects Disney stuffed animals. Angel imagined her mother pausing in the doorway, her shock at the bare walls and cleared shelves. Angel knew from posters at school that one of the warning signs of suicide was giving away treasured belongings, and Angel liked the idea of her mother's distress. Probably, though, Angel thinks now grimly, her mother isn't even aware of the warning signs of suicide. Probably her mother can't wait to move in her hoard of Disney characters, let them colonize Angel's bed and shelves with their creepy grins and plastic eyes and solid, oversized heads. Or worse, give Angel's room to Mike for a home office, let him turn it into an altar to his own anal-retentiveness, with his rolls of blueprints and fussy metal protractors and the expensive Japanese pens that no one's allowed to use even to take one tiny telephone message.

The road makes its gentle curve, and now the village is in sight. Las Penas consists largely of abandoned buildings, blank sockets where windows used to be. In front of the locked church, there are a few nearly intact squares of sidewalk stamped *WPA*. All around is evidence of better times and failed enterprise: boarded-up windows, painted letters barely visible on the broken plaster. *Grocery. Cash Store. Hamburger.*

Las Penas in the Ass, her mother calls it, but she means Amadeo and not the town itself. Even on the full-sized New Mexico state map her grandmother got from AAA, Las Penas is marked in the tiniest font imaginable. Most everyone works in Española or Los Alamos or, like her grandmother, in Santa Fe. Anything that needs doing can be done better elsewhere.

Angel hasn't spent much time here—usually when she sees her grandmother they get dinner in Española—and most holidays are spent with her mother's parents, Ramon and Lola, who have been so disapproving of Angel's situation that you'd think they'd forgotten that their own daughter was once in the same boat. Rather, Grampa Ramon has been disapproving; Gramma Lola is so out of it, she doesn't even recognize Angel. Angel has been avoiding them because, frankly, she doesn't need that kind of energy in her life.

The Idle Hour Cantina is her turnaround point. It's five thirty now, and the sun is slipping down the sky. Angel walks briskly back down the length of the village. She'll make dinner—she needs to tell her dad they're low on vegetables—and she'll do her homework. She'll stick a star into her planner.

At the curve, her phone vibrates in her pocket. She is filled with that buoyant fizz she always gets when someone tries to reach her. It has to be her grandmother. But, no, even better: it's Lizette from school.

What u up 2

She smiles. Lizette Maes is a year older and significantly more badass than any of Angel's old friends at Española Valley High School, yet for some reason Angel cannot divine, she's decided she approves of Angel. As far as Angel knows, Lizette is an orphan, and has lived with her brother and his girlfriend ever since her mother OD'd three years ago, but she never seems to feel sorry for herself, doesn't even seem to care. This makes Angel feel babyish, because if she were an orphan, she'd always be thinking about it. Look at her now: both parents alive and still she spends half her time feeling neglected and unloved.

Angel replies to the text hungrily, like a castaway snatching at any hope for communication. *Nothing much. You?* Last week Brianna had a mini breakdown over some text-speak that had made it into a few of their reading responses, and ever since Angel's been trying to spell and punctuate her texts properly, but it's hard to do without looking uptight, and Angel especially doesn't want to appear uptight to Lizette. *Bored lol*, she adds.

Angel keeps her phone out, waiting for Lizette's reply, but there isn't one. She shouldn't take it personally—Lizette is, if anything, undependable. But why ask what someone's up 2 if you don't actually care? Then Angel wonders if that text had even been intended for her. Just because Angel no longer has friends outside of Smart Starts! doesn't mean Lizette is equally pathetic. She probably has tons of friends. Maybe she's going out tonight. The thought makes Angel feel even lonelier.

In the last month, she hasn't called or texted one single person she used to hang out with. Why would she? She's zitty and bloated, and their lives have moved on.

"Sex complicates things, both practically and emotionally," Brianna told them in class yesterday, and boy, is she right on that first count. But for the first few months of her sexual career, emotionally, at least, things were pretty simple for Angel. Her crushes were light and transient, swiftly extinguished.

Even when Ryan Johnson from her geometry class asked her to be his girlfriend last spring and again in the fall—actually phrased it that way—and seemed truly sad when she rejected him, Angel hadn't, herself, felt any complication at all.

Angel isn't like the knocked-up teens in movies whom audiences can sympathize with because they've had sex once and even then it was with their best guy friend or some jerk taking advantage. Angel enjoyed letting it be known around school that she was doing it—that she was *active*, as Brianna would say. It made her feel voluptuous and powerful and musky and mysterious.

Angel has never been, strictly speaking, boy crazy. Not like Priscilla, her best friend since fourth grade—former best friend—who's been dying for a boyfriend forever, even, last year, spent part of her birthday money on a subscription to a bridal magazine.

"A *bridal* magazine? Are you joking me?" Angel asked, lounging on Priscilla's bed and flipping through the glossy pages. "Don't you still get *Highlights*?" She didn't, and Angel knew that because when they were younger Priscilla had always passed her back issues on to Angel, who loved the Hidden Objects feature and whose mother would never waste money on a magazine except *People*, which was practically a necessity for any informed citizen. "You don't even *talk* to Kevin Gabaldon, Cilla. Don't you think you should, like, say hi before you order the cake?"

Priscilla pressed her already thin lips almost out of existence. "Just 'cause your mother didn't value marriage. Ever heard of thinking about the future, Angel? It can take, like, four years to plan a good wedding, and if I have all the dresses and decorations picked out, I'll have a head start." She leaned over Angel, placing a finger on a page featuring a blond bride running through a lush garden, lifting her skirts and laughing over her bare shoulder, looking ever so slightly demented, the quarry in some hilarious chase. "Plus, I like the pictures."

Angel nearly pointed out that dress styles were likely to change between now and whenever Priscilla found someone to marry her, but then, turning another page, reflected that the dresses all looked basically the same, so maybe not.

But even without an interest in a real, honest-to-goodness boyfriend, Angel enjoys—enjoyed—sex. Or rather, she enjoyed what sex did, the way it established an invisible connection between her and the guy, a secret knowledge. She remembers after the first time, last summer, when she'd been eager to transform herself and get this part of high school over with, she couldn't believe how easy and unremarkable it had been. So much hoopla over *that*? It didn't even feel like a sin. But after, she'd see the guy around school, and she'd *know* certain things about him: his secret sounds, his self-conscious laugh. She felt powerful, getting these guys—who'd once been so swaggering—naked, with their zitty backs and needy, nosing penises. They were pathetic in their grunting urgency and in those slack, defenseless minutes after.

"You're lucky," complained Priscilla as they walked through the briny-smelling halls of the school when it started up in August. "People know who you are now."

"They know who you are, too," Angel said kindly, but Priscilla was right: once you'd proven that you were desirable, you actually became more desirable. Older kids called out to Angel in the parking lot. They invited her to parties. With Priscilla and among their friends, Angel became both an expert and worthy of discussion. Soon she pitied these other girls their hopeless innocence.

Eventually, at least in her relationship with her best friend, things *did* become emotionally complicated. Priscilla is skinny and tough and sometimes not very nice, and as the fall semester wore on, she got nastier.

"It's crazy that you became such a slut," Priscilla told her as they fixed their makeup at the trough-like bathroom sinks. "Not in a bad way. But it's not like you're as pretty as, like, Kylie or Sabrina." The Española Valley High School bathrooms could be in a prison. There were no doors. Instead of mirrors, which could come in handy in a riot, smeared steel plates were screwed to the walls. The whole architecture of the place put you in mind of mutiny, escape.

Angel peered at her blurry, distorted reflection. "So? I'm okay-looking."

"I just never would have guessed it in middle school. Remember what a nerd you were? Also, isn't it kind of rare for a fat girl to become a slut?"

"I'm not fat," said Angel, and she wasn't, just didn't happen to be a skinny old bone bag.

So it felt good when, after Priscilla had called her fat for the millionth time, Angel found herself drunk at a party and talking to surly Kevin Gabaldon with his stupid patchy upper lip, whom Priscilla had liked since seventh grade without ever actually making a move. And it was so easy to make him smile, then to step closer, to go from talking to kissing to the urgent press in the dark laundry room of the apartment complex. Angel loved that urgency, garment after garment dropping away as though they'd always been extraneous.

Priscilla was mad enough when she heard about Kevin that she texted around the school a headless naked picture claiming it was Angel. Angel had seen the pic and the text, thanks to Ryan Johnson, who intercepted her in the library after school.

"Hey," Ryan Johnson said, and shifted his weight uncomfortably from one Converse sneaker to the other.

Angel looked up from her math notebook and rolled her eyes. "What do you need?" He'd already asked her out again twice this year and she'd declined nicely, but her patience was wearing thin. The guy couldn't get it through his knobby head that a hookup was just a hookup. He'd been trailing her like a lost fawn.

Ryan palmed his thin blond hair and bit his cracked bottom lip. Hadn't he ever heard of ChapStick? "Um," he said, then shoved his phone at her.

It was all pretty laughable. *Look what someone sent me poor angel!!!! I feel so bad!!!!* The person in the photo had a body twenty times better than Angel's, a body that was at least semiprofessional, given the spherical breasts and the blond landing strip between her spread legs.

"That's not me," Angel made herself say. She felt very cold and sick with the sense that her life was on a precipice and that everything would soon become very, very horrible. The library was mostly empty except for three girls on yearbook conferencing in the far corner, but still Angel covered the screen with her hand. "That's not me," she said again, voice hoarse.

"*I* know that." Ryan blushed.

"No you don't. Delete it."

"Of course. I just thought you should know. See? I'm deleting it." And he did, right in front of her, which was pretty considerate of him, except that it was also the bare minimum of human decency.

If Priscilla had been hoping the pic would go viral, she was disappointed, because all the people she'd implored not to show anyone hadn't shown anyone, which, when you think about it, kind of makes you feel good about the teens of today.

Angel was nonetheless humiliated. Every one of the recipients of the text—maybe about twenty people, Angel's classmates and friends—must have imagined Angel naked, must have compared the image in their heads to the image on their phones. Every one of them must have wondered if posing in such a way was, indeed, something Angel might do. And it scared Angel to think, given how easily she'd hooked up with guys she hardly knew (mostly with protection), that maybe she might actually have allowed herself to be photographed or filmed—or, even scarier, how easily she might have been photographed or filmed without allowing it at all. She'd seen how swiftly girls' lives got ruined. It took a fraction of a second.

Even now, thinking about what might have happened, Angel feels the heat of humiliation spread through her. Priscilla denied originating the image—"Don't play like that! We're best friends!"—and Angel pretended to believe her red-faced denial, but who else could it have been? At any rate, when Angel discovered she was pregnant, it was an easy choice to drop out of school and deactivate her social media accounts and flee. She even felt grateful; if she had to be punished, pregnancy was preferable to showing up on the internet.

"By the way, Cilla," Angel said as a parting shot, on that last day at school, her belly already swelling beneath her sweater, "you should probably know that Kevin's the father."

Kevin wasn't the father—they hadn't even had full sex, just some groping—but Angel said it to ruin Kevin for Priscilla. No, the father is Ryan Johnson, oblivious Ryan Johnson, and only Angel knows this fact.

Even before the Kevin episode, even before she found out she was pregnant, Angel had had moments when she really did feel kind of filthy and used. Certainly, in a few instances, it was tricky to tell who was using whom. Is it possible that Angel got so carried away with her own power that she actually did give something up—not her virginity or (she touches her belly) her freedom, because, yes, obviously those are long gone—but something hard to articulate between desire and dignity and choice?

One night last summer at a party, a senior girl who must have heard of Angel's reputation brought her into the pink-tiled bathroom and gave her three condoms from her purse. "You don't *have* to do it, you know. Only do it if you want to," the senior told Angel, and Angel was so touched by the concern that she blushed. Then the older girl offered her heroin, waggling a little baggie, and, when Angel declined, smiled and shrugged and gestured to the door with her chin.

She was a little fool, Angel understands now. She'd felt chosen and desired, granted access to a rarified world. But all that time, she'd actually been excluding herself, incrementally and irrevocably, from the life of school and friends and teenage concerns.

And now here she is in Las Penas, wedged up in the mountains, cut off forever from that life. All around: piñon and juniper and crumbly pink dirt. She's so far out here that no future could find her even if it came GPS-equipped. Again she scrolls through her texts to see if she missed one from her mom. Not one single person knows where she is right now. Angel is a minor! Shouldn't *someone* be keeping an eye out for her?

The clouds behind her grandmother's house are blush pink, reflecting the sunset. Deep blue shadows gather under the juniper, and in the falling light, everything seems very defined and clear and sad. Through the barred window, Angel can see her father moving around the kitchen. If she's alone for one more second, she'll cry, so Angel jogs down the driveway toward him.

Amadeo is on the couch with a Coke and the remote balanced on his thighs when his daughter comes in. Her cheeks are flushed and she's sweating at her temples.

"Hey, don't worry about me," she says lightly. "I got a ride home from school."

"It's a busy time, Angel. I told you that." Amadeo chews his lip. "Did Tío Tíve say anything about me?"

"Like what?"

"Did he mention anything about—" He glances at her stomach.

Angel widens her eyes pointedly. "So I'm guessing you had work and that's why you couldn't drive me? Where you working now?"

"It's slow."

Angel drops beside him, then scoots down so her neck is cricked and her belly high.

"Huh." Her disapproval sounds remarkably like Marissa's.

"It's called a recession, Angel. Besides, I'm getting together a business. Windshield repair. I have a kit and everything." The truth is he doesn't have the kit, not yet. He saw it advertised on a late-night infomercial and has been waiting for his mother to get home to help him buy it. For $1,199.99, there are enough supplies for four hundred repairs. Amadeo has done the math: if he charges fifty bucks a repair— and that's a bargain, people would easily pay twice that to not have to replace their windshields—he'll make twenty thousand. Twenty thousand from an eleven-hundred-dollar repair kit.

"I've always been an entrepreneur," he tells his daughter. He loves the early stages of creating a business.

"Yeah? Like your Amway?"

Mostly he'd sold to his mother and his mother's friends. If Amadeo's stint as a salesman didn't last long, though, the industrial-sized bottles of product did. Even now he'll occasionally come upon an old blue bottle of window cleaner or shampoo tucked under a sink or at the back of a cupboard. The truth is that the products aren't very good. One acrid-smelling shaving cream gave him a rash over his entire face.

Then there was the time he started outfitting cars for the races down in Albuquerque with his friend Charlie Vigil. Amadeo enjoyed working with Charlie, and was good at it, re-boring the engine, replacing the metal front and sides with fiberglass, removing what wasn't essential, making what was essential as light as possible. Yolanda hadn't been happy about the prospect of fast cars, but she was glad Amadeo was "getting involved" and had offered to give them what she could afford to start them out. But in the end Charlie partnered with his cousin. "No offense, man, but in a business you got to know your partner's going to show up."

"Windshield repair is where it's at," Amadeo tells his daughter. "Look around: this whole state is rocks and dirt. I got to be my own boss." Amadeo imagines windshield repair is a trade Jesus might get behind. It is, essentially, carpentry for the twenty-first century. "It's about showing people a clear way forward, about helping them get to where they need to go." It's about repairing shattered lives. There's a possibility Amadeo is overthinking it, but he's pretty sure he's not.

"Windshield repair." Then, after a moment, Angel asks: "You still sing ever?"

"Nah." Not for years, though at one time he'd thought he could actually go somewhere with it. He's grateful to Angel for remembering. Amadeo offers her his Coke.

She shakes her head. "It'll dissolve his baby bones."

Amadeo remembers when Angel was younger; he looked forward to the weekends when she'd come from Española to stay with him and his mom, enjoyed taking her out for the day, showing her off to his friends. He felt like a good influence, teaching her how to check the oil and eat ribs and not to listen to Boyz II Men. She was sweet then, eager to please, riding in the truck, fiddling with the radio, asking him at each song, "Is this good?" When he'd nod, she'd settle back and try to sing along, listening intently, each word coming a little too late. Sometimes Amadeo would sing, too, his voice filling the cab, and Angel would look up at him, delighted.

She still resembles that child—cheeks full and pink—but there's something frightening about her. It's as though she's a full contributor to the world, proud to be a member in good standing. Now she regales Amadeo with facts she's learned from her parenting class, about fluids and brain stems and genitals. "Like, did you know he had his toes before he even got his little dick?"

Amadeo looks at her, surprised, then back at the TV. "Why you have to tell me that?"

Angel faces him enthusiastically, grinning around her big white teeth, one foot tucked under her belly. "Weird, huh, that there's a dick floating around in me? Do you ever think about that? How Gramma is the first girl you had your dick in?"

"—The fuck. That's disgusting."

"Jesus, too," she says, singsong. "Jesus had his stuff in Mary." She laughs. "Couple of virgins. There's something for your research." She settles back into the couch, pleased.

Angel has seemed only mildly interested in Holy Week, which is a relief to Amadeo, and an irritation. "So it's like a play?" she asks.

"It's *not* a play—it's real." He doesn't know how to explain it to her. As real as taking communion, Tío Tíve said that day at Dandy's Burgers when he offered Amadeo the part. Tío Tíve said, looking at him severely, "You got a chance to feel a little of what Christ felt. You can thank him, to hurt with him just a little."

Angel asks, "They're going to whip you and stuff? Like, actually hard?"

He's proud, can't keep the smile from creeping in. "Yeah."

"My friend Lizette cuts, but she just does it for attention."

"It's not like that. It's like a way to pray."

Angel whistles low. "Crazy." She seems to be thinking about this, turns a pink cushion slowly in her hands.

Amadeo waits, exposed.

"So it's gonna hurt."

He tries to formulate the words to explain to Angel that the *point* is to hurt, to see what Christ went through for us, but he's as shy as he'd be if he were explaining it to his old high school friends. And he isn't even sure he's got it all right.

When he was a kid, singing at family parties, watching Yolanda smile at him across the room, he'd been sure something dazzling was coming his way—and he kept waiting for it. For a long time he didn't realize it wasn't just about being chosen, but about recognizing his opportunity, and when he saw it, he'd better throw himself at it as though it were the single open boxcar in the last train out of here. And here it is: his chance to prove to them all—and not just them—God, too—everything he's capable of. "But it's a secret, right? You can't go tell nobody back in Española."

"Who'm I gonna tell?" she says bitterly. "Anyways, why?"

"Tío Tíve wants us to keep it on the DL. You just can't say nothing."

"Can I see it? The morada?"

He'd like her to see what he's the center of. "Tío Tíve don't let women go in there. You can go to Mass at the church. You can be in the procession."

Angel scrunches her face. "Can't I just see it once? You're *Jesus*, aren't you?"

"Tío Tíve would kill me."

She's good-natured in her pleading, all smiles. "Come *on*."

"Women can't go in. And besides . . ." Before he can stop himself, he glances down at her belly. Her face slackens and she turns back to the TV. When Amadeo looks again, she's crying soundlessly, face blotchy and ugly, mascara running down her cheeks.

It's not his fault. He didn't tell her to be a girl. He didn't tell her to get knocked up. They were doing so well, she was showing interest, he was feeling so good. "It's just an old gas station. It's mostly empty anyway."

But now Angel's shoulders rock. Her fist presses over her mouth, and she's still not making a sound.

"Hey. Hey." He turns awkwardly on the couch, pats the shoulder near him.

When she speaks, it's with a gasp. "I'm too dirty for your morada. Is that it?"

An image flashes: Angel naked, sweaty and grunting with some boy. "You're not dirty."

———

LATER TONIGHT, the hermanos will gather for the last vigil, but for now the parking lot of the morada is deserted.

Amadeo unlocks the door and steps aside for his daughter. He watches Angel take it all in. On one of the benches is a canvas jacket, left last night by one hermano or another.

She walks the periphery of the room, stopping at various points to consider the man on the cross. His suffering is garish under the buzzing fluorescent bulb: blood flows down his pale neck and torso and knees, every wound deep and effusive. This statue's pain is personal and cruel, and he's not bearing it with perfect grace. The figure on the crucifix is a living man, a living witness to Amadeo's transgressions. Amadeo looks from the statue to Angel, then back, hands trembling.

The artist did not stop at five wounds, but inflicted his brush generously on the thin body. And there are the nails. Three. One in each hand, one skewering the long, pale feet. Amadeo feels his own palms throb.

Angel tips her head, impassive, and Amadeo is disappointed that she isn't impressed, that for her, it really is just a gas station.

When he hears a creak, he thinks for a moment it comes from outside, but it's closer, within the morada. Amadeo looks from his daughter to the statue.

"There aren't any Baby Jesuses here, are there?" Angel observes. No Blessed Mother, either, no audience of saints. Amadeo is alone here with his daughter and the statue. "I guess it's not a good idea for Baby Jesus to have to see himself later." Her voice is tired. She taps her belly distractedly, walks a few steps, stops. "I wouldn't want my baby to know."

Amadeo waits in dread for the statue to move, to lift his head. To fix Amadeo with his eyes.

Angel makes her slow way around the room again, stopping every few feet, head tilted. She turns to him, face pale, and he is startled when she asks, "So you really want to get whipped? To know what it feels like?" With her finger she traces a trickle of blood down the bound wooden feet. "Why?"

The room waits, but Amadeo doesn't have an answer. What he thinks about are the years passing blunts and working on cars with old friends now mostly married and supporting families, watching TV at night with his mother. Whole weeks go by without him remembering he has a daughter. Now here she is, standing before him under the eyes of Christ, and he doesn't know what to tell her. Too much time has passed. He thinks about the shadowy memory of his own father, wonders if the man ever felt this lost for words, this insufficient.

Though he can't articulate it to Angel, his answer is this: he needs to know if he has it in him to ask for the nails, if he can get up there in front of the whole village and do a performance so convincing he'll transubstantiate right there on the cross into something real. He needs to know if he can face that pain, straight on and with courage, without dodging it as he did on Ash Wednesday. He looks at the statue. Total redemption in one gesture, if only he can do it right.

"You never asked me why I came here," Angel says.

"You told me. You and your mom got in a fight."

"You never asked about what."

Amadeo is suddenly afraid. "Was it about me?"

She stares at him. When she speaks again, her voice is strained. "I thought you'd care."

"Of course I care. Tell me. I just assumed it was some girl thing."

"Some girl thing. I guess." Angel turns to the door.

As he watches it shut behind her, the longing that wells in him is so intense he must touch the wall to steady himself. At the front of the room, Jesus hasn't moved, wholly absorbed in his own pain.

Amadeo switches off the light, checks the lock on the morada door.

Angel heaves herself into the cab of the truck, looking like a kid in her too-large jacket. She gazes out the window all the way home.

"I want to know, Angel," he says.

She smiles at him sadly. "Tomorrow's a big day. Thanks for showing me the place."

Her ability to wrong-foot him is staggering, and he can't even tell if she means to. Long after she's gone to bed, after he's returned to the morada for the vigil, then come home again, he stays up, clicking through online videos, guilt and unease sloshing in him. One beer, then five.

―――

THEY GATHER AT the base of Calvario. A mile to the top, and Amadeo will walk barefoot, dragging the cross. He trembles and his upper lip sweats, though the morning air is cool. The hermanos help Tío Tíve unload the cross from the bed of his Ford. When the pito sounds three times—the cock's crow—Tío Tíve steps forward, Pontius Pilate giving his sign, and the hermanos seize Amadeo. Tío Tíve places the crown of thorns on his head, and tears leap to his eyes. Amadeo turns and hoists the cross onto his right shoulder, stooping under the weight, and the procession starts. The hermanos walk in two lines behind Jesus and begin to whip themselves. Then the women and children, the bright clattering colors of them, so distinct from the neat dark and white of the hermanos. Amadeo cannot see her, but he knows Angel is there.

He feels like a star: he is young, he is strong, he could carry this cross all day. The sky is the deep blue of spring, the air still cool and spiced with the smell of piñon. The fluting notes of the pito sound thinner up here, competing with the breeze and the birds.

Soon, though, the cross grows heavy. He tries to get into the part. He was up all night, he tells himself, in the garden, crying out to God. He remembers to stagger: his first fall. The crown of thorns is pulled tight, so it pierces the skin at his temple, the stinging sweat slides down, but Amadeo is just not feeling it. He is still himself, leaden and slow, his brain hungover and filled with static.

Angel comes up alongside him on the right, panting in her sneakers and tank top. "Shoot. I should get two stickers today. I can't believe I'm hiking up a mountain at eight months. This must be a record." She pats her belly. "Your mama's breaking the Guinness World Record, baby."

"Get to the back," he tells her. "You can't be up here."

She swigs water, holds the bottle out to Amadeo. Her cheeks and arms are rosy. "Want some water?"

Amadeo shakes his head fiercely, panic rising, and heaves the cross up the slope after him, wishing she'd leave him alone, wishing she hadn't come to ruin his performance with her pregnancy and personality. He needs to concentrate!

When the lashes come, Angel clamps her hands over her mouth. She looks like she might be sick, and Amadeo is glad.

He scrapes his shoulder under the edge of the cross, wincing when the wood breaks skin. The hot blood rises, his own blood, his own heat. He must leave his body, become something else. Behind him, the hermanos sing the alabados.

His second fall is not intentional; neither is his last. He has forgotten to pick up his feet, and he stumbles, the cross heaving down with him.

"You got to have water." She opens the little plastic top and pushes the bottle into his hands, but he doesn't take it.

In the brush, birds chirp and little lizards dart, then freeze, from rock to rock. He watches Angel follow one with her eyes. Inside her, the baby twists and turns—he can almost sense it—hot in her flesh and under the sun. For the first time he's glad she's here: more than anyone, he realizes, he wants Angel to see what he's capable of.

At the top of Calvario, the hermanos lift the cross from his shoulders and rest it on the ground. Amadeo straightens, an unbelievable relief, and the word *good* thrums in his head: *good, good, good.* The hermanos help him down, position his arms along the crossbeam, his feet against the block of wood that will support his weight. Amadeo spreads his arms and looks up into wide blue sky; there is nothing in his vision but blue. As they bind his arms and legs against the wood, lines once memorized surface: *With a word he stilled the wind and the waves.* But the wind skates over his body, drying his temples.

Then the hermanos lift the top of the cross, and Amadeo's vision swings from sky to earth. Upright, his weight returns; his torn heels press into the wooden block. The cross sways as the hermanos anchor it in the hole they've dug, packing dirt and stones around the base. Below him, on the distant road, a few glittering cars wink behind the trees, oblivious. He sees distant mesas and pink earth, piñon and chamisa. The air tastes of salt.

Angel stands before him, holding her hands under her belly. The nails, the nails. He is not sure if he says it or thinks it. Tío Tíve looks surprised, but nods and reaches into his pocket for the paper bag. The hermanos pour rubbing alcohol over the wood and Amadeo's hot hands. The alcohol burns cold and clean.

They hold the tip of the nail against his palm, and he feels it there a moment, light as a coin, and then they pound it through.

The pain is so immediate, so stunningly distilled, that Amadeo's entire consciousness shrinks around it. He is no longer a man: only reaction, outrage, agony.

He imagined the pain spreading through him like silent fire, unbearable in the most pleasurable of ways, like the burn of muscles pushed to their limits. He imagined the holy expansiveness that would swell in him until he was, finally, good.

But instead there's only this confused searing clamor, out of which rises a voice he only dimly registers as his own. "The other! Give me the other!" His voice sounds out over the heads of the onlookers, rolls down the slopes of Calvario.

Briefly Amadeo registers dismay in Tío Tíve's face, and Amadeo is proud of himself, because even though he hurts so bad, he's about to hurt worse.

———

IN THE CROWDED ER waiting room at Española Valley Regional Hospital, Angel sits beside him in cold silence, flipping angrily though a ragged parenting magazine, while Amadeo cradles his hands in his lap, marveling at the bright stickiness of his own blood soaking the towels.

The doctors are taking forever. He's been sitting under the fluorescent lights in this plastic chair bolted to the floor—leaning forward so as to protect his scourged, tender back—for nearly two hours. Through the automatic doors, the sky is already pink.

"Hey," he tells a nurse rushing past in scrubs printed with Easter eggs. "How long's it going to be? Because this is really serious." He indicates his hands, but the nurse regards him with only the barest tightening flicker around her mouth, then rushes on, consulting her clipboard.

Most of these people don't even seem sick. Not a single other person is losing blood. Where are the gunshot wounds, the heart attacks, the massive head injuries? Where is the carnage? Would someone please show him a single emergency greater than his own that might explain this unconscionable wait? He is *Jesus*, for Christ's sake.

"Whoa," he tells Angel. "I'm feeling really light-headed." But she doesn't even glance at him.

Across from them, a woman scrolls through her phone. Her young daughter—seven, eight—swings her feet restlessly, and a rhinestone-studded flip-flop drops to the teal epoxy floor. With both hands she grips a bag of cherry cough drops. Her eyes are wide and fixed on his bloody towel.

"Are you sick?" he asks the girl as nicely as he can, trying to rein in his annoyance.

The girl raises her eyes from the gore in his lap with some reluctance. Her hair is ratty and she wears a pilled yellow pajama top. "I might have foot-and-mouth disease."

The mother looks up warily from her phone.

"Maybe I could go before you, then?" Amadeo raises his swaddled hands, shrugging regretfully. "I'm bleeding out."

"We been here three hours," the woman says, voice flat, and she returns to her phone.

"You are not bleeding out," says Angel, louder and meaner than necessary.

But what does she know? Angel is a high school dropout, not a doctor. People die all the time from slit wrists, and the palm is basically the wrist.

He moves in his chair and gasps when the bandage on his back shifts. After the second nail, the hermanos helped him right down and gave him water, offering their congratulations. At first his hands didn't even hurt—his feet did, from clinging to the block on the cross. Al Martinez had bandaged him up gently. "Keep pressure here and here," he said, his voice low. "You did good, son." Still, the man is no professional, and Amadeo can already feel the medical tape coming unstuck.

To Amadeo's surprise, Tío Tíve didn't show any of the kindness of the other hermanos, didn't even seem proud. And the old man didn't call him an ambulance, either, just got one of the hermanos who lives in Española to drop them at the hospital. "Nail gun," Tío Tíve warned. "You got in the way of a nail gun."

"Anyway," says Angel, turning the page of her magazine, "it would serve you right if you did bleed out."

He looks at her, disbelieving. "Hey. Come on." What a thing to say. "Where did that come from?"

All of a sudden, he remembers that today is Angel's birthday. Sixteen. She didn't mention anything this morning; he wonders if she forgot herself, or if she wanted the day to be his.

"Listen, Angel. I'm sorry you had to be in the emergency room on your birthday. I apologize. Is that your problem? Is that what's bugging you, that you're not getting the attention? Listen, I wouldn't have asked you to come if it wasn't *an emergency*. I'm *wounded*."

Angel says nothing. Thank god she'll have the baby soon, Amadeo thinks, because he's not sure how much more he can take of these moods.

"Did you see the whole thing?" he asks in an undertone. He wishes he'd had her take pictures, but, he reflects, that wouldn't have been in the spirit of the occasion. Still, he wishes there was a record of his success.

Angel riffles through the magazine too fast to be reading anything. Amadeo watches the article titles as she flips past them: *Oral Fixation: Take-Along Snacks Your Child Will Love!*; *Milking It: Your Toddler and Lactose*; *I Feel You: Raising Empathetic Children*.

Amadeo taps this last article, and Angel pauses her frenetic page-turning. "Hey, that one looks good. Wish I'd known about raising empathetic children."

Angel gives him a shriveling, disgusted look. "You got to be joking me."

He turns away from her and looks instead at the television mounted in the corner. Cable news plays too loud. A cruise ship has lost power and is floating free in the Caribbean; the toilets have flooded and the king shrimp have gone off. Big deal, thinks Amadeo. So they get a longer cruise. So they eat Fritos. It's not like they're facing a medical situation. It's not like there is blood involved.

In the corner, a skinny tecato with patchy facial hair clutches himself, shivering and moaning, his eyes squinted as if under full sun. "I'm hurting so bad," he mumbles to no one. He smells like he's shit himself. He extends his legs and then draws them in again, shifting on his skinny butt, as if he can't find a position that doesn't cause him agony. He's got las malias, heroin withdrawal, and Amadeo turns away. He thanks God that he can't stand needles.

Amadeo hurts much worse than after the cutting of the sellos on Ash Wednesday, worse than after those lashes. Earlier, on Calvario, he seemed to have risen to some heightened space that pain didn't penetrate. He was cloaked in grace, he supposes.

But now he really, truly hurts, and Angel is giving him neither the praise nor the sympathy that he deserves. The pain clusters in his palms, shimmering, ever-changing. The blood is messy, coagulating thick and black, ruining his white pants. He wants, suddenly, to put his daughter in her place. "Don't you even got a boyfriend?"

Angel turns and looks at him like he's stupid. "What do you think?"

"Didn't your mom never teach you not to sleep around?"

"All the girls in my parenting class, not one of them has a guy that matters. Not one. You think you mattered?"

"You shouldn't have come. You think you have a right to just barge into my house and make yourself at home."

Angel's eyes widen, and then she narrows them. "It's my grandmother's house. You don't have a house." She turns back to her magazine, resolute.

At long last the girl and her mother are called. Amadeo looks at them piteously, and the girl looks back at him with interest, but the mother gathers their things and walks away, refusing eye contact.

"Hey," he says, ready to reconcile. "Why are you so mad at me? I did good today."

Angel finally sets the magazine on her lap and turns to him. "So," she says deliberately, "tell me: What was that? You never said anything about actual nails. You never said anything about actually getting crucified. What good is that to anyone?"

Her words are like a slap. "What's it to you, Angel?"

Her voice thickens and lowers. "In three weeks, I'm due. Three *fucking* weeks." She swallows and turns away, and her eyes rest unseeing on the television. For a moment Amadeo thinks Angel is going to cry. When she turns back, however, her eyes are dry, her face splotchy, gaze shuttered. Very quietly, so quietly he has to lean toward her to hear, Angel says, "How're you going to hold the baby? Or didn't you even think of that?"

t's Easter Sunday, the day of the Lord's Resurrection, and in honor of that, and of her own return home, Yolanda is going to gather her children around her, feed them the perfect Easter dinner, and break the news that she is dying of a malignant brain tumor.

When she pulls in front of the house and cuts the engine, Yolanda thinks, So this is what it looks like: her home without her. She's lived here her entire adult life, and has been away for less than two weeks, but somehow the house seems lower and drabber than she remembered it, crouching among the dusty juniper. It's an adobe-style house, soiled pink with iron bars on the windows that her daughter Valerie says will trap them all in a deadly inferno should there ever be a fault in the wiring, but that make Yolanda feel safer just the same.

Anthony built it in the first year of their marriage, while the two of them shared her childhood room at her parents' house. "You'll have a washer and dryer, babe," he told her. "Dishwasher, picture window, any color carpet you want."

She remembers bending over the plans with Anthony and her parents after dinner, clutching his hand under the table: the three little bedrooms, the dining nook. At his happiest, Anthony could be genial and loving, laughing too loudly at family parties, keeping up affectionately with old aunts. She'd grown up with him—he'd been her cousin's best friend—and she'd loved the clarity of his vision of their future together. Finding the land had been so easy it had seemed fated: four beautiful acres surrounded by hills, just outside of Las Penas, the asking price five hundred dollars under what they'd decided they could manage. Each day, while she went to answer phones and sort paperwork at the legislature in Santa Fe, thrilled with the importance and glamour of her first job, Anthony drove out to the land with the bed of his truck filled with cinderblock and cement. Yolanda sometimes forgets how competent and hardworking her husband could be—talented, even, she thinks, looking at the flagstone steps he fit together with geometric precision—and she feels sadness—less at his absence, than that all those good memories were overwritten by what came after.

Stop, thinks Yolanda. Above all she must not let herself get depressed. But who wouldn't be a little blue? Three days ago, she was a woman with a boyfriend and a normal life expectancy, a woman vacationing in Las Vegas.

For the last month Yolanda has been holding the headaches at bay with increasing doses of Aleve. Headache, singular, really, since it never actually goes away, and has, in fact, worsened.

"You're stressed," Cal said two weeks ago, always chivalrous, over a too-expensive dinner at the Steaksmith in Santa Fe. She'd set down her fork to press her head into her palms when the pain nearly scooped her eyes from their sockets. "Come away with me." And he described the fountains and lights, the shows and the escape. Cal is thin, a carpenter with shot knees. His jowls hang loose and pink and clean-shaven, giving him the kindly sad-sack look of a basset hound, and Yolanda agreed.

Who wouldn't agree to a vacation in Vegas, to being cared for so completely by a good man? She met Cal when he came to install the new prefab shelves in the chief clerk's office (a job unworthy of his talents, she discovered later when she saw the shelves in his own house), and for over a year now, he's treated her to dinners and movies and taken her back to his tidy condo, where he lets her pick the show they watch and then, after, is incredibly attentive in bed.

He is so easy to be with, and Yolanda is impressed with the version of herself she is when she's around him: laughing and quick and unencumbered by the past. Unlike any man she's dated, he's never expected her to cook for him, has never asked anything of her, except once, when he was remodeling his master bathroom and wanted her to weigh in on whether he should get a Jacuzzi tub. "I don't have an opinion," she said, because it wasn't fair to let him make permanent decisions based on her preferences.

Cal is, in fact, so perfect that Yolanda cannot understand why she can't love him. Yet the more time they spend together and the more he seems to love her, the more aware she becomes that part of her remains remote.

When she went to Urgent Care in Las Vegas, it wasn't for the headache, but for her acid reflux, which had gotten bad enough that she was eating only saltines. She couldn't enjoy the seafood buffets or the inexpensive cocktails, or even drink coffee anymore, and the caffeine withdrawal certainly wasn't helping her head. Twice she woke in the night so nauseated she had to throw up in the tiny cardboard bathroom of Cal's travel trailer in the Mojave Oasis RV park. Each time she was afraid Cal would wake up and find her, but he was always dead asleep when she crawled back in beside him.

Her acid reflux was not acid reflux, but an ulcer. "Why are you taking so much Aleve?" the RN asked, alarmed. "That's fully six times the recommended dose." When she explained about the headache, he sent her down the road for a CT scan, just to be sure.

The technician blathered cheerfully about her son's trip to France. "I've never been, myself," she said, inserting the needle into the top of Yolanda's hand for the IV of contrast dye. "Why go, when we've got an Eiffel Tower right here in Vegas?" Woozy, Yolanda tried to determine if she was feeling the tug of the needle or of the tape. "You'll feel a little warm when we get this dye flowing, and then you'll roll right in. Just follow the instructions over the speaker." Yolanda barely heard the technician shut the door behind her, because a strange metallic heat grabbed the back of her throat. Before she'd even processed this, the heat shot down her torso, settling in her groin like a violation.

After the scan, doors began whooshing open to welcome her. She was ushered from the dingy emergency facility to a fancier wing of the medical center with grassy courtyards and curving palm trees, where she, Yolanda Padilla, VIP, was treated to an immediate MRI. As she rode the elevator up and down from chilly floor to chilly floor, from

Radiology to Lab to Neurology, receptionists treated her kindly, nurses told her not to worry, medical assistants brought her little Dixie cups of cold water to sip. At first Yolanda *hadn't* worried. She read magazines in the plush chairs and ate a peanut butter cup from the vending machine and rubbed her sleeveless arms, wishing she'd brought a sweater. How pleased and impressed she was with the health care offered in Nevada. What speed! What service! Las Vegas was surely a special place, with its apparent surfeit of doctors and their wide-open appointment books, with its hale and hearty population kept busy at the slots.

But the growing tightness in her stinging, sour stomach belied Yolanda's understanding that such attentive patient care could only mean bad news.

Oncology was located on the top floor of the medical center. A great deal of effort had been expended to mute the essential horror of the place. At either end of the hallway was a cozy little alcove with couches, dim lights, every surface punctuated with tall pink vases of dried pussy willows. Sheer curtains covered the large windows overlooking the city, as if an unimpeded vista might taunt patients with the world they were so close to losing. Or, thought Yolanda, her heart urging flight, inspire them to jump. A small room near the reception featured calming classical music, cushions on the ground, reclining loungers. *Shh . . . Meditation Room*, read the sign on the door.

In the examination room, the comforts were fewer. Pink and green linoleum floor tiles. On the walls, disconcerting desert landscapes of nowhere in particular. And it was even chillier here, the air-conditioning cranked high against the hot atmosphere that pressed itself into the bowl of the valley. Yolanda shivered in her sleeveless shirt.

The appointment could be said to have gone well, insofar as it started on time and the conclusions were clear. Pressing on the left frontal lobe of her cerebral cortex, the scans revealed, was a tumor the size of an almond.

Her oncologist, Dr. Mitchell, sat beside the examination table and pointed out the various fuzzy regions of her brain on the scan. "Here you see the occipital lobe, which is responsible for converting light on the retina into images in your brain. And this is your frontal lobe, which is responsible for voluntary movement and other higher functioning, planning, social navigation, and whatnot." Even Yolanda could see the problem: a mottled white island in her brain.

"Unshelled or shelled? The almond."

Dr. Mitchell paused and smiled. "I always get those confused. Shell on."

Behind Dr. Mitchell stood a very young Chinese man who'd introduced himself with an impossible accent. Dr. Mitchell had explained that he was a med student from UNLV. The boy kept tugging at his stethoscope.

"Can I have a blanket or something?" she asked. "It's cold in here."

Dr. Mitchell looked vaguely at the student. "Get her a covering cloth." He waited, sympathetic and patient, while the cloth was found, and then he unfolded it and set it across Yolanda's shoulders as though she were his date to the opera. Yolanda was grateful that she was in her own clothes, hadn't been made to undress and put on a gown.

Dr. Mitchell scooted his rolling stool closer. He was just below her eye level. He might be about to propose to her or fit her with new shoes. It seemed absurd that she was sitting so close to this glossy man—she could lean down and kiss him.

Yolanda had a lot of respect for the medical profession—for professionalism in general—but she found herself looking hard at this man with his tanned face and lean body. His gray hair was as short and glossy as a squirrel's pelt. There was something suspect about Dr. Mitchell, and maybe that something was that he was a doctor in Las Vegas, where everything was show and surface. Maybe Dr. Mitchell was just playing the part of doctor, and really behind the scenes he was a craps dealer at Harrah's. Or a Chippendale in a little zebra-print loincloth. Yolanda could picture that. From her perch on the high bed, she looked out the window; no sheer curtains in this room; this room was all about facing facts. Below her, lush green golf courses spread like patches of carpet across dry desert floor, and swimming pools were blue lozenges pressed into the dirt.

"This is serious." Dr. Mitchell tapped the brain scan with his ballpoint, leaving little hatch marks on the tumor. "Given the size and the worsening of your headaches and fatigue and the rest of your symptom-atology, I'm concerned. I understand you're on vacation. Do you have anyone who can be here with you?"

Yolanda shook her head. "I'm fine," she said. She couldn't bear Cal's sad eyes, his big dry hand squeezing hers, his assumption of their inti-macy. He'd spent the whole vacation doing nice things for her: getting up early to bring her muffins, proposing dinner at fancy restaurants on the Strip, walking proudly past their neighbors in the RV park with his hand around her waist. He thought they were headed toward marriage. "Please just tell me what I need to know."

She remembered an appalling joke Amadeo had brought home from school when he was nine. *Do you have HIV? Are you positive?* She'd whirled on him, her own son, breezily bringing such terrifying, hurtful words into her kitchen. "Never, *ever* joke about that," she'd said, and his smile had vanished at the urgency of her tone. "People *die* from that." She'd known the word *die* would frighten him, and she was glad to see his stricken expression. "But not you, right, Mom? You're not going to die?" Amadeo had asked, and she'd relented. Of course not, she'd said.

Behind Dr. Mitchell, the med student had removed his stethoscope and was now occupied with stretching the headset wide, then bringing the ear tips to meet each other, over and over.

Dr. Mitchell inhaled. "Based on the presentation, my guess is that this is a glioblastoma multiforme."

The med student stopped fiddling with his stethoscope and looked up, alarmed.

"Are you sure there isn't someone who can be with you?"

Yolanda shook her head tightly.

Dr. Mitchell nodded once. "Well. This is a serious diagnosis. Glio-blastoma is aggressive. It's uncommon, maybe one in every fifty thou-sand people, but when it hits, it works quickly."

Yolanda forced a laugh. "One in fifty thousand. Wish I'd been so lucky at the slots last night." She'd never given much thought to her brain. When she thought of organs, Yolanda thought of her stomach usually, with its seething acids, or of her heart, always straining, always ready to be broken. Not her brain. "Can't you just take it out? Don't they have real good surgeries now?"

"Given the location, total resection probably isn't an option—it would almost certainly damage the brain tissue. I recommend we remove part of it to reduce pressure and buy you time, but glioblastomas have deep roots." These roots, Dr. Mitchell explained, were tapping into the blood her brain needed. Yolanda imagined her tumor like a squatter siphoning electricity from neighbors with extension cords. She imagined the blood vessels thickening, tightening into a wicked net, choking off her poor brain until it spluttered and twitched. "They almost always come back."

There were, unfortunately, no good options, he explained. Treatments included radiation and chemo.

Yolanda had heard on some commercial or other that humans only used five percent of their brain's capacity. "What about that? What about my other ninety-five percent?" Wasn't that enough to keep her alive?

Dr. Mitchell smiled sadly, as if she were making a joke. But she wasn't joking—she wasn't!

"So what does this mean?" Yolanda asked.

"It means you're dying." He said this simply, gently, and Yolanda was grateful for his clarity. This was the one thing she truly understood since this whole rigmarole started. "With surgery and treatment, median duration of survival for aggressive tumors like this is a year, fifteen months."

"And without treatment?" Yolanda's voice sounded very dry and calm to her ears, and she was proud of her composure.

"No one knows the future, of course, but we could be looking at as little as five months."

Yolanda slumped, the paper crinkling beneath her. "I'm not good at games of chance. Last night I lost two hundred dollars in twenty minutes."

Dr. Mitchell smiled sympathetically. "Keep that sense of humor. It'll be a blessing to you."

So: brain tumor. That was how she was going to go. No one in her family had ever died of such a thing. People in her family either lived forever, growing smaller and crankier, still baking and cleaning and hauling wood—take Tío Tíve, for example—or they died in some preposterous and untimely way: car accidents (Anthony), falls from roofs (Yolanda's second cousin), overdoses (Elwin). These were idiotic, wasteful, hapless deaths, and they could, in certain retellings, be darkly funny. Never anything so bland and dreary as a body turning against itself, of resilient, inventive cells dividing industriously, spreading and conquering as in a game of Risk. These cells were the American Dream. They were the Sam Waltons of cells, the Starbucks, starting small and taking over vast swaths of territory, leaving destruction and foreclosures and empty storefronts in their wake.

Because of the location of her tumor, Yolanda could look forward to loss of fine motor ability—goodbye typing, goodbye cooking—as well as of speech and balance and more primitive functions. Seizures. Personality change.

In the end Yolanda slid off the table. She folded the cotton cover neatly, snapping it. Dr. Mitchell and the med student watched her.

"I'm going home," she told them both. "Back to New Mexico."

"I don't recommend that. We need to bring in a neurologist and should schedule surgery and start a course of radiation immediately. We should operate now, relieve the pressure on the brain."

"I don't live here!" Yolanda whipped her head around, afraid of being grabbed and wheeled away.

"We can see about arranging for a medical transfer."

"I'm fine. I got myself here, didn't I?"

Dr. Mitchell looked at Yolanda, then stood, pushing himself up on his thighs. He ran a hand through his molded gray hair. "I can't keep you here against your will. But I need to impress upon you the severity of your condition. I urge you to get treatment immediately when you get home. And no driving—coordination, cognition, it's all affected, and the risk of seizure is high." He left the room, the med student hurrying after. When Dr. Mitchell came back he was alone, armed with a sheaf of

50

papers, including an AMA, Against Medical Advice, which stated that she, Yolanda Padilla, had been informed of the risks of her voluntary discharge and was operating with full knowledge of those risks. She would not sue Las Vegas Medical when her seizures set in.

This was only the beginning of her medical journey, Dr. Mitchell said as he handed her a list of referrals in Santa Fe and Albuquerque. She should be in touch for as long as it took for her to find a doctor she trusted, and once she did, Dr. Mitchell would work with her team in New Mexico to sort out what was best for her. When he left, Yolanda flipped through the pages. On the last page, under the innocuous heading *Further Resources*, was "Hospice of New Mexico."

Yolanda dropped the packet on the examination table. When she rubbed her arms, she found that she couldn't feel her palms against her skin. This was why they kept it so cold in here, she realized. So that people would be too slow to react with violence against the news, too numb to feel despair.

Instead of telling Cal about the tumor, she paid a shocking amount for a dye job and dramatic jagged layers, packed her bags, rented an absurd convertible, and announced she was leaving. Poor Cal, baffled behind the steering wheel as she jumped out and slammed his truck door. He waited, watching from the curb as she went into the Hertz office, thinking she'd turn around, give him some explanation, and she did turn around, told him to *just leave.*

How good it felt to be driving yesterday! Top down, phone shut off, map flapping crazily on the seat beside her. She was, for the first time she can remember, completely untethered to anyone. As she left Las Vegas, the Mojave spread wide around her, Yolanda combed her fingers through her spiky new haircut, feeling like a starlet, like the lovely title character in some movie about rebirth and reinvention.

At first she truly didn't think about her diagnosis. She sped over the blacktop as if her tires would stick if she slowed. Sage-scented wind caught in her hair, pressed her into the seat like firm hands against her chest. Higher crept the speedometer: eighty, ninety, ninety-nine, and then, for a moment, a hundred. The car trembled, buffeted by the wind, and Yolanda wondered if this was the kind of loss of self Anthony had been seeking all those years, driving fast, soaking himself in alcohol. It was exhilarating even to stop to pee in those dinky desert towns with their overpriced gas, and she found herself flirting with the grubby and slightly threatening men who seemed to be the only permanent inhabitants of these outposts. She could be kidnapped, Yolanda thought with an oddly light heart, murdered, left for dead among the sagebrush, and not a soul would know where she was!

But the thrill had worn off, and the vast deserts began to feel just desolate. The landscapes changed, from sage and scrub brush to agave, briefly to dry ponderosa forest, then back to stunted prickly pear and yucca, but to Yolanda, it all looked dead. Her brain was heavy in her head, her tumor pushing against the walls of her skull. She put the top up, then down again, hoping to recapture some of her earlier elation, but now the air just felt thin and dusty and too bright.

Finally, after a sleepless night in a motel outside of Shiprock, she is home, but she sits rooted, her hands still gripping the steering wheel at ten and two. Her armpits are damp, her sundress wrinkled, her gut hollow. The engine ticks.

Near the steps, partially screened by her rosebushes (which do not appear to have been watered in her absence), another palm-sized piece of stucco has dropped off the cinderblock. The morning sun glazes the picture window with a wobbling reflection of piñon and piled white clouds and sky—and there is Yolanda herself, a blur in her red convertible—obscuring what awaits her inside: demands and expectations and drama that she is not ready to contend with, but that will, nonetheless, be dropped squarely into her lap.

Soon, she thinks melodramatically, her reflection won't be here, won't be anywhere on this earth.

Now, bursting out the front door, stomach huge, wet hair combed and dripping spots into her T-shirt, is Angel. "Gramma!"

Yolanda arranges her face into a smile, steps out of the car to meet her granddaughter's vigorous embrace. "Look at you! How are you feeling?"

"Look at *you*! Look at your hair!" Angel cries, laughing. "Where *were* you?" Then Angel bursts into tears, and Yolanda is home.

———

"ANYWAYS, I DON'T *GET* IT," says Angel, her tone belligerent. She leans over the breakfast bar. "My thing is, it's stupid, hurting your-self like that." When Yolanda doesn't respond, Angel pops her eyes at her. "Well?"

Yolanda's never seen Angel like this. Usually she's sweet-tempered and ebullient, always kissing Yolanda's cheek and reaching for her hand. But for the last hour, the girl's been trailing her, full of indignation over Amadeo, certain of Yolanda's agreement.

Yolanda shakes her head, tired. "I don't know, mi hijita." She doesn't have it in her, she really doesn't. Her head is killing her, and she's too tired even to be stunned by the news Angel has reported, that her son went and got himself nailed up there. Amadeo himself is at Easter Mass, another surprise. "I didn't think he'd . . . go so extreme." She's impressed, actually, and thinks if he can apply that kind of determina-tion to a job—any job—he might be okay.

"He thinks he's so tough. He's just showing off."

"It's an old tradition, honey," says Yolanda. "A sacred thing."

"Maybe for other people," Angel says. "*He's* showing off."

Yolanda hasn't even unloaded the car, and already here she is, with her head in the fridge. What was she thinking, after twelve hours of driving, arranging Easter dinner? Frozen meat they have, a five-pound bag of wrin-kled potatoes. On the counter, a head of garlic has sprouted green scapes that arc toward the window. Sticky spills on the linoleum, the trash over-flowing to the point that it no longer fits under the sink. The brown living room carpet is littered with gum wrappers and mysterious threads. Every surface is covered with abandoned soda and—she sighs—beer cans.

Once, just once, Yolanda would like to have a perfectly clean house, every dish and glass washed and dried and waiting in the cupboard. It will never happen.

Yolanda shakes out a new trash bag and starts clearing the refrigerator: slimy bags of greens, sour milk, liquefied tomatoes. She throws out whole Tupperwares, too, because she can't bear to face their appalling contents, remnants of meals she herself cooked for Amadeo weeks ago. There aren't any fresh vegetables at all.

"Why wasn't your cell on, Gramma? I tried calling you a thousand times."

"Bad reception in Nevada." Please, she thinks, please just leave me be. Yolanda feels for the girl. The procession is startling, especially the first time. She presses the heel of her hand into her forehead. "I don't know what to tell you. It's an important part of who we are, and it keeps the men out of trouble."

Yolanda sees the hermandads scattered through the mountains as pure spots of hope, now that the communities are dwindling and drug-blighted. She's glad her Aunt Fidelia isn't here to see her son Elwin's story reproduced over and over in houses all through these hills. Passing the syringe in a kind of communion. Sometimes three generations at once, slumped in their living rooms with needles in their arms, eyelids fluttering. Grandmothers with naloxone in their purses tucked among the used tissues and lipsticks and EBT cards. The *Rio Grande Sun* is packed with obituaries of young people: *Died suddenly at home. Passed away unexpectedly. Entered Eternal Rest.* She has always lived in terror that Amadeo might find himself on that path, is so grateful that he hasn't yet.

"There was blood everywhere." Angel's voice rises. "A kid shouldn't have to see her dad like that. Why would you let him?"

Yolanda takes in her granddaughter's soft brown eyes, the stubborn jut of her chin. She's surprised that Angel has somehow divined her role in the whole business. Yolanda didn't just *let* him; she actually begged her Tío Tíve to give him a chance, a detail she prays never gets back to Amadeo.

After his DWI in December, he stormed around the house and tore up all his citation papers so Yolanda had to call the courthouse to request copies, claiming to have accidentally thrown them away. She did it because she loves him and because she'd felt guilty; he accused her of lying about not getting his voicemail when he was arrested, and the fact is that she *didn't* hurry down to the police station, that after she got his message the next morning she'd taken an hour to compose herself because she'd been so angry. At the station, she was apologetic and submissive around the police, as though she'd been the one driving drunk.

"Please, Tío." She stood in her uncle's living room. Velvet sofa, gold-framed mirrors on the wall, a topless, armless plaster goddess on the sideboard; despite being dead for twenty years, her Aunt Fidelia is still a presence here. Her uncle's country CDs and insulin vials rest among dusty plastic grapes in cut crystal bowls. She remembered being a child, playing Yahtzee with her beloved older cousin and Anthony in the back bedroom, their patience with her as she laboriously tallied the points. "Amadeo is like his dad, I think. In that much pain. Like Elwin."

Tíve grunted and pushed at the air in annoyance. "Your boy doesn't have nothing to be in pain about."

"Oh, Tío. He lost his father. That's a trauma for a five-year-old."

"Well, Elwin didn't lose his father, and neither did Anthony. Those boys made their own problems."

"I guess we don't always know what our kids go through. They were good boys underneath. Like my Amadeo." She wanted her uncle to remember Amadeo as he once was: his black-lashed eyes and round open face, his easy affection. He held her hand until he was fifteen with such trusting ease. Even into his teens, he spoke to Jerry, his pet corn snake, with the tenderness of a mother. But she couldn't describe Amadeo without making her uncle think of his own lost son.

"Well," Tíve grumbled, but then he took Amadeo out for burgers and made him a novicio.

"Your father is a grown man, Angelica," Yolanda says now. "He makes his own choices." Yolanda's tone is harsher than she intends, a tone she's never, to her recollection, used with the girl before.

Angel flinches, the hurt plain in her face. She stalks off to the living room couch and settles among her papers and folders.

Yolanda begins to tackle the pile of dishes, cramming them into the already-packed dishwasher. She drops a ham in the sink to defrost, enjoys the solid weighty clank when it hits metal. Easter. As a child, she loved the candy and new dresses, the white shoes and short gloves. The hats with their white netting and ribbon flowers. But since then, the holiday has meant work. Eggs to hide, baskets to assemble, heavy dishes to cook.

Growing up, Yolanda had felt rich in family, because she'd had Elwin and that dense network of cousins and aunts, everyone streaming in and out of each other's houses, rooting through each other's refrigerators, the women gathering to wrap tamales and sip their whiskey-and-waters. But her generation hasn't been a productive bunch: a child here and there, dispersed all over the state and country. And Yolanda's own children actively dislike each other. If not for Yolanda's dinners, when would Valerie and Amadeo ever see each other? When will they see each other when she's gone?

"I am sick," she'll tell them tonight. Yolanda shuts the refrigerator and steadies herself against it. She cups her head, squeezes as hard as she can, but gets no relief.

She catches herself in the mirror by the door. Yesterday, she loved her hair: its interesting purple-red hue, the way the stylist had gelled it spiky and mussed. But now it looks garish and artificial, and Yolanda herself, beneath it, is drawn and pale-lipped. She runs a finger along the crepey skin beneath her eyes, and the skin holds there, gathered where her fingertip had been, before slowly sliding back.

On the couch, Angel frowns down at her notebook. Her hair is pulled into a ponytail, her legs spread, belly sagging between them.

Having children is terrifying, the way they become adults and go out into the world with cars and functioning reproductive systems and credit cards, the way, before they've developed any sense or fear, they are equipped to make adult-sized mistakes with adult-sized consequences.

She's filled with sad affection for the girl, and also remorse. She should have brought presents. Oh, god. Angel's birthday was on Friday.

"Hijita," Yolanda calls. "Do me a favor and bring my purse."

Angel gets up and makes her way over. "I like your haircut," she says as she sets the purse on the counter. "I meant to say before. It's very punk. Sorry I made you mad, Gramma. I forget you had such a long drive."

Yolanda touches her hand to her new short spikes and smiles at her granddaughter. "Oh, hijita, I'm not mad. Just tired." Yolanda pats Angel's hand, flooded with love for her. "Listen, about your dad, don't take it personal."

Angel nods as if to shake the tears back into her head. "Tell me about your boyfriend," she manages. "Is he nice?"

"Oh," Yolanda says lightly, grateful to her granddaughter for letting her off the hook. "He's just a friend."

Angel's eyebrows tip in real concern. "Did you guys break up?"

"No, it was just time to come home. You know men." Yolanda grins and bats away Angel's pity. "Sometimes you need a break."

Right now, Cal is probably outside his trailer in the shade of his blue-striped awning, lawn chair anchored in the dirt. He's probably trying to read the paper, calling friendly greetings to neighbors on their way to the park's pool. He'd tell them Yolanda had been summoned home early by a family emergency, and he'd agree to pass on their good wishes.

"I'm sorry, Gramma. That really sucks."

"We're fine. But I missed my kids. I missed you. So I hit the road." She laughs, and it sounds convincing to her ears. "Listen, about your dad. He hasn't been like this for a while, but when he was a kid he used to be very religious. He'd pray all the time, before breakfast, after breakfast, on and on. I had to get rid of his children's Bible because he'd get all worked up. They're just stories, I told him, and he'd get even more upset. *What if God decides to flood us out again?* he says. *He won't*, I say. *He promised the people.* But does a promise from God comfort your dad? No way. *Yeah, but what if he changes his mind?*"

Angel laughs and then says soberly, "Maybe he was worried because his dad died."

Yolanda nods. It hurts her how obvious Angel's need to forgive Amadeo is, hurts her that she, Yolanda, is pushing for this forgiveness, when the girl has every reason to be upset. "Probably he was. Probably he's always felt something missing." She fishes in her bag for her wallet, withdraws three hundred-dollar bills, which she slides over. "A little something, hijita. Happy birthday."

"Whoa. Gramma, this is too much! Thank you!"

Yolanda is cheered by Angel's smile.

"It's really nice. Thank you." But then she says worriedly, "I think this is too much."

Yolanda leans forward in confidence. "I won big." It's remarkable, how easily this happy grandmother act comes to her, even feeling as bad as she does. She plucks a number at random. "Three thousand dollars."

"Are you *joking* me?" cries Angel. "Three *thousand* dollars?"

"I'm glad you're here, honey. This is your home, too." She comes around to hug Angel and pats the girl's stomach. What a wonderful, necessary, joyful distraction she and her new baby will offer. "I'll give you more when the baby comes."

Outside, tires crunch as Amadeo's truck pulls in. "Wope," says Yolanda, looking to the window. "Your dad's here."

Amadeo is in high spirits. "Mom! You're home!" he cries, hugging her. "What happened to your hair? I didn't know whose car that was." He's shaved and smells of soap and cologne. Both hands are bandaged, the stubby tips of his fingers peeking out of the gauze.

"It's a rental. You look nice, hijito."

Amadeo beams. "I just went to Mass. It was great. I'm starving, though, you know, from fasting. You should've come, Angel." He shoots his daughter a pointed look.

"Ha," she says flatly. Angel holds up her bills. "Look what Gramma gave me. Isn't that nice?" There's an edge of cruelty in her steady bland smile.

Amadeo looks to Yolanda in horror. "What's she going to do with that kind of money?"

Angel grins. "*And* she's going to give more to the baby. She won three thousand dollars!"

Yolanda avoids her son's eyes. "I just thought we could give him a little start," she says apologetically. Now's the time for her to give Amadeo a gift, and they both know it, but part of Yolanda stands aside and watches with a kind of gleeful defiance as she busies herself with wiping the counters. The moment stretches and passes.

Amadeo turns away and looks out the window. "You rented a *Mustang*?"

Yolanda shrugs. "I wanted a convertible. Wanted to see the sights."

She ties up the trash bags, then sets them at Amadeo's bare feet. "You can take these out for me, honey."

"I can't." Amadeo holds up his bandaged hands. The medical tape is grubby around the edges. "I got the nails on Friday."

"I heard." Yolanda pats his cheek, then turns to fit a last glass into the dishwasher. "I'm proud of you, hijito. Bring in my luggage, too, will you? Be a nice chance for you to look at the car." Yolanda measures detergent, clicks shut the dishwasher.

"I've seen a Mustang before." His tone is hurt.

"How was the procession, hijito?"

His shoulders hunch and he scowls, and Yolanda sees him, as she so often does, as the three-year-old he once was. It pains her to think of him so overgrown and vulnerable.

"It was fine," he snaps. He makes no move to leave with the garbage bags. Instead he announces piteously, "I'm getting sick." He clears his throat. "I'm coming down with something. Maybe from the stress of Lent and Calvario and everything." Amadeo coughs into a bandaged hand. At first it sounds dry and unconvincing, but he tries again, and this time he taps into something.

"Well, then stay away from me," says Angel. "I don't want to be doing no labor breathing with snot coming out my nose."

From the bowl on the counter, Amadeo fumbles a softening orange. Bracing it against his middle, he manages to remove two sticky chunks of peel, juice dripping into his bandage and his shirt, then glares at the overripe flesh. The too-sweet scent fills the kitchen.

"Help me clean up and I'll make you both some honey and lemon. We have a lot to do before Valerie and the girls get here."

Amadeo's head jerks up. "You invited *her*?" He tosses the orange back in the bowl. Fruit flies rise in irritation, then settle. "What about a quiet night, just *us*?"

Yolanda snatches the orange and drops it in the trash. "Of course I invited Valerie. She's my daughter. She's your sister. You need to be nice." As an afterthought, she dumps the rest of the contents of the bowl, too, then looks at each of them sternly. "This place is a mess."

"We didn't know when you were getting home," Amadeo says. "You could've called. Things were really busy here. With Good Friday and all. And it's hard for me to clean and stuff." He lifts his hands. "Plus, it wasn't just *me* making a mess."

Angel casts him a dirty look across the counter. "*I* tried to keep it clean, Gramma. I did the dishes literally eight times in a row, but he had to take a turn, too. And I have my program and I'm doing my GED, and Brianna says we got to prioritize—"

"They're the same thing," Amadeo interrupts. "The program is *for* the GED."

"No, it's also to learn baby development. Also my back's been hurting and I'm tired all the time. *You* know how it is, Gramma."

They both feel entitled to be here in her home, and it surprises Yolanda that she doesn't necessarily think they are. "Things have to change around here. By the time this wonderful little baby comes, we are not going to be living like animals."

They groan, but without conviction. Really, they're relieved. They've been waiting for her, Yolanda realizes, waiting for her to put their lives in order. She will right what's wrong, referee their contests, soothe their hurts and uncertainties. She's raised babies before. No one loves these two more than Yolanda does, and she will know how to proceed. She looks into their grouchy, childish faces, and sighs.

Amadeo's sister apparently doesn't notice that he isn't speaking to her and hasn't since her obnoxious gift last Christmas. When Valerie comes in, her arms filled with bulging shopping bags tearing at the sides, the first thing she does is drop it all and hug him before he can dodge. Still gripping his arms, she steps back and takes Amadeo in. He almost can't look at her: the absurdly long hair hanging loose, the oversized earrings, her draping black dress, the ambiguously ethnic scarf. And that superior forbearing expression, as if she's willing to humor him, but only up to a point. "Good to see you, little brother."

Amadeo nods coolly but she misses it, because she's already turned to Angel. "Oh my god, Angelica! Let me *see* you! You're enormous!"

Angel ducks her head, pleased and a little shy. "Hey, Aunt Val."

Valerie hugs her, then crosses the living room to switch off the television. Two years ago Valerie got rid of her TV. If she's not making a big show of ignorance whenever someone mentions *The Bachelor* or a piece of celebrity gossip, then she's going on about some project one of the girls has done with the endless stores of time and intellect and creativity endemic to television-free households. "I don't know how you guys can hear yourselves think with that thing going all the time," she says, dusting off her hands.

Armed with a brand new master's degree, Valerie is now a counselor in the Albuquerque public school system, and is therefore an expert on everything. She took night and weekend classes for three years, and for three years she swanned around, sighing and rubbing her temples, talking about how overworked she was. "Full-time job, full-time school, full-time single mom." She tosses around theories and diagnoses, pressing her lips. "Hmm," she says, nodding knowingly. "Ah-*hah*." She has the maddening tendency to read into even the most banal comments. If, for example, Amadeo says that he wanted to kill the lady with the six hundred coupons in front of him at the checkout, Valerie's eyebrows will pinch in concern. "Are you having urges to hurt other people, Dodo?" Amadeo's theory—and god knows he's no school counselor—is that Valerie never got over his birth, which means she's spent all but five years of her life resentful.

Only three things make Valerie bearable: First, she's gotten fat and she's self-conscious about it. Second, she was hit by her ex-husband, which makes her skittish around any displays of masculine strength, so Amadeo need only flex his fist or massage a bicep to disconcert her. Third, her kids are pretty cute.

Or used to be. Now that she's twelve, Lily acts just as superior as her mom. She reads far beyond her grade level, no surprise, given her glasses and frizzy mop of hair. She and her little sister are still standing in the doorway, the screen propped open against their bottoms, staring solemnly at his beer and his bandaged hands, as if they're afraid to step all the way into the house with Amadeo there. Uncle Amadeo, erratic, mean drunk. He can imagine what Valerie tells them: watch out for Uncle Amadeo, never get in a car with Uncle Amadeo, whatever you do, don't end up like Uncle Amadeo.

Before he can help himself, he is making a nasty face at them, mouth wide, tongue nearly to his chin. "Rah!" he snarls, raspy and sudden. Lily flinches, then regains her composure and rolls her eyes behind her glasses, but Sarah, the seven-year-old, breaks into a delighted gap-toothed laugh. She's an adorable child, large-eyed, with a sweet black bob, skinny legs poking out of soccer shorts. Amadeo grins back, his irritation transformed into affection for this niece who is, it seems, still too young to despise him.

"Hijitas! Get in here!" cries Yolanda, and they rush their grand-mother, the screen thwacking.

Angel grins at her cousins. "Holy crap, you guys are big!"

"Man," says Amadeo, slouching against the wall. It's not easy to grip his beer around his bandage, but he's managing. "Today really took it out of me. They got me on painkillers and everything." He holds up his hands, but no one sees. At Mass this morning, several people touched his sleeve with reverence. "You done real good," Shelby Morales murmured, and he and Amadeo hugged gingerly, each careful of the other's tender back. Al Martinez rested a gentle hand on Amadeo's wrist. "God bless, son."

His performance wasn't just a performance, but a true crucifixion. How many people can say they've done that for God? Though Amadeo will never admit this to a living soul, while the priest droned on about joy and resurrection, he allowed himself to fantasize about being invited to the Vatican. Saint Amadeo. It has a dignified, archaic ring to it.

Maybe his hands are infected. In fact, they probably are. He unwraps the left bandage, which is moist and smelly. So is the wrinkled, pale flesh of his hand. The nail hole itself doesn't seem too bad, though—just boiled-looking. The holes didn't even require real stitches, just a kind of paper tape, a tetanus shot, and a prescription for antibiotics. "Keep the wounds clean," the nurse told him, "and they'll close right up."

"That is disgusting," Angel says. "Don't do that crap in front of us."

"How'd it go on Friday, Dodo?" Valerie calls. Cupboard doors open and shut. She's grazing; she's got a handful of chips, which she eats swiftly, one by one, her fingers delicate pincers.

"Oh, it went just great," says Angel aggressively. "Ask him how his hands are."

"I heard," says Valerie. "Unbelievable."

Yolanda glances at Lily and Sarah and says with guarded cheer, "We don't need to talk about this now. How's school, girls?"

His mother might have slapped him. "Are you *ashamed* of me?"

"Of course not, honey, but blood and whatnot, not at dinner. Careful, Valerie. Watch your Points. We'll eat soon."

"I'm not doing Points anymore." Valerie pushes a cookie into her mouth whole.

"I'm an atheist," brays Lily. "I believe Jesus was a person, but that other stuff just got made up."

"Oh," says Yolanda mildly, "let's not talk like that, either."

"My question is, what's the point?" Angel says. "Life doesn't suck enough?"

Amadeo's hands, thick in their bandages, don't fit in his pockets; he can't think what to do with them. He wishes his uncle were here to explain. They take it seriously coming from Tío Tíve. His mother's proud of her uncle's role in the tradition. In Tío Tíve, it's noble, authentic. He's heard both his mother and sister bragging to people, usually other women, usually Anglo transplants, people from their great wider worlds of college and the legislature. They brag about it the same way they brag about their Spanish blood, about having been in America for four hundred years, about the fact that they still live in their *ancestral village* (Valerie's term). But somehow, in Amadeo, they can't believe the feeling is genuine. Somehow, in their eyes, his participation tarnishes the tradition, degrades it from the romance of sepia to garish cereal-box color, from true religious conviction to pathology. "I thought you were *glad* I was in the hermandad."

"Oh, hijito, I'm very proud of you."

"It's cool you're keeping the tradition alive—I mean, it's our family history. And community is great." Valerie eyes his bandages. "Just maybe don't go overboard. Do you have to do physical therapy or anything?" She shuts the cupboard, then crosses the living room. She settles herself into an armchair, tugging the fabric at her boobs. "I don't know, I could never believe in a God who wanted me to hurt myself."

God doesn't *want* it, Amadeo longs to explain. It's something *you* want to do *for* God, if you care enough. He'd like to argue with Valerie, but knows that she, with her college degrees and intro religious studies classes, can out-argue him. "No one's telling you to believe nothing," he says. A familiar sense of drowning helplessness fills him, and he kicks a stack of catalogs waiting to be recycled. They slide smoothly across the carpet.

For Christmas Valerie gave Amadeo a hardback book called *Mastering Ares: Breaking Free from the Prison of Male Rage*. This is why he isn't speaking to her. The cover—fiery splashes of red and orange—features the naked, muscled god of war looming over an exploding volcano and looking pissed, with a little smiling cartoon man in a business suit stepping out of a doorway in his chest. "The author is very well-regarded," Valerie told him primly, as he sat there turning the thing in his hand. Thanks to that book, Amadeo has discovered new depths of male rage. He will never forgive his sister, ever.

"Yeah, that's not a great present," his mother conceded when Amadeo cornered her in the kitchen. Amadeo had, for a moment, felt vindicated, until she paused, hands motionless in the dishwater, and ventured, "It's maybe worth thinking about, though." That was a terrible night, that Christmas Eve, and Amadeo is glad Angel wasn't there. He only hopes Valerie hasn't told her about it.

Now, they've all turned their attention smoothly away from him so as not, he supposes, to set him off.

From the kitchen doorway, he watches his sister and daughter on the couch uneasily. The house is itself once again—vacuumed, table extended and set with a plastic lace tablecloth, femininity reasserting itself. He wishes things were right between him and Angel; it makes him nervous to have no one on his side. Angel and Valerie laugh.

"Oh!" Valerie leaps up. "I brought you some stuff." She drags the bags across the carpet. "It's from when Lily and Sarah were babies, but you know babies, they grow so fast they never wear anything out."

"That's really nice!" Angel looks truly touched, her smile slow and big and clear. Amadeo is surprised to find that he's envious; why did it never occur to him to buy her baby things?

Valerie starts dumping the bags on the living room floor, and the females converge on the pile like zombies, rendered powerless in the presence of tiny pants.

"And," says Valerie, "I found Sarah's old car seat in the garage."

Angel kneels beside the bounty. In spite of himself, Amadeo leans over the breakfast bar to watch. Stained onesies and shorts, misshapen little T-shirts, individual peanut-sized socks floating around everywhere. When she speaks, Angel's voice is muted. "Thanks, Aunt Val."

"This stuff was mine?" asks Sarah, digging. She sticks a fist out of the neck of a yellow smocked shirt and waggles it like a head. "Hello!" she squeaks. "I am a shirt mouse!" She turns to her mom. "Hey. What if I want to keep it?"

Lily is the only one not interested in the mound of stuff. She has tucked herself into a corner of the couch under a crocheted afghan where she's been scowling into the pages of a fat young adult novel. Now, though, she withdraws her thumbnail from her mouth and informs her sister, "Actually, most of it was mine. So."

Middle school isn't easy for Lily. Last year there was a scandal when she reported several classmates for sexual harassment to the president of the school board. The boys had, it seemed, been rating the girls, with separate scores for body, face, and overall fuckability. ("What was Lily's score?" Amadeo made the mistake of asking, and his mother just narrowed her eyes at him.) The firestorm ended, predictably, with Lily's complete ostracism from the seventh grade. She was featured on the evening news in a segment called "KAQB Celebrates Kids Who Can," and the family gathered to watch as Lily explained with unnerving monotonic eloquence to a reporter that a middle school that isn't safe for one girl isn't safe for anyone. If Lily had been cuter or less self-righteous or less articulate, she might have come through the ordeal all right. But as it was, she cut a singularly unsympathetic figure, a pint-sized nag pushing her glasses up her nose, and it hurt Amadeo to think of his sister allowing his niece to expose herself like that. When, at the commercial, he suggested that maybe Lily shouldn't have gotten involved, Valerie turned on him. "This is *why* I fought tooth and nail for full custody and a lifetime restraining order." She jabbed a finger at Lily, who sat hunched against the armrest. "She's growing up to be a powerful woman, and I'm proud of that," Valerie declared, and Lily, powerful woman, picked miserably at the thicket of her eyebrow.

"Technically," Lily tells her mother now, lowering her book with forbearance, "you should have asked us before giving away our stuff."

"Angel's baby doesn't have a lot of nice things. And since we do, we're going to share."

Angel scratches at something crusted on a miniature UNM sweatshirt, then folds it into a teensy square. She picks up a lavender pinafore and folds that, too. There are several dresses in there, Amadeo sees now, frilly floral pinks and purples. It seems Valerie just brought the whole lot of crap from her house without even bothering to go through it, as though his home were a Goodwill dumpster.

"You know she's having a boy, right?" Amadeo cracks open another beer. He's getting better at maneuvering around the bandages.

"I thought I'd let Angel choose from all of it." Valerie grabs a fistful of hair and winds it over her shoulder into a long glossy rope, her old nervous gesture. "Babies don't understand gender, Amadeo. They don't know what they're wearing."

Angel's cheek and neck are flushed, and, watching her, Amadeo is seized with an urge to defend her. "Did you even *wash* it?"

"No, no," Angel insists. She won't look at him. "It's really nice of you, Aunt Val." She smiles bravely across the pile.

Valerie narrows her eyes at Amadeo's beer. "Haven't you already had one tonight? Aren't you on Percocet?" She points to the prescription bottle on the breakfast bar. "You have to be really careful with that stuff. I'm amazed they prescribed it to an alcoholic."

His daughter's lips part, pale.

"You're lucky I never got into chiva." His voice is louder than he intends.

"Actually," Valerie says, consonants snipped, "you're lucky you didn't."

"It's an epidemic. You see it all over the papers. The whole county is fucked." He glances at Angel. "Screwed."

"Yeah, thanks, I'm aware. You're not seriously asking me to commend you for not being a heroin addict."

Amadeo sets down his empty can, hard. "Well, it's not nothing."

"Mazel tov, little brother."

Amadeo inspects his bicep, flexes, and Valerie looks away, biting her lip.

His mother is touching tiny garments, smoothing them gently in her lap. "I had no idea you saved all this, honey." Something in her voice makes Amadeo look at her, but she lifts her head, blinks, and smiles serenely.

"Are you scared of labor?" Valerie asks Angel, shifting on the floor, her short legs not quite crossing. "I was scared out of my mind. Both times I just wanted to give up and leave them in there." She pulls Sarah onto her lap and says to Lily over the girl's head, "Aren't you glad I didn't? I'd have to open a middle school in my uterus."

"Sick." Lily glances up just long enough to grimace, draws her knees closer to her chest, and goes back to chewing her thumbnail. Sarah wriggles away from her mother.

Angel reaches over her stomach and lays the pinafore carefully on the far side of the pile as if it's contaminated. "I'm not that worried. I'm in my prime childbearing years. Body-wise, I mean, not society-wise. Probably labor won't be too hard."

"Don't you kid yourself," says Yolanda darkly. "I was young, too, and it hurt like heck."

"It's true, Gramma. Studies have shown that it's easier for teen-agers." Angel has brightened. "My teacher, Brianna? She told us that younger girls have less C-sections. All these old ladies waiting 'til they're forty, they're the ones who make problems for themselves. I see them in the grocery store, looking at me all judgy, but they're jealous."

Valerie shoots a worried glance at Lily. "Well—"

But Angel is already telling them about her friend Lizette's birth-ing experience. "It only took her an hour. She wasn't even sure if she'd make it to the hospital before the baby slid out. Not to be gross, but she said it was like taking a crap."

Lily sets down her book and regards her cousin with interest. "Nast."

Angel looks at each of them, bright-eyed. "Have you heard about olive oil? Brianna invited a guest speaker about natural birth. This lady didn't use drugs at all, just did yoga the whole time and rubbed olive oil on her junk. She didn't even have to get snipped."

"Snipped?" asks Amadeo faintly. When Marissa was pregnant, they didn't talk like this, at least not in front of Amadeo. Something's hap-pened to society in the last sixteen years, though. Now it's like these women just can't stop themselves.

"The perineum," Valerie explains. She gives Amadeo a bland smile. Revenge.

"Disgusting, right?" says Angel, warming to her subject. "'Cause if you tear, then it don't heal right and you're all stretched out and you won't give good sex ever again."

"Okay." Amadeo giggles, high and nervous. "Stop." He looks at his mother and sister and is surprised to see revulsion in their faces, too. Lily, on the other hand, regards her cousin with fascination. Maybe they aren't a united front of womanhood after all.

Valerie winds her hair around her hand again and takes a deep breath. "First," she says, pulling out her school counselor voice and preparing her air quotes, "Angel, it's not your job to *give good sex*. And second—" Her fingers go motionless in the air, and Valerie glances again at her eldest daughter.

"Don't get pregnant," Angel tells Lily dutifully. "It'll ruin your life."

Lily looks insulted. "God! I would *never*. God." She scoots back on the couch, away from her cousin, as if screwing up might be contagious. "I'm going to college."

"Well, Angel might go to college, too." But Valerie's voice is chipper and unconvincing.

Yolanda looks at her progeny worriedly and touches her spiky new hair. "So, the cooking olive oil? Just regular stuff from the kitchen?" She shakes her head. "No, thank you very much. I want real hospital-approved stuff on my shee-shee."

Amadeo slaps his hands over his ears. "Mom!"

"Just call it a vagina, Mother."

Yolanda waves Valerie away, laughing. "I hate that word. It's dirty."

"Dirty!" cries Valerie. She leans in, her deep, disturbing cleavage tipped forward. "How can it be dirty? It's an *anatomical* term. *Shee-shee*. Ugh."

"Well," says Yolanda, "I think it's cute." She gets up and circles around to the kitchen, where she begins banging pots, spooning food into serving dishes, opening and closing the oven door. Crisp golden potatoes fragrant with rosemary, the salty ham. Amadeo's mouth waters. He's starving, he realizes. It's been almost two weeks since he's had a real meal, unless you count Angel's bizarre food combos, and Amadeo doesn't.

"Cute! It is a part of a human body, and it does a hell of a lot of work. Just because it's on a woman we should devalue it, make it *cute*?"

"Mom," says Lily. "Stop."

"It is *not* cute," says Angel, pushing herself up. She starts to set the table. "It's gross. But anyways, what I was saying. This guest speaker didn't feel any pain because she self-hypnotized herself and breathed right through it. Did it all in a horse trough right in her living room." She arranges silverware on folded paper napkins.

Panic rises in Amadeo's chest. "Don't do that, Angel. You gotta be in a hospital."

"*Obviously* I'm going to be in a hospital." For the first time this evening Angel looks him full in the face. "You think I'm going to give birth *here*? With you as my breathing coach? No thanks, Captain Hook. I want professionals." She pats her stomach. "Only the best for you, baby." Now her tone is without malice. She resumes placing the dishes around the table, bored, apparently, by her own anger.

Valerie tips her head. "Good for you, Angelica, sticking with your program. It'll make going back to school so much easier."

"I didn't even know I liked school," says Angel. "But now there's a real actual point, you know? Brianna teaches us useful stuff. Maybe all those years I wanted to be learning about baby development and how to make a good life for myself and not the history of the Constitution or whatever stuff they make us learn."

"You can't be a good citizen without understanding the Constitution," Lily informs them.

"All those years," Amadeo repeats to Valerie and his mom with a laugh. He jerks his thumb at Angel. "She talks like she's an old lady. You've done one year of real high school, Angel."

"A year and a half. Plus middle school counts." Angel stops beside the table, holding the platter of ham. It's pink and rich, curls of burned flesh at the edges. "I learned tons of stuff in middle school I didn't care about. Brianna says we have to discover our passions. Like you, Lily: I watched your news clip online. You were amazing, standing up like that."

"Brianna, Brianna, Brianna," says Amadeo. "You in love with this lady?"

Angel thumps the ham on the table. "She's a *role model*. Which, in case you can't tell, I could use."

Amadeo holds up his beer and realizes that he's a little drunk. "To role models." He throws it back and tosses the empty across the room and into the trash. He makes the shot and looks to each of them, grinning, but they're all staring at him like he's committed a felony.

"Do you need to belittle her experience?" Valerie asks the question sincerely.

This isn't who he is! he wants to protest. These women are putting him on the defensive, and it isn't his fault, it just isn't. He's afraid Angel will cry, clinch the case against him.

"I'm sorry." The apology startles him, startles them all. Yolanda's face smooths. "You're doing great," he tells Angel softly. Goodness swells in him, and the feeling is intoxicating. The feeling is a fuck you to Valerie.

Angel raises her head, and now her eyes fill. "Yeah?"

Amadeo isn't seeing Valerie, isn't seeing his mother. Just Angel. It takes so little to make her happy, and he can do it. He'll make his daughter happy, he pledges. "Yeah," he says. "Really great."

———

AFTER A TENSE, quiet dinner, Valerie reluctantly agrees to allow her girls to watch one show, so they're on their bellies, blank-eyed before some sitcom. They munch on the contents of the plastic Easter baskets Yolanda produced, slurping the gunk from Cadbury Creme Eggs, crunching on candy-coated chocolates, while Angel sits above them on the couch, doing her math homework.

All night his mother has been quiet, rubbing her forehead. But now, at Valerie's urging, she retires to her own bedroom to watch her stories, while Amadeo and Valerie clean up, Valerie having volunteered for both of them. "We'll have dessert after, then," his mother says. "I want us to talk."

"Fine. I'll help, but I can't really use my hands." He pops a Percocet, because it's time, and also to remind his sister of his injuries. She says nothing.

While he's putting away leftovers, Amadeo takes the opportunity to get himself another beer. It's number four maybe, or five. He gropes at the tab under his shirt to muffle the pop and fizz and swigs fast, blocked by the refrigerator door from Valerie's critical eye. And because he needs to keep up his strength if he's going to be enclosed in the kitchen with his sister, he tosses back another, placing the empties in the crisper.

"I am so impressed with Angel," Valerie says over the running water.

"Yeah." Amadeo wipes his mouth on his sleeve and starts scraping plates into the trash.

"She seems like she's got a solid head on her shoulders. She'll need that. She's got a tough row to hoe." Valerie laughs. "It just shows how long it's been since I've seen her, but, god, she's grown up."

Amadeo looks over the breakfast bar at the girls in the living room. Angel seems absorbed in her homework. He is entering that stage of intoxication where everything is hazy and bearable.

"Some of the girls I work with in the schools are so unrealistic. They think being pregnant makes them special, like they're one of these celebrity pregnant teens and should get their own shows just because they had unprotected sex. But Angel seems to be engaged in her classes and taking it all really seriously."

Blabbity-blab-blab. The woman doesn't stop. Her forehead is shiny with steam or sweat or both, her black sideburns damp.

"I guess she turned out pretty good."

Valerie shuts off the water and turns to him. She pokes his chest gently with a wet finger, looking up into his face with moist earnestness. The water spreads through his T-shirt and a few tiny bubbles of dish soap collapse into the fabric. "And I'm proud of you, too, brother. You're stepping up. I have to admit, I didn't think you would."

The fuzzy sense of well-being washes away completely, replaced by blurry rage. Amadeo palms his scalp and pulls it toward his shoulder, cracking his neck. First one side, then the other. "I have to admit, Valerie, I didn't think you'd make it through tonight without being a bitch."

Valerie steps away from him and holds up her dripping hands. "I didn't drive all the way from Albuquerque to be verbally assaulted, Amadeo. I don't need your hostility."

"Why do you have to be like that, Valerie? Don't be like that." He gathers more plates from the table.

"Like what? I just said a nice thing. You read insult into every single comment."

Assault, hostility, insult. Valerie buries these accusations in her speech, planting them like land mines. If Amadeo were to press on any one of them, uproot or deny it, the word would detonate, and he'd be blamed for the fallout.

Well, he wants to lean on one of those words, wants to let it blow for the sheer pleasure of the explosion. The universe tends toward chaos, he's heard, and he feels the pull of it, the seductive tug of destruction. He teeters on the edge, and then, with a kind of relief, gives himself to it. "What about you? You feel so great about yourself 'cause you bring some truckload of shit-stained baby clothes. Like Angel's going to be so grateful for your charity. You think we need your secondhand shit?"

He's holding the stack of streaked plates—scraps of fat, blobs of mustard. His bandages are grease-spotted. He watches himself look at the plates, watches himself make the choice. He holds them aloft, eyes on his sister, and then lets them fall. The noise is terrific. Shards spray across the kitchen.

For a moment everything is still, and then his sister's expression makes its way through stages: shock, fear, fury. "You're drunk. Oh my god, you're *drunk*." Valerie rushes from the room. "Mother!"

Yolanda runs from her bedroom, hand on her heart. "Who's hurt?"

Angel, Sarah, and Lily cluster around, looking gape-mouthed at Amadeo and the mess he's made.

In a moment Valerie has gathered her daughters, dragged them outside. "Come *now*, girls." Her voice is low and taut with fear.

Yolanda and Angel follow, barefoot, alarmed. The door slams.

Amadeo alone stands in the bright kitchen, surrounded by shards of porcelain, his heart hammering. Around him the counters are bright and glaring and clean: the green teakettle, the row of cereal boxes on the counter, the bowl of new fruit. Beyond the breakfast bar, the television carries on. From the full sink, the sound of quiet settling as the bubbles melt into the cooling water. And outside, voices.

They're lit by the porch light. Valerie has a daughter pulled tight under each wing. He can't hear them over the laugh track in the living room, but he knows it's the same old conversation. "He's an alcoholic, Mother. He's an alcoholic and he's dangerous."

He leans his forehead against the cool wall. Amadeo doesn't feel remorse for smashing the dishes; he's just sad for his mother because once again she's in the position of having to defend him, to tell Valerie that he's getting better, that he's a good boy at heart.

Amadeo closes his eyes, concentrates on the cool solidity of the wall. Around him the black universe spins.

Yolanda takes a sleeping pill and then a second. Breathe, she instructs herself. Usually just being alone in here calms her, in this bedroom that is all hers. All the beautiful objects she wanted as a child and bought herself as an adult: a canopy, a pink satin bedspread, a skirted dressing table.

But her pillow is flat, her blankets too hot, the room too cold. The pain in her head is too large to be contained by her skull. She wants to open a window for the fresh air, but she doesn't want to hear when Amadeo gets home. Tomorrow, she'll be firm, tell him he needs to quit drinking and to start earning a living. But god, she dreads it.

"I'm sorry, I'm sorry, I'm sorry," he'll intone, and Yolanda will be expected to tip him back into balance. She wants to skip this stage: the apologies, the begging and remorse and entreaties.

"I hate Valerie," he'll whimper into her chest. "She always blames me."

And Yolanda will have to comfort him. "I know," she'll say, patting his head. "But she's right. In this case, she's right."

Ah, well. The cycle won't last forever. She imagines her tumor as a mass of wires, snapping electricity from the raw ends, sending little shocks into her bloodstream.

All night she'd worried about how to tell them about her diagnosis. She watched them squabble, waiting for an opening. As the night progressed, she even began to look forward to her announcement. She enjoyed the thought that with a single sentence, she could blow the whole gathering apart.

But then, as usual, Amadeo took the stage. And Yolanda, who ought to have been surrounded and petted, wept over and adored, was once again backed into the same tired role of defending the indefensible. What does Valerie want her to say? Yes, Amadeo is a disaster. He's a failure. And Yolanda has failed, too, for raising him to be this way.

Poor Valerie. When Valerie was a child, she'd strain over her homework, scowling and nail-biting and breathing fierce taurine breaths, until she was nearly done, just a problem or two from the end, and then she'd burst into tears, melting over the worksheet in anguish, ready to give it all up. Every night, she'd be nearly across the finish line when she'd fall apart, and every night Yolanda would have to come to her rescue, lift her up, praise her and reassure her and promise her that she was smart and capable. And Valerie would argue, because what did Yolanda know about fractions or the Revolutionary War?

Valerie has never forgiven Yolanda for making Anthony move out, has never stopped missing her father. She all but stopped speaking to Yolanda in that time after the separation, whereas little Amadeo would climb into her lap and pat her cheek anxiously, asking, "You okay, Mama?" Valerie baffles Yolanda, moving as she does through the wider world, grasping hold of projects Yolanda doesn't understand. She knows the girl feels hurt by Yolanda's closeness to her brother, but the fact is that Amadeo, for all his malefactions, has been easier for Yolanda to mother, his needs so much clearer.

Yolanda had *liked* Valerie's ex-husband, had been impressed by his job as a network specialist, and grateful her daughter had found a man who knew computers and had a steady job, and at the UNM law school, no less. She liked his easy flirtation with Yolanda herself, the way he never failed to kiss her cheek and always helped bring dishes to the table. Yet all the while, he'd been hitting her daughter, and Valerie, proud Valerie, so intent on being the family's success, hadn't said a word until the bruises had already been documented and charges pressed, when divorce proceedings were already underway. It had chilled Yolanda to realize that her instincts were so blunted, that she'd been so susceptible to that charm.

Yolanda should have known better. For the eleven years of her own marriage, Anthony teetered on the brink of destruction or self-destruction—both options seemed equally likely. When he was really bad, she hid the guns in her uncle's garage, and refused through tears to tell Anthony where they were. She still remembers retrieving them from closet and drawer, toolbox and shed, working quickly, while Anthony was at a job site, placing them all on the floral bedspread: both handguns, three rifles, the BB gun he'd been given as a boy. She remembers their terrible weight, their dull metallic gleam, the sense, as she packed them carefully into a cardboard box, of their killing potential, each one heavy and wound tight, ready to explode. For months at a time, when Anthony was in his dark moods, weeping and raging about matters large and small, threatening to kill himself, Yolanda would drive to work with her trunk filled with every sharp object in the house.

For those months, she was unceasingly aware of skin: her children's skin, Anthony's skin, her own, so thin and easily torn, so unequal to the threat of blade and bullet. To let her children out of her sight was like a physical wound, even to send them on the school bus. Now, Yolanda can't believe she allowed herself to live like that, and for so long. Every evening, she'd run out to the car, retrieve a paring knife from the trunk, chop the onions or trim the pork with furtive haste, then wash and dry and stow the knife before Anthony got home. She wonders now whether she was overreacting or underreacting. Yolanda can never be sure if her responses are appropriate to the situation, which is maybe a result of living in fear for so long. She used to catalog those knives religiously, but now it is obvious how misplaced her efforts were. As if Anthony couldn't pick up a knife or a box cutter at any hardware store. As if he couldn't borrow a gun from any one of his friends. As if he didn't have others tucked away that she didn't know about.

It embarrasses Yolanda now to remember how entirely her field of vision narrowed, how, in her efforts to keep her husband away from weapons, she repressed her own intelligence, and her dignity, too. For eleven years she was a neurotic caged creature, like one of Amadeo's feeder mice, obsessively arranging and rearranging her nest, unaware of the snake waiting in the terrarium next door.

Yolanda grew weary of the responsibility. Anthony wasn't her flesh, yet he demanded the same constant supervision that even her children had begun to grow out of. He was like a child, but without the sweetness and vulnerability that enchanted her in Valerie and Amadeo. Every time, Anthony would pull out of his dark periods, beg her forgiveness, promise to never scare her like that again, and she'd relent, relieved to give the guns back.

For a long time it was just alcohol, at least as far as she knew. But one night, unable to sleep, she went out to find Anthony watching TV in the living room. It wasn't long after eleven, though the kids had been asleep for hours, and Yolanda always went to bed early. She'd imagined curling up next to him, resting her head against his chest. He'd put one arm around her, his other hand on her bare leg. They'd watch whatever he was watching, and maybe, maybe, she could bring him back to bed with her. It had been so long since they'd held each other, since they'd spoken to each other with anything other than impatience or anger. Yolanda loved her husband, and this is why she tolerated his tantrums and his dark moods, his occasional rough pushes or slaps.

He was asleep on the couch—or rather, not quite asleep. Even in the cool light of the TV, she could see that his forehead was flushed, his eyes slit. His belt was loose around his bicep. Spread on the coffee table, all the props: square of foil, lighter, black-stained spoon.

When Yolanda approached, Anthony did not raise his head. She stood there in one of his undershirts.

"Not that," she whispered. "I told you never that."

"Yeah," he murmured agreeably, then drifted off. The slack pleasure in his face almost made her envious. How dare he find such cheap satisfaction when all she did was work and worry? How dare he do what Elwin had done when he knew how much it had hurt them all?

She plucked the needle from where it had fallen on the couch cushion, imagining her own skin pierced, the skin of her sleeping babies. She turned slowly in the kitchen, queasily regarding the tip, uncertain how to throw it away, until she finally dropped it into an empty beer bottle, wrapped the whole thing in half a roll of paper towels, and double-bagged it. She took the bundle out to the trash can. After she'd cleaned up the mess, she paced the rest of the night, her blood coursing with the astonishment that her marriage was over.

When it was time to get the kids up for school, she covered Anthony with a blanket to make his sleep seem normal, and ushered them through their cereal and tooth-brushing as fast as she could. Once the bus had taken them away, she shook him awake and told him to move out.

There were entreaties, of course, tears, but Yolanda never wavered. The relief of having him gone was too powerful, a drug in itself. She braced herself for his incessant begging, but after the second visit and the fourth phone call, he quit trying. He was at his little brother's house, his mother told her, where, no doubt, the two of them were drinking and shooting up to their hearts' content, and, his mother made sure to point out, Yolanda was the one who'd driven him to it.

Nearly six months later, when she got the call from the police informing her of Anthony's car accident, she'd been terrified at first that one of the children was with him, forgetting—stupidly—that they were never in his care anymore.

"Valerie! Amadeo!" she cried, flinging open doors, pulse throbbing in her head. When Yolanda burst through her bedroom door, Valerie looked up, her face open and surprised and then, very swiftly, irritated. "I'm *working*," she said, then bowed over her notebook.

But Yolanda could not find five-year-old Amadeo. She ran around the house, then across the road to the Romeros', calling wildly. Finally she came upon him and the other kids in the arroyo, rolling dump trucks through the sand. Only now did relief flood her, because what she'd feared for so long had finally happened. Wordlessly she grabbed Amadeo by the wrist and dragged him home while he fought and yelled and resisted, then just cried, until finally, bewildered at his mother's strangeness, he fell silent.

Thank god Anthony hadn't killed anyone else. When she thinks of him driving off the road, sailing through the air, Yolanda imagines that with all the alcohol in his veins, he must have caught alight himself, a falling, fiery star, leaving nothing, but she knows that isn't true; she was at the funeral, saw his casket. She stood beside his mother, patting her as she wept. His mother wrenched away. "You drove him to this!" she cried, and then clung to Yolanda again. They'd been separated, but not divorced, Yolanda on the hook for truck payments and credit card bills, for his myriad debts to their friends and family.

Yolanda is an optimist. Yolanda considers herself a happy person. Her life is filled with love and family and friends. She *likes* people, believes that they are basically good. But this doesn't change her simultaneous belief that the universe is essentially malevolent, life boobytrapped with disaster. The evidence is clear: so many bodies damaged and beaten and destroyed, washed up on the shores of her life. And her own body, harboring its deadly secret knot. It doesn't seem normal, the sheer quantity of awfulness crowded into her family. Sure, every family has its problems, but her family problems are uglier.

She knows what Valerie's take on it all would be: that somewhere buried in their past someone committed the first act of violence, and every generation since has worked to improve upon that violence, adding its own special flourish. She thinks of that first man, a conquistador, here in this dry new land for the purpose of domination and annihilation, yanking on the arm of his newly christened Indian wife, and from that union a son was born. Generations of injury chewed like blight into the leaves of the family tree: shaken skulls, knocking teeth, snapped wrists, collisions and brawls and fatal intoxication.

Sometimes during her lunch hour, Yolanda walks from the Capitol building to the cathedral, not to pray, but to sit in the bright, airy quiet. She refuses to look at La Conquistadora, the wooden statue of the Blessed Mother tucked high and snug in an opulent niche in her chapel to the left of the altar. The conquistadors brought her from Spain, hauled her around with them like a lucky charm as they invaded the peoples of the New World, and she served as a placid, unmoved witness to the violence they wrought. No wonder the Spaniards loved her so: O Conquistadora, Our Lady of the Rosary, Blessed Mother, Adoring Mother, Our Mother of Excuses and Turning a Blind Eye, Our Lady of Willful Ignorance and Boys Will Be Boys, Our Lady of Endless,

Long-Suffering Hope. In the nineties, in a belated acknowledgment of the Church's violent past—or, more accurately, a feeble revisionist cover-up of that past—the bishop renamed her "Our Lady of Peace." But there's never been peace in this land, not then and not now, not for her family and not for Yolanda.

Yolanda rolls onto her side, presses her cheek into the pillow. This is her favorite position, the one she allows herself only when she really needs comfort. For years she's tried to sleep on her back, because she heard that sleeping on your side gives you wrinkles, that long vertical one down the cheek. But Yolanda doesn't have to worry about that vertical wrinkle now.

At the Rosary for Elwin, when Yolanda was fourteen, Yolanda's mother advised her not to look at him spread out in his coffin. "If you do, you'll always remember him dead, you won't be able to help it." So Yolanda hadn't approached the coffin, but her mother's warning had been a kind of curse, because she still can't conjure the living face of her favorite cousin. What remains vivid is the scene of his death, a scene she invented from the adults' whispers. The blue truck marooned in the dirt parking lot; beyond, the flashing neon sign: *Engine RX*. In her mind she approaches the truck, knowing what she'll see. Elwin's arms are spread, as if he's opening himself to the stars, but the stars have been blotted out. His face glows orange, then pink, then green, eyes blank, rolled up to the whites.

Thirteen years later, at Anthony's Rosary, there had been no viewing. Just the gleaming casket clamped shut. Although he didn't actually die the night she caught him passed out in the living room, that's the image that persists in her mind: the blue light from the television playing on his slack features. For thirteen years, it seems, Anthony had been chasing Elwin.

She never said goodbye to Anthony, not truly. She'd imagined that he might return to her as the person he'd once been, that she'd once imagined him to be.

Her biggest fear is that her son will get sucked down this same road, a fear compounded by the fear that her very fear makes it inevitable, and this is why she's done everything she can to shield Amadeo, to provide a buffer against the consequences of his own bad choices. She can't do otherwise.

How little they know her, her children. They are incapable of seeing her as anything but strong and nurturing and living only for them. Yolanda, a terminally ill cancer patient? Whose every thought must center on her own survival? No; it would be far too great a strain on their imaginations. They would never guess she was capable of such dark thoughts. This understanding makes her so angry she has to sit up.

She won't tell them about her tumor, not until they have to know. She'll buy herself as much normalcy and privacy as she can.

The decision comes as a relief. It's for their own good—this crosses her mind, less a thought than a reflex, and she knows it's a lie.

I don't care, she thinks. I don't care. Finally, mercifully, her mind slows and sleep pulls her under.

Long after her aunt left and her grandmother took her sleeping pill and kissed her good night, Angel sits on the floor against the couch, her homework on negative numbers abandoned beside her. She scratches a pimple at her jawline and glares at Valerie's car seat.

The baby is active tonight. He is active every night, which doesn't bode well for Angel's postpartum sleep. For now, his ruckus is more or less muffled, but still when she drifts off, he kicks her awake, demanding even at age zero—age negative 0.075—her constant attention. Tonight he's throwing punches and turning tense flips, as if he, too, is on the point of angry tears.

It was nice of Valerie, bringing these baby things—of *course* it was nice of her—but Angel glowers at the car seat with hot eyes. It reclines among the piles of baby clothes, sticky and encrusted with sand and lint and grime. There are still Cheerios caught in the crevices between the blue velveteen pads. Just because she's sixteen and jobless doesn't mean that she doesn't deserve nice things. These disadvantages should mean she deserves them even more.

She understands now that no one will be throwing her a baby shower. Sure, once the baby is born, Angel will get the little party at Smart Starts!, with hummus and lemon poppy-seed muffins from the grocery store and paper towels from the bathroom dispenser for napkins. Everyone will go around the circle telling her what they value about Angel and their wishes for the baby, the same predictable things. *I value that you're a good friend. I hope he is happy and smart and goes to college.* At the end they'll present her with a brochure on early literacy and a wrapped board book donated by Ready Readers, either *Goodnight Moon* or *The Carrot Seed* or *If You Give a Mouse a Cookie*, the only titles they have.

But Angel wants a *baby shower*. She wants a duck-shaped cake with *Welcome baby!* spelled out in frosting and silver balls, wants laughter and a sunny room filled with ribbons and streamers and flowers. She wants piles of pastel-wrapped gifts—fleecy footed sleepers, gauze receiving blankets, baby toys that rattle and crinkle and squeak. Angel wants games, too—Pin the Pin on the Diaper, nursery rhyme bingo, that one where they swing the wedding ring in front of your stomach to determine the sex—and she wants to pass around her sonogram to laughing, photogenic, mimosa-drinking friends, the whole thing orchestrated by her dearest friend of all, a busy, effusive, adoring friend, the friend who is also her baby's godmother. But Angel doesn't have a wedding ring, she already knows her baby's sex, and she doesn't have friends anymore, not really, and certainly not a best one.

It pains Angel that she is thirty-seven weeks pregnant and still hasn't found a suitable godmother for her baby. Angel needs someone affectionate, competent, and supportive, someone who will be a good influence when, inevitably, Angel isn't.

She's run through the possibilities: her mother and grandmother are already grandmother and great-grandmother, her old best friend Priscilla hates her, and wouldn't have been up for the job anyway. All her friends from school have been distressingly easy to fall out of touch with. The girls from Smart Starts! offer support and understanding, but they are not godmother material. Take Lizette, for example. She's full of bluster and brassy humor, and pretty, too, but she got pregnant because she was raped by her uncle. And she smoked weed pretty much her entire pregnancy, except for one weekend when she did meth—actual meth!—with some guy she met on the Rail Runner. So it's no wonder, really, that Lizette managed to crap her baby out, because Mercedes was underweight.

Aunt Valerie was, until tonight, a possibility. But Angel's baby needs someone who will make him feel special. Above all, Angel's baby must believe he was anticipated, longed for, even *tried* for—she thinks of those pitying women, skinny middle-aged loose-skinned white ladies with their yoga pants and their Chinese babies in their grocery carts. And Angel does want him! When her doctor reminded her that adoption was a possibility, Angel shook her head stoutly. Even in the thick of her fear, she couldn't imagine giving him up; he was already a part of her.

Angel will never, she vows, remind her child of what she missed because of him. "I would've gone to college," her mother says constantly. "I would've moved to New York." Well, her mother was free of her now. She and Mike are probably home watching some television drama, Mike waxing poetic about how amazing TV writing is nowadays, like he's the only one to have ever made the observation.

Angel sits in the cold white circle of the halogen lamp, feeling abandoned, and afraid, too, of the vast dark wildness around the house. She should go to bed, but she knows that the baby will keep her awake, and if she's lying prone and undefended, worry will descend in earnest, will grip her by the throat and drag her under.

She could take one of her grandmother's sleeping pills or one of her dad's Percocets. Angel wonders if the baby would drop off into a floating slumber, his lips parted, his little fists unfurling, or if the drug would only affect her, and he would continue to somersault and karate-chop her unresponsive body.

One thirty. She didn't realize how long a night could be, how capacious and elastic.

Her father is wrong in thinking that Angel feels entitled to be here. She doesn't feel entitled to be anywhere. What no one appreciates is that it takes courage—and considerable dramatic flair—to show up and insist you belong, to invoke genetic claims and demand food and love and housing. Angel falters, Angel worries, Angel lies awake, hating to be a burden, afraid they'll send her away, but every morning she gets up and busies herself in the kitchen like it's hers. She comports herself as though she isn't some needy disgraced teenager, but a treasured, helpful daughter filling her rightful place. *Fake it 'til you make it*, Brianna told them.

Earlier, when her father left in his truck—stamped past them as they all stood outside shivering in the driveway—Valerie shook her cell phone and threatened to call the police, to alert them that he was on the road, "plastered out of his *mind*," but Yolanda had begged her not to, saying he couldn't afford a second DWI. Angel hadn't even known about the first.

"So you want *me* out there on the road with him?" Valerie shouted, pulling her cardigan tight against the wind. "You want the girls out there? Even if you don't care about us, how will you feel when he kills some stranger's family?" But she lowered the phone.

Yolanda blinked helplessly before her daughter's outrage. Angel stood with Sarah close along her thigh, stroking the little girl's tangled hair, but Sarah brushed her hand away. "Come inside with me," Angel said. "I'll read you a story."

"No," Sarah said easily, big eyes on Valerie. Beside her, Lily also looked from her mother to her grandmother with interest, but no surprise. Clearly this fight had occurred in some form before.

Angel thinks that Valerie's reaction was overblown. Her father didn't seem *that* drunk, and kids at school drive buzzed and stoned all the time. It's how you get between parties. Beer isn't black tar, it isn't meth, it isn't even vodka. And these roads are so long and so empty. But she also feels pricked with injustice because someone should have told her about the DWI. She had a right to know.

"You can't keep enabling him, Mother. At some point it has to stop. What does he *do* all day? Does he just sit around drinking *all day*? Do you ever ask *anything* of him?"

"He's trying, hijita. He's starting up a business fixing windshields. We've just been talking about it."

"*Windshields?* Christ."

Yolanda dragged her hands down her face. "Why can't you help him instead of getting mad at him? You're the counselor. You should help him."

Valerie exploded with a long, garbled wail. "*Help* him? You think that's what *you're* doing? He's thirty-five years old and unemployed. He still gets an *allowance*. That hasn't helped him yet."

"He's thirty-three."

"He should go to college," Sarah volunteered.

"Stupid," said Lily to her sister. "You can't go to college when you're thirty-three."

"You were always so mad at Dad, but you let Amadeo and his addiction run roughshod over this family."

"Your brother is sick, Valerie." Yolanda's voice is barely above a whisper.

"I *know* he's sick. So was Dad, but you never had any sympathy for him. Did you ever *help* him?"

Angel stepped closer to her grandmother.

"I cannot believe it's come to this. But until he gets help, or moves out, we're not setting foot in this house. Get your things, girls, get in the car." Sarah and Lily trotted inside. "The girls have seen enough violence, Mother; I'm not going to expose them to any more."

Valerie was calming down now, bolstered by her plan.

"And *you*, Angel." Valerie fixed an accusing expression on her. "I think you should seriously consider whether you want to bring a baby into this house."

"Okay," Angel said obediently, despair seeping through her like black ink. How many options does Valerie think she has?

"He's a good boy," Yolanda kept saying.

Somehow they'd split into teams: on one side, Valerie and her daughters, and on Team Amadeo, Angel and her grandmother. But Angel didn't want to be on her father's team. She was *glad* he was gone. She'd been scared, and even more than scared, embarrassed by his behavior. But, she supposes, the fact of her embarrassment only underscores her connection to him.

On Friday, when they'd cut him down, he'd swayed on his legs, then dropped to the dirt. "It hurts," he kept whispering through chapped lips, looking up at her through tear-clotted lashes. "It hurts." She'd felt the weight of his need settle across her back.

———

SHE MUST HAVE FALLEN asleep, right there on the living room carpet, because she wakes to a car crunching up the drive. Headlights brighten the living room window, an engine idles, a door slams, heavy, metallic. Fear grips her as the headlights swing around, grazing Angel's body where she leans against the couch, and the rumble of the engine recedes. Her father's steps on gravel, and then he's inside. Behind him the screen door gives its pneumatic wheeze, then snaps shut.

He gropes the wall and then flicks on the overhead.

"You're up," he says, surprised, and for a moment they regard each other. "What time is it?" His face is puffy.

Angel doesn't answer, but glances at the television's digital display. Three thirty. The baby somersaults.

He steps closer until he stands above her. Her father's gaze is clouded, and he lists just a bit. He toes the pile of baby clothes. "Jesus. What a load of crap."

Angel wants to get away from him. His eyes are red-rimmed, and she's afraid he's going to cry. Again the thought hits her, how little she knows her father, really, how rarely she's been alone with him, and with this thought, a taut thread of fear vibrates in her veins. She flashes on Mike, his hands around her throat, then bats that memory away. Sweat trickles down her sides.

Angel begins to gather the baby clothes into a bag. "I have to go to bed."

Her father swoops down and Angel is briefly and irrationally afraid that he is going to claw her with the fingers that emerge from the bandage, claw his nails down her face and throat and belly, but instead he grabs the lavender pinafore and shakes it in Angel's face. "Dresses? She thinks a boy is going to wear dresses?"

Angel snatches it from his hand, shoves it in the bag. "It was nice of her," she mutters.

"She's a fucking bitch."

Suddenly Angel is so angry at him the surprise catches in her throat. She staggers to her feet. "Valerie's right. You're a drunk."

"Angel," he says, reaching for her upper arm. "Listen."

She twists away. "Don't *touch* me." She jerks back and stumbles down the hall.

For a long time, Amadeo holds his head in his hands. He has sobered considerably, but still the room rocks and rotates into place when he opens his eyes. The living room is still scattered with the detritus of dinner. On the counter sits an untouched lemon meringue pie, the meringue collapsed and the filling shrinking from the crust.

The house is so unchanged he almost can't believe that the last several hours happened. But they did. Just two days after enduring the nails, Amadeo has his second DWI and spent three terrible hours in jail.

Well, at least it wasn't as bad as Christmas Eve. Then he had to spend a whole night in jail, because, his mother claimed, she didn't get his voicemail message. Yolanda had been out driving, looking for him, worried, she told him later, that he'd hurt himself on the icy roads. Amadeo suspects that she left him there overnight to teach him a lesson. Why else have a fucking cell phone, if not for crises like that? He still doesn't forgive her.

That night in jail was awful beyond words—smelly and dirty and the cops spoke to him like he was scum, and he'd had to puke in that seatless metal toilet and they wouldn't even give him toothpaste to rinse his mouth, though one of the cops did give him a Quarter Pounder and even paid for it himself.

Tonight, when the cop asked him which number he wanted to dial, Amadeo hesitated. In the end, he called his uncle, who'd picked up on the second ring, despite the hour. He expressed neither anger nor surprise, just said, after a pause, "All right. I'm coming."

The moment Amadeo caught sight of his uncle, he flung himself at Tíve, sobbing, clinging tighter the more Tíve tried to shake him off. "I wasn't even that drunk." The unsmiling lady police officer shook her head contemptuously and left them in the tiny windowless lobby, which smelled of disinfectant.

On the way home, Amadeo waited for his uncle to reprimand him. The old man squinted myopically at the dark road, driving fifteen miles under the speed limit. Amadeo's hands lay in his lap, useless, the bandages filthy.

The silence stretched, itchy and intolerable. Finally Amadeo said, "I know what you're thinking. I'm not like my dad. I'm not like Elwin." The words were lumpy and malformed in his mouth.

His uncle lifted his foot from the gas and looked at him. Even in the light of the dashboard, Amadeo could see the hurt that flared across the old man's face. "Don't be," Tíve said. "Your mother don't deserve that." He straightened, accelerated again, and was silent until they reached the house.

As Amadeo was about to open the door, his uncle said, "Tonight you make a change." He gazed into the pool of the headlights.

Amadeo was surprised by his tears, which seemed to have sprung from some new source. "Yeah," he said, and for a moment, the word swelled in him, a bubble of possibility, then deflated, because just a few hours ago he'd promised himself he'd be worthy of his daughter, and already he'd let her down.

From where he stands, Amadeo can see Elwin and his father on the living room wall, aged eighteen, in the only picture his mother will display of her husband. It was taken not long before Elwin died. They're sitting close together on the steps of his uncle's house: wide smiles, disturbing black mullets. Amadeo steps closer. His father's face is round and dark, his hair gelled and wet-looking, curling at the nape. Amadeo used to stand before this younger iteration of his father, trying to reconcile the smiling boy with the man who scared him with his rages and his silences, and scared him more with his bouts of desperate affection. Amadeo remembers his father grabbing him and whirling him around, that terror and exhilaration.

With a cold flush, Amado is reminded that his father was thirty-three when he died, the same age that Amadeo is now.

Amadeo looks at the time above the stove. Four o'clock on a Monday morning in April. The house is silent. Outside, a coyote howls, and it sounds like a woman crying out in pain. It's been hours since Mass concluded, since the church emptied itself into the bright day, and children and adults alike returned to their homes to glut themselves on Peeps and cheap grainy jelly beans. The austerity of Lent is past, the countless lapses and broken promises forgiven, Christ's sacrifice forgotten.

His mother and his daughter are enclosed in their rooms at the back of the house, unreachable. Amadeo's hands ache. He picks up the bottle of Percocet, rattles it, then, with difficulty, twists off the lid. Before he can stop himself, he pours them down the drain and switches on the garbage disposal.

Part II

ORDINARY TIME

The mission of Family Foundations is to improve outcomes for at-risk children in the greater Española Valley. Smart Starts! is the teen parenting and high school equivalency program, now in its third year, and, thanks to both a federal and a foundation grant, it is the jewel in the agency's crown. The year-round program accommodates eight students, eligible from pregnancy through their nineteenth birthdays, with on-site child care. When BriannaGruver was interviewing for the teaching position last year, the application included a fill-in-the-blanks component.

"There are no wrong answers," the administrator assured her, which made Brianna nervous, because in her experience "no wrong answers" really meant that the range of possible wrong answers was unimaginably broad. After all, the questions on her dating profile were also supposed to have no wrong answers, but hers couldn't have been right because, apart from some dick pics, they have gotten her exactly nowhere.

> *Families should _____.*
> *I get angry when _____.*
> *I fear _____.*

Brianna majored in biology precisely because in biology nothing is subjective. There were cell functions to memorize, complex neural pathways to map. When Brianna assisted in a lab studying chromosomal mutations in fruit flies, the procedures were clear and invariable. But these vague fill-in-the-blanks? What was she supposed to do with them? Be original? Be *truthful*?

There are a lot of things that make Brianna angry that she didn't want noted in her HR file. Being talked over, being mistaken for a high school student, being subjected to couples making out in movie theaters when she's trying to pay attention. In the end she settled on bland earnestness, which is more or less her default around people in authority. *Families should focus on the needs of the children. I get angry when children are hurt. I fear not being able to make enough of a difference.* So much of adult life, Brianna was discovering, was about pretending to be the person people wanted you to be.

Brianna was particularly proud of her last answer: *I believe _____. I believe every young person is capable and precious and can change her life regardless of the circumstances she was born into.* She's pretty sure this answer is why she got the job. And it wasn't just pious posturing, either. Brianna *did* believe this; if she hadn't, she wouldn't have been interviewing for jobs at nonprofits in Española. The whole country is suffused with hope: smiling, kind-eyed Obama is in the White House, progress unspools all around them, the bad old years of struggle and war and intolerance are, if not gone for good, at least on the wane.

Brianna is proud of her first year at Smart Starts! When she toured the classroom during her interview, the atmosphere was one of utter airless boredom. Eight teenage girls slumped at their desks, with their push-up bras and lip liner, paging hopelessly through their workbooks. She was surprised by how closely they resembled her own high school classmates, except that some had to squeeze pregnant bellies behind their desks and others had babies in the nursery down the hall. The walls were bare. Bookshelves in the back were filled with GED workbooks and nothing else, not even a dictionary. Above the whiteboard in the front was a single tiny American flag.

When Brianna got the job, she brought in art posters, books, a globe, an entire set of encyclopedias. She purchased bright rugs and a ficus plant. She sought donations from local businesses, and she spent plenty of her own money, too, including her grandparents' birthday check. And it was worth it. The classroom is now colorful and invit-

ing, the girls are engaged in daily journaling and simple science experi-
ments. She even negotiated a deal with the president of the community
college to allow those girls who receive their GEDs before they age out
to take up to five credits' worth of classes. Brianna has created a safe
and positive learning environment.

The Smart Starts! schedule is flexible, to allow for the necessities of
feeding and child care. The curriculum, derived from research-based
best practices, leans heavily on self-reflection, the idea being that this
particular population could use practice in stopping to reflect. In the
morning, the focus is on academics and GED test prep, two pursuits
that often seem in direct opposition to each other; the afternoons are
for parenting- and life-skills. It's a student-driven curriculum, at least
in name. Students give presentations on aspects of parenthood: early
literacy, benefits of breast-feeding, introducing solid foods. Contracep-
tion. Today, Friday afternoon, class will end with their weekly Community Meeting.

The girls have surprised Brianna. She expected more behavioral
problems, certainly problems more serious than gum-chewing and
cell phone use. She expected these girls to be surly and oppositional.
Española being Española, she expected heroin addicts (though many
of those kids are referred to the city's single overburdened addiction
clinic). She expected, frankly, that since they were having sex so young,
these girls had to be bad. But, with only a single, infuriating exception, they're not. Brianna is amazed at how willing they are to engage
in even the most inane group activities, activities that Brianna feels
embarrassed even proposing, but that are part of the curriculum suggested by experts. Nutrition collages, for example: on the classroom
wall are poster boards covered in examples of Always Foods and Sometimes Foods.

Their stories pain her, actually keep her up at night—the histo-
ries of abuse and family violence and addiction. Brianna doesn't tell
the girls about the studies that haunt her as she gazes over their carefully made-up faces in the classroom, showing that maternal stress can
flood the bloodstream with hormones that poison the prenatal environment, making the babies over their lifetimes more prone to anxiety and

depression, more likely to be born early and underweight and to die early and overweight.

So she teaches them meditation techniques. She drills them in power stances: legs planted apart, shoulders flung back, arms akimbo. She shows videos of the little monkeys desolate in their cages with their wire mothers and enjoins them to hold their babies, talk to their babies, sing to their babies, and the girls actually take her at her word. Just last week, from the bathroom stall, Brianna overheard Tabitha narrating her makeup routine to her belly.

She's a good person, Brianna. She tries!

I believe every young person is capable and precious. Ha-freaking-ha, thinks Brianna now, as from the staff room window she watches Lizette Maes give a blow job to a banana. Brianna notes that Lizette has opted not to peel the banana before pleasuring it. Good, thinks Brianna, I hope the pesticides make her puke.

In the courtyard, the other girls surround Lizette, leaning in, spluttering over their juice boxes. Even through the closed window, Brianna can hear their boisterous laughter. It's impressive, really, a full-body performance: the girl straddles the picnic bench and her eyes are rolled back ecstatically, big breasts heaving in a more or less convincing imitation of arousal. On the ground, from her infant carrier, Lizette's three-month-old daughter Mercedes peers up at her mother with cross-eyed fascination. Up and down the length of the banana Lizette runs her tongue, encircles the black tip with languid caresses.

Brianna can't stand this girl. As far as she's concerned, Lizette is neither capable nor precious, and to be honest, Brianna can't muster much sorrow for what the girl has gone through—incest, rape, poverty, god knows what other horrors—a fact that disturbs her enormously. Lizette is unpleasant and aggressive, with a sly gleam in her gorgeous, heavy green eyes. Mercedes, Brianna feels sorry for, but to be brutally honest, she's even written off the baby as a lost cause.

"Charming," says Raquel, who manages Family Foundations' Family Food Security program. She has paused on the way to the microwave, Lean Cuisine in hand, and followed Brianna's gaze to the courtyard outside.

"And you wonder how she ended up in her particular predicament," says Brianna, disliking herself.

There are two picnic tables in the Family Foundations courtyard, between which the girls used to distribute themselves more or less evenly, depending on shifting alliances, but ever since Lizette joined the class a few months ago, all eight girls crowd around one. That's Lizette for you: the great unifier.

Ysenia weighs her own banana in her hand, as if trying to determine whether she should contribute her own take on fellatio or remain in the audience. At the end of the table, only Jen remains aloof, frowning fiercely into her compact as she applies lip gloss so pale it might as well be Vaseline. She'll disapprove, Jen will, but she won't leave the circle. Instead she clings to the bench with a single clenched butt-cheek. Even Angel, earnest Angel, is laughing, which irks Brianna still further, because Angel is one of her favorites and should know better.

There is no need for Brianna to go out there. Her lunch break isn't over for another twenty-five minutes and she still has to put in a call to her dentist's office to see about scheduling her cleaning. Still, she sighs an aggrieved sigh, pitches the remains of her lunch into the trash.

"Good luck," Raquel says grimly.

Brianna reminds herself that she is a twenty-five-year-old adult tasked with this girl's well-being, an adult with all the advantages in the world, including but not limited to: white privilege, a stable, middle-class upbringing, a bachelor's degree, a teaching license from the State of New Mexico, and a certificate attesting to the fact that she's completed training in teen outreach. She can be generous, she tells herself. She can be the bigger person.

Outside, the spring warmth envelops Brianna. Most of the girls are alerted to her approach by her clicking heels and freeze, but not Lizette, who has now set to moaning. Up close, the performance is even more disgusting. The banana is slick, and saliva shines at the corners of Lizette's mouth. Trinity elbows Christy. The girls fall silent, watching Brianna watch Lizette gyrate like a porn star. Angel looks positively stricken as Brianna advances. With a rapturous groan, Lizette thrusts the banana down her throat. A remarkable length disappears from sight.

She slides it in and out until, finally, Brianna snaps. "Lizette. Are you going to eat that? Or just slobber on it? Because that's a grant-funded banana."

Lizette removes the banana with a pop, slurps and swallows. "Hey, miss. I was only playing." She wipes her mouth with her sleeve, then dries the banana neatly on the hem of her sweatshirt.

Brianna smooths her wool skirt, one in a series of frumpy and seasonally inappropriate pieces she bought in hopes of looking older and establishing her authority. "You probably aren't aware that someone has to apply annually for state, federal, and foundation grants to bring in the money to buy that banana so that you can have a well-balanced, nutritious, no-cost meal. You probably aren't aware of the number of people working for slave wages who have sweated to deliver that banana from a plantation in Guatemala to this table." She jabs at the picnic table.

Through all of this, Lizette regards Brianna with her lovely, half-open eyes. In general, she doesn't put much effort into her clothing, seems to have near-total disregard for her self-presentation—today she wears shapeless black athletic pants and a hooded sweatshirt—but her green eyes, with their fringe of heavy black lashes, are always made-up. Mascara, lavender eye shadow, smoky liner. They're her best feature, and she turns them on people like weapons. The other girls watch Brianna, too: Ysenia places her own banana carefully among the wrappers on the table and sits up, nodding attentively. Beside Lizette, as if burdened with the shame that Lizette has refused, Angel looks at her lap, her ears pink.

"I'm not *wasting* it, miss." Lizette peels the banana and offers it to the table at large. "Anyone want this? I don't eat bananas. They make my tongue all weird."

Squeals of disgust all around. "Gross," says Corinna.

Brianna exhales, and only then does she realize that she is trembling. "Lunch is over, ladies," she says without looking at her watch.

"Are you for serious?" says Lizette. "We still got like fifteen minutes."

"Lunch is over."

Brianna turns away, leaving the girls to gather their wrappers, but not before she sees Lizette toss the banana into the planter.

———

THAT AFTERNOON at Community Meeting, after the girls have arranged their chairs in a circle and Brianna has reminded them to note the date of the Open House next month, she asks if anyone has anything they want to check in about. Lizette is the first to raise her hand.

Instead, Brianna calls on Tabitha, who sits up straight and smooths her curly hair before talking. "Yeah, miss, I got a headphone issue. I don't get why they're not allowed, because, like, when we're studying, it's easier to tune people out with headphones. My thing is, if people are talking to each other, it's easier to concentrate with music."

Brianna smiles hard, aware of Lizette's hand swaying. "Those are valid points, Tabitha, and I appreciate you bringing them up. Our classroom rules make the classroom similar to a workplace. At a job you can't answer personal calls or use headphones. The point is to give you what you need to succeed in the world outside the classroom. But during lunch and breaks, you're welcome to listen to music."

Tabitha flops back into her chair, dissatisfied. "Okay," she says, unconvinced.

Lizette's head is cocked in challenge.

"Yes," Brianna says coldly. "Lizette?"

"Hey, miss. I really feel you weren't fair, cutting our lunch short. We need nutrition."

Brianna forces herself to look at the girl, and to her dismay, her heart kicks with agitation. She hopes the movement isn't visible through her sweater. Every single thing about Lizette bugs Brianna: those pretty eyes, that insolent fat slouch. Brianna can sense Lizette fungating, sending out spores of toxic attitude. She's just so—*sexual*. "Well, I feel you were misusing your lunchtime. Lunch is for eating, and you were not eating that banana."

Lizette rolls her eyes. "You're just all—*I feel* you're just all butt-hurt because you can't take a joke. Just because something's not funny to you doesn't mean it's not funny to other people."

"Lizette, that behavior was not school-appropriate." Brianna taps the classroom rules printed on the piece of butcher paper behind her. "You weren't respecting yourself or your classmates, who deserve to eat lunch without being subjected to that kind of display. Your behavior might even be construed as sexual harassment."

"Sexual *harassment*?" Lizette hoots. "Who'd I harass? The banana?"

Brianna takes a deep breath. "Sex is not a performance or a joke. It is something that should occur between consenting adults."

Ysenia raises her hand tentatively, and with relief Brianna nods to her. "Yes?"

"I mean, it *could* be a performance or a joke, right? Like, if we want it to be? Didn't you say that we're in charge of our bodies? That we should be sex-positive?"

"It was *inappropriate*," Brianna says too loudly. Sweat trickles between her breasts. Indeed, the front of her sweater wavers with each heartbeat. "Any future behavior like that could be grounds for expulsion from the Smart Starts! program, which has, as you all know, a zero-tolerance policy for behavior that could negatively impact members of the community. I suggest you all bear this in mind. And now, Journaling Time." The relief in the room is palpable, and the girls drag their chairs to their desks and pull out their journals.

Oh, it's ironic that Brianna Gruver is teaching in the Smart Starts! program. In college, Brianna took an evolutionary biology class, and the entire semester turned out to be one long source of sorrow to her. Every lecture, every theory, every finding of every study, emphasized that Brianna Gruver had none of the traits signifying fertility, none of the bosoms or hips or plush ample fragrant femininity that the male of the human species, despite what the fashion magazines indicate, is looking for in a mate.

Brianna's roommate and supposed best friend Sierra (a double-D whose biological viability had by junior year already been twice proven, both times requiring Brianna's presence at her side in the waiting room of Planned Parenthood) was also enrolled in the class, and each night over dinner at their co-op, she reported the day's highlights to their male housemates. For instance, wasn't it amazing that during ovulation, women's voices increased in pitch? And wasn't it more amazing that when played audio recordings of women's voices and asked to rank them by attractiveness, heterosexual men picked the ovulating woman? Every time! Sierra's high, vivacious voice would go on and on, the pheromones rolling off her like heat, enveloping and intoxicating the rapt boys surrounding her, while Brianna, deep-voiced, narrow-hipped, glandless virgin that she was, shoveled forkful after wretched forkful of quinoa into her mouth.

The term had culminated in Brianna's conviction that she might actually have ended up with a tricky dissembling Y chromosome, like those Olympic athletes who, despite their convincing vaginas and outward appearance and gender identification, are actually genetically male. These things happened all the time! Or at least to one in thirty thousand people. Brianna's doctor had shaken her head, dismissing the studies on Swyer syndrome Brianna had printed out and presented her with. "People with Swyer syndrome do not menstruate regularly," she said, and refused to order any tests, instead writing a script for Ativan.

Brianna's Smart Starts! students are designed for reproduction, every last one of them. Every day in the classroom, she sees the biological markers of fertility: those high baby voices, the curves in their ill-fitting skinny jeans, the plunging necklines that emphasize their young full breasts. The absolute recklessness. Of course these girls were desired. This classroom is the single realm in which Brianna might feel grateful—smug even—that her own biology and family history and social context and personal decisions didn't predispose her to this fate. Instead, Brianna is acutely aware that she is, on the deepest level, unqualified for her job, and she's always waiting to be found out. On her worst days, like today, she looks at her students, not with compassion, but with envy.

Brianna isn't hideous or sickly-looking. She is clear-skinned and intelligent, reasonably socially adept, reasonably well-adjusted, employed, possessed of her very own double bed. Everywhere you look, people are having sex—in books, in movies, in the bathrooms of

Blake's Lotaburger—her own students have had sex in the unlikeliest of places—but Brianna is trapped by her own cowardly nature, her terrible reserve, and also, she likes to think, by her competence.

The girls start rustling and packing away their journals and books, despite the fact that there are still eight minutes left of class, but Brianna doesn't bother to correct them. They swivel in their seats, talking to each other, and begin to stretch and stand, while their teacher sits glum and distracted at her desk.

Brianna aligns her pens, closes her grade book and centers it with precision on top of the *Nurture Now* textbook. The school day is almost over, thank god, and Brianna thinks with longing of home. She'll sit in the garden outside her casita with her novel, unless her landladies are puttering about back there. In that case, she'll take her book and her vibrator into the bath and then think about dinner.

Brianna doesn't feel the need to bear children. She doesn't feel any urgency to disperse copies of her genetic material into the world. She just wants to have full vaginal intercourse with an adult human male at least once by the time she turns twenty-six.

Amadeo's mother wakes at five every morning to get to the Capitol building in Santa Fe in time for her job as a secretary—nay, administrative assistant—in the office of Monica Gutierrez-Larsen, Chief Clerk of the House of Representatives of the State of New Mexico. Amadeo has never met Monica Gutierrez-Larsen, but she exerts a force in their house. Yolanda isn't typically awed by other people, but her boss is the exception. "That Monica is wonderful," she says frequently. "So educated. Work always comes first for her." Yolanda shakes her head and concludes with admiration, "A real professional."

Amadeo has always considered his mother a professional, because she sits in a climate-controlled office all day and has a gaggle of work friends—"the girls"—but when he hears her praise Monica—her intelligence, her capability—he wonders if maybe she had other ambitions than being an administrative assistant. She loves her job, though, loves dressing up for work, loves the endless, breathless days of the legislative session.

Amadeo stretches in bed, remembering being a child, the comfort of being awake in the early morning, the sky outside still mysterious and dark, television news murmuring indistinctly from his mother's bedroom. He would listen to her click around the kitchen in her work heels. Warm light spilled from her bedroom into the hall, fragrant steam from the shower. Amadeo would wait for her kiss, knowing that even as he reached his arms around her neck, he'd shrink from her coffee breath and the abrasive scent of her perfume.

Then she would pull away (heels muffled on the carpet, snapping free and sharp when she reached the linoleum). At the front door, there was always a pause, and a bright note of hope would ring in Amadeo's chest, but no, she was only buttoning herself into her long coat. The jingle of keys and the sound of the lock turning, and then the car would start up, the headlights briefly brightening the edges of his bedroom curtains, and Amadeo would follow the sound of the car until he couldn't any longer. Alone, with two hours before his own alarm would sound in the blue light of the house (Valerie already up and buttering his toast), Amadeo would snuggle down into the blankets, trying to find that coziness, but it was gone, had left with his mother and was now speeding south toward Santa Fe.

These memories sting because that little boy was superior to the Amadeo now. That little boy thought he was going places.

Neither his mother nor Angel has mentioned the DWI. Still, when Amadeo thinks of it, he breaks into a full-body sweat, shame leaking out of him like effluent. And anger, too, because how hard would it have been for the cop to have been looking the other way? And how fucking stupid of Amadeo to have been speeding. He should have just pressed the fucking cruise control—it's not even like he was weaving or anything. He got comparatively lucky: a six-month license suspension, community service, DWI school, at which they berate you for six straight hours and force you to watch gruesome movies about people killed by drunks. Amadeo doesn't much relish the prospect of sitting in a classroom again at the community center with the other lowlifes.

He owes Tíve for bail and his mother for the fee to get his truck released from the impound lot, plus the fine and the cost of DWI school—the whole thing is outrageously expensive, and it strikes Amadeo as pretty shitty that the State of New Mexico thinks it can make money off people's honest mistakes.

Nonetheless, this morning, after he hears his mother back down the dark driveway, he springs up—before his alarm, before Angel has stirred—and starts the coffee. He can't help feeling hopeful, because he hasn't had a drink in over a week, and because today's the day his windshield repair kit will arrive.

Angel pinches the underside of her chin as she thinks. It's Journaling Time, and Brianna has told them to make a list of things they each need to make their own and their babies' lives better. The first few are easy.

1. *GED <u>OR</u> high school diploma <u>AND</u> college degree*
2. *A godmother*
3. *A support system*
4. *A car*
5. *A driver's license*
6. *A house*
7. *A job*

Here Angel is stumped. If she got a job, who would take care of the baby? So she adds:

8. *Free babysitter. A good one.*

But there is no such thing, not really, not unless your mom or grandma doesn't work. Even Angel knows that. Briefly she considers her father, then dismisses the thought.

Christy and Trinity are whispering. They are best friends and knew each other from before Smart Starts! "We got pregnant, like, the same month," they're always telling people, which is either a crazy fluke or an organizational feat. Both possibilities depress Angel.

"Who'd like to share?" asks Brianna. Today she wears her clunky sandals and a shapeless maroon sweaterdress that is too heavy for outside, but perfect for the chilly canned air of the Family Foundations building.

Jen raises her hand, tucking her silky mousy hair behind her large white ear, preparing herself for the stage. "An education." Jen smiles, anticipating Brianna's praise. A cross dangles from her neck, and in the lobes of those stuck-out ears, diamond studs glint. Even though Angel knows they probably aren't real, knows she could get a pair herself at the mall, she's still jealous.

"Right," drawls Lizette. "*Education. I forgot* that one." Angel grins and tries to telegraph her approval to Lizette, but Lizette's beautiful green eyes are half closed like a lizard's.

On her left hand, Jen wears a promise ring with a dinky little amethyst. "It's my birthstone," she said, as if none of the rest of them were born in months with birthstones. She is going to marry her boyfriend Jared, whom she met at church and who picks her up every afternoon when Smart Starts! lets out. He's a senior and works after school installing car stereos, and once he's paused at the curb, he never gets out of the car or even looks up, just attends to his own stereo while Jen climbs in.

Not that Angel's own child's father is any better than a car-stereo-installing Christian. Her stomach churns whenever she thinks of Ryan Johnson, the way, in geometry, he always sat in the front row, grimacing up at the board. He always raised his hand to answer questions, but was only correct about fifty percent of the time. It seemed crazy to Angel to keep putting yourself out there like that, but the next time Mrs. Esposito asked a question, there he was, long skinny arm swinging in the air.

"Hey," he told her breathlessly once in the hall after class. "I thought of a name for you. A math name." For weeks he called her Angle. Or sometimes, delighting himself still further, Obtuse Angle. He was so persistent she felt embarrassed for him, which, along with the tequila shots, explains why she slept with him. Her embarrassment also explains, perhaps, why she hasn't told him the baby is his.

Angel's back aches, her legs ache, she has to pee every four seconds. She's a manatee. She doesn't know how she can stand to get any bigger.

Jen sits up straighter in her seat and her frown deepens. Speaking directly to Brianna, she says, "For success, I also need to maintain my relationship with Jesus and make my baby have one, too."

Angel pictures Jen forcing a recalcitrant toddler into the arms of a horrified Jesus. The Jesus looks exactly like her dad, and she laughs out loud.

Brianna catches Angel's eye and betrays the tiniest smile, and Angel's cheeks heat. "Thanks, Jen," says Brianna, and writes *Education* on the whiteboard, the felt-tipped marker squeaking.

Jen's parents are still together and teach at the community college, where Jen, their only child, can go for basically free once she gets her GED. They've already started a college fund for Jen's baby. She's always bragging about how in the beginning her parents kept trying to buy her an abortion, but she wouldn't let them because she is a Christian now.

"Could you please put up the part about Jesus?" Jen strokes her tidy belly through her pink-striped maternity shirt. "I've been entrusted with this beautiful little life, and if I'm going to be a success, I need to love and care for it as Jesus loves and cares for me."

Lizette snorts. "Was Jesus loving and caring for you when you were bumping uglies with that dumb boyfriend of yours?"

"Lizette," warns Brianna, syllables clipped, but a surge of dislike has already been unleashed among the members of the class.

"You're not *special*, Jen," says Christy.

"Yeah," says Trinity. "We're *all* Christians here."

"Ooh, umbers," singsongs Lizette. "Jen's getting taught."

"No," says Jen, face flushing. "Like half of you are Catholics, and Catholics aren't Christian, exactly."

"Are you *joking*?" Angel surprises herself with her cry of incredulity, but, after all, she is something of an expert after her father's Good Friday shenanigans. "Anyone who believes in *Christ* is a *Christian*. It's the main definition."

Now Lizette looks over her shoulder at Angel and gives a wry half-smile. Angel's happiness is like a ball popping to the surface of a clean pool. It bobs there, glinting in the sunlight. Jen stares forward, face splotched.

"That is true," says Brianna. "And anyway, I'm agnostic. But, girls, let's please stay on task. What's something else you can do to make your futures better?"

"Sleep," says Tabitha sadly, aged seventeen and due next month, already possessed of a nineteen-month-old who is known in the baby room for his powerful lungs and disinclination to nap. "I never get no sleep."

"Good. Yes, sleep is essential. Self-care in general. Other thoughts?" Ysenia raises her hand.

Brianna nods encouragingly. "Ysenia."

Ysenia is a pretty girl who, in Angel's opinion, shouldn't try so hard. A tiny pimple on her chin is more noticeable for having been spackled over in foundation, and her mascara is clotted so thick that it seems an effort to hoist her eyelids open. Her black hair is streaked in dramatic blond highlights that her sister does for her with an at-home kit Ysenia claims is just as good as a salon. "Marry a rich guy," she says.

This sounds good to Angel. Her mother once told her that it's just as easy to fall in love with a rich guy as a poor one. Not that Marissa would know—along with the rest of his personality deficiencies, Mike isn't rich. The problem, her mother conceded with a sigh, is meeting one.

Angel starts to add *rich guy* to her own list, but catches Brianna's expression. Instead of that smile of bright approval with which she usually rewards classroom participation, Brianna presses her lips and gives an equivocating waggle of her head. *Marry a rich guy* is, apparently, the wrong answer.

"Well," Brianna says, "that's one thought, Ysenia. I like that you're thinking of The Practicals, of how to get the resources you need to live day to day. But if you're dependent on someone else for those things, then you aren't developing the skills *you* need to provide for *yourself*. And if that rich guy, I don't know, leaves or dies or divorces you, or proves to be a bad partner so that *you* have to leave *him*, then you're right back where you started."

"But he'd have to give me alimony," Ysenia points out. "He'd have to pay child support."

"Sure," snorts Christy, scratching flakes of neon orange nail polish off her stubby thumbnail. "Because guys pay child support. Guys are super at that."

"He'd be *rich*. Of course he'd pay. It would be no big deal if he was rich."

"If he was rich," Christy says, "he'd have lawyers and he'd know how to get out of it. *You* wouldn't see a cent." She goes back to denuding her nails. Her desk and thighs are covered in orange flakes.

"True," chimes Trinity.

Brianna's head is tilted thoughtfully. Angel presumes she is trying to work out how to validate Ysenia's point and at the same time crush it and move on. The girls are aware that Brianna handles them with kid gloves, acknowledges points of view that are foolish or plain wrong, lets slip pretty gaping lapses of logic, just to instill in them some sense of self-efficacy. Sometimes they say dumb stuff on purpose, just to watch her perform the intellectual acrobatics necessary to at once validate and correct. It can be very entertaining.

Angel is pretty sure they're all imagining this man in his slim wool suit and narrow black shoes, looking like a Banana Republic model, and it strikes her as unfair that they're passing these judgments on him just because he's square-jawed with soft-focus eyes and a leather wallet filled with platinum cards.

Angel also feels sorry for Ysenia, having to defend what is, objectively, a good idea. Because who's to say Mr. Banana Republic would definitely be a dick? He might be decent. And they're all speaking hypothetically anyway—any discussion of their futures is by definition hypothetical—so why not let Ysenia marry some hypothetical rich guy who happens not to be a dick?

If they're going to be strictly realistic, then, yes, Mr. Banana Republic probably has other plans for his life than taking care of Ysenia and her not-very-attractive eight-month-old infant, and if by some miracle Ysenia *does* convince him to marry her, then, yes, it's probably just a matter of months before he fucks her over. But if they're going to be strictly realistic, then they might as well acknowledge that number seven on Angel's list, *A job*, is unlikely to end up being the kind of job that will cover food, rent, health insurance, child care, utilities, and car payments, and also allow her to sock ten percent away into her savings account. At least not at first.

Angel tries to get up the courage to defend Ysenia—after all, Brianna has told them that *It takes a village*, and *Don't underestimate the power of community*, and *Remember, people are resources, too!*—but the thought of contradicting Brianna makes her nervous.

Lizette takes a long drink from her water bottle before dropping it hard on the desk. The gesture isn't aggressive, simply careless, but it's loud. "You're the one who said we had to get us a support system, miss," says Lizette. "I don't see what's the matter with getting a rich support system."

Yes, thinks Angel, vindicated. Her point exactly.

"There's nothing the *matter* with it, Lizette. Please raise your hand." Brianna moves over to the list of rules, which they arrived at collaboratively with quite a bit of directorial input from Brianna, and taps number three: *Raise your hand during discussion so we all have a voice.* Brianna turns to the class. "I hope you'll all be fulfilled in your relationships, but today I want us to focus on the things that you, right now, can do to improve your lives and your babies' lives. We're going to set our goals and lay out a game plan for how to achieve them." She smiles expectantly.

Ysenia slouches in her chair, her gold-digging aspirations deflated.

Angel watches Lizette, who gazes out the window, conveying with her posture, her expression, her every cell, that nothing will make her ever care about anything, ever. In the curve of her cheek, the full poutiness of her lips, she looks younger than seventeen. Angel wonders when Lizette was last hugged, when someone last made her dinner.

All this talk of marriage is depressing. Angel is a kid. She doesn't want to get married, not yet, maybe not ever, not even to a Banana Republic model. She wants to be in her house, her own house, with her mother, wants to make hamburgers in the frying pan and eat them together out on their little concrete patio in the white plastic chairs that warp when you sit. They'd bring the whole jar of pickles, dig them out of the juice with their fingers, the way they used to before Mike moved in and informed them it was disgusting.

9. *My mom. I need my mom.*

The other girls rustle their backpacks, and Angel looks with disappointment at the clock. Apparently, they'll have to come up with their game plans another day, because school's over. These activities always seem to end just before Angel learns exactly *how* to reach her goals. All around her, the girls are jabbering and slamming their desks, rubbing pregnant bellies and going to fetch babies from the nursery. Angel doesn't close her journal yet.

Sometimes she imagines grand successes for herself. She'll take her free five credits at the community college, become a doctor and, from there, a consultant on talk shows. She'll have beautiful clothes and a stylist. She'll listen sympathetically to the guests, then offer compassionate and intelligent advice, using her own difficult youth as an example. The faces of the audience will soften in admiration and sympathy as she puts forth her story with matter-of-fact grace.

More often, though, she spins a romantic story around her failure: the tragedy of her wasted gifts and a youth cut short. It'll be hard, raising a baby. Everyone says it, and Angel believes them. But raising a baby has to be easier than figuring out what her gifts are. She's pretty good at algebra, for example, and likes solving logic puzzles, but are these enough to build a career? With a baby on the way, a lot, suddenly, is settled. It turns out Angel will not be graduating with her class or moving to Albuquerque or New York. Chances are, Angel will not, as her aunt and cousin have surmised, be attending college.

At the front of the classroom, Brianna arches into a graceful yogic stretch, her thin ponytail tracing down her spine. Then she swings her enormous backpack over her shoulder.

"You okay, Angel?"

Angel is surprised to find her chin trembling, and then her eyes spill over.

"Hey. What's up?" Brianna moves swiftly toward her and places a hand on her back, peers into her face.

"I don't have my game plan." Angel brushes a tear off her cheek with the back of her hand. "My mom won't even call me." The baby twists in her womb.

Brianna is watching her, holding her in her attention, and the sadness in her expression sends a shock of fear through Angel. "I know." But then she seems to rouse herself. "Listen," she says with urgency. Her smile has vanished. She sets her backpack on the carpet. "I need to say something. I know that what you're doing is fucking terrifying."

Angel is surprised by the swearword, but more by the vehemence in her tone.

"But you're doing it, and I know you'll continue to do it. I know that your living situation has changed, Angel. But you need to make a commitment to yourself that when the people around you let you down, you will not believe you are a person who deserves to be let down, that you will not in turn let yourself down." Brianna stands with her hand clamped on Angel's shoulder, and Angel can't meet her teacher's eyes. She stares at her journal, her words smeared.

"You're already making good choices. You're here, aren't you? You're staying away from drugs and alcohol, you're eating well and getting good sleep for that baby, you're making plans for a future that's worthy of you both."

"But I made bad choices."

Brianna laughs. "Everyone has. You're a good kid, Angel. I *like* you." She gestures around the classroom. "Your friends like you."

Brianna's kindness is like the too-rich chocolate lava cake Angel had once with her mom and Mike in Santa Fe, when things were still good, delicious and too sweet to take in. She nods, her throat clotted with sadness and joy and fear and exhilaration.

Brianna squeezes Angel's shoulder again. "But now it's time to go home."

Angel places a hand at the top of her stomach, right where the baby's rump is wedged. Seeing her goals listed there, on the notebook in front of her, it all seems manageable. Not easy, of course—Angel is no fool—

but manageable. She has her learner's permit, after all, and just needs to take her test for her license. And she's well on her way to a GED right this minute. She thinks about the day when she'll be able to cross each item off her list.

And number nine: *my mom.* The baby will be born soon, and then her mother will have to come find Angel. She'll be so happy to see the baby that she will see how wrong she was about Mike. She'll scoop Angel up and bring her home, bring both of them home. The chasm of silence will close over. Her mother will teach her what she needs to know to raise this baby. Angel just needs to hold out until then.

She shuts her journal and tucks it into her purse. She's still blinking away tears, but her spirits are high. There were times in this last year when she'd lie in bed at night, rigid with worry because she couldn't imagine knowing how to do adult things like balance a checkbook or get a lease, much less find a job or go to college in Albuquerque or in some other, bigger city she knows even less. But everything she needs is enumerated in nine points on a piece of ruled paper in her composition book, and the list seems only barely more daunting than a grocery list. In Brianna's class, the forbidding requirements of adulthood—and not just adulthood, but parenthood—are a matter of incremental, deliberate steps.

Brianna. Brianna will be her baby's godmother. Angel is amazed that this hasn't occurred to her until now. Brianna is inspiring. She knows everything about babies and about The Practicals, she's childless, and she likes Angel. And in choosing her, Angel will lay claim to her, make her more hers than any of the other girls', ensuring that Brianna will stay in her baby's—and by extension, Angel's—life forever.

t's late afternoon when the UPS truck eases down the driveway. Amadeo meets the guy outside and circles to the back with him.

"It's going to be a big box," Amadeo says helpfully as the UPS man—Darnell, according to the name tag—raises the back with a clatter and starts inspecting boxes. "It's my new career."

Darnell shrugs, probably pissed about having to drive his giant truck all this way on the broken-up old roads.

"My business is called Creative Windshield Solutions. Windshield repair. If you ever need any work done, let me know."

The UPS man nods agreeably but doesn't smile. "Got it." He hands down an unwieldy and suspiciously light carton.

"Hold on, hold on. Let me get you my card."

Amadeo leaves the carton on the step. By the time he returns with the brand-new box of a thousand business cards, Darnell is backing down the driveway.

"Here! Wait!" cries Amadeo, and runs after him waving his card, but Darnell merely glances at him, shifts into drive and takes off, sending gravel shooting behind him.

Inside, Amadeo drags the box across the living room carpet and slits it open to reveal a large gray plastic toolbox.

As he snaps open the flimsy latches, he's filled with excitement. The toolbox is divided into compartments, and there's a sheet of labels to stick on each compartment according to a diagram. Everything is individually wrapped in plastic: the awl, the little bottles of resin, suction cups, and sheets of plastic film. A palm-sized battery-operated drill, a clear box full of razor blades. Amadeo bought the add-on, too, the long-crack repair kit in what looks like a pencil case, for three hundred bucks more.

Amadeo reruns the calculations, and it comes out the same: fifty dollars a pop for four hundred repairs, and he'll clear twenty thousand. And now that he owns the kit and the tools, he need only buy new supplies and resin. In a year, Amadeo figures, he can repair twice or even three times that number. Once he's taken care of all the windshields locally and in and around Española, he can work his way south. Just think of all the cracked windshields in Santa Fe and Albuquerque, in all of New Mexico.

Sixty thousand a year isn't bad, not at all. He can help out with the baby, start a college fund for him, and one for Angel, too, and still have enough left over for a new truck. Also he wants a Suzuki four-wheeler, but he'd be fine with a used one. Maybe he'll charge a hundred bucks a repair and clear a hundred and twenty thousand. People will definitely pay a hundred bucks for his services—people drop a hundred bucks on lots of things on a daily basis: traffic tickets, groceries.

His prospects look excellent. For the first time in a long while, since Good Friday, in fact, Amadeo is happy—happier even than on Good Friday, because then he was worried about his performance. Now, though, he is filled only with certainty. There was a time when he would have been afraid, embarking on a new business venture like this. But that was before Amadeo asked for the nails, before he flushed his painkillers and gave up booze; anyone with that kind of courage is a man who can succeed.

It feels good to be an entrepreneur, to be a mover in the world, to be a man who plans and creates and gets things done. For so long he's resented people in power, but now he's seeing the world through new eyes, and everywhere he looks is opportunity.

Amadeo crawls through the plastic wrappings to the television and loads the instructional DVD. The video opens with five minutes of footage of happy people driving and their windshields being pelted. "You're minding your own business," the voice-over says, "when trouble is thrown up in your path, and before you know it, *you have a crack*."

"Dang!" says the mustachioed businessman behind the wheel. He swerves dangerously and claps a despairing hand over his head.

In the next scene, the businessman has pulled onto the side of the road. He bends over the shoulder of a happy and helpful windshield repairman. The repairman grins into the camera. "Bingo!" Behind him, a flawless windshield glints.

The production is low budget—in the background is a whirr of white noise and the shots are overexposed, and the editor has leaned heavily on canned effects for transitions (yet another picture explodes into a starburst)—but Amadeo is trying his best not to see that. Now a new guy in a striped polo shirt and gelled hair stares dead-eyed into the camera. "Not many people know that windshields are actually made of two panes of glass sealed together," he says in a monotone. If the delivery leaves something to be desired, the information is solid, and Amadeo grabs a notebook from the coffee table. In the majority of cracks, the man explains, only the outside layer of glass is damaged. The key is to fill in and smooth that top layer, to restore the windshield to its original appearance, preserve its integrity.

Amadeo likes these words: *restore, preserve, integrity*. He jots them down. He's always known he wasn't the type to sit in an office or follow orders. An independent contractor, a small-business owner, that's him.

Angel bangs into the house. "Did Santa come? What is all this crap?"

"Shh." Amadeo indicates the TV. He's taking notes.

"Simply scrape the excess resin off the windshield with the razor blade," intones the man on the video, "and the repair is invisible." It *does* look simple. Amadeo can't tell from the video, though, how invisible the crack really is. It looks pretty invisible.

"Hey," objects Angel. "That's my math notebook."

Amadeo looks up, hassled.

"It's fine, whatever. Just don't use too many pages." She drops onto the couch and unties her sneaker one-handed around her bulk, grunting.

Amadeo explains the finances to his daughter. "So in a year, I can be clearing a hundred and twenty thousand dollars. That'll be good for the baby, no?"

"If it's such a great business opportunity, why aren't more people fixing windshields?"

This stops Amadeo. Maybe people *are* doing it. Maybe the world is glutted with windshield repairmen, all of them working from the same kit they ordered from the same late-night infomercial, and he just doesn't know it.

Angel nudges her chin at the pile on the floor. "How much was that stuff?"

"A thousand." He intends his tone to be casual, easy, to convey how seriously not a big deal the sum is in light of the vast profits he's about to reap.

"A *thousand*?" Angel toes the toolbox with her bare foot. The lid bobs precariously on cheap hinges. "As in a thousand *dollars*?"

"Angel, the average start-up cost for a small business is over *thirty* thousand dollars. Look it up."

"Yeah, but that's, like, for a store or something. Or a software company. Maybe that's the start-up cost for whatever company sold you this crap." She raises a skeptical eyebrow at the molded plastic mass on the carpet. "I doubt it even cost them that much, though."

"It's called an investment, Angel."

"Where'd you get the money?"

"Mind your own business."

"Oh god, Gramma. How'd you convince *her* this was a good idea?"

Actually, it was easy. He simply told his mother about the infomercial, and she nodded tiredly and gave him her credit card. Amadeo began to launch into his calculations, but Yolanda waved him away, saying, "Just stick with it." Amadeo felt deflated as he typed her credit card number into the website.

Outside, his mother's car trundles up the drive. From the window Amadeo can see her bend to root around for her purse and coffee mug and water bottle and the rest of the millions of items she drags along every time she ventures off the property.

Quickly, because he wants this sorted before his mother gets in, he sternly reminds his daughter, "You know, my mother gave you a pretty hefty sum not two weeks back. And I don't see you starting no business."

"Right. I'm just saving it. To pay for college for the human being I'm growing. No big deal."

"Hey, hijitos." Yolanda pulls the door shut behind her quietly. She glances at the mess in the living room. "So it arrived." She lets her bags and jacket slide off her shoulders and onto the floor. She drops even her keys and travel mug onto the pile at her feet. Closing her eyes, Yolanda presses the heels of her hands into her temples.

Amadeo feels a thread of alarm—she looks exhausted. "Maybe one day I'll have a shop," he says to cheer her up. "My own windshield repair shop."

Yolanda seems about to say something, then shakes her head ever so slightly. "Well, good. If it'll get you on track, hijito."

Angel stands to hug Yolanda, then starts gathering the stuff by the door. She deposits cups in the sink, hangs Yolanda's purse off the back of a kitchen chair, then goes back to wash up.

"Oh, I'll get all that," says Yolanda, but she makes her way to the couch. She sits gingerly on the edge of the cushion, hands planted squarely on her thighs, as though she's waiting at the dentist.

"I've got it. You want a drink, Gramma? I can make you some chamomile tea."

"My mother used to make that from the flowers. Used to grow them in the garden." Her voice is thin and high. Amadeo peers at his mother. There's a thin stripe of silver along her part. The skin under her eyes is purple and dented.

"So you want some?"

"No. Thank you."

The ice machine growls, and Angel emerges with a glass of water, which she hands Yolanda. Without taking a sip, Yolanda places it on the coffee table. On TV, the polo-shirted man is frozen in his explanation of the nuances of windshield repair. The ice crackles as it settles.

"If you guys don't mind, I'm just going to keep watching?" Amadeo hits PLAY.

"Oh, sure. Anyway," says Angel as though continuing a conversation, "it's cool that Gramma's your investor. So now she gets a cut of your earnings."

Amadeo pauses the DVD again. This has not occurred to him, and it probably hasn't occurred to Yolanda, who is accustomed to investing in him without any return. Now that Angel has said it, Amadeo can't *not* give his mother a cut, not without looking like an asshole.

"Of course I'll pay her back." Already Amadeo can see his income being eaten away. He thinks with despair about advertising. And taxes. Why hadn't he thought about taxes? "You think I won't? I'll pay you back," he tells his mother.

He waits for her line—No, mi hijito, you save your money—but she doesn't say it. Instead she looks at her hands, traces the veins that pop out. "Okay, honey."

His mother doesn't have savings beyond her retirement fund; he's aware of that, but, especially when he's thinking of borrowing money, he prefers not to think too closely about her financial situation. "Look, here. It's all official." He arches his ass off the couch to slide some business cards out of his back pocket and hands one to her. She turns it in her hands, smiles dimly, and places it beside her glass on the coffee table.

His only hope is if she doesn't cash his checks. Or if he gives her a payment the first couple months and then they both gradually forget.

Angel shrugs. She's enjoying this, he can tell. "You don't just got to pay her back. You got to pay her back, then give her a cut of every repair. So, like, if you charge ten bucks for each windshield, maybe you give her, like, five. She did cover all your starting costs. That's how investment works."

He looks at her, incredulous. "You learn this shit at Smart Starts!? Your precious Brianna teach you all this?"

Angel twists her mouth. "Don't you know anything? Don't you even pay attention when you watch TV?"

What he wants is for his daughter to be on board, to support and cheer him, to admire him and believe in his business. He wants the same from his mother, but he can understand why her faith in him might be faintly shaken.

"So, what," Angel says, "people are just going to, like, stop by Las Penas to get their cars fixed? Because it's such a thoroughfare? How're you going to do all this with a suspended license?"

Amadeo freezes. Somehow he'd overlooked the fact that his suspended license would make it virtually impossible for him to get the business off the ground. "Ten bucks?" he says. "You think you can get a windshield repaired for *ten bucks*?"

Angel regards the kit spread out across the carpet, the empty little baggies. "Just keep that crap away from my baby. I don't want him choking."

Mike moved in with them nearly two years ago. He was supposed to be the good guy, the sensible choice. He doesn't smoke pot or drink overmuch. He isn't handsome, like the men Angel's mother often goes for. Mike is forty-five, fourteen years older than Marissa, with a soft belly and a baby face, thin brown hair flecked with gray at the temples. He is an architect and works for the state, working on teams to design various nondescript buildings: rest stops and DMV satellite offices and the like, buildings that Angel hadn't even realized required architects.

He and Marissa had been dating for three months before Angel met him, and for all that time, Marissa had been giddy, buying forty-dollar face creams and new lacy underclothes, which she would hand-wash and leave dripping from the shower curtain rail. Those months were suffused with festivity, and Angel felt close to her mother, proud of her beauty: her full lips, shining dark eyes, her thick, glossy hair. Before her dates—three or four a week—Marissa modeled her outfits and con- sulted with Angel on eye shadow colors, and then Angel stayed up as late as she could, usually falling asleep on the couch, so she'd know when her mother got home and could ask how it had gone. This business with Mike seemed to Angel to be a joint project, and her advice was crucial to the success of the courtship. She also had the sense that she was her mother's apprentice; now that she was in eighth grade, Angel must pay attention, keep alert, learn what she could about relationships.

The evenings Marissa stayed home, they ordered pizza and rented movies. If it was a weekend, Marissa let Angel invite Priscilla to sleep over, and all three of them would stay up late, laughing and baking cookies like girls in teen movies.

"Architects are rich, right?" Angel asked on one of these nights, made braver by Priscilla's presence.

Marissa explained regretfully that, sure, Mike made decent money, but he owed it to his ex-wife in California. He had two kids, teenagers, a boy and a girl, whom he saw only rarely, and though Angel hadn't even met Mike yet, the mention of this distant, nameless daughter caused a fillip of envy.

Mike lived in a tiny apartment in Santa Fe, a quick bike ride to his office. "It's nice, though," Marissa assured Angel. "Right downtown. He just doesn't care about things."

"Do you think you'll get married?" Priscilla asked.

Marissa laughed. She always pretended nonchalance when talking about Mike, but then would be unable to stop herself. "Maybe? Who knows! But the other night we were watching this movie set in India and he said, 'Let's go there for our honeymoon.' "

"What movie? Did you go to a movie theater or did you rent it?" Angel asked, not quite liking the thought of her mother snuggled up against a man in an apartment in Santa Fe she'd never seen.

"Oh!" cried Priscilla. "You could do an India-theme reception! Like, bright silk tablecloths and little wooden elephants for centerpieces. The cake could be, like, spicy."

Marissa pushed her hair back from her face, seeming to take Priscilla's idea seriously. "I don't know, I've just always thought a traditional wedding is better. What do you think, Angel?"

"Oh, *definitely*," said Priscilla. "I'm totally going traditional. Next time I'll bring my magazines and we can plan it!"

Angel loved this new, delighted version of her mother and also felt repulsed, because now she had to think about her mother and this Mike character having sex. A region between her stomach and her pelvis quivered, as though a dozen flashing silvery sardines were flipping around there in the dark.

Angel frowned. "Why doesn't Mike see his kids?" This seemed to be a warning sign.

Marissa shrugged. "His ex-wife's kind of a control monster. And Stockton is far."

The first time Marissa introduced them, it was at Serafina's, a nice restaurant just outside of Santa Fe. "It was Mike's idea," Marissa said, looking around the patio strung with white lights while they waited for him at the table. "He wants to do things right."

Her mother was stunning in a burgundy dress with a deep neckline. Angel had also dressed up for the dinner, in a flattering sundress and the shoes she'd worn to the eighth-grade end-of-year dance; Serafina's wasn't the kind of place she and Marissa frequented. The sun had set, though the sky was still bright, and Angel felt glamorous, here among other well-dressed people, sipping her ice water.

"Can I get you a drink while you wait?" the waiter inquired, but Marissa shook her head tightly, as if afraid that Mike might not show.

But he did show, looking round and tidy in a V-neck sweater and khakis. He pulled Marissa in for a kiss on the mouth and extended a confident hand to Angel.

"The famous Angel. You look just like your mother. And *that* is a compliment."

When the waiter came again, Mike took charge, urging Marissa to get a drink and then ordering guacamole, which, to Angel's astonishment, was made fresh from a cart, right there at the table. The waiter sliced and scooped avocados into a molcajete with quick, practiced motions, squeezed limes, then mashed it all up and served it to them with a bowl of hot, salty chips. It was the most delicious guacamole she'd ever tasted.

Angel felt shy, but she answered Mike's questions about school and hobbies with the pleasant carefulness she used when addressing teachers. To her relief, he soon turned his attention to her mother, and Angel was allowed to sip her lemonade and watch them laugh.

Her mother was a fresher, more alive version of herself with Mike, Angel decided that first night. The tension that sometimes made Marissa's face rigid at the nostrils and along the jawline, as though a complex network of wires were stretched just beneath her skin, had gone. She looked soft and radiant, and Angel saw her as she'd been when she was young, as Marissa still must see herself. "You don't know what it's like, always doing things alone," she'd once told Angel, looking up from an impossible spread of paperwork, but Marissa was wrong. Angel knew exactly what it was like. Hadn't she been coming home to an empty house since she was seven? Also, her mother *didn't* do things alone. What about Angel, who took on fully half the chores and did her best to be a friend to her mother?

But that night at the restaurant as they ate their enchiladas and fajitas, Marissa laughed and joked, and her jokes seemed more sophisticated than Angel would have given her mother credit for. When Mike started complaining about the Republicans for blockading some bill or other, Marissa joined right in, adding facts and perspectives of her own, though Angel hadn't known her mother followed the news or cared much about politicians. They're all assholes, she'd once told Angel.

"I shouldn't have had a second one," Marissa said, tapping her empty margarita glass. The straw was waxy with lipstick and most of the salt had been licked off, but still, Marissa extended the tip of her tongue shyly to the rim.

Mike laughed. "Better for me. I get to enjoy your company until you sober up."

So Marissa and Mike each had a third, and Angel tamped down the flare of worry as she watched her mother sip, and they ate their dinners slowly and then ordered sticky flan and creamy chocolate cheesecake and the fanciest, most delicious pile of churros, chewy and crunchy, with cinnamon sugar that spilled on Angel's dress. On the side of each dessert plate was mounded whipped cream so thick it was almost cheesy, and Angel, imitating her mother, ate the whipped cream one delicate and distracted half-spoonful at a time, setting the spoon down after every creamy, dreamy bite, as if each extension of the spoon was singular and decadent and they had no intention of gobbling the whole mound, though Angel knew they both did.

"Taste it," Angel urged Mike, but he patted his stomach.

"Alas, no. I have genetically high cholesterol."

Finally all the dessert plates had been scraped clean and the cappuccino cups stood empty but for some drying foam on the rim and the thick dark circle in the bottom (Angel had never known her mother to drink coffee after dinner). It hadn't felt as though they were biding their time until Marissa's tipsiness faded. They'd had so much fun that, in the end, they were nearly the last to leave.

Mike slid his credit card into the folder without even looking at the bill—Angel had hoped to catch a glimpse of the total—the dinner must have cost a fortune. After he'd signed the slip, he walked them to their car and opened the passenger door for Angel, handing her in.

Then he went around to the driver's side, where, aware of Angel watching, he and her mother shared a laughing, awkward kiss that melted into something longer and less awkward.

Sitting there, Angel was embarrassed by how dingy their car was— twenty years old, stained upholstery, used napkins in the cup holder, the dirty floor mats worn bald. She wished Mike didn't have to see it, but he wasn't looking. His hand was deep in Marissa's hair, Marissa's head tipped back.

Finally they pulled apart and Marissa got in, giving a single self-conscious giggle and then falling silent.

"Do you like him?" Marissa asked worriedly once they were on the highway, her nostrils tensing, the wires already beginning to tighten below the surface of her face.

"Definitely," said Angel, and Marissa had looked over at her and flashed a sudden radiant smile, and Angel was so lifted by that smile that she didn't ask her mother if she was okay to drive.

"I'm really glad. It's important to me that you like him." Marissa paused. "We were thinking he might move in with us. At the end of the month."

And Angel had been so happy about her mother's happiness that she hadn't even minded that the plan had already been made and that she hadn't been consulted.

The first few months Mike lived with them, things were great. Angel felt that they—she and Marissa—were rising, occupying a more stable position in the world, even if their actual circumstances hadn't really changed. They still lived in the same house, but it felt tidier, and with the second income, the rent didn't feel like such a burden. Marissa had never fallen seriously behind in rent, but the worry that she might preoccupied her and sifted like sand into Angel's sense of home, a constant itchy grit.

There was more money for dinners out and movies and little spontaneous gifts from her mother—a lip gloss here, a new outfit there. On Angel's fifteenth birthday, Marissa and Mike presented her with a laptop computer. "You have to have one now that you're in high school," Mike said.

He didn't ignore Angel, as some of her mother's boyfriends had, as if by ignoring her she'd simply disappear and they'd have Marissa to themselves. And he never seemed creepy, either, like these guys who seemed to regard a single woman with a daughter as a twofer. That's how one of them actually put it, joking about his "girls," when Angel was eleven. Marissa had turned on him savagely. "That's fucked up. Never, ever say that."

No, Mike was a good guy. He seemed like a *dad*, cracking corny jokes, chiming in on whatever subject her homework was about. He was well educated, he subscribed to boring thin-paged magazines with lots of news and commentary and not many pictures. And he seemed to care for Marissa. He was always slipping his arm around her waist, commenting on her sexiness, grabbing her boob, and Angel would avert her eyes or hang out more with friends. He supported Angel when she lobbied to be allowed to go to parties. "She needs her freedom." Marissa agreed, flushed and happy and, after fifteen years of single-parenthood, relieved to give up some of the burden of parental responsibility to someone else—someone older, with kids of his own, a man.

So Angel began going out more, staying out later. "We trust you," Mike said over and over, and Angel, thrilled and uneasy with the sudden freedom, would look for confirmation to her mother, who would lift her head, nod, then lay her head back on Mike's chest. Not long after, they announced with clasped hands that they were engaged.

Mike's personality began to change the summer before Angel's sophomore year, when he was tasked with designing picnic ramadas in a park in Roswell. This was a big deal, he emphasized to Marissa. "I do this right, and it's a whole new ball game. They'll give me more projects, a promotion. We can move out of this craphole." He looked around Marissa and Angel's little living room, with the bent venetian blinds and the shelf of Disney animals, the friendly polka-dotted rug and the suede-like microfiber couch that Angel and Marissa had chosen together with great enthusiasm several years earlier, but that hadn't, admittedly, held up well.

He started spending days at a time at the job site four hours south in Roswell or in meetings in Santa Fe. When he got home, he was grouchy and constantly on his cell phone. The board hadn't liked his design—too ambitious, unrealistic for the budget—and now he was being asked to work with another architect senior to him. "*Collaborate*," he spat. "They're giving me a fucking babysitter." He and Marissa began fighting—about money, about the state of the house, about the hours Angel was keeping. It was true that she was spending two and occasionally three nights a week out. A few times last summer, Marissa, bleary and nearsighted, had come out of her bedroom at the sound of Angel quietly letting herself into the house at dawn. "What time is it? Have you been drinking?"

"*No*. God," Angel would say, pushing past her mother into her own bedroom. And, doubtless because it was the easiest course, Marissa decided to believe her.

One evening during one of Mike's trips away, Angel had come home from Priscilla's house to find her mother, in too-short sweatpants and her hair in a rough ponytail, standing over a pile of laundry in the hall. Marissa was inspecting what Angel realized in horror was a pair of her own—Angel's—underpants.

"Are you having *sex*?" Marissa demanded. She looked angry and old, her skin discolored and dry, her mouth warped into an ugly little curl.

"That's disgusting, Mom." Angel snatched her dirty underpants from her mother's hand and slammed her bedroom door.

Her head throbbed. What kind of sick Sherlock did her mother think she was? Of course she'd been having sex. And how hypocritical! It wasn't Angel who dangled her disgusting, lacy panties from every towel rack in the house. It wasn't Angel who left her stupid diaphragm on the edge of the bathtub, where it winked lewdly at Angel like a fleshier and less amiable version of one of those Scrubbing Bubbles from the commercial. It wasn't Angel who hung on the neck of her smug, jerky architect boyfriend, and who cracked sly innuendos as though Angel were too stupid to pick up on them.

She waited all that night for her mother to come in after her, to lay down the law, and, in the nights that followed, she kept waiting. She was ready to be defensive and angry, but she was also relieved to have been found out. Maybe her mother would start behaving like an actual mother—ground her, keep her safe in the house—and Angel would have no choice but to get off this increasingly troubling train she'd found herself on.

But Marissa didn't come into Angel's room. And in the weeks following, did Marissa, even knowing what she knew, ever once talk to Angel about birth control? About abstinence? Did it, in those days, ever occur to her to just *not let* Angel go out every night? No, it did not, because Marissa was preoccupied with Mike, who, it turned out, hadn't given up the lease on his Santa Fe apartment—the revelation had resulted in a massive fight and a smashed kitchen chair—and was now staying half the week there. Marissa was spending her energies dressing up for him, trying to cajole him back into his former good mood, then breaking glasses and yelling at him and at Angel, too, when her attempts failed.

So Angel went out more and more to parties in people's parentless houses or in empty buildings and construction sites or at the end of long roads in the empty desert. She lost herself in hysterical drunken laughter with friends, in the pleading pressure of someone's body against her own, and also in the long, sad days after that were muffled by irritability and hangover, when memories of things she'd said and done would detonate in the smog with radioactive clarity and, always, shame. Her own stupid plays at self-assuredness were laughable and wrong, and, tense with humiliation, Angel would relive moments from the previous night's party and the many parties leading up to it: laughing meanly at Priscilla for saying *taken for granite* or calling some other girl a bitch behind her back or giving some guy a blow job through the pee-hole of his boxers.

Three missed periods later, after Angel could no longer ignore it—and after confirming it with both a drugstore-brand and a name-brand pregnancy test, wrapping the packaging in a black garbage bag and pushing it deep into the trash can outside, not even recycling the paperboard—Angel confessed to her mother. It was late on a school night, just the two of them home, and they were washing their faces at the sinks in the bathroom. After Angel uttered the words, she nearly cried with the relief of handing her burden to her mother.

Her mother looked up at Angel in the mirror, her face streaming, hairline wet. "Wait. You *think* you're pregnant?" She looked very young and frightened, which wasn't the reaction Angel had hoped for.

Angel's mouth went dry. With shaking hands she spread toothpaste on her brush, and tried to steady her voice. "I guess I don't just think it."

"Oh, shit. Oh shit." Marissa's face dripped into the neckline of her pink pajama shirt. "Mike's not going to be happy about this."

Angel put down her toothbrush and stepped back. "Mike's not the one who's going to have to go into labor."

Marissa snatched the towel and rubbed her face vigorously. Then she folded it with great precision and hung it on the rack. "Let's not pretend this isn't going to affect Mike. And me, too. Who's the father?"

Angel was still too stunned to speak, but Marissa must have interpreted her hesitation as not knowing, because she let out a long keening whimper.

"Oh god, how stupid could you be? Messing up all of our lives!"

"What about me?"

"Your life, too! Especially your life! Oh god."

She seemed about to go on, but Angel left the bathroom without brushing her teeth, and shut herself in her bedroom. She curled on her bed, waiting for her mother to come in and make things right, waited and waited.

———

"SHE'S GOT TO GET an abortion," Mike said when, a full three weeks later, Marissa finally told him. Angel overheard the conversation from her bedroom.

She might have gotten one, too, *would* have gotten one, except that her mother never suggested it and Angel was somehow afraid to bring it up, because her mother must have thought it was a sin. Why else wouldn't she mention it? And it was a sin, wasn't it? Except that she can't believe that God would be so unfair, letting guy after guy get off scot-free, while saddling girls with either lifelong responsibilities or mortal sins.

At the same time, Angel had a sense that she should suffer for her mistakes, see them through. Now she wonders at the inertia that somehow allowed her to ignore what was happening inside her week after week and the self-loathing that insisted she be punished.

Mike was already looking up clinics. "Call them," he ordered Marissa, waving the phone in her face. "Now." Angel was flooded with relief, because even if he was a jerk, Mike was an adult, taking charge, and Angel was about to get a second chance at a normal life.

"It's too late," Marissa said in a small voice. The disappointment was like a sack of sand in the gut. Angel hadn't actually known it was too late until now.

She could hear Mike's long exhalation. "What the hell do you mean, *it's too late*." It was a statement. "How long have you been keeping this from me?"

"Maybe if you'd been around. You were staying in Santa Fe! Anyway, it's Angel's business and she's my daughter. And besides, you know we're Catholic. We don't believe in abortion. I didn't give up my baby, did I?"

He gave a short mean laugh. Angel could picture him exactly: tipping his round head, smiling wryly. "Do you really not believe in it, Marissa, or do you just think you don't, because then you'd have to admit you made the wrong choice?"

"Gee thanks, Mike," Marissa said bitterly, lamely.

"I guess I should be congratulating you," Mike said when Angel finally ventured out of her bedroom. "I guess the stork's bringing you something *extra* special for your sweet sixteen." He looked at the swell of her stomach, his lip twisted in revulsion, and Angel wrapped her arms around herself.

Amadeo knew it was coming, but still, when Angel goes into labor, it's somehow a surprise. There's a window in the delivery room, but it seems to have been tinted with some UV protectant so that everything—the parking lot, the mountains, the sky heaped with clouds—is violet-blue, the whole world on the verge of evening even now, in the heat of the day. Angel is yellow and drawn, and her hair frames her face, frizzy against the pillow.

They're waiting for her to dilate, the nurse tells him, which makes Amadeo think of a giant dark eye between his daughter's legs, an infant bursting through the fragile, unblinking tissue. She's resting, her belly a mound as high as her propped head, but it's only a matter of time before it all starts. A nurse has supplied him and his mother with blue papery smocks and shoe covers like shower caps.

"Ungh," grunts Angel as a contraction comes, then she relaxes. "Where's my mom? Is she here yet?"

"We left messages, honey," says Yolanda.

As if Angel has just noticed Amadeo there, she turns on him. "Could you say something at least? If you're gonna be standing there? Tell a story? Crack a joke?"

A joke. Nothing comes to mind. "Why did the chicken . . . Shit, I don't know, Angel."

She pushes her face away in disgust and grimaces into another contraction.

Yolanda says, "I heard on the news where a little boy—" Her voice breaks, but is strong when she starts again. "A father shot his own son. The little boy was hiding in the closet. Seven years old."

"What's the punch line, well?" asks Angel.

"That's just the story I heard. I can't stop thinking about it."

"God, Mom. Not the time." Amadeo looks at his mother in surprise. Her judgment's been a real issue lately. Just the other day she left the burner on under the kettle for four hours. The kettle was so hot the enamel flaked off.

"Well, it's a terrible story," says Yolanda. "Really terrible! Why shouldn't we think about that poor baby? Terrible things happen in this world and we can't just pretend they don't. We can't turn our backs on people who are scared and in pain."

"Ungh," moans Angel again.

Three hours they've been here. When he got the call this morning that Angel was in labor and was being driven to the hospital by the Family Foundations receptionist, Amadeo had to get Tío Tíve to give him the ride. It's not the first ride Amadeo has had to beg from his uncle since the night Tíve bailed him out. Each time it's a profoundly humiliating experience, having to wait outside the community center or probation office, and then climb into the passenger seat like a twelve-year-old. Generally Amadeo endures these humiliations in silence. Today, he asked, "Can't you go any faster?" and his uncle growled, but sped up.

Amadeo was the first of the family to arrive, and was, gratifyingly, the sole beneficiary of the relieved smile Angel beamed onto him as he came toward her in the waiting room. She waved from her wheelchair.

"Why's she in a wheelchair?" he asked the woman who drove Angel. The woman's purse strap crossed her chest like a bandolier of bullets. "Why's she need a wheelchair?"

He'd expected to be ushered into a sterile delivery room in time to see his scarlet screaming grandson lifted triumphantly over the doctor's head. But Angel was still in her jeans and Pumas, her big gold purse hanging from her knee.

Angel shrugged. "They just gave me one." She maneuvered forward and back, flexed her bicep. "I'm going to get me some guns, lose this baby fat."

"Well, I'll duck away now that your dad's here," said the receptionist.

Angel looked up in alarm. "Tell Brianna I'll keep up with my journal. Tell her I'll call the minute the baby comes."

The receptionist laughed. "Catch your breath first."

"And tell her there's no way I'm missing the Open House! I'll be there, and so will my dad. Right, Dad? You're coming? So you can meet Brianna?"

"Relax. You're good, Angel," Amadeo said. "You'll be good." Of course she would be good: her father was here. But then the receptionist shook his hand and passed through the automatic doors, leaving Amadeo horribly in charge.

"Brianna's like my personal hero."

He pictured a competent, gray-haired woman with a shelf bosom. She'd be a hugger. "Hey, what about me?"

Angel laughed, full-throated. "Oh yeah. You, too."

Now, she groans.

"You're okay, hijita," says Yolanda.

Amadeo peels the hefty Band-Aid off his left hand. Maybe a nurse can check out his injuries, wrap them up professionally. They haven't healed entirely, but it's clear that he's not permanently wounded. Now he can more or less do the things he used to do, though his writing looks like shit. He's forever knocking the back of his hand into things and making himself yelp.

"Weird that we've both been to the hospital lately," Amadeo remarks to his daughter. "Who'd have thought?" He pushes the Band-Aid back on, but the stick is ruined.

"Huh," says Yolanda.

She pats Angel's hand, the hand Amadeo can't bear to look at because of the IV needle pushed under her skin. A piece of curling tape keeps it from getting wrenched loose, but, Amadeo thinks, the needle must shift around in there. Woozily, he imagines the tip grazing the thin walls of the vein, scraping bone.

From the television mounted in the corner, Judge Judy snaps at bedraggled defendants who don't even have the wherewithal to pick a nicer sweatshirt for their televised court appearances.

"Where's my mom?" Angel asks her grandmother with a little whimper. "I thought she'd be here by now."

"I left a message." Yolanda checks her phone, then both her hand and the phone drop back to her lap. "She'll be here."

"She hasn't seen me in over three weeks."

When he looks at his daughter, Amadeo sometimes has the sense that he's looking at one of those holographic postcards—she's a woman, she's a child, she's the tiny kid she once was. He can't get her image to hold steady.

"Hey, you're okay. You got us," Amadeo reminds her.

What Amadeo didn't expect was how boring it would all be. It wasn't so bad when they let Angel walk the halls, but as soon as a bed became available, they stuck her in it and plugged her into machines. For long periods nothing happens, just the tedious comings and goings of people with brisk walks. They write baffling things—numbers and abbreviations and impossible-to-read drug names—on the whiteboard opposite her bed, check dials and digital displays and make marks on plastic clipboards.

A heavy lady packed into banana-printed scrubs—nurse, nurse's assistant, doctor?—pats the arm of a chair. "Why don't you take a seat, Dad, out of the way?" Amadeo sits obediently, the vinyl exhaling under him.

But Amadeo is still in the way, and it doesn't matter where his chair is. "Excuse me," says first one medical professional and then another. "Excuse me." Amadeo scoots this way and that, and each time he moves he loses one shoe cover or another. His big feet in their yellow leather work boots stick out into everyone's path. Finally, he wedges himself into a corner next to a red biohazard bin and behind the swinging IV line. A nurse administers an injection, and with a rapidity that can only be carelessness, passes the needle under Amadeo's nose on its way to the biohazard bin. She pops the bin open with her foot and then lets the lid drop, subjecting Amadeo to a puff of contagion.

Everything becomes hazy; sound is fuzzy, his vision clouded. The vinyl of the chair is damp beneath his thighs. He looks at the floor, the walls, the arms of the very chair he's sitting in, and because he just saw a segment about it on the news, he thinks of the MRSA bacteria that must be coating every surface. The Band-Aid on his hand flaps off.

"I gotta go," Amadeo says, and murmurs something about the bathroom to a medical assistant as he staggers into the clean bare cold of the hall. He leans against the blank wall, breathing heavily, willing himself not to vomit.

If only Angel could be like her friend and just crap the baby out.

After taking a spin around the hospital, though, he feels better. He goes down to the cafeteria, pressing the elevator button with his elbow. He feels useful, trucking around like he has a purpose. "I got you a Jell-O snack," he informs Angel, pushing back into the room.

His daughter turns a dark look on him. "I'm about to blast a watermelon out of my pussy and you think I want a Jell-O snack?"

Yolanda flinches. "Angel, mi hijita, please."

"Fine." Amadeo places the Jell-O on the rolling tray. "You could have it, Mom."

"You go ahead." But there's no way Amadeo is going to carry a spoonful of Jell-O snack through this thick viral air and into his mouth.

A nurse assures them that Angel is dilating, slowly but surely, not that Amadeo wants to know the details. He sees very little change in Angel's state, except that she is becoming increasingly irritable.

When Angel was being born, Amadeo remembers, he sat in the waiting room watching VH1, clutching a package of peanut butter crackers from the vending machine and concentrating very hard, as if he were going to be quizzed later on the video for TLC's "Waterfalls." The whole time, Marissa's mother had been in there with Marissa, and her sister and Yolanda, too. All those women united over Angel's birth as they never would be again once, just a few months later, things began to disintegrate between Marissa and Amadeo.

He doesn't know why he wasn't there with Marissa. He'd wanted to be—or part of him had wanted to—except that the prospect felt scary and intimate and he sensed that the women would have been surprised if he'd presented himself at the delivery room door.

Now, five hours in, Yolanda stands, presses the heels of her hands into her eye sockets. She unties her smock and folds it neatly, removes her shower cap. "I'm going to go home for a while, hijita."

"Wait, what?" Angel scoots up, alert. "You're *leaving*?"

"What can I do, honey? I'm not helping anything, just sitting here. It could take hours and hours. And you've got your dad." She gathers her purse. "I have a headache. I just need to lie down. I'll be back in an hour or two. Call if anything changes," she tells Amadeo.

"*You're* not leaving, are you, Dad?" Angel's hair is tangled, her face pale. The caked mascara looks ready to crumble into her reddened eyes. She looks a little unhinged.

"No," he says meekly. He hadn't known leaving was an option.

They both watch in shock as Yolanda follows through with her threat, pulls out her car keys, plants a casual kiss on Angel's head, and is gone.

"What the hell?" says Angel. "What is *with* her? What is with *all* of you?"

"Hey now. *I'm* right here."

Angel is right. Yolanda has been strange. For instance, her comment earlier: What was she thinking, bringing up some kid's murder at a time like this? And then up and leaving at maybe the most dramatic moment of their lives, the moment when Amadeo is going to become a thirty-three-year-old grandfather? Yolanda is not behaving like the mother he knows, the one who cooks for them and buys them socks and hands them money when they need it. She has a responsibility to be the mother they've come to expect.

He nearly says something along those lines to Angel, but a parrot-faced guy with the wavy hair of a rock star hustles past him to check his daughter's blood pressure.

Amadeo dawdles at the end of Angel's bed, watching the nurse pump the blood pressure cuff. Despite his profession, he's still a man, the guy's demeanor seems to convey. There's something delicate and efficient and assured in the way he pumps the bulb. He juts his chin and stares thoughtfully into the middle distance, as though posing, listening through his stethoscope. As Angel gazes through tears at the ceiling, waiting for her arm to be released, Amadeo thinks about blood pressure, about the actual pressure of blood—thick blood, red blood—pulsing through his own veins, and he thinks about needles. He eyes the biohazard bin grimly.

"Would you just relax?" snaps Angel. "Sit *down*."

"Sure." His voice sounds faint in his ears. "I'm relaxed." He doesn't want to blame Angel while she's lying here frightened and in pain, but no one can deny that it's because of her that he's in this hospital teeming with hordes of pathogens. Why none of this occurred to him when he was sitting in the ER on Good Friday is beyond him.

"Looking good," the guy tells Angel, marking the number on the clipboard.

"Hey," says Amadeo. He tugs the nurse's sleeve, hampering his rush from the room. "Do you think everything's been sanitized? I mean, what about MRSA?"

The nurse shakes his head warningly. "We have very few cases here, sir."

"What the hell is mersa?" Angel looks from the nurse to Amadeo and back, her face alight with terror.

Amadeo turns to his daughter regretfully. "It's this infection that's totally drug-proof. Hospitals are full of it. You can get it from, like, a hangnail, and they usually have to amputate. Don't you even watch the news? They're always talking about it."

"Dad!"

"You don't need to worry," says the nurse. "It doesn't help to worry."

Amadeo's knees liquefy and his vision wobbles. Come on, he tells himself. Get a grip. He must be strong. "Don't worry," Amadeo tells Angel, and then he leans over and vomits.

The vomit slaps the linoleum and achieves an impressive range, splattering the far wall, Angel's sheets, even the biohazard bin.

Angel wails.

"Okay, sir," says the male nurse firmly, leading him away by the elbow from the awful intimate sight of fully formed corn kernels and diced tomato. He deposits Amadeo in the hall before calling for backup, as if they have to get rid of Amadeo before they can begin to get rid of his mess.

———

TWO MORE HOURS PASS. Amadeo sits in the corridor on a plastic chair in his smock. He slouches like a disgraced child, cast out of the classroom. Throwing up had a salutary effect; he feels strong now, actually, and clearheaded, despite the scourging taste in his mouth. But it doesn't matter, because he is not allowed back in the delivery room. Of course, *of course*, he puked in front of the one male nurse.

His mother returned, summoned on her cell phone by both Amadeo and Angel, and is in there now, in her rightful place. Amadeo expected to be reprimanded—I can't leave you for a *minute*—but she just patted Amadeo as she passed. "It's okay, hijito. Your dad almost fainted when Valerie was born, and he wasn't even in the room." Then the door clapped shut behind her, leaving Amadeo with this comparison to his father. He knows they will hold this fuckup against him forever, his mom and daughter. In the decades to come, they'll laugh at him, shake their heads, but deep down they'll see it as the deeper failing it is.

He jabs his hand. The crucifixion feels very far away, not at all like something that happened to him in his own life. Angel is right—there's enough pain in the world, lurking darkly at the edges and poised to spring. Shame floods him; his limbs are engorged with it.

The whole hospital seems to be buzzing and beeping—the lights, the intercoms, the computer monitors, the phones at the circular nurses' station. The place is a complex machine, and at the heart of it is his Angel, his beautiful child in pain.

Amadeo peers at his daughter through the narrow window in the door, sees the spasms that tighten her pale face. She lapses into a light, drugged sleep before being yanked awake once more.

Amadeo pokes his head in. "I remembered a joke. Did you hear about the hurricane that passed through Española?"

A nurse is doing something between Angel's spread legs, so Amadeo rushes. "Ripped right through town and did two million dollars' worth of repairs."

A smile passes over Angel's face, as brief and pained as a contraction. "You shouldn't be talking crap about Española. It's my hometown. And you went to high school there." Then she looks beyond him to the hallway, carts and gurneys and visiting families passing. "I'm practically naked! Shut the door!"

Amadeo withdraws his head. Now other jokes present themselves to him, jokes he remembers from his own high school years that he'll never tell Angel. Why'd they cancel the driver's ed program? They needed the cars for sex ed. Why wasn't Jesus born in Española? Because God couldn't find a virgin.

Amadeo is filled with an electric jangling fear that doesn't expend itself. He presses his thumbs into his palms and prays to Jesus, but he isn't comforted. What does Jesus know about waiting for one's daughter to give birth? Nothing. So he prays to God, who's a father, too, but he can't picture God except as a woolly jovial guy. He'd pass out cigars, clap Amadeo on the back, call out hearty congratulations, and Amadeo doesn't trust that. Finally, he prays to Mary, who does know what he's talking about, having had a kid herself and having had to watch that kid go through big troubles. *Let her be okay*, he begs. *Please let her be okay.* But he can't give the prayers the kind of lift they need, the lift he was able to give his prayers in the morada. Amadeo can almost see them catch in the drafts from the air conditioner and drift to the floor, skate around the linoleum like dust bunnies.

Amadeo remembers praying as a child, listing the people he wanted God to bless. He lay in the dark, stiff with anxiety that he might forget a name, scouring his mind for even the most forgettable of his classmates lest God, to punish Amadeo for his omissions, take that person out. Amadeo still remembers the Technicolor cartoon violence of those visions: anvils plummeting from heaven, chasms splitting the floors of buildings, fires leaping unbidden from the sidewalk. It must have been boring for his mother, having to sit there at the edge of his bed, holding back her final kiss until he'd finished droning. But these prayers were important, because hadn't his father—whom Amadeo hated, whom he feared for his rages and silences, whom he intentionally left out of his prayers starting the year he turned five—died just such a Looney Tunes death? Descending La Bajada on I-25, crashing through the guardrail, the car (as Amadeo imagined—still imagines—it) flying in slow motion through sky until the tires once again touched earth and the car erupted in flames.

Even now when he thinks of his father, Amadeo remembers with a pang his little vinyl case of Matchbox cars, which he'd left in his father's trunk and which never made it out of the wreckage. He'd loved those cars, each of which somehow had its own personality—the serious, studious police cruiser and the sassy delivery van and the peevish chipped blue convertible with the doors that opened—those beloved cars that had met their own miniature fiery ends. He wept a lot for those cars, though even at age five, he knew better than to let on. Surely he'd been weeping for his father, too. But amid those memories, Amadeo remembers the exhilaration of his own power, the sense that God was listening carefully.

Fuck, Amadeo thinks now, looking at his palms, disgusted with his exaggerated sense of his own importance in the eyes of God.

He wonders now how things between him and Marissa would have turned out if he *had* been in the delivery room with her. If they'd held hands, united and ready to welcome their daughter, while their mothers waited outside, would they have moved in together? Would they be together to this day?

As if conjured, Marissa stands above him now, a purse and a canvas tote bag over her shoulder. She's put on a little weight since he last saw her, nearly two years ago, but she's still hot, in tight black pants and a sweater that slides off a shoulder. She wears glasses now, oversized and hip. Her skin is smooth and flushed, her hair pulled back into a coarse ponytail. A few strands, too short for the rubber band, fall around her face. "Hey."

"Oh. Hey. You're here." He straightens, runs a hand down the front of his shirt. Of course Amadeo knew he'd see her today, but he didn't expect this nervousness. "She's dilated to three centimeters. I was in there a long time."

He smells the cigarette cloud on Marissa. Amadeo is about to tell her she'd better not go in there smelling like that, that it will snag in Angel's lungs, make the breathing even harder on her, but he doesn't want to start a fight, and he also isn't sure she won't go in anyway just to spite him.

Marissa tips her head and gives a bleak half-smile. "She okay?"

Amadeo nods with more conviction than he feels.

Marissa pauses before the door and seems to gather her forces. Is she nervous? Amadeo wonders with surprise. She repositions her purse strap higher on her shoulder and then turns the knob and goes in.

Amadeo jiggles his leg and regards the wide hall and the other loitering men. They all look unkempt. Shirts untucked, assorted smudged shoes, exposed hairy arms. They tug at sideburns and uneven facial hair, they wander out to the elevators and back. A few talk on phones, but their voices are muted, as though they're aware that this place is not theirs.

"You threw up?" Marissa says when she comes out after only ten minutes. She seems cheered. "Why? She hasn't even started pushing. There isn't even any blood yet."

"I'm not good with needles. You know that."

"I didn't know that." She drops into the chair beside him. "It's a real hurry-up-and-wait, huh. It's good to see your mom." He feels her studying him. "It's good to see you."

"How's Angel?"

Marissa's expression tightens. "She's fine," she says testily.

"She was waiting for you. For hours. We must have put in twenty calls."

"My cell was out of juice. No one tried me at work until your mom just this minute, and then I came right over. Smart Starts! has my work number, so I don't know what's up with that. Plus, you know where I work. I've been at the same damn place for ten years."

Amadeo should have tried calling her himself. Or suggested his mom stop by Marissa's house and office, neither of which is more than ten minutes from the hospital.

After a moment, she says, "Really, she was waiting for me?" She indicates a tangled wad of lavender acrylic at the top of her canvas tote. "I'm knitting her a blanket. For the baby. A lady at work is teaching me. I hate it." She positions the mass on her lap, scoots the loops up and down the needles, then gives up and spears the snarl.

All at once Amadeo is struck by the oddness of the fact that it's been so long since he's seen his daughter's mother. Their visitation schedule was always casual at best, and these last few years, Amadeo has hardly seen his daughter, despite the fact that she lives just forty minutes away, in a city he goes to literally all the time. Marissa never asked him to do pickups or take Angel to doctors' appointments; she turned instead to her mother and his. She never had the faintest flicker of faith in him, and was right not to. Again that hot wash of guilt sluices over him, and sorrow, too, because all those years he could have known Angel and didn't.

Two years younger than him, just a year behind him in school, yet Amadeo used to be in awe of Marissa's determination. She did better in school than Amadeo, and he always figured that she'd end up a successful real estate agent or lawyer. He figured she'd move up and away and marry someone equally successful and sneer from her great heights at that first boyfriend—that mistake—who didn't know how good he had it.

From Angel, Amadeo has gathered that Marissa has never been lacking for romance. He hopes Marissa doesn't ask if he's seeing anyone. Occasionally a woman at a bar will catch his eye, and they'll chat, and even more occasionally he'll go home with her. His last actual girlfriend was four years ago. She moved in with him and his mom for about twenty minutes before getting fed up. Since then, he's spent a certain amount of time on free dating websites, carrying on endless text conversations—conversations that are less conversation than clumsily phrased juvenile flirtation and premature disclosures of sexual preferences and deadly serious negotiations over what each person is looking for in a partner—over the course of which the relationships rise, peak, and crash, so that he already feels smothered or rejected or resentful before the women have even consented to meet him.

There's something defeated in Marissa's manner that he's never seen before, in her slump, even in the snarled knitting on her lap. Amadeo finds himself feeling generous, sorry that she didn't achieve the astonishing future he always imagined for her. He doesn't even feel compelled to make up a girlfriend.

"You look good."

"Thanks." Marissa regards him. "What happened to your hands?"

"Nail gun."

"Both of them? Shit."

Apparently Angel hasn't said a word to her mother about the procession. Amadeo is peeved for a moment, before he remembers he told her to keep it a secret, and then he is filled with admiration for his daughter.

Marissa pinches her hairline, then yanks a long strand out of her ponytail, inspects it. "So you're doing construction again?" Amadeo is surprised to see gray at her temples. She's only thirty-one.

Amadeo shrugs. "You're still working at State Farm?"

"Yeah. Same old. I'm office manager now, though." She jerks her thumb at the delivery room door. "I can't stand it in there. It's ten times worse watching than going through it yourself."

This is the same thing Amadeo's been thinking all afternoon, but hearing Marissa say it now rankles him. "Angel is terrified," he says, indignant. "Poor kid."

"Remember how little she was? God, she was cute."

"I always thought she looked like a naked mole rat. At first."

Marissa laughs. He wonders if they could ever end up together again and then wonders if the possibility has occurred to her, too. Amadeo imagines wrapping his arms around her, being naked with her, wonders if it would feel familiar. It would make a good story: Angel's parents brought together after sixteen years over the birth of their grandchild.

"Hey, has she ever said anything about the"—he lowers his voice—"the father?"

Marissa flattens her lips. "No. I don't get the sense that he counts for much." She clears her throat. "I'm not even sure she knows who it is."

"Not something a dad wants to hear."

Marissa laughs harshly. "Yeah."

"I guess it's better than some guy trying to control her." He thinks of a guy he knew in high school, a dealer who did well for himself, who was always demanding that his babies' mothers dress the kids better, criticizing their mothering, even as his own contributions to their upkeep were paltry and inconsistent.

"You don't think anyone"—he forces himself to say it—"hurt her?"

Marissa shakes her head, twisting the hair around her fingers. "She'd have told me."

She stretches the hair in and out, as though putting it through a stress test. "I just hope she's okay. I don't know what I'll do if something happens to her. Nothing will happen to her. Still. Things aren't great between us now. As I'm sure she's told you." Marissa slumps.

Amadeo nearly asks what happened—it's gratifying to know that someone else has screwed up with Angel—but he's afraid. "She'll be okay." He nudges Marissa's soft upper arm with his elbow. "She's in her best childbearing years, did you know that?"

Marissa looks at him quickly, alarmed. "Did you tell her that? Is that why she went and got herself pregnant?"

"You think *I* encouraged this?" No way is Amadeo going to be blamed. "Before she showed up I didn't see her for a year. There's no way this is my fault. You're her mother."

Marissa sighs. "Fuck. I know."

This baby is amazing. His tidy red ear, his miniature round nostrils, his funny flattened nose. The flimsy little nails. Those perfect Cupid's-bow lips. There's a kind of scrim on his face, like the white coating on a purple plum. Angel palms Connor's clean new skull, feels his pulse through his soft spot. *Fontanel*, it's called, and Angel loves this word, thinks it would make a beautiful name for a baby, if Connor were a girl. *Fontanel.*

They've both been cleaned up. Angel is wearing the most enormous maxi pad she's ever seen in her life, a pillow wedged in her crotch. A mattress. But even this is a kind of comfort, buoying her. She is floating, as though this bed were set adrift in a wide, warm ocean. The two of them, Angel and Connor, and for a moment it feels as if they are all either will ever need.

And her father is with them, asleep in a chair in the corner. His features are smushed comically where his cheek is propped on his hand.

Angel closes her own eyes.

"Sweetheart?" A nurse drums her nails on the doorframe and glides in. "Time to give this little one a test."

"What kind of test?" Angel asks, determined to advocate on behalf of her child, to be an informed consumer of health care.

"PKU."

Angel tries to remember which one this is. Brianna gave them a handout that enumerates the newborn screenings, but Angel doesn't have her binder with her, and she forgot to ask her dad to bring it. "PKU?"

"Phenylketonuria. If he's got it, it means there are certain foods he won't be able to process. Just getting the info we need."

There have been so many nurses and medical assistants. At first, bearing in mind something Brianna said about the importance of always trying to use people's names, Angel did her best to remember them, but every few hours a new batch descends, and she's so tired. This one is animated and wears scrubs printed with fruits and vegetables. She leans over and lifts Connor away from Angel, unwraps a minuscule purple foot from the flannel swaddling. "A li'l pinch," she says, and jabs him with a pin.

"Oh!" cries Angel. Connor's features freeze, as if he's surprised by the existence of pain. She is shocked by how deeply she feels his hurt.

And another shock: her dad leaps to his feet. "What the fuck are you doing?" Connor's face splits and pours forth red, bleating wails.

"It's fine," says the nurse soothingly, speaking at once to Amadeo and to Angel and to little outraged Connor. With one expert hand, she pinches Connor's heel and dabs the blood onto a strip of paper. "Just making sure he's doing okay!" And the nurse is already coming toward Angel, rewrapping the baby, smiling cheerily.

Angel reaches for Connor and pulls him close to her, patting and rocking and murmuring until his cries quiet.

"It's *bull*shit, stabbing a baby that little," Amadeo says after the nurse leaves. His eyes are bright with tears. Amadeo jingles the coins in his pockets, looks around, tense, as if searching for someone to punch.

"Definitely better to stab a bigger baby," Angel says, trying for levity, though she, too, is rattled. "It's okay. Look, he's calm again."

Amadeo gives his hands a shake, as if ridding himself of some uncomfortable thought, and then leans over Angel to peer into Connor's pinched face. The baby's color is subsiding and he blinks his nearly closed eyes.

If her father has surprised Angel with his immediate interest in the baby, her mother has been, on the other hand, a disappointment.

For weeks Angel was waiting for Connor's birth, not just because she was excited to meet him, and sick of being fat and gassy and sour with heartburn, but because she'd been certain he'd be the occasion for reconciliation with her mother. Even as she spent all those weeks in a silent rage, refusing to speak to her mother, all the while she believed this particular fight would end once the baby was born. She expected her mother to swoop in with apologies and love and firmness, to take charge and comfort her and fill her rightful role as joint caregiver of this creature.

Instead her mother chose to wait outside while Connor finally forced his way through those last inches of the birth canal. Her mother had, in fact, waited until Angel and baby were cleaned up before stopping in, and even *then*, she stood barely inside the door, shifting her weight from foot to foot, as if she were only an acquaintance, offering the most generic and self-evident observations a person could come up with. "God, he's little, isn't he?" and "I can't believe you have a baby, Angel."

When Angel asked if she wanted to hold Connor—she couldn't keep the chill from her voice—her mother smiled and looked so grateful and pathetic that Angel relented toward her. Angel's seen her mother with babies over the years, and she's never looked this uncomfortable: stiff, cautious, terrified. Her cradled arms were somehow too high and tense, and Marissa had looked down at him, rapt and unsmiling. Watching her mother with her son, Angel felt compassion that vexed her, because she doesn't owe her mother anything—compassion least of all. Is this what motherhood means? Being suddenly able to pity the adults in your life?

Shouldn't her mother have had something to say to Angel? Shouldn't she have offered her own story of childbirth and given advice? She should have filled her role as grandmother. Instead Marissa seemed almost deferential to Yolanda, who sat in the chair next to Angel and held the baby with ease and compared him knowledgeably to other babies she's cared for. "You had those same long legs, Angel."

Marissa leaned over Yolanda. "And Angel had a potbelly like that, too, didn't she?" she asked, as if she'd hardly been present for Angel's babyhood.

"Listen, Angel," says her dad now. "I had an idea. When you're feeling better, when you're up for it, would you want to be the Creative Windshield Solutions driver?"

Angel looks up at her father, at the sweet uncertainty in his face, and she can't help smiling. "Sure, okay, but you'll have to pay me."

"I know that," he says, and she laughs at his discomfort. "Of course I will."

"Me, Gramma: you're going to be cutting checks left and right."

———

Now EVERYONE IS gone and Connor has fallen asleep, his little pursed mouth sucking industriously at nothing.

She just changed his diaper for the first time, under the supervision of the nurse, gently swabbing with alcohol the swollen blue nub of umbilical cord. Her son's penis is a healthy little grub nestled between his red thighs.

He's wrapped snugly in flannel, all his skinny flailing parts contained and safe. Angel frees one arm from underneath Connor, and reaches warily for the oversized plastic sippy cup of ice water they left for her on the rolling tray. All the while she expects Connor to open his eyes, catch her out. But no! He sleeps on, as if he trusts she's actually doing the right thing.

Angel is so happy. She never knew she could be so happy. Lying here against these pillows, Connor bundled to her chest, the body heat passes between them, indistinguishable. The dim afternoon light slants through the thick pane of the window. They feel clean and warm—she is sure she is feeling for both of them—swaddled by this hospital, with the nurses just outside the door, ready to make sure they're okay. She could stay here forever, lying on these fresh sheets, looking out the window at the wide blue sky.

This person was in her, part of her, and now he's not. He was once hers alone, and now, for the rest of her life, she'll be sharing him with the world. It's amazing to her how the human body can stretch, and she thinks that if the heart can, too, maybe it can stretch big enough to fit them all.

t's late, long past when Amadeo should be asleep, but he's pacing the living room, the grin pulling at his face. When he and Yolanda left the hospital this evening, Angel had been dozing, the baby asleep beside her in the Plexiglas bassinette. His mother, who had been quiet all night, went to bed almost immediately, neither eating dinner nor preparing anything for Amadeo.

Amadeo posts online about the birth. Within an hour, two distant cousins and a friend from high school whom he hasn't spoken to in years like his post. He refreshes his social media pages again and again, but no new congratulations come in. He flips through channels, pages through *The Santa Fe New Mexican*. He needs fresh air, he needs to leap and run. He needs to drive fast down dark roads. He's a grandfather!

Amadeo lets himself out quietly, taking his truck keys from the hook by the door. His mother will kill him if she hears he was driving. If he gets caught, he could spend a year in jail and lose his license for three. But that old Amadeo already doesn't exist anymore. Out here, nearly two in the morning, there's no one to catch him, and the night is bright with stars, a fattening half-moon high and small in the sky. The cool air smells of juniper and seems saturated with possibility.

He starts his truck and, without headlights, reverses down the dirt drive. He turns onto the cracked paved road, and then he is on his way, heart full and airy.

When he's out of sight of his house, he flicks on his headlights, piercing the darkness. Not ten feet in front of him is a coyote, head canted over its pointed shoulder, red eyes. It's small, thin, its wiry fur too white. There is something malicious and hungry in its narrow face.

Amadeo slams on the brakes. The coyote stares through the blinding brightness of the headlights and right at him in the dark cab of the truck, though of course that isn't possible.

Amadeo taps the horn, once, twice, but the coyote doesn't flinch. "Scram," Amadeo says, his voice strange and quiet. He considers rolling down the window and yelling, but an irrational fear tightens like a cord around his chest. Amadeo can't explain the way he feels; he has the sense that an unseen hand took a scalpel and cut a hole into the fabric of the night, letting in something supernatural.

When the coyote still doesn't move, Amadeo eases off the brakes, and the truck advances slowly. He wants to scare the coyote off the road, tip this moment back into normalcy so that the night can resume. But instead of fleeing, the coyote takes a step toward the truck, eyes glowing.

With shaking hands, Amadeo flashes his brights, but the coyote doesn't flinch. He snaps his headlights on, off, on, off. The coyote remains there, motionless, until, in the space between light and dark, it vanishes.

———

AND THEN Angel and the baby are home. Angel lays Connor out on the couch and peels the diaper off him. Black tar-poop is smeared across the narrow red bottom.

"Come on, Angel. Do you have to do that here?"

Angel lifts her head from her scrubbing with the baby wipe to train a look of contempt on her father. "When you change his diaper, you can do it wherever you want."

Amadeo is disturbed by Connor's soft spot. The *fontanel*, Angel insists on calling it, pronouncing it with panache, like it's a French pastry. Amadeo watches it throb. It's sickening that a child should be born so delicate and precisely formed, bluish red with such long thin limbs, obscenely fragile fingers, the veins on his temples and across his skull netted and pulsing under the impossibly thin skin. Even wrapping him in a blanket could cause injury, let alone lifting him.

He's not a beautiful baby, despite what they all keep telling him and each other. Connor Justin Padilla has patchy long dark hair over a peeling, crusted yellow scalp ("crib crap," Angel pronounces with authority), cheeks so full they squish his lips, and an oddly dented skull that narrows at the top. His unnervingly large black eyes make him look like some nocturnal woodland creature, except that they're unfocused and slightly crossed. Two weeks old, and he already has a little mustache, heavy eyebrows, a furry forehead. His grandson is a manimal, thinks Amadeo.

And yet, Amadeo can't stop looking at him. The second the baby falls asleep at her breast and Angel deposits him in the crib, she collapses on the couch into the sleep of the dead, unwakeable by ringing phones or television commercials or conversation, until Connor's piteous little mewl breaks through.

As his grandson sleeps, Amadeo stands over the crib, watching: the little frowns and smiles that pass over his face like thoughts, the pursed, suckling lips. Once, as though he hasn't been asleep at all, the baby opens his eyes and Amadeo's breath stills. Before the baby can scream, Amadeo lifts him, holds him against his chest. The baby's eyes are murky brown, the edges of the irises touched with blue, like the eyes of a very old man. He frowns at Amadeo, head wobbling, his eyes crossed with the effort of pulling his grandfather's face into focus. All at once, those eyes roll in his head, and he is asleep again.

This baby: such a massive force with so little actual personality. Everyone is in a foul mood. Yolanda keeps giving Amadeo jobs to do while she's at work—laundry, dishes, trash duty—then getting mad if he forgets to do them. Angel, home for a month on "maternity leave," as she insists on calling it, has been storming around, snapping at Amadeo, the limp baby a permanent fixture in her arms.

She cries at minor frustrations—when the hot water in the shower runs out, when she can't find the ointment for Connor's scabby purple belly button—and instead of telling her to get a grip, his mother will pull her into long hugs, letting Angel soak the shoulder of her shirt with snot and spit and tears. Only when visitors stop by does Angel cheer up, long enough to accept their good wishes and gift cards and to snooker them into believing she's bright-eyed and balanced and worthy of their gifts.

The house has been transformed. A woven fabric basket slouches by the couch, filled with baby toys that his mother or visitors will shake in Connor's face until he blinks his cloudy eyes or yawns or registers some other minimal awareness of their presence. Irritating classical music plays on the radio constantly, the first time ever, to Amadeo's knowledge, that classical music has been played in the house. Connor's belongings are everywhere: seats and bouncers and changing pads and wadded spit-up rags patterned in goldfish and dinosaurs. Crowding every surface are canisters of butt wipes and lint-covered pacifiers and board books that Angel insists on reading to his unresponsive form, to, she says grandly, "promote early literacy." Then she follows up with viciousness: "Not that you cared about *my* early literacy."

Amadeo feels squeezed out and retreats to his bedroom. Usually when he's feeling like this, Yolanda notices. She'll sit on the edge of his bed, say, "Tell me what's wrong, hijito," or "You have to get up; look, I made you beans." And she'll talk to him and try to make him laugh, and when he snaps at her, she'll be hurt, and then he'll apologize, and sometimes he'll lay his head in her lap.

But none of that happens, not with the baby screaming and Angel sobbing and all of Yolanda's friends coming by with their beribboned gift bags to fight over who gets to hold him and to congratulate Angel and stroke the silken head. "Oh, he's such a little miracle," his mother's friends say again and again. Right. A miracle that a sixteen-year-old figured out how to fuck. The thought shames Amadeo. But still.

At least he has Creative Windshield Solutions. He's read and reread the booklet and committed the DVD to memory, but he's nervous about actually attempting a repair. Now, though, with everyone so grouchy, he's got to escape the house.

Fortunately he has two dings in the windshield of his truck. He gathers his kit and heads out into the bright day, leaves Angel with her bad temper and the sweet milky smell of spit-up. He'll start with the little one near the bottom right corner.

The procedure is simple enough. You're supposed to align the suction cup over the divot, inject the clear resin into it, then cover it with a sheet of film to preserve the surface. When the resin is dry, you peel off the film and then scrape away the dried excess with a razor blade.

The result isn't invisible to the naked eye, as in the video, but it's definitely better than it was, a shining uneven mound of clear resin that could almost be a floater in one's vision. He does better with the second, larger chip. When he's done, he sits in the driver's seat and watches the sunlight ripple through the gelatinous-looking patch. He'd like to show off his accomplishments, but Angel and his mother aren't a receptive audience right now.

———

EVER SINCE THE BIRTH, Marissa has been calling Angel on her cell, and then, when Angel disregards the calls, on the landline. Amadeo listens to Angel's monosyllabic responses to whatever her mother says. He wonders if Marissa ever asks after him, but Angel just hangs up and returns to her grumping. Since their pleasantly unconflicted interaction at the hospital, he's found himself thinking about Marissa; she's cropped up here and there in his idle sexual fantasies. He can only think that his newfound interest in her has something to do with his heightened role as Angel's preferred parent; they're equals now; Angel herself proved that he's no longer a deadbeat when she moved in with him.

One evening Marissa arrives unannounced, bringing a plastic bag filled with rattles and blocks and musical stuffed animals, toys that even Amadeo can tell are for a baby much older than Connor, a baby with some modicum of control over its own limbs. For Angel she brings fancy truffles in a golden box.

"Super," Angel says, not getting up. "I've been trying to get fatter." She flicks her eyes to her mother and then back to the TV.

Marissa's face falls. She sets the truffles on the coffee table.

"Hey now," Amadeo tells his daughter. "Your mom's just trying to be nice." He hopes Angel will open the chocolates now and offer him one.

"Which is more than I can say for you," Angel shoots back. "How old's he going to be before you change a diaper?"

Amadeo tries to meet Marissa's eye, ready to shrug. *What can you say, she's a teenager.* It could have been a nice moment, the two of them united by Angel's brattiness. But Marissa bites her bottom lip and frowns, deepening the two creases between her brows.

"I'll change him," she says. "Give him here."

"He doesn't *need* changing."

Marissa digs in the bag and holds up a painted wooden stacking tower, shakes it weakly. "You used to have a toy almost exactly like this. There was this one blue ring that you especially loved to chew. I was always afraid you were going to get splinters in your gums."

"Lucky Connor. Lead poisoning and gum infection. Thanks a lot, Granny."

"Can I hold him?" Marissa's voice is pathetic, supplicating. She gazes at Connor as though she might absorb him with her eyes.

"Whatever." Angel sets Connor on his back beside her on the couch and looks away. The baby kicks and flaps his arms as if trying to take flight.

Marissa approaches and gathers the baby to her chest. She's hunched so far over him Amadeo can't see her face.

The television keeps jabbering away relentlessly, spewing the screeching announcers' voices and frenetic jingles. "Wanna shut that thing off?" asks Amadeo. "So we can talk or something?"

"No," says Angel aggressively. "I don't *wanna*. Taking a cue from Aunt Val?"

Marissa kisses Connor once on the forehead, her lips lingering, eyes closed. There's an almost religious solemnity to her manner with the baby, which seems too weighty, too private for Amadeo to witness. In embarrassment he counts the small items scattered on the carpet: a plush Very Hungry Caterpillar, a bootie, a plastic ring of clacking keys, a used diaper wrapped tightly on itself that he wishes they'd thrown away before Marissa's arrival.

"Well," says Marissa, after many long minutes have passed without

Angel speaking. "I guess I better get back home." As if she'd just stopped by on her way. As if Las Penas was on the way to anywhere.

Angel doesn't shift her eyes from the TV as she accepts the baby from her mother. "Mike needs his dinner?" she asks bitterly.

"I made him move out." Marissa stands in front of Angel, awaiting her pardon or approval. She clasps and unclasps her hands, then crosses her arms as if shivering. "I wanted to tell you that."

Angel's eyes dart almost imperceptibly toward her mother's face, then back to the screen.

Marissa kisses Angel on the head, but Angel doesn't move. "I love you." Marissa pauses, and then, when she gets no reply, gives a strand of Angel's black hair a gentle tug and crosses the living room, her steps jerky and self-conscious. "Take care, Amadeo," she says from the door. "Say hi to your mom for me."

"What was *that* about?" asks Amadeo. "Why'd she make him move out?"

Angel's gaze is locked on the television. For a very long time she says nothing, cheeks flushed and eyes dry and bright, until Amadeo figures she's ignoring him. Then she says, "How should I know."

———

THREE WEEKS AFTER the baby's birth, Tío Tíve agrees to come for dinner. Amadeo's mother, has, of course, arranged it, with her usual optimism that *this* time everyone might get along. Angel's been stomping around in the same puke-covered cupcake-print pajamas, but today she showers, blow-dries her hair, puts on a strange shimmering mauve shirt with blousy sleeves and a bow at the neck and a line of unnecessary buttons up the back. "What?" she challenges Amadeo when she catches him looking at the bow. "Gramma loaned it to me. She says it draws the eyes up. Away from this." She thumps her soft middle with real hatred. Honestly, if Amadeo didn't know better, he'd think she was still pregnant.

In the kitchen, Yolanda is whipping potatoes with butter. Amadeo swipes his finger in the bowl. Uncharacteristically, his mother doesn't swat him away. Instead she waits for him to remove his hand a second time before grinding pepper. Without raising her head she says, "Your sister's coming to meet the bobby, so you need to be nice to her." She pauses. "The baby," she corrects slowly. "She's coming to meet the baby."

Amadeo snorts so vigorously that a droplet shoots from his nose to his shirt. "What happened to *Amadeo is a drunken psycho*? Jesus, Valerie can't stand to miss nothing." He yanks open the fridge and all the jars clank in the door. He searches the shelves. His mother's back is tense over the bowl. "You *hid* the fucking beer from me?"

"It's not there?" asks Yolanda in a voice so transparent he almost laughs again. "Well, a night without beer won't hurt any of us. And you're being sober now."

Maybe he wouldn't even drink it, but it's up to *him*. Hasn't he been sober since Easter? Hasn't he been doing fine on his own? He doesn't need her condescension, her punishments, as if she's withholding a treat from a bad dog. "One mistake and you think I'm a fucking alcoholic." He slams the refrigerator so hard the ceramic fruit and vegetable magnets drop and scatter.

"I told Valerie you weren't drinking, honey. She's proud of you. We're all very proud." He feels a pang when, with a sigh, she kneels to gather the magnets herself. He's relieved that the beer is gone, because it's out of his hands.

"And otherwise, what? She wouldn't come meet Connor? She'd punish a little baby to make a point?"

"Otherwise I'd have to ask you to leave for the evening. So be good." The firmness of her tone stuns him into silence.

When Valerie shows up, she takes one look at Amadeo, then grabs each daughter protectively by the hand. His nieces gaze up at him with clear, distant eyes. "Hello, Amadeo." She arches a skeptical eyebrow, then turns smoothly away. However, her stony face softens when she sees Connor lying in his little bouncy seat. "Oh, *look* at you." She drops her daughters' hands, leaving them to fend for themselves in the presence of their monstrous uncle, and advances on the baby.

Because Amadeo's plan for the evening is to prove to all of them what a good grandfather he is, he gets to Connor first. He lifts him by the butt and head, supporting the fragile little neck the way he's been instructed. Connor makes fists and squints crossly into the overhead light.

"Oh, let me *see* him," croons Valerie, arms extended, crowding Amadeo.

"I've got him." Amadeo swivels, blocking his sister with his back.

"Jesus, Dad," says Angel, pulling plates from the cupboard. "You can hold him whenever you want."

Connor gives a twitching half-smile. "See?" Amadeo says. "He wants to stay with me. He's smiling."

Angel glances. "Gas."

"Bullshit. No one smiles when they got gas."

"Seriously, Dad. Give him to Valerie."

Amadeo complies grudgingly. "You got to hold his head. He don't like to be held too loose."

"*Doesn't*," Valerie corrects automatically. "*Loosely.* I've held babies before, Amadeo." But her voice is sweet, because she's already nuzzling Connor.

Amadeo has a memory of Valerie hugging him tightly on the couch when they were kids. After their father died, they did this every day when they got home from first and sixth grade: had their snacks— ramen noodles or cheese melted on their grandmother's tortillas—and then just clutched each other as if their lives depended on it while they watched TV. They never, as far as Amadeo can remember, spoke about their long silent hugs. Amadeo remembers his arms reaching up and around his sister's neck, his own neck cricked, his hand turning numb from where it was caught between Valerie and the back of the couch, remembers not wanting to shift even a fraction for fear of reminding them both of the strangeness of what they were doing. Eventually they must have untangled themselves, because certainly they'd have parted by late evening when their mother got home from Santa Fe with cold caught in the seams of her coat, kissed them tiredly and started dinner. Amadeo wonders if Valerie remembers any of this—she must, she's vain about her ability to remember obscure moments from her childhood. He wonders if, as she's treating him like shit, she thinks of it.

He watches his sister cradle little Connor, her face bright with happiness, and misses her, misses himself as he once was. When he was in elementary school, he'd depended on his big sister; while his mother was at work, Valerie helped him get ready in the morning, assembled his lunches, after school she helped him with his fractions. Even when she bossed him, she'd been there for him, which is maybe why he resented her so much when, as a teenager, she became focused on her own life, on getting herself into college and away from Amadeo and his mother.

Tíve shows up late and grunts in reply to the women's enthusiastic greetings. Honey the dog pokes her long snout past the door, eager to join the party, but finds herself forced back by Angel, who briskly latches the screen.

"Hey, Uncle," Amadeo says, but Tíve just nods and allows Yolanda to kiss his cheek and take his jacket.

The food, as always, is perfect: the mashed potatoes, of course; also gloriously crunchy green beans and slivered almonds sautéed in butter; golden pork chops with a mustardy breadcrumb crust, edges caramelized; and, because it's Angel's favorite, a whole baking dish of red chile enchiladas, the heat of the chile tempered by the tang of the cheddar. Amadeo's mother has always been able to pull together varied and flavorful meals with barely any effort at all.

All through dinner, Amadeo feels an itchy unpleasant impatience as the voices swim around him: Angel's high, Yolanda's oddly muted and careful, Valerie's fake and patient. Periodically one of his nieces will pipe up with a precocious observation that will be met with enthusiasm only by their mother.

Lily holds her speared pork chop aloft, regarding it with skepticism, then drops it back on her plate. "Do you know pigs are smarter than dogs?"

"Smarter than most humans, probably," says Valerie. "So when are you going back to your program, Angel?"

"Our Open House is next Friday." Angel looks from her grandmother to her father. "You guys remember, right?"

Amadeo rolls his eyes. "Yes, Angel." The Smart Starts! Open House is a very important event, Angel has informed them. She's kept the flyer on the kitchen table and has read it aloud to Amadeo and Yolanda. *Come meet the Smart Starts! family! Get involved! See why EVERYTHING starts at Smart Starts!!*

"I was so worried I'd have to miss it due to labor, but we'll be there. And then I'll start up again on Monday." She ducks her chin to address Connor's head. "And so will *you*. You will start school, *too*." Angel turns to Lily. "Have you read anything good lately?"

Lily pushes her glasses up her red nose, as if trying to determine whether her cousin is making fun of her. Reassured, she tosses her thick hair. "Of course. There's this one book? Called *Into the Breach*? It's about a World War II girl who disguises herself as a soldier"—and for the next ten minutes she recounts the intricacies of the plot.

Amadeo sips his soda, sets it down. What's the point of being sober if no one notices?

Tíve has planted a hand on either side of his plate, and he scowls at his food. Since Easter, Amadeo can't stand to be around Tíve, who has been privy to Amadeo's most recent major failures. Over and over he is beset with shame flashbacks: his uncle standing in the bright glare of the police station, checkbook in hand; his uncle waiting in the truck to ferry Amadeo to one court-mandated appointment or another. Even more shameful is Amadeo's memory of his own earnest absorption in his role of Jesus, his immersion in—what? Hope? Prayer? No, Amadeo was immersed in something even more ludicrous than that: belief in himself, belief that he might actually succeed at something difficult and pure. Night after night in the cement quiet of the morada, Tíve witnessed Amadeo trying to lose himself, on his knees. Amadeo wouldn't be more humiliated if his uncle had caught him masturbating.

Tíve's hands are unsteady as he lifts his laden fork. His uncle's mouth waits, agape and straining, for the trembling mound of potatoes.

Panic swipes at Amadeo's heart. His uncle is aging. One day soon, he will die, when Amadeo has yet to earn his good opinion. As a kid, he had a fantasy that his great-uncle would one day treat him like his missing son, a fantasy encouraged by Yolanda, who is always putting Amadeo in Tíve's way like some kind of irresistible treat. An inheritance, it's true, was also part of his fantasy. But what Amadeo really wanted was a father figure. Isn't that how things should be? That the man who'd lost a son and the boy who'd lost a father should find each other? Now the thought occurs to him, as though it was original, that there *is* no way things should be, only the way things are, and the way things are is going to keep changing.

His expression must be bleak, because across the table his mother tips her head inquiringly, but Amadeo turns away.

After dinner, as they eat cake and coffee ice cream in the living room, Tío Tíve leans across the couch to peer into the baby's sleeping face. "He's a looker, ain't he?"

"Want to hold him?" Angel turns the sleeping Connor face-out, gripping him under the armpits so his onesie rides up and his limp, dimpled thighs dangle. His jowls droop over her fingers as if his entire musculoskeletal system were composed solely of dried beans. At his perfectly formed lips, a single bubble rises and pops.

"He don't want to go to no old man," Tío Tíve says, but he smiles, showing his teeth worn to brown nubs. The skin cinches around his eyes. He sets his untouched slice of cheesecake on the end table.

Angel lowers Connor into his arms. With a deep shuddering breath, the baby settles against the old man's skinny chest.

"You okay? I know he's heavy."

Tíve waves her away with his wrinkled chin. "He's just a little thing, ain't he?"

The room is silent as Tío Tíve regards the baby, bewitched. He holds the baby in a stiff high cradle and looks down at the creased little face, the swollen eyelids. "I haven't held a baby in a hunnerd years." His knees in their polyester pants are large and square. His shiny black socks have sagged, revealing thin, nearly hairless ankles.

When the old man looks up at Angel, it's with a kind of open amazement that strikes Amadeo as *sweet*. His sister also watches their great-uncle, as surprised as Amadeo by his interest in Angel and her kid.

"Tío," announces Valerie from her cross-legged posture on the floor. "Lily's doing a report on New Mexico statehood. I'm sure she'd love to include oral history from her great-great-uncle." Valerie always tries to make their uncle map the family's genealogy and asks earnest prying questions about life in the olden days. Her interest in the plumbing of his childhood is depthless. "What *were* those early years of statehood like?"

"He's not a hundred and thirty years old, Valerie. He wasn't keeping no journal of his thoughts in 1912."

Lily drags her eyes from the cooking show on the mute television. "It wasn't a report," she informs her mother. "It was a *work*sheet. Just some stupid random worksheet. It wasn't even for a unit."

Amadeo catches his uncle's eye, and is startled to see the hint of a smile tugging the old man's mouth.

Flustered, Valerie turns her attention to her younger daughter, who is going through the baby toys, methodically rattling, squeaking, and crinkling each one. "How're you doing, bean?" Sarah declines to answer her mother, allowing Amadeo the novel experience of feeling sorry for his sister.

"Oh my heck, I just realized—" Angel crows to the baby, "That's your great-great-*great*-uncle."

"Holy," says Tíve.

Valerie shakes her head. "That's crazy."

"Great-great-great-great-great-great-great," chants Sarah. She gives a plastic rattle a celebratory fling into the air. It hits the ceiling with a crack, drops to the carpet.

"Quit it," says Lily. "Mom, tell her."

Yolanda has finished the dishes and joins them now. She lowers herself onto the couch beside her uncle and the baby. "Whew."

Since when did his mother start moving like an old person? Amadeo scans them all with alarm: his suddenly frail mother, her hair full-gray at the roots; his daughter, whose bright features have become puffy and pale; his rickety uncle; his sister slumped on the floor, her ridiculous woven scarf hanging from her stooped shoulders. Even his nieces, homely and intelligent and socially deficient enough to eventually find success in tech or academia, seem doomed. Connor, the newest and theoretically least doomed among them, can't even hold his own head up. Since when did everyone around him become so *fragile*?

Yolanda waggles one of Connor's fat feet, and his red-blotched arms and legs recoil briefly before relaxing again. "Does he remind you of Elwin?" she asks her uncle with tenderness.

Tíve looks up sharply. "No."

"What about me?" asks Amadeo, aware that he sounds desperate. "Does he look like me when I was a baby?"

Tío Tíve frowns as if Amadeo's question is an insect buzzing around his head. "I can't remember that long ago."

Amadeo is jealous of a baby. The humiliating realization zings through him. He has the sense of being the least necessary person in the room, the person they'd all be justified in cannibalizing in the event of a nuclear apocalypse.

Amadeo would not have noticed anything at all amiss about his uncle if Angel didn't exclaim, "Wait, are you *crying*?"

"Nah," says Tíve, eyes swimmy.

"What's wrong, Tío?" Yolanda touches his arm.

"He's just a real cute little guy," Tíve says, dipping his head.

Everyone lowers their eyes to the baby. Tíve's arms tremble. Connor starts fussing noiselessly, grimacing in his sleep. Tíve jiggles him. Connor struggles to pry his eyes open, and when he does, he squints up at the light fixture and, to everyone's relief, lets out a howl.

Angel reclaims the baby and kisses the old man's cheek, which hangs brown and loose and clean-shaven. Amadeo imagines that it would be cool against her lips.

Back in her seat, she pulls up her satin shirt and unhooks her nursing bra. Only a few days in, Angel is no longer self-conscious about baring her breasts. She just pops one out, blue-veined and swollen, brown nipple jutting, and draws the baby toward her. Connor shakes his head furiously, trying with his open mouth to get at the nipple, milking her flesh with a tiny red hand as wrinkled and dexterous as a monkey's.

The routine is impossible not to watch, and it's embarrassing to be caught watching, but they'd all rather focus on the baby than on whatever sour vulnerability has blown into the room.

"I'm *so* glad you're breast-feeding," Valerie says.

"I already know about the research, Aunt Val," Angel says testily.

Amadeo marks another point in his column, but derives no pleasure from it.

Connor snuffles away, kicking like a drowning victim.

"Welp," says Yolanda into the silence. The cheer in her voice is at odds with her grim expression. She stands. "There's more cake."

Without any provocation, she seems to lose her balance, sways first one way and then another, as if playing a drunk in a comedy act. Her eyes and mouth open in terror so pure and magnified that it can't be real. And then, as if the ground has summoned her, she tips forward onto her face.

"I'm okay," she cries. And then she's laughing, tears running down her cheeks, as her nose begins to trickle blood. "I'm okay!"

Yolanda doesn't forget about her brain tumor—she couldn't—but somehow she allows herself to slip back into her life. She goes to work as she always has, makes dinner. All the while, she is waiting for someone to notice that she's dying. It seems ludicrous to Yolanda that no one checks on her to make sure she follows up on Dr. Mitchell's diagnosis. Did she expect official calls? A summons to the hospital as if to the principal's office? Yes, actually.

Even Cal, attentive Cal, hasn't called. In their one conversation after her return, she told him in the vaguest, most clichéd terms, "I need time. To figure out what I want." After a pause, during which she could hear the long inhalation whistling in his nostril, and then the long, resigned exhalation, Cal said, "Take your time. I love you, but I'll give you time." And true to his word, he hadn't tried to contact her since.

She should get her affairs in order, but the practicalities of her own funeral arrangements and finances are boring and unreal.

Yolanda watches herself for worsening symptoms, and indeed they come. Words—nouns especially—become maddeningly elusive, ducking away as she reaches for them, leaving her with other, unsuitable nouns to slot into their places. Periodically the world swirls, as if God has decided to give it a stir around her. She drops things. Multiple times throughout the day, fatigue crashes into her, and she rests her head on her desk, flickering out of awareness. Soon, she'll fall again. Soon, she will no longer be able to work, will no longer be able to leave the house alone, and the prospect of this new, diminished existence terrifies her. She especially worries about letting down Monica. It's fortunate that the chief clerk's schedule is so packed, because somehow, miraculously, Yolanda doesn't get caught.

So she continues to work, simple tasks looming large. She needs to reorder letterhead for three legislators, and then she's supposed to put in a request to Building Services to have a flag flown over the Capitol, which will then be sent to a new senior center in Alamogordo. She needs to prepare a certificate and letter of authenticity for that flag. It's not complicated work—just a matter of filling in dates and names and affixing seals—but it's overwhelming. Also, what's the point? Who cares if a flag has been flown over the Capitol? Do any of the little old people who gather for their mediocre two-dollar lunches of posole and green Jell-O even notice the flag?

She thought, during her long, juddering drive back from Las Vegas, that she might refuse treatment, pretend nothing is wrong until the day she is struck dead. But though her mother had a friend who approached cancer like that, to save her family the pain, and though this seems both admirable and courageous, and smacks appealingly of martyrdom, Yolanda understands that she is afraid and she will get professional support, because her need to talk to someone about what is happening to her is stronger than her need to avoid it. Still, somehow, she finds it impossible to pick up the phone.

On her way back from the bathroom, one afternoon in June, Yolanda discovers that she doesn't know where her office is. The Capitol is a perfect circle, and the hallways go all the way around, punctuated by offices and occasional corridors to the chambers. The curved walls are endlessly beige; above, the fluorescent lights hum. Over thirty years she's worked in this building, and now it's like the stage of a nightmare. Be calm, she tells herself. If you can make your way back to the bathroom, then you can make your way. But the bathroom doesn't reveal itself, either. Doors, doors, on either side of her, but none opens onto that short hallway and her own snug, familiar office.

During the legislative session, these offices are all open, bustling, people rushing briskly by with folders tucked under their arms. The House chambers are cheerful, the curved benches decorated with fresh flowers and little flags and jars of candy. Now, though, the place is deserted, the offices dark through the panes in the doors.

Panic starts beating its wings in her chest. Finally she stumbles upon an elevator. Above the panel of buttons is a map showing fire exits and egresses, and she peers at it, hoping it will illuminate her current position, but the map is confusing and unlabeled and she can't make the green arrow line up with anything she sees around her.

"Making sure our emergency exits are in order, Yo? Or you just lost?" asks Sylvie Archuleta. She presses the elevator button, then bends to pull her hose up her leg.

Sylvie Archuleta is an old friend, another of the year-round employees. She's older than Yolanda, thrice married and flamboyant, and her politics change with each new husband. She works in the House Speaker's office, despite the fact that she's currently a Republican. She still has her West Texas drawl, though her family moved to Roswell when she was a teenager. She's Anglo with big blond hair; her second husband, the one who died on her, was the Archuleta. "He was my favorite," she says. "The love of my life. I like him even better than Willy." Willy Greene is her current boyfriend, who also works in the legislature, though just during the session.

For a moment Yolanda considers confiding in her. Yes, I am lost, she'd say. I don't know how to handle this.

"Just taking a breather." Yolanda laughs, and the sound is false in her ears. This is it, she thinks. Game over.

But Sylvie Archuleta does not appear to notice that Yolanda is adrift. She fluffs the back of her hair and with her chin gestures down the hallway on the left. "I just saw Jim Gordon lingering around your office. He wants to ask you about Monica's schedule next week."

"I'll try to catch him." Yolanda sets off down the hall. A few seconds of disorientation, and then, as if someone rotated the focus on a camera, everything is clear. She pushes through the door to the suite of offices.

She sinks into her desk chair, gripping the armrest, filled with an overwhelming urge to sob. That afternoon she calls the first number on Dr. Mitchell's list of resources.

———

MORE TESTS ARE ORDERED, and Yolanda is required to fast for ten hours. They call the night before to remind her. Maybe it only takes a bite of oatmeal or a piece of toast or a single grape to throw the test results, to cheat fate and orchestrate another diagnosis for herself. Maybe, with the right breakfast, she could walk out of here with a normal life expectancy. But with her luck, she'd probably only further diminish her paltry allowance of days, so she fasts as instructed.

She spends a lot of time in various waiting rooms at the Cancer Center, which is not, as Yolanda expected, part of the St. Vincent's campus, but rather in a separate location behind the Albertsons. She avoids eye contact with the other pallid patients who are squandering their last precious hours in this sucking, air-conditioned sterility. They are bundled in sweaters and scarves, and it's only when she makes this observation that Yolanda realizes that she, too, is wearing winter layers, that she, too, has been feeling an insidious chill along her spine. Some of the other patients wear knit caps on their heads, some pull oxygen tanks, some vomit weakly into pink kidney-shaped tubs. Everyone but Yolanda is accompanied by frightened spouses or heavily accented caregivers or adult children with set jaws, determined to advocate. A gray-haired Native American woman with a windbreaker spread over her lap smiles at Yolanda, and Yolanda looks away.

Near the reception is a table spread with hats. A framed placard announces that every patient is entitled to a free hat, handmade by volunteers and available in two equally ugly styles: stocking caps knit in rainbow variegated acrylic, or the cotton calico (cats and florals and Lobos are popular prints), reminiscent of the floppy bonnets Yolanda's grandmothers and great-grandmothers used to wear when working in the gardens so that their skin wouldn't darken. It seems that dying people are expected to relinquish any sense of style along with their plans for the future.

Yolanda's new oncologist is Dr. Konecky, a tall woman in her thirties with very fine hair held back with a too-large purple velvet scrunchie, a girlish, outmoded choice of accessory that irritates Yolanda. Dr. Konecky confirms the diagnosis of the shellacked Dr. Mitchell.

Many of the neurological tests are the same that Amadeo endured in the drunk tank and later railed against: walking a line, touching finger to nose. "They think I'm a fucking idiot?" he demanded.

"How many fingers am I holding up?" Dr. Konecky asks, and Yolanda says with relief, "Four."

"Good," says Dr. Konecky.

As a rule, tall people make Yolanda nervous, looming above her, but it isn't just the lanky, stooped height or the scrunchie that seems off about this oncologist. After she takes her seat behind the desk, Dr. Konecky gazes at Yolanda with pale lashless eyes. Yolanda keeps looking at those eyes and then having to look away as Dr. Konecky reviews with her the results of the scans and the blood tests. That blue—clear and nearly dead. Yolanda's own eyes water, and she grips the strap of her purse.

This new MRI—performed a mere seven weeks after her first—shows not one but two tumors. The almond, now a Brazil nut, has been joined by a marble. The marble presses on the occipital lobe, which explains the results of the vision exam, results that Yolanda, strangely, hasn't noticed: the entire right field of her vision has vanished. This may be playing a role in her loss of coordination. She has begun to list, and she steps heavily with her right foot, like a green sailor on a rough sea.

"As you can see," Dr. Konecky says, sliding over both the new image and the Las Vegas image, which Dr. Mitchell had sent, "the first mass has grown significantly, and another has established itself. I wish you'd come right in. We need to get you started on radiation to try to arrest the growth." *Arrest*: Yolanda pictures the biggest tumor being hand-cuffed and read its Miranda rights. The lump takes on the image of her son. "Radiation won't eradicate the tumors, but if we're lucky it will slow the growth. Surgery is the best option. Either way, we're looking at a matter of months, not years." The doctor clears her throat and seems to labor to make her voice soothing. "I'm so sorry."

"It's okay," says Yolanda, then wonders where this sangfroid came from. "It's what I expected. I mean, it's what I knew." She realizes that she was hoping for a do-over, that maybe this second death sentence would be accompanied by plaintive strains of music that could, if not make the situation okay, at least make it lovely.

Dr. Konecky looks relieved: evidently not everyone takes the news so well. She puts her fist to her mouth and burps quietly into it. "Excuse me." She taps her narrow breastbone, and Yolanda imagines her eating her lunch at this desk an hour ago—something vegetarian, surely—flipping through Yolanda's file, thinking what a drag it is that once again she'll have to spend her Friday afternoon in the role of the Grim Reaper.

"I don't want surgery. Not if there's no chance. Not if I'm going to die anyway."

Dr. Konecky shakes her head, back and forth, back and forth, and keeps shaking as she speaks. "I do not recommend forgoing surgery. It will buy you time."

"No," says Yolanda with a certainty she didn't know she felt. Surgery would mean telling her family, would mean the whole business of dying had begun.

Dr. Konecky asks if she'd like to speak with a counselor. "Some people find it useful to process the information with someone trained in these things. I'll page someone."

"No," Yolanda says, straightening her purse on her lap, drawing herself together in preparation for leaving. "I don't need a counselor."

"I think it's best." Dr. Konecky picks up the phone and calls for a floater. To Yolanda, she says, "Someone will meet you in 209, just down the hall. And it goes without saying, I hope, that driving is out. With the loss of vision and coordination—"

"Right."

On her way to reception, Yolanda passes Room 209, head down, expecting to be caught, but she escapes without a hitch. As her copay is being processed, Yolanda gestures vaguely at the line of photos on the wall above reception. Dr. Konecky is frozen in a wan, stretched smile. "That Dr. Konecky doesn't look so healthy herself."

The receptionist laughs, then composes himself. "You be safe out there," he says, handing her the receipt.

Friday afternoon, and Angel is curling her hair in preparation for the Smart Starts! Open House. Connor fusses on a receiving blanket on her bedroom floor. She thinks of it as her bedroom—hers and Connor's—despite the fact that the bookshelf holds an array of Valerie's yearbooks and plastic Garfield figurines, about thirty years of Yolanda's *Cooking Light* magazines, and a couple of indeterminate glazed clay mounds made by Angel herself, if the initials gouged into the base are to be believed. Angel loves this room more than she ever loved her bedroom at home, perhaps because she hasn't ruined it with her personality. She especially loves the mirrored bureau and matching nightstand, cream with gold accents and curved legs, which Valerie declared she'd always hated. The sixties-tackiness makes her feel bohemian. She likes to imagine them in the brick loft space of her future, which will be spare and tasteful with maybe a single bright silk scarf dropped lazily on the gleaming wood floor.

Even in these long, exhausting days, when she's constantly yanked by the needs of the baby's body and her own, Angel keeps the duvet smooth, her lotions and baby toiletries lined up on the bureau, label out, as if they are still on display in the store. In this tiny enclosed piece of the planet, she is in control of her life.

Connor squawks from the floor, first experimentally, then warms to a sustained wail.

"Simmer down, hijito." She subjects a piece of hair to a mist of hairspray and then coils it around the hot iron until the scorching chemical whiff reaches her nose.

She's nervous, because it'll be her first day back at school in a month, and because tonight's the night she's going to ask Brianna to be Connor's godmother. Brianna likes her. Brianna at least likes her more than she likes rebellious Lizette, or sanctimonious Jen. She's made Connor as cute as possible for the occasion. He's wearing a mite-sized turquoise polo and tiny plaid golf pants with a little fabric belt, and socks that actually match for once in his life. Earlier, she sprayed his whole head with water, which made him flinch and sneeze, then combed his hair so the long strands at the front cover the bald spot at the back. "Zero years old, and you've already got a comb-over. Not good, baby." His eyes are slits, as if he's considering sleep but is still interested in the world's goings-on. He is irresistible. Brianna won't be able to stand it.

The other part that makes her nervous is that she's going to be driving the whole way. It will be the longest drive she's made, and she can do it, of course she can do it. Angel is pretty sure that driving with her father is not technically legal, since her father isn't technically a licensed driver, at least not until November, but her grandmother is coming straight from work. Her father argued that in a larger sense he *is* licensed, that his license is merely suspended, not revoked or canceled. Her father *knows* how to drive. And he's been sober since Easter—two months—her grandmother and dad have both been making a big deal about it—so that's a comfort. Anyway, all Angel needs from him is another set of eyes and maybe a pointer here and there. Angel gets quite a bit of pleasure out of driving her father's truck, because he's always been so vain about it. She knows it bugs him, riding impotent in the passenger seat as she presses inexpertly on the gas and they lurch forward.

Angel peers at her face in the dresser mirror. She got all-new makeup for tonight: foundation, lipstick, eyeliner. The purchases are technically Wants-Not-Needs, a designation Brianna kept harping on during their budgeting unit, but, looked at in another light, they *are* needs. Angel *needs* to feel put together. Angel *needs* to look and feel like an adult. Angel rubs the foundation along her jawline and down her throat, trying to blend it, which is a technique she read about in *Seventeen* when she was in middle school. It's a little dark. And she's still fat, obviously. But she's pretty! She's okay-pretty, anyway.

Angel is generally not impressed with good looks; god knows good looks haven't gotten her mother anywhere, though Marissa still seems to think her beauty should qualify her for something the world is withholding. When they watch TV, Marissa can't even enjoy the storylines, she's so busy evaluating the faces. "I'm prettier than her," she'll say with dissatisfaction. Her mother should know that she's old now, thirty-one, and it's pathetic to still be waiting around to be plucked up into some romantic story.

She's going to see her mother tonight, unless Marissa blows it off, and the thought makes Angel so anxious her stomach flops. She thinks of Mike, his hands on her throat. Her mother asked Mike to move out, which is exactly what Angel wanted, yet Angel is still angry with her, and she isn't entirely sure why.

We are fam-i-ly! asserts her cell phone. Connor stops screeching and listens, frowning at the ceiling, so she lets the phone go for a second longer. The Sister Sledge ringtone is the only ringtone she ever hears nowadays. Her father. A flare of exasperation bursts behind her sternum, because they are due to leave for Española in five minutes.

"Where are you, Dad? We got to be going."

"Chillax," he says, to drive her nuts. "I'm outside. I got something to show you in the truck." Sound of tapping at her window, and there is her father, waving like a goof.

"We don't have time," Angel says into the phone, eyes on him. "I can't be late for this."

"Just come outside."

"Fine." Angel drops her phone into her purse and hooks it and the diaper bag over a shoulder. There's already a rut pressed into the muscle there that Angel fears might be permanent. She straightens and gives the mirror one more determined grin. "Let's go, baby." When she swings Connor up, he lets out a delighted cackle that makes Angel laugh, too.

Her father looks surprisingly nice, standing beside the truck he is no longer allowed drive. He's got on a striped polo and khakis and his good work boots. And cologne, Angel discovers as she approaches. She feels a pang of remorse for snapping at him. And then she has the thought that slithers through her awareness whenever they're alone now, that if her father wanted to, he could strangle her. The thought leaves her feeling disgusting and guilty.

"What's up?" She jostles Connor. "You two are dressed the same. Ready for a day on the links."

Her father glances into the truck, then steps aside, rubbing his hands nervously. There, hogging most of the narrow back bench seat and sporting a confusing network of straps and buckles and clasps, is a brand-new infant safety seat. It's as opulent as a throne, all molded plastic and velvety plush cushions, and it is exactly what Angel wanted.

She feels her blood thicken with the sweetness of the gesture. "What'd you do with Valerie's?" she asks dumbly.

Amadeo jerks his thumb at the road, where the nasty old car seat sits forlorn beside the green plastic garbage bin.

"It's a Graco. One of the best rated. Not *the* best rated, 'cause that one was like five hundred dollars, but it was in the top three." He scuffs the gravel. "I put it in backwards; did you know you're supposed to put them in backwards when they're little? The lady told me."

Angel nods. The old one was also backward, she nearly says, which he'd know if he'd ever buckled Connor into the car. Or even bothered to look in the backseat. She shifts Connor to her other hip and places her palm against the velour where he will go. The seat is upholstered in sophisticated gray, as though designed for a business-class traveler. There's even a matching curved neck pillow to nestle around his floppy head.

"We should probably keep the old one. For Gramma's car."

"Oh, yeah. And I got you this, too." He doesn't meet her eye as he hands her a wrapped box. He takes the baby and busies himself with mussing his hair.

Inside is a pair of tiny black basketball shoes. Soft leather booties with little laces, and there, on the side, is the leaping silhouette of Michael Jordan.

Angel takes them from the plastic box, pushes a finger into each one. She walks them up her arm, jumps them into a layup.

"They're old school. They cost fifty dollars." He shrugs, puts his free hand in his pocket, then removes it again. "I was like sixteen when I got my first pair. I don't want my grandkid going through that kind of deprivation."

Angel stands there, smiling stupidly. She can't look at her father, so she focuses instead on the black fuzz at the back of Connor's head, which looks moth-eaten. "He can't play basketball. You know he just lays there, right?"

Why does she do this? Rankle against her father, resent him for not caring, for never being who she wants him to be—and then when he *does* do something kind and fatherly, something that another, better father would do for another, better daughter, her happiness is too bountiful to bear, the pleasure intolerable. She must thrust it away from herself, must rush through the moment.

"Tíve drove me out to the mall in Santa Fe," says her father. "He complained, but when I said it was for you, he agreed. Don't know what you did to that guy."

She runs a finger along the stitching of the bootie. Her father is looking at her too closely, and she sees herself: errant and undeserving. "Thanks," she says, her voice stiff, even though she *is* grateful, *is* pleased, even though that car seat is exactly what she wanted and the miniature basketball shoes are the most perfect things she can imagine.

"I just thought he could use some new stuff." He shrugs, embarrassed. "Ready to go?" Her dad puts Connor into the seat and starts fiddling with the clasps. Then he backs away and dusts off his hands. "You're going to have to tie him up in there. It's too much for me."

Angel leans over Connor, pulls his limp little arms through the harness, fastens one clasp after another. He smacks his perfect drooly lips, but submits to the manhandling. When he's been thoroughly trussed, Angel and Amadeo stand side by side, regarding him. He's dwarfed by the cushions.

"He could go to space and he'd be safe," says her father. "Anyway, it's the least I can do, with you being the official Creative Windshield Solutions driver."

Amadeo and Angel don't talk on the way to Family Foundations, which is just as well, because Angel needs to concentrate. The low sun is heavy on the alfalfa fields and on the apple and apricot orchards, leaves and trunks glowing reddish gold. In a corral, two skinny horses tear listlessly at grass, and their dusty coats shimmer like velvet. During a straight section of road, Angel cranes to see Connor, who has fallen asleep. His mouth is tethered to the clean upholstery by a cord of drool. She can't help but smile.

The traffic is light in Española, and she navigates her way easily to the shopping center where Family Foundations is located.

In the parking lot, Angel gets out stiffly and unhooks the baby carrier from the base. Connor shifts and grunts in his sleep. "Dad, wait," she calls after her father as he strides toward the door. He turns. "Thanks." She hugs him, and when she pulls back, she's surprised when he holds on tight.

Here they are, crowded with the other families into the Smart Starts! classroom, drinking neon institutional lemonade from waxed paper cups. With the cheerful bulletin boards, it resembles an elementary school classroom more than any of the bare utilitarian classrooms Amadeo remembers from high school. There's even a reading nook with beanbags, where, presumably, the girls can go beach themselves with a magazine while they nurse. Across the whiteboard is written *Welcome, Families!* and, in every color marker, the signatures of the girls: *Ysenia, Corinna, Jen, Lizette, Christy, Tabitha, Trinity.* The signatures all look bubbly and optimistic, and while no one has dotted their *i*'s with hearts or stars, hearts and stars wouldn't look out of place. Someone has also drawn an unsettlingly sexy-looking baby with anime glints in its giant eyes and a single long ringlet sprouting out from the top of its head.

"This is all beautiful," Yolanda tells Angel. She gestures vaguely around the room, holding her head very still. When she turns, her upper torso moves first right, then left with a slight robotic jerk. Amadeo wonders if his mother has a crick in her neck. Certainly she looks tired, the skin under her eyes bunched and fragile. Her nose is still bruised, as though from a punch. She's tried to cover it, but the makeup has flaked off.

Angel beams shyly. She seems not to know what to do with her hands, keeps resting them on her hips and then letting them circle around her back. She gives one a good shake, in a gesture of excitement Amadeo recognizes from her early childhood.

"Angel!" cries one of the girls, advancing on them with a dry-erase marker. "You're here! You gotta sign your name!"

Yolanda removes a stockinged foot from her shoe and rolls the ankle. When she teeters, she grabs Amadeo's arm.

"Watch yourself, woman! You gotta stay on your feet." He circles his arm around his mother, and she leans her whole weight against him, laughing quietly.

There are only a few other men. A teenage boy in jeans and flip-flops carries a baby one-handed, with an ease that amazes Amadeo. An older man with a big belly and skinny hips stands near the door, holding up his pants. He peers into the hallway, as if looking for his chance to flee.

It's obvious who's a Smart Starts! student: girls swollen in pregnancy or with babes in arms. One girl is both, her round body canted under the weight of an overgrown, tangle-haired toddler who keeps arching his back and squealing irritably. They're all made-up, several of them in short stretchy black dresses that would be better suited for a nightclub. A few grade school kids run around, brandishing markers, spinning the globe, flinging themselves onto beanbags. These must be the little brothers and sisters of the students. The adults themselves— mothers, mostly—hold back, gripping their paper cups, either admonishing the little kids or smiling determinedly at them, avoiding eye contact with the other adults. They're made-up, too, many in similarly tight dresses, and they have a heavy aura of resignation about them, as though they're waiting to be reprimanded.

Angel, however, is in her element, hugging her friends, showing off Connor. The second she walked in, she made a beeline for the young woman who could only have been Brianna, and presented her with the baby carrier as if it were a gift basket. The teacher of Angel's parenting class is not, as Amadeo expected, a starchy gorgon in a pantsuit. She's young and earnest in floral rayon, and, Amadeo knows from Angel, childless. Angel stood there, flushed, as the teacher hugged her and admired the baby.

Now the girls cluster around his daughter, oohing and ahhing over Connor, and Amadeo can't help but feel proud, because, despite the baby acne and patchy hair and plentiful eyebrows, Connor is the cutest one here. Those wide, clear, nearly black eyes, his steady, knowing wisdom: none of these other babies even come close. Amadeo has the urge to move into the festive knot of students, pick up his grandson, kiss and bounce him. He'd turn the baby face-out and make him wave at each of the girls with his little wrinkled hand. Maybe he'd even do funny voices. But Amadeo doesn't, from shyness, maybe, or from some adult awareness that this isn't his show.

As if she's read his mind, Angel waves him over. "I want to introduce you guys. Ysenia, Christy, Trinity, Corinna, Tabitha." Tabitha is the especially fertile one. Her toddler is asleep now, straddling his mother's pregnant stomach, splayed-armed across her breasts.

Angel touches the arm of a heavyset girl holding a baby, then cups the baby's head with a hand. "This is Lizette. And this little cutie is Mercedes." Ah, Lizette. Mercedes, then, must be the baby she crapped out.

Lizette turns lazy green eyes on Amadeo and smiles. The lashes are thick and dark. The baby has the same eyes—enormous on her—and also a frilly headband strapped to her bald head. "Nice to meet you, Mr. Padilla." Lizette's voice is slow, taunting, disturbing. She blinks.

Angel laughs. "Mr. Padilla!" She's so innocent, so oblivious to the look Lizette is giving him. Amadeo wonders if his daughter could be putting it on, that guilelessness, but no, the laughter is burbling up, genuine. "No one calls him that. Have you ever been called *mister* in your life, Dad?"

Not by anyone who isn't a telemarketer, but Amadeo still bristles. After all, he is an adult, a father and a grandfather. Why shouldn't a teenage delinquent show him respect? Except that he knows it isn't respect Lizette is showing. "Nice to meet you girls," he says, coming at each of them with a firm handshake.

"Connor looks like you," Lizette says. "Same head shape."

"Well," Amadeo says, with a jocular nod, "we are related."

The little girl gabbles and grabs at Lizette's hair. Lizette turns an annoyed grimace on the kid and unhooks the sticky-looking fist.

Amadeo backs away and joins his mother, who is inspecting a poster of the periodic table. He's aware that he's disappointing Lizette, that she'd like to keep up the limp repartee. He feels sorry for her, poor sad kid, spending her days in a girls' school, saddled with a baby. Of course she wants to flirt with one of the few men she runs into, even if he is completely unsuitable. Her attention is gratifying, he won't deny that.

When he looks up, Marissa is hovering at the classroom door, tugging at her wrap dress, almost an hour late.

He wasn't sure if Angel even invited her mother tonight, but didn't want to ask. Whatever's going on between Angel and Marissa, it doesn't make sense, because Angel has always been so forgiving and eager to please.

"Marissa's here." Amadeo nudges his mother and she looks at him blankly, then waves. Marissa's shoulders drop in relief and she makes her way over to them.

"Hey." Marissa watches Angel, who is swinging Connor gently in the carrier and laughing with the other girls. His daughter looks so at ease, so in control, that Amadeo marvels that he and Marissa managed to create her.

Amadeo's aware of a contest between him and Marissa, possibly one-sided, to be the lesser fuckup. For years Marissa was ahead. Amadeo understands that his successes are somehow worth more points than hers—that his recent minor achievements (the little sneakers, his punctuality this evening, Angel's decision to move in with him in the first place) are, at this late date, rivaling Marissa's sixteen thankless years of basically competent single-parenting.

"I got Angel a new car seat," he says, gesturing to the carrier in Angel's hands. "It's a two-in-one." He almost says that he didn't even ask his mom for the money, either, but actually sacrificed, sold his electric guitar on Craigslist to pay for it, but is aware of how lame that would sound.

Marissa nods. There's an apologetic, furtive slump to her shoulders. Nonetheless, she looks great—hair up in a complicated-looking twist, her color high, and that dress, which is snug in the right places. He wonders, with a proprietary twinge, if she has a date after this.

"I'm also starting up a business. To support them more."

"Oh," says Marissa.

He looks to his mother for backup, but Yolanda is failing to take charge. Lips parted, she stares into space. It's not possible, is it, that Amadeo is the most socially adjusted adult representative of the family?

Just as Amadeo is getting restless, a man rises and clears his throat. He introduces himself as Eric Maxwell, the Family Foundations president. He's short and exceedingly handsome. His athletic build is tucked neatly into his khakis. He's left his mandarin collar unbuttoned. "On the first anniversary of our beautiful new building, I'd like to thank everyone who has made this possible, including the Gerald Family Foundation and United Way." He turns to the teacher. "And mostly, *mostly*, I'd like to thank Brianna Gruver, who has brought her considerable knowledge and talent to the Smart Starts! program."

Brianna Gruver stands before a bookshelf in her loose dress, blushing and waving away the attention. Brianna's only authority with these girls must come from the fact that they are so young that *any* adult seems old. Also, judging from the ages of the adult women standing around, many of the students' own mothers had them when they were teenagers, so these girls' perceptions of age have naturally undergone a kind of inflation.

"Brianna has done great things with our unfortunately limited funding. We are lucky to have her." Amadeo wonders idly if they are sleeping together. This is an interesting thought, and he looks at her more closely. There is something appealing about her, something wholesome and kind. Her hair is cut in a pallid little bob, her forehead high and square and shiny. His daughter beams at her teacher, and in the light of Angel's admiration, Brianna is almost pretty.

"*Mostly*"—here Eric Maxwell sweeps his hand across the gathered girls, in their short dresses and shiny black slacks, their makeup, all of them trying to look professional, but succeeding only in looking a little slutty—"I'd like to thank these industrious ladies, who have worked hard on their presentations. And now, I turn the stage over to them."

"Wait, what?" Amadeo says to his mother. "There's presentations?"

Lizette and a blonde take their places before the whiteboard. The girls in the audience whoop their support. "Yeah Lizette! Yeah Corinna!"

Lizette pulls at her skirt, which has worked its way around her waist. He's surprised to see her looking so uncertain, after her swagger earlier. Angel is holding Mercedes; she waves one of the baby's hands. "This is a talk about nurturing discipline," Lizette murmurs. The paper trembles in her grip.

The blond one—Corinna—nudges her. "You gotta *project*."

Lizette raises her voice for a few words before sinking back into inaudibility, so the blond one grabs the paper and takes over. "Discipline is a problem issue every mom from age thirteen to sixty has to face at some certain point in her lifetime."

Brianna has a pleasant, attentive look plastered on her face, but Amadeo notices when she pulls a book from the bookcase and reshelves it. The blond girl drones on about time-outs and consistency. The information seems to have been copied directly off the internet.

"Because think about it," says Lizette belligerently, reclaiming the stage. She's found her voice, she's going off-script. Brianna Gruver bites her lip, poised to intervene. "Say your kid is screaming her head off. You think she's going to *stop* screaming if you spank her?" She jerks her chin at her child. "As an example, Mercedes doesn't know what a spanking means. She's too little to know what anything means."

The event is catered by Food King. As the girls talk, Amadeo munches from the veggie tray, using carrots to scoop quivering quantities of ranch dressing. Some splats onto the carpet. He looks around and scuffs the spot with his shoe.

"In conclusion," Lizette says loudly, "discipline isn't about hurting. It's about loving correction." She and Corinna grin, count three nods, then give deep, campy bows.

After, Amadeo brings Angel a plate of veggies. She thanks him but sets it on a desk, her attention entirely absorbed by her friends.

"That was *awesome*," Angel tells Lizette as she hands Mercedes back. "Thanks to you, I'm going to quit throwing Connor. Maybe just a gentle toss now and then."

Lizette ducks her head, pleased. "It was stupid."

"I did most of the research," says Corinna. "Actually."

Angel hugs Corinna. "You did so awesome. And you projected really clearly." Corinna lights up, and Amadeo's eyes prickle with pride.

After, there's a tour of the baby room (rocking chairs and mobiles and rows of clean white cribs, colored floor mats to cushion tiny bodies during Tummy Time) and everyone mills about.

There's something irritatingly democratic and condescending about Eric Maxwell, the way he hobnobs with his target population, engaging with the scattered siblings and parents of the teen mothers. You can almost see him gathering anecdotes of improved lives for the annual report. He shines his sympathetic attention first on one woman, then on another. And then, having discharged his duty, he gives Brianna a little salute and slips out, presumably to get in his Volvo and hightail it back to Santa Fe.

Amadeo's mother slumps at the desk, her cup of lemonade forgotten beside her.

"Hey, you tired, Mom?" He touches her shoulder.

She gives him a blank look, then nods like a sleepy child.

"Go home, then. We'll meet you there."

As she bends to gather her purse, her arm slow and jerky, he has the uncomfortable sense that something's wrong, but then across the room in the knot of girls Lizette laughs wildly.

After his mother leaves, Amadeo also slips out, ostensibly to find a restroom, but really because the shrieking of babies and teenagers is getting to him. In the hallway, he peers into offices, where the other earnest work of Family Foundations gets done—food stamp outreach, free tax prep for qualifying families, therapy. Under a sign that reads *Resource Library* is a single jammed sagging bookshelf. Amadeo reads the spines. *The Sexual Male.* Now that's one he wouldn't mind taking a look at. Next to it, *The Male Conundrum. Men Vanquishing Darkness.* Who knew there were so many books devoted to the difficulties of being a man? He wonders if they have a copy of *Mastering Ares.* Another shelf is packed with books with titles like *Family Violence* and *Black and Blue and Baby, Too.* Amadeo straightens and moves quickly away.

All over the walls are signs for school supply drives and helpful posters in English and Spanish explaining how to prevent fetal alcohol syndrome and shaken baby syndrome and SIDS, syndrome after horrible syndrome.

Amadeo inspects one on early-childhood dental hygiene. *Caries,* apparently, is another word for *cavities.* Another poster details ways you can ensure your child's success, and he is stunned to discover that his daughter is considered an at-risk child. Divorced parents, born to a teenage mother, unemployment of one or more parents, minority status, family discord. On the plus side, neither of her parents is incarcerated, currently.

Marissa and Angel appear beside him. Angel's holding Connor, who's gripping Marissa's index finger and trying to focus on her face.

"So, do you like it, Dad? What do you think? Isn't Brianna great? And my friends?" Her grin is expectant.

Amadeo touches the back of her hair. "It's real nice. I see why you like it here."

"Is your mom okay?" Marissa asks him. "She seems kind of out of it."

"What? Yeah. She's good." His daughter looks so adult and poised, her shoulders straight.

"How old is that Brianna, anyway?" Marissa asks. From the classroom, a baby squalls.

"I don't know. She went to UNM. She was even on the dean's list."

"The dean's list of what?"

"Ugh, it's like the honor roll."

"She *told* you that?" Marissa says, just as Amadeo says, "Nerd."

Angel looks from one to the other, her face screwed up in a particularly teenage expression of annoyed disbelief. "No, I looked her up. And some people might think it's a *good* thing to succeed in school. Some people might respect that and not go around calling other people nerds."

"I was kidding." Amadeo smiles, fatherly and indulgent. "You can be on the dean's list, too."

"Shit," Marissa says, tapping the poster over Amadeo's shoulder, "who knew? I used to let Angel fall asleep with a bottle all the time." She gives Connor's hand a waggle.

Angel's mouth twitches and she detaches Connor from her mother. "That's why I got so many cavities."

"You lost those baby teeth anyway. There were things we didn't know back then. Like, you drank formula. I even smoked when I was pregnant." Marissa laughs, then, catching sight of Angel's face, says more soberly, "Like, a couple times."

But Angel's lips tremble. "It's not *funny*. It was *1995*, Mom. They knew that smoking during pregnancy was bad." In her arms, Connor starts up a fuss, as if also registering his indignation. "Why can't you just act like a grandmother?"

Marissa extends her palms, helpless, beseeching, the very image of innocence attacked. "How is a grandmother supposed to act? I don't know what you want from me, Angel."

"You know exactly how a grandmother acts. If you don't, then you've never seen one or had one or turned on the TV. I'm not an idiot. I'm not one of your boyfriends who can be manipulated. You forget that I *know* you."

"Yeah, they definitely knew smoking was bad," says Amadeo, trying to pull the conversation onto more solid ground. "Remember all those commercials when we were kids? *If you smoke, I smoke*."

"Ugh!" Angel storms off down the hall, her body tipped to the side to counterbalance Connor's weight. Connor's shrieks rise.

"You turned out *fine!*" Marissa calls after her daughter. "So I'm shit! I admit it! I ruined your entire life!" But Angel veers into the baby room, Connor's cries cut by the slamming door. Marissa turns on Amadeo. "Oh, *fuck* you."

Amadeo puts up his hands. "I didn't say nothing."

"Don't you dare preach to me about how to parent." She flaps her arms once and storms off the other way.

The festivities are still going strong when Brianna ducks out. In the bathroom, she plucks at the wet spots in her armpits and peers at her face. She is gratified to see that her eyes are bright and clear, her skin even, and her hair has some fluff to it. Authority becomes her, she thinks.

She's enjoyed meeting her students' families, though she admits to herself that at least some of her enjoyment is voyeuristic. Ysenia's mother has a vacant quality about her. When Brianna told her that it was a delight having Ysenia in class, Ysenia's mother responded warily, "Okay . . ." It made Brianna sad to think of spirited Ysenia growing up with this woman. All night Jen's parents have sought Brianna out to repeat how grateful they are that Jen has this opportunity. "It's not a situation we expected she'd ever end up in, but we're so appreciative of this resource," her dad said, pumping Brianna's hand. Lizette has not brought anyone with her. Brianna gives herself a shake, but cannot shake away the disagreeable guilty pang.

As she makes her way back to the classroom, she sees Angel's father inspecting a poster in the hallway. The sleeves of his polo shirt are tight around his biceps, his thumbs hooked in his pockets. He rocks on his feet as he reads.

She noticed him earlier, during the presentations. He's not exactly handsome, and he's just a couple inches taller than Brianna herself. But his eyes are warm and brown and thick-lashed, and he seems easy in his body. Her nerves vibrate, alert.

Emboldened by her professional role, she smiles and sticks out her hand. "So. Angel's dad, right? I'm Brianna."

He turns slowly. "Angel's an at-risk child?"

"Well, her baby is," she says. "Angel is technically an at-risk *youth*."

"At risk for what?" He bites his lip.

"Pregnancy, for one." Brianna gives a quick rueful laugh. "Drug and alcohol use, dropping out, being a perpetrator or victim of crime. Ditto child abuse. Teenagers who have babies are at risk of reduced future earnings, less educational attainment, having children who are underweight or have serious health problems." She catches his stricken expression and tries to right the ship. "I mean, not always, of course, but those are the statistical outcomes we're trying to prevent."

"Not Angel. Angel's going to college. She may even get her master's. Her aunt's got hers. And Connor was seven pounds three ounces. Just right. He's healthy as anything."

Brianna smiles gently. "Angel's great. She shines. If she keeps on like she is, she'll achieve whatever she wants."

"You mean it?"

She feels a wave of tenderness for this father who is looking to Brianna for assurance. "Sure, I mean it. Some of these girls I worry for, but not Angel."

"I just bought Angel and the baby a new car seat. A Graco." He shrugs, like it's no big deal. Is he trying to impress her?

"Rear-facing?"

"Of course. It was the third most expensive one in the whole Babies 'R' Us."

"What really matters is that it's rear-facing and secured. I'm sure it's great. Reputable outlets only sell AAP-approved models."

"Yeah, I know, that's why I went there." He nods, grinning. "I'm Amadeo."

"So, Angel gave you the tour?" Brianna gestures nervously. "Right here is our conference room. Where we hold mock interviews. All the girls do it, you know, for jobs."

It's a bleak room with a brown laminate folding table, the kind used in Brianna's childhood cafeteria. The building is new, but the funding ran out by the time they got to this room. Mismatched chairs are arranged haphazardly; three more folding chairs lean against the wall.

Affirming stickers have been pasted to the table and peeled off with varying degrees of success. From where she stands, Brianna sees a nearly intact cartoon thumbs-up in an orange star: *My Feelings Are Okay!*

At the window, Amadeo surveys the shopping center that shares the parking lot. A Dollarland and a nail salon, a Jack in the Box and a liquor store. "Nice," said Amadeo, gesturing at the flashing neon sign: *LIQU–R.*

"I know," says Brianna, joining him. "But it's on the bus route. We had to be on the bus route."

"You must see some rough stuff."

"Oh, yeah. You wouldn't believe the family situations some of these girls have to contend with. The worst things you can imagine. I had one student when I did my internship in Albuquerque? Twelve years old, brand-new mom. Guess how old the grandma is. Twenty-four. A year younger than me! Can you imagine?"

Amadeo whistles low. "Shit."

"It pisses me off. It really——" she falters. "It makes me so mad. These girls deserve better." She laughs, embarrassed. Why is she saying these things to this man? After all, he's young to have a teenage daughter. She wonders how old he is. "I know I'm not supposed to have favorites, but if I did Angel would be one of them. I bet you're proud of her. She's smart." This is all true, but she recognizes that she is saying it to please him.

Amadeo smiles. "She's amazing. Best kid I could ask for."

"I like your name," Brianna says thoughtfully. "Amadeo. Like Modigliani. Amadeo Modigliani was an Italian artist. He did a bunch of portraits. Women mostly."

"I know that. I've googled my own name. How do you know I'm not an art lover? Hell, an art *collector*."

Brianna's face heats with deep shame. "Oh." What an idiot, assuming that he didn't know Modigliani. It's the worst kind of patronizing, exactly the kind of misstep they'd been warned about in her training and she thought she'd never make.

"Hey," he says. "It's okay."

"I apologize," she says.

Amadeo nudges her with his elbow. "That Eric Maxwell. Are you two, like . . ."

Brianna regards him quizzically, then flushes. "No! No."

"Sorry. That was—Angel just thinks you're the best. Like, I feel like I know you from everything she says. She said you made the dean's list. She's always telling us about your good advice. She said you're her personal hero."

Brianna dips her head in pleasure. "She said that?"

"Hey, let me give you my business card." Amadeo pulls out his wallet, rifles through it. "If you ever need a repair, let me know. I'd give you a deal. My number's right there."

Has he given her his number? Or is he really just trying to drum up business? Brianna turns the card in her hand.

"Listen. We should hang out sometime. Get to know each other."

Her breath is still in her throat, and before she can even muster her courage, she blurts, "I'd like that."

"Okay! Okay." He looks at his watch. "We need to get Connor to bed. It's late." Brianna is grateful to him for taking the initiative in putting a stop to this awkwardness. He pats her on the shoulder, then strides into the hall.

Angel finds Brianna in the conference room looking out the window onto the dark parking lot. Her affection for Brianna is so intense it's an ache. Angel would like to hug her teacher, to lean her head against Brianna's shoulder. Soon, thinks Angel. She pictures the two of them out for dinner, laughing like sisters or friends.

Earlier, in the baby room, Angel cried. She and Connor had been alone, the festive sounds from the classroom deadened. She doesn't know where all that emotion came from, because she'd been having a good evening.

She shouldn't let her mother destabilize her like that. But her mother's comment really hurt—and not just because her mother smoked when she was pregnant, but because she treated it like some kind of joke. And worse is how her mother makes Angel out to be so critical and unpleasant: like, if only Angel hadn't been so humorless they might chuckle together about Marissa's ineptitude. Angel knows that back then her mother was young and alone and dealing with a tough situation, but knowing this doesn't make it easier to forgive her—mostly because her mother is so willing to forgive herself. *It was a different time, I was alone, your dad never helped at all, I was young.* She always has an excuse. And she's not young now, but she's still screwing up, still refusing to take care of Angel.

Marissa's own mother, Angel's Gramma Lola, contributed enormously to Angel's upbringing, both financially and in child care, until the dementia set in, and if this somehow slipped Marissa's mind, then she's an idiot.

Now Angel squares her shoulders. She will not be like her mother.

She will not blame everything on Connor. She'll give him what he needs, even if those are things she never got herself. And she'll start by getting him a good godmother. She looks down at him, asleep against her chest, then at Brianna's back. There's something private and delicate and almost sad in her teacher's posture, the way her fingers rest on the sill. Angel expects Brianna to see her reflection, to turn with a smile, but apparently she is looking beyond reflections. Angel takes a deep breath. "There you are!" she calls. "I was looking all over for you!"

"Yes?" Brianna pushes herself off the windowsill, and Angel wonders if she startled her. "What can I do for you, Angel?"

Angel falters. "It's okay. I can ask you later. I just had a question." She is more nervous than she expected, because Brianna is more distant than Angel's ever seen her. She tries another approach and turns Connor. "I realized I never told you his full name. Brianna, this is Connor Justin Padilla. The First." She laughs lamely. "You can hold him if you want."

Brianna gives Connor's socked foot a little shake, but her eyes skate over him toward the door. "That's a nice name. A nice, real name. It's good to meet a baby who isn't named after a rapper or a car."

Angel laughs uneasily. A knot of something in her chest is as hard and pointed as a nectarine pit. "You mean like Mercedes? Lizette's loved that name since second grade. Plus, it was a name before it was a car."

"I shouldn't have said that." Brianna smiles brightly, just a flash, and then is remote again. "I was kidding. Mercedes is a lovely baby."

The pit is still wedged up under her rib cage. "She really is."

"And so's this little guy." Brianna shakes Connor's foot again. "We should wrap up in the classroom, Angel. We have to be back here before we know it."

"There was just something I wanted to ask." Angel reaches out to touch Brianna's cardigan sleeve, but doesn't make contact. This isn't going at all the way she'd hoped, but she plows forward because she's waited too long as it is. "I wanted to ask, would you be Connor's godmother?"

Brianna's distant, private expression shifts. A gleam of alarm—fear, almost—and then her face is sunny, enameled, professional. Angel didn't understand until now that the face she knows so well *is* a professional face. The corners of her own smile tremble.

"Oh, Angel. That's so nice."

"Thanks," says Angel.

"I'm afraid I can't accept the offer." Brianna now turns professionally sympathetic, mouth downturned.

"Okay," says Angel, stung. "Sure." Every part of her feels cottony and numb. It had never occurred to Angel that her teacher might decline. Angel had assumed Brianna would be flattered. She'd assumed that she'd be *grateful* for the honor. Angel pictured Brianna pulling her in for a hug, both of them happy and safe in the understanding that they'd be bound together long into Connor's adulthood.

"I hope you understand." Brianna tips her head and adjusts her loose dress. The flowers are large and pink and ugly. They belong on a grandmother's curtains, a grandmother with less taste than either of Angel's grandmothers. "It's nothing personal, Angel. I just have to be careful of boundaries. When Ysenia asked, I told her the same thing." Brianna smiles again, a quick, indifferent stretching of her mouth.

When Angel was a child, four or five, she discovered that she was possessed of a minor, yet astonishing, magical power. If—say, when she'd just woken from a nap—she watched the closed blinds or the dots on the couch, and yielded to a certain tug on her eyes and allowed her vision to slide out of focus, then the stripes of the blinds or the white dots on the couch would lift, levitate apart from the object, until eventually Angel blinked, and everything snapped back into place. This power was a marvelous secret that the universe offered up just for her.

She depended on her secret power. When her mother was giggling with this or that boyfriend in the living room, or, just as frequently, weeping and yelling, Angel would go to her room, lie with her cheek against her comforter, and focus her attention on not focusing at all. Her vision would blur but for the tiny pink fleur-de-lis pattern on her sheets, and the sounds outside her bedroom door would fade. Two or four or five fleurs-de-lis would rise off the percale, hovering there until Angel released them. Angel could control and dismantle the world in her tiny, secret way.

Then, when they were nine, Priscilla had shown Angel a large soft-cover book of 3-D Magic Eye illusions, colorful stereogram images that looked like wrapping paper but concealed silhouettes of sports cars and cats.

Priscilla, bossy as ever, had shoved the book into Angel's face and launched into detailed instructions. "It'll take a while, but you'll get it."

"Yeah, I see it," Angel said, cutting her off.

"Well, what is it, then?" Priscilla challenged.

"A mushroom." Angel traced the outline, her forefinger passing through the translucent, floating image.

Angel was astonished to learn that others shared this gift, then stricken, because she now saw her superpower for what it was, a phenomenon as common as it was unimportant, good only for selling cheap books and posters of tacky mall art.

This is how she feels now, standing with Brianna in the dark conference room. This precious, secret thing—the intimacy she's felt for Brianna—has been exposed as tawdry, unreciprocated, shameful. She thought Brianna cared for her, when Brianna was just doing her job.

"I hope you understand," Brianna says again.

"Oh, yeah, course. I get it." She didn't know she was crossing boundaries inappropriately, didn't understand that all of Brianna's warmth has meant nothing—and it smarts that Ysenia had the same idea and got there first, all those months ago.

Brianna smiles. "Shall we go back to the Open House? I think people are starting to leave."

"Okay." Angel stares down at Connor's fuzzy, scaly head nestled in the crook of her elbow. He is fast asleep, his pursed lips slick with drool. He has no idea that he's been rejected. The abashment turns to indignation, because little Connor deserves only love and goodness. He will never, ever know about this, Angel vows.

Brianna is already at the door. She switches off the conference room lights. "You working on your book report?"

"Yeah," Angel says stiffly. "It's this World War II thing."

"Terrific."

Angel presses her lips against Connor's scalp as she trails Brianna down the hall. It's amazing to her that someone so little can create so much heat.

———

"THAT WAS AWESOME," her dad says when Angel starts the car. "You got a really good thing going." He's energized and grinning.

"I guess. It was fine."

He peers at her as she pulls onto the road. "You tired?"

"I guess."

"Well, you had a long night, showing Connor off to all those people. He was cuter than all those other babies put together, did you notice?"

Angel thinks for a moment about this image: a baby that's really eight babies mashed together, a colossal, multi-limbed monster of need, all its mouths wailing. She drives silently. Eventually her dad gets the hint. He leans against the window, a little smile on his face, as the headlights sweep past the dark trees along the road.

"Are you asleep?" she demands.

"No," her dad says, surprised. "What is *up*, Angel?"

"Nothing." It's not fair. The night started off so well. It should have been perfect. The girls all seemed happy to see her, and Angel felt like a truly essential part of the school. Lizette, usually so undemonstrative, even called out "Hey, biatch!" and hugged her. The lights before her slant and blur. She wills her father not to turn to her.

She squeezes her eyes to clear her vision and inhales deeply, and all at once a flash of white darts across the road. Angel yanks her foot off the gas, swerves, stomps the brake, then lets up.

"Whoa," cries her dad, grabbing at the dashboard as the truck lurches. "What the fuck?"

Angel yanks the truck to the shoulder, fear slamming through her. The wheels grind the gravel. She squints wildly into the dark on the left and right of the road, but sees only the black outlines of the trees against the depthless starry sky. At first she had the impression that a naked child had flashed in front of the car—she has a distinct image of a round face and big eyes—but she doesn't know why she thought that, because whatever it was was bigger, longer, four-legged. A dog or a wolf.

"Did you see that? What *was* that?"

"What was what? What happened?"

"Didn't you *see*? I almost hit something. A wolf or something." The weak headlights illuminate only a swath of crumbly pink soil and the nearest trees, the night crisp against their ragged edges. No glowing eyes, no movement at all.

"There aren't wolves out here," he says uncertainly. "It was probably just a coyote. You didn't hit nothing. We're fine."

"Why weren't you *looking*? You're supposed to be looking! That's the whole point of you being the licensed adult driver." Angel cranes around. In the back, Connor is still asleep, a plug of mucus clinging to one nostril. She wants to get out, to hold him to her. Angel drops her head to the wheel. Wracking sobs clutch at her. She's shivering, freezing suddenly.

"Hey now." Her dad's voice is calm, but he looks shaken. "Hey now." She presses her forehead into the steering wheel until it hurts. After a moment, he opens the door, and Angel almost cries out, afraid he'll let whatever is out there into the truck. But he shuts the door. She listens to his steps outside. He opens the driver's-side door. "Scoot over. I'm driving us home."

"You can't!" But she slides over and buckles herself in obediently. "You'll go to jail," she says, muted.

"No I won't." His tone is assured and calm, the voice of a father. He cranks the heat and adjusts the blowers so they hit Angel full-on.

She tries to relax her body, part by part, the way Brianna taught them in Guided Relaxation, but her rigid muscles won't release. "Probably it was nothing. Just a coyote or something. Maybe a big rabbit."

Her dad looks both ways down the long empty road and pulls back onto the hardtop. At the edge of the road, the shadows swing to avoid the headlights. He drives smoothly, his speed restrained.

"Close your eyes," her dad tells her, and she does, feeling the warm sway and rumble pressing into her back as the truck carries her toward home.

She wakes to her dad shaking her. Angel lifts her head. The house is waiting for them, yellow light at her grandmother's bedroom window.

"I'm tired."

He laughs. "I know you are." He gathers her purse and backpack, the stack of informative handouts and the free picture book about alligator pilots that each family got as a party favor. "I'll get the door, you get the baby."

Under the dim orange of the dome light, Angel blinks her sticky eyes and grapples with the straps. Connor's eyes open and he squints up at her. His face is pinched and he begins to whimper.

"Oh, calm yourself," she murmurs. "You'll give yourself a stress disorder." Her memory of whatever shot in front of the truck—a vague impression of light and speed and fur and sentience—hasn't faded, but it no longer seems as terrifying. She can think about it later or not at all. She fusses with the plastic handle, trying to release the carrier from the base. When she tugs, the entire contraption shifts forward.

"Oh, god, Dad!" Angel cries. "Look." In a flash, he's at her side. She lifts her head, stricken. "Look what we did."

Her dad follows her pointed finger to the seat belt that dangles against the back of the seat, the metal buckle glinting. Connor is strapped into his car seat, packed as snug as an egg in its carton, and the seat is snapped securely into the base, but the base itself rests loose on the bench. In a collision, Connor might have been pitched forward onto the truck floor, pinned beneath the immense weight of safety features.

"Oh," her father breathes.

A wave of despair crests, but her father reaches past her to release the baby and settles him gently at his shoulder. Sinking back into sleep, Connor exhales long.

"He's fine," her father says firmly. "Look at him. We made a mistake, we both did, but he's fine. We're lucky we're both such excellent drivers."

"I could have killed him. I'm a horrible mother."

"Listen." He takes her chin and turns her face to him gently, a gesture he's never, ever made. "It was a mistake. Every parent makes them. That don't mean it's okay, but we're not gonna ever make this one again."

July is hot, but Yolanda shivers in her sweater. Somehow she manages to schedule and attend all these appointments—chemo every other week, four hours at a time, plus scheduled labs—without arousing any suspicion in Amadeo or Angel. They're so incurious, her offspring.

And Monica Gutierrez-Larsen, too, seems to believe her when she explains her days off as "a minor medical thing." Monica searches her face, as if to check for signs of lying or plastic surgery. "Of course, Yo. Take care of yourself. Just make sure the agenda for the meeting with the governor is good to go."

She supposes she can't blame them, these young people with their faith in the body, their faith that the world will keep providing what it always has. Was Yolanda ever so oblivious to death? No, but then, she'd been the only child of old parents, one of just a few children born to all those uncles and aunts and second cousins, and sometimes it seemed barely a year went by without someone in that once-vast family dying, a long parade of death headed up by Elwin and punctuated most dramatically by Anthony.

On the way out of the Cancer Center parking lot, Yolanda flinches at the sun glinting off the hood of her car. The whole landscape—the streets and stucco medical buildings, the piñon-dotted hills to the east—is achingly bright, like an overexposed photograph of another, less habitable planet. Realizing she is trembling and nauseated from hunger, Yolanda stops at the Tortilla Hut for a milkshake and an enchilada. It's two in the afternoon, still plenty of time to make it back to work and finish some tasks there, but Yolanda is sapped.

At a table near her booth, a red-faced girl gazes into her computer screen and chews her three middle fingers. The fingers are in deep, to the second joint, and the girl works away at her big drooly mouthful, heedless of the people seated all around her. Yolanda feels a rush of compassion for this girl wearing her private face, forgetful that she is more than a mind perched on a body. Yolanda tries to freeze her own expression, to catch herself in her own private face, but the muscles in her cheeks and forehead tighten with awareness, composing themselves into something to be observed, if only by herself. The girl removes her slick fingers to type something, then plugs them back in her mouth.

Yolanda will soon be like one of the patients in the Cancer Center waiting room, one of the thin chalky-faced people hunched in their wheelchairs, the tubes of oxygen hissing in their nostrils. With a shock Yolanda realizes that many of those people will outlive her.

Not ten minutes ago, Yolanda thought she might pass out if she didn't eat. But now, faced with her enormous, high-caloric meal, that urgency has fled. She drags her fork through the chile at the edge of her enchilada, then sets it down, sips her milkshake, pushes it away. She stands, hooks her purse over her arm, and leaves.

In the car, Yolanda crosses herself, then raises her head, the sunlight stabbing at her eyes, and pulls out. She backs into a parked car, then brakes hard. Her heart sloshes and she looks around. No alarm sounds, no one shouts. No one is in the lot at all. The bumper of the sedan behind her is dented.

Driving in her state is, she knows, deeply unethical. One day, one day soon, she will have her first seizure, and if it happens while she's behind the wheel—and the chances are fairly good that it will, given that she commutes over two hours every weekday—she could kill someone. Yolanda registers her hypocrisy, judging her son for his drunk driving, but continuing to drive herself. Somehow, though, despite the headaches and the spotty gray brain scans and the grim assurances of Dr. Konecky that she is, in fact, dying, she can't believe that her body could betray her so spectacularly.

Still, she vows, she won't drive the baby, won't drive Angel. This resolution has required some quick footwork and creative excuses at home to dodge her son and granddaughter's demands. They're a family of barely capable drivers: an old man, a teenage girl, a lady with a glioblastoma pressing on her brain, a drunk. Connor's practically the most qualified member of the family to shuttle them all around.

In her previous life, Yolanda would have left a note on the dented sedan. It would never occur to her to not do the right thing. Now, though, she straightens out and drives away.

Amadeo calls and leaves a message for Brianna on her line at work.
"Hey. It's Angel's dad. From the Open House? I was wondering how you are."

It's the middle of the day, and he thinks of her standing in the classroom in front of all those teenagers, doing good. He feels as if, having called her, having pictured her and those girls hard at work, he is a part of that good, hard work. Energized, he does twenty push-ups on the living room carpet, then, further invigorated, he does ten more.

When Brianna doesn't call back that day, he's surprised by his disappointment. Since the Open House, he's thought of their encounter in the conference room with fondness—he liked talking to her about art, this girl who is clearly intelligent, who recognizes his daughter's gifts—but it's when Angel mentions her teacher, when he sees her through his daughter's eyes, that he experiences a rush of warmth. His crush is fueled by his daughter's admiration, a strange and unsettling dynamic.

Last night, for instance, after she'd put Connor down, Angel marched into the living room, dangling a blue plush rabbit. "Who put this in his crib?" she demanded, looking accusingly from Amadeo to his mother. "We can't leave crap in his crib or he'll *die*. Ever heard of SIDS? I mean it: Brianna said."

"Okay, hijita," Yolanda said mildly, while at the mention of Brianna, Amadeo just grinned.

"I'm *serious*!" Angel cried, flinging the rabbit at his chest.

He's still thinking about his phone message the next day. He does what he always does at home, but daytime TV depresses him and so do the internet and video games and the endless meandering stroll through product reviews and skateboard fails. On their social media pages, his high school classmates, the ones that haven't been destroyed by heroin, show off their full lives—their adorable children, their trips to Disneyland. There's so much to want out there—trucks and computers and vacations and a new house—and all of it requires money.

He must get started with CWS. But no one has responded to his ads on Craigslist or in the *Rio Grande Sun* or in the church bulletin, and he still can't drive. He'll need to talk to Angel tonight about getting started, now that she has her license. He reads some websites about business start-ups and takes notes in Angel's math notebook.

As if rewarding his industry, Brianna phones that afternoon. "Mr. Padilla? This is Brianna Gruver, returning your call." Her voice is swift, but not assured.

"Oh, hey." His heart picks up speed. "I was just calling to say hello."

"So it's nothing to do with Angel or Connor?"

"No, they're good. I wanted to see if you wanted to get a drink sometime."

A long pause. "I guess I could do something Thursday."

"Cool, cool," says Amadeo, his own voice jovial, as if to make up for her doubt.

That evening he says nothing to Angel about his plan with her teacher, an impulse he decides not to think too deeply about.

And again he says nothing when, on the appointed day, Tíve, grumbling, drops him in Española. He's early, so he wanders around, then stops in at the bar at El Paragua. Leaning on the sticky counter, he orders a whiskey. It's the first drink he's had since Easter—over ten weeks—but instead of feeling guilty for falling off the wagon, he's proud that he can order a single drink in public like a normal man. The bartender scarcely glances at him, just delivers his drink and goes back to rolling place settings. In the corner, a woman in a floury apron operates a tortilla press, flattening each ball of masa before slapping it on a wood-burning stove. She flips it neatly with her bare fingers. A steaming, even pile of tortillas rises on the table before her.

The lunch rush is over. Amadeo catches the eyes of the two men at the table under the big artificial tree, who are having tacos and beer.

Contractors, Amadeo guesses, from their air of competence and the hardness of their forearms.

He prods the scar in the center of his left palm, then the one in his right. In each palm is a shiny purple bean of raised skin. He could have severed a tendon, could have had lasting problems, but he was lucky.

He raises his glass and smiles at the contractors, and then, because he's nervous and because there's still another hour to kill before Angel's school lets out, and another twenty minutes after that before he's allowed to present himself at Family Foundations, per Brianna's instructions, he orders a second whiskey, and a beer, too.

"What kind?"

"It doesn't matter," he says magnanimously. "Whatever they're having."

By the time he sets out, ambling along Riverside, the sun is heavy on his face, and he's relaxed and happy. Brianna is waiting for him in the doorway of the building with her backpack, and when she catches sight of him, she rushes over, as if to intercept him. She's wearing her floral dress and vivid lipstick.

Her smile wavers. "Let's go," she says, sounding not the least bit glad to see him.

"My truck's in the shop," he lies. "Mind driving?"

"Sure." She heads across the lot, hunched under the straps of her backpack.

Brianna drives a sea-green Beetle, the girly kind from the early aughts with the plastic flower in the vase on the dashboard. When she starts the car, some folksy music blares, but she switches it off. Amadeo's legs nearly touch the dashboard. He notes the aggressive cleanliness. Box of Kleenex, hand sanitizer, and in the drink holder, a plastic canister of hand wipes.

He flicks the hand sanitizer. "You're prepared, huh?"

Brianna chews her lip as she pulls out of the lot, her face and throat streaked red as if from a histamine reaction. "So, where should we go?"

Why hadn't he thought of this? There's Saints and Sinners or the Dive, but they hardly seem suitable for Brianna's air of scrubbed sweetness, and besides, he doesn't need a drink right now. "Are you hungry? We could go out to eat."

"No," she yelps. "Someone might see us."

If it weren't for the drinks, he might be on the verge of panic now. He looks down into the wheel well at her hiking sandals.

"Want to drive somewhere to watch the sunset?" It's a romantic gesture, unlike anything he's ever suggested, and he's certain she'll like it.

"Okay," she says skeptically. "God. I really shouldn't be doing this. Going on a date with a student's father. It's incredibly unprofessional."

"Are we on a date?" He tries for a teasing tone, but distress suffuses her face.

"Oh."

"Hey, no, it's all good." He touches her shoulder. "It can be a date if you want it to be a date. And if not, we're just hanging out."

"Right." She relaxes, and beside her, Amadeo does, too.

As they drive, Brianna tells him that she rents a casita from some rich lesbians near Chimayo. "We could go there," she says.

The property is surrounded by a well-maintained latilla fence. Up a dirt drive and then the house itself becomes visible: large and modern and adobe with a generous tiled porch and carved double front doors. Brianna parks next to a pair of matching Priuses and yanks the emergency brake. As they follow the brick walkway that leads around the main house, automatic lights snap on, though the sun hasn't yet set. Amadeo looks into the bright windows, curious to glimpse the lesbians, but sees only stainless steel track lighting and corners of large abstract canvasses. Beyond the piñon-scattered hills, the sky is turning orange. Brianna leads him through a garden to a little cottage with a blue door flanked by terra-cotta pots of geraniums. She looks around, as if seeing her house for the first time. "It's a little more than I wanted to pay, but I figure it's safer here than right in town. And I get free Wi-Fi and laundry."

She unlocks the door, then hesitates, as though realizing she's brought a complete stranger to her threshold. "Do you mind taking off your shoes?"

As he stoops to untie his boots, Amadeo looks around. Inside, everything is cheery and tidy and almost belligerently feminine. The tiny kitchen is accented in red: red dish towels, red trivet. Not a crass plastic bottle of dish soap by the sink, but a red ceramic dispenser. On the stove, a gleaming red enameled pot appears to have never been used. Books on a shelf, arranged in blocks by color, spines lined up (no *Mastering Ares* in the red section). Candles and little accents everywhere: a vase of twigs, a bowl of quartz, and on the windowsill, an antique mason jar filled with clear colored marbles. In the corner, partially obscured by a woven screen, is a low bed with a fluffy white duvet and a scattering of throw pillows. He sees the place through his daughter's eyes—Angel would love every inch of it. Amadeo stands in the doorway in his gray socks, feeling like a hulk. He could use a drink now.

"Excuse the mess." Brianna indicates the single rinsed cereal bowl in the sink.

"These your parents?"

Brianna confirms that, yes, the athletic gray-haired people on a trail in an Oregon rain forest are her parents. She stands in the middle of the tile floor, wringing her hands, then, all at once, rushes at him and clamps her mouth on his.

Amadeo backs up in surprise, thumping his elbow against the doorknob, and the shock of pain makes him gasp, which she seems to take as encouragement. Brianna's kisses are fierce and involve a lot of assertive tongue.

He cups her face and tucks a strand of hair behind her ear, but she bites her bottom lip and doesn't meet his gaze. Instead, almost with impatience, she takes his hand and leads him to the bed.

Brianna clutches herself as, grinning, Amadeo unbuttons his shirt and shrugs it onto the braided rug, kicks his feet out of his khakis. Shirtless, he's as muscled as she'd imagined, his skin smooth and brown and taut, and his masculinity gives her a thrill—an illicit thrill, because as a feminist, shouldn't she interrogate her attraction to this kind of masculine display? The tattoos are a surprise: the bloody red heart above his own heart, the line of thorns encircling his bicep. She finds them alarming and appealing in equal measure. Last, he removes his socks. Brianna herself is now wedged up against her bureau, arms clamped around her middle, nearly paralyzed with nervousness. She tries to slow her breath, but it's bunched high and shallow in her chest. She has no idea what to do.

"Can I?" he says, and steps toward her, lifting her dress over her head, exposing her newest blue cotton underpants and her red satin bra.

Amadeo's erection pushes against his boxers, angling toward her. He must see her doubtful expression, because he drops a hand to cover it, looking a little dashed.

This isn't going well—self-consciousness is spreading between them like a contagion. But Amadeo saves the situation. "Hey, come here." He wraps his arms around her and rubs her back vigorously as if she's cold, and together they fall onto the bed. Brianna gives a short giggle of relief, then kicks herself under the covers.

It's a Thursday evening, not quite a weekend, not quite a date night, but close enough that Brianna is considering this a date, which is, in fact, what she texted to her friend Sierra not one hour ago: *oh gotta run, date tonight!* She has, as yet, opted against answering Sierra's insultingly incredulous reply: *???!?!?!?!?!!!??!* Then, *You're not gonna tell him you're a virgin, right???*

The scene that ensues is without the gentle insistent urgency of a sex scene in a Merchant Ivory film. No soft candlelight or slow kisses or close-ups of smooth, indistinct body parts, no slow inevitable easing together, murmuring and rocking as one until the breathless culmination. Instead, a lot of effortful thrusting, their rhythms off until Brianna stops her bucking altogether. She shuts her eyes and tries to set her expression to one that looks simultaneously relaxed and engaged.

When he finishes, he drops onto her, his breath hot on her cheek, as if he's fallen into a narcoleptic sleep. Brianna rubs his arms uncertainly, and finally he raises his head and rolls off her.

"How was it?" he asks. "For you?"

She's glad for the thick blue twilight that has filled the cottage and that now shields her face. Words feel almost impossible to utter. "Great." Through the window, the trees are black lace against darkening sky. After a while, because it seems strange that they aren't talking, she says, "Did you know that heterosexual men are naturally more attracted to women who are ovulating?"

He sits up, switches on the bedside lamp with its yellow embroidered shade, and regards her with alarm. "I used *protection*. You're fine."

"I know that," she says, blinking into the light.

He gestures to the limp, tied-off condom on the bedside table, next to her book and water glass. "I always use protection."

"You put that *there*?" She yanks one Kleenex after another from the box beside the bed and thrusts a handful at him.

He wraps the condom and, looking around, opts to place it on the floor. He falls back against the pillow. "I see where Angel gets her thing for factoids."

"Ha. My major was human biology. Angel might like that. She's really into science and math. We have to encourage her. She's smart, you know."

"I know. She must have gotten it from her mom. I had no patience for school." He grins up at the ceiling, totally unself-conscious in his nudity, sweating into the duvet beneath him.

Brianna props up on her elbows, back arched, aware of the long curved line of her back and bottom, the lushness between her legs. She catches a glimpse of herself in the mirror on the bathroom door, and is, for once, pleased with what she sees. Her cheeks and lips are makeup pink, the sheet is wrapped pleasingly around her lower back. She feels little beside him, sexy and quick and lithe.

Brianna touches the scar on his right palm. "What happened to your hands?"

Amadeo regards them, front, back. "Oh, it was an accident. Carpentry."

"Whew." She smiles. "I really worried you'd been abused."

"No. God, no." He tucks them under the sheet.

"Could you turn that light off?" she asks, and when he does, she leans into him. They kiss a little more, and he touches her.

When she comes, a breathy little whimper, she strokes and strokes the same part of his bicep. Real affection for him seems to have bloomed out of nowhere. She tucks herself around him in the humid little eco-system beneath the duvet.

"I'm glad we did this." She burrows her face in his shoulder, then lifts it. In a rush she says, "So, until just now I was a virgin."

His face flickers in the twilight, and he looks at her quickly, then away. Otherwise, his face betrays no feeling at all, which is how she knows he's dismayed.

She flops back on the pillow, stomach clenched. Whatever composure and loveliness she possessed just a minute earlier has vanished. "I knew I shouldn't have told you. My best friend told me not to. Sometimes I do this thing where I know what not to say and it's like I'm thinking so much not to say it, that it's the only thing on my mind and then I say it."

"That's no big deal." Now he turns to face her. Why does she care what this guy thinks of her? But why would she reveal herself to him? He smiles, and this sickens her, too.

"But, I mean, you're twenty-five, right?"

"I'm not religious or anything like that," she says defensively. "It's just more of an opportunity thing."

"Weird."

"It's not *weird*. You can't tell anyone."

"It's just crazy that you teach all these teen moms and you were a virgin."

Brianna has the sense that she's drowning and the only one who sees her flailing from the shore is this ding-dong. "I mean," she says firmly, "that you can't tell anyone about this at all. I'd lose my job." She's almost afraid to say this next thing, afraid that she's making an unreasonable demand that will cause him to pull away from her. "I mean Angel. Angel can't know."

Amadeo regards her for one beat, then another. "Hey, hey," he says, pulling her in. "I won't tell no one nothing."

For a moment, relief. But, then what? Are they going to keep doing this and never tell anyone? Is this—secretive sex with the fucked-up father of one of her students—even what Brianna wants? She wonders if she used him for sex. What if he wants a relationship? The possibility fills her with a kind of warm excitement.

What am I doing? she wonders. A student's father—a student's deadbeat father, no less—though he *is* back in the picture now, and seems committed to being in Angel's baby's life. But who knows what kind of person he is? He doesn't have a job, didn't go to college. And now he is her First.

Although why she is thinking in these absurd terms, Brianna can't imagine. She is a health educator. A teacher licensed by the State of New Mexico. She likes to think of herself as knowledgeable and unembarrassed, yet compassionate. A mentor. And here she is freaking out over a guy. A man, she amends.

Because Amadeo *is* a man, bulky, muscular, an unemployed male on the social margins, unable to provide for either mate or offspring, with the porous roseate beginnings of an alcoholic nose. But despite all this, she finds him very, very attractive.

"It's cool," he says, smoothing her hair.

She submits to his comfort, resting her head against his chest, feeling him hard now between her legs, feeling herself open smoothly to receive him.

"I won't tell."

"Thanks," she says softly.

He chucks her under her chin. "If we can do this again."

"Yeah," she breathes. She grins into his shoulder.

Everything pisses Angel off these days, even the good things. At Tabitha's birth party, Brianna said the exact same empty, encouraging things she'd said at Angel's party. She and Connor and the incredible physical feat she's performed are old news. Even the little basketball shoes irritate her. They keep falling off and ending up under the sofa or in the gravel, and who ever heard of spending fifty dollars on sneakers for a baby that just lies there? She's so, so tired—it seems Connor wakes up every few minutes throughout the night, wrenching her from sleep, and then when he finally settles, she's tense under the blanket, eyes open in the dark, her heart hammering.

When Smart Starts! lets out, Angel's mother is waiting for her on the concrete portico outside the agency. Fear seizes Angel like a claw in the chest, and her first thought is that her mother's been fired.

She's in her work clothes, tight black pants and heels and a drapey blouse, hair blown smooth. She looks put together, as she usually does for work, and thinner, too—Angel notes with envy that her shoulders are sharp and glamorous under the silky fabric—but her expression is wary. Her big purse is over her shoulder, and she's gripping it with both hands, one arm crossed protectively in front of her body.

It's an old fear, dating back to when Angel was five and Marissa actually was laid off when the car dealership where she'd been working closed down. It was a scary time. For six months, they lived with Marissa's parents. Her grandmother Lola had been showing the first confusing and erratic signs of early-onset Alzheimer's—loving one minute, spiteful the next, panicked the minute after that—and her grandfather was still disapproving of Marissa for not marrying Amadeo, all of which had resulted in fights that made Angel, even at five, pity her mother.

Since then, Marissa has had the same job at the State Farm office, and there's never been a real danger that she might be fired, not really. Her boss loves her. But still the fear has lingered, because where would they go, now that Marissa's mother is near comatose with dementia and Marissa's father has fallen into baffled, resentful depression?

Whatever, Angel reassures herself, her mother isn't her problem now. But even thinking about that time, thinking about Marissa's stubborn, unhappy face when she was back in her parents' home, makes her soften toward her mother.

"What are you doing here?" Angel cups Connor's head protectively, but he peers with solemn interest at his grandmother.

"Hey, Angel." Marissa comes in for a hug, but they're as self-conscious as strangers. She presses her palms together. Angel has the anxious sense that her mother is about to deliver bad news.

She jiggles Connor, though he isn't fussing. "What? What's going on?"

"You want to get a milkshake or something? Or whatever. I could take you out."

Angel shrugs, noncommittal. "I should get home. I promised my dad I'd help him today."

Marissa shifts her weight uncertainly, wipes her palms on her pants. She nudges her chin at Connor. "How's he doing? Can I hold him?"

"Not sure if he'll go to you. He's been weird about strangers lately."

Marissa looks so hurt that Angel relents. "Sure, here." She passes him over, and Marissa clutches him to her. Connor, the little turncoat, beams radiantly. Marissa's face lights up, her mouth rounding to mirror his.

"How's your grandmother? She doing okay?"

"My grandmother?" What about me? Angel wants to ask. What about how I'm doing? "She's fine."

"I just thought she seemed strange at the Open House. Tired. I don't know. Just, remember when Gramma Lola—"

"Of course she's tired. We're all tired. There's a little baby waking us up every five minutes."

"Listen." Marissa's voice cracks a little. "What I came to say, I'm sorry I told you I smoked when I was pregnant with you. At your Open House. I didn't actually."

"Oh. Okay."

"I was jealous of you."

"Jealous? Of what?" Angel is surprised by the bitterness of her tone.

"I don't know. You belong." Marissa waves a hand at the Family Foundations building. "You belong at this school. You belong with Yolanda and your dad. They love you. It's obvious. I mean, you belong at home, too, obviously."

Amazing that her mother might be envious of her. More amazing that Angel should appear to belong anywhere in the world. How can her mother not see how alone she truly is? How her teacher rejected her and her baby? Nevertheless, Angel's heart goes out to her mother, who hadn't had Smart Starts!, who'd had to navigate young motherhood and a GED on her own.

"I've always been amazed by you. When you were three you said, 'Mama, can you tell me all the things I don't know?' You were so impatient to learn and make your own way."

Angel smiles. "I don't remember that."

"Just—I'm sorry, Angel. It's all been tough on me. I'm an idiot, but I really thought Mike was the one. Finally. But now that's over, and I'm a grandmother. I'm too young to be a grandmother!" Marissa's chin ripples and she wipes at her eyes with both palms. "But I am one." She laughs. If this were a movie, they'd laugh together, but Angel sees nothing funny. Does she expect Angel to feel sorry for her?

Marissa clears her throat. "Would you come home, Angel? I've been wanting to ask you to come back home. I miss you."

This is what Angel wants, isn't it? Isn't this what she's been waiting for? For her mother to admit she was wrong, to admit she misses her, to beg her to come home? Yet she's unmoved by her mother's hopeful eyes. Angel wants so much to soften, to mend the rift between them, but something in her won't allow it. Why?

"It's a little late, isn't it?" Angel takes back Connor, pulling more roughly than she intends. She winces at the naked hurt on her mother's face.

Marissa stands with her empty hands out. The hurt closes over, those wires under her mother's skin taut and vibrating. "You can be such a hard little bitch."

Angel reels as though from a slap. As heated as their fights have been in the past, her mother has never called her a bitch. "Oh, that's great. A sign of a real great mom."

And now Marissa is crying, her face screwed up, mascara running. "I'm sorry. I don't think that! I don't think that at all. I came here wanting to make things better!"

Angel is so, so tired. Gently, without rancor, she says, "Thanks for trying, Mom."

"Why can't I make things better, Angel?"

They stand looking at each other for a long moment, Marissa's eyes full and imploring. Angel almost relents and steps forward to hug her, but then her mother turns away, gripping the top of her purse as if it's a life preserver.

———

THINGS WERE TENSE after Mike found out about her pregnancy, but as Angel's stomach grew, mostly he just ignored her. One afternoon, however, she let herself into the house to find that Mike was working from home. He was at his drafting table, which took up a wall of the living room, absorbed in his silver laptop. He was spooning blueberry Greek yogurt into his mouth, mawing it distractedly. He'd just showered, probably after a run; his hair had grown out and was wet, curly at the nape. He was in his faded jeans, the heels of his cowboy boots hooked on the rung of the stool. When he finished the yogurt, he stacked the container inside another empty one beside him, then ripped the foil off a third and started in.

"Hey," Angel said. "That's my yogurt."

Mike didn't look at her. Spoon still in hand, he typed a few words.

"Mike. That's my yogurt."

"I'm working, Angel." He scooped another bite, spoon rasping the plastic.

"Okay, I'm just saying you're eating all my yogurt."

Very slowly he set the container down and turned to her on his swivel stool. He swallowed with exaggeration and then asked, "Do you do the grocery shopping?"

"Yes. I went with Mom. I picked that yogurt, because I need protein and calcium." She indicated her stomach.

Very slowly, as if she were a foreigner, Mike said, "Do you, with your hard-earned income, purchase the groceries for this house?"

"No," said Angel.

"Then don't fucking interrupt me when I'm working to tell me I can't eat food I bought."

"I'm not saying that. I'm just saying please don't eat my yogurt that *my mom* bought me."

His face went rigid. "You think your mother's salary covers all the expenses in this house? You think it paid for your computer? You think it'll cover your little teenage pregnancy? It sure didn't cover a box of condoms, did it?"

"Why you gotta be such a dick?" Angel was electrified by her daring. She'd never sworn at an adult, never challenged anyone so directly. "You shit on everyone. Sorry your boss doesn't think you're as smart as you think you are. Sorry you're not some big-shot architect, but ever think it's maybe 'cause you're just not that good?"

And then he was up and moving swiftly toward her. Angel backed up, but there was nowhere to back into, because the couch was behind her. Mike kept advancing. He put his hands around her neck. He didn't squeeze; the gesture might have been a performance for someone else's benefit. Her hands flew up to meet his.

"You piss me off so fucking much," he said softly, and shook her, like a cartoon throttling.

Angel was more surprised than anything. Strangely, she wasn't scared, not yet, though that would come in the moments after. Some part of her was exhilarated, because despite the fact that he was looming over her, his hands almost gentle around her throat, despite the fact that he was bigger and stronger than her, she understood that she was the powerful one in this scenario. She'd enraged him.

Her hands were on his, clutching at them, and even now she remembers the odd intimacy of the pose: his shampoo smell, the dryness of the stretch of skin between his thumbs and forefingers, his trimmed nails smooth as river stones, the rough spots on the knuckles of his thumbs. His face was almost touching hers, his mouth contorted, his even, yellowing teeth bared, each whisker rooted black in its pale pore.

Angel's mouth was open, but before she even thought to try for a breath or to scream, he released her. She fell back into the couch.

"Just kidding," Mike said flatly. And this is when the fear flooded in. As Angel lay on the couch trembling, he kicked the bare bottom of her foot with the pointed toe of his cowboy boot. "You're lucky you're pregnant," he said, his voice low. "Just kidding." His eyes slid from her.

He wanted her. This understanding arrived whole and obvious. He controlled it, yes, he was disturbed by it, but that didn't change his desire, and the fact of it now lay bare. And as they held each other's gaze—his thick brown lashes, his brown-green irises, a red vein stretched across the white of his right eye—she saw this understanding pass between them. She saw that he was terrified.

He swiped a palm over his curly hair, touched the collar of his shirt, as if to make sure he was still there.

He turned away as if he couldn't stand to look at her—on her back like a bug, her legs now curled up protectively, her own hands around her throat—then slammed out the door. From his computer on the drafting table, an email arrived with a cheerful chime.

———

EVEN NOW, watching her mother cross the Family Foundations parking lot to her car, Angel can feel Mike's fingers around her neck, the pressure of his thumbs above her windpipe like meat lodged in her throat. She trembles, the panic coursing through her, even though she is fine. Fine! He didn't even squeeze. She didn't even have a bruise after.

Marissa's gait is stiff and truncated, and Angel knows her mother is still crying. She wants to call her mother back, but at the same time, Angel is glad her mother feels bad. She should! But instead of bustling in with energetic competence to make everything right, Marissa seems defeated, and this scares Angel, because she doesn't want to see her mother powerless in the face of what Mike did. Her mother's manner conveys that she is sorry, but that she has been crumpled by what happened. And if her mother is crumpled, doesn't that mean, by extension, that what Mike did was awful and permanent, and that Angel might be forever damaged? Doesn't it mean that her relationship with her mother might never go back to normal?

Angel tightens her hold on the baby and turns her back on her mother. As she makes her way to her dad's truck, Connor pats her cheek, his brow cinched with worry.

Tío Tíve has given Amadeo another ride to his DWI class. After, they stop at the drugstore. As they wait in the checkout line, Tíve peers into Amadeo's packed cart.

"You didn't get no diapers," he says critically. His own handbasket contains a single canister of Tums.

"Right, hang on." Amadeo takes off, running down aisles to grab a package.

"That your mom's?" Tío Tíve asks as Amadeo, winded, swipes his credit card.

"We share one," Amadeo says lamely. He expects his uncle's characteristic grunt of disapproval, but the old man just looks at him with pity.

"I appreciate the ride," Amadeo says on the way home.

His uncle doesn't respond, but then he says, "Good to see you providing. Trying to, anyway. Call next time you need a ride."

Was that praise? Amadeo grins out the window. The afternoon light is golden on the fields. The green leaves shimmer and dance, and in the acequias, the blue sky flashes.

He's been in an excellent mood since his date with Brianna. Amadeo is surprised that he enjoyed himself as much as he did; this skinny Brianna girl, nervous and clean-living and with an untended patch of pubic hair, is not his type at all. Despite the fact that she is so thin, there's something a little piggy in her appearance: the button nose, the pale firmness of her skin. A skinny pig in hiking sandals. She's kind of adorable.

Angel's admiration is contagious. He wants Brianna to like him, wants her to understand that he's a good guy, and he's allowing himself

219

to believe that he's trying to win her over for Angel's sake. When you think about it, it can only benefit Angel, having her dad and teacher sweet on each other—maybe, if Amadeo plays things right, Brianna will give his daughter extra help getting into college.

Amadeo is feeling optimistic. It's been a while since he's slept with a new woman whom he wants to see again; usually he cycles through a few predictable old connections, or meets strangers in Española or, at least before his friends started settling down, at liquor-fueled parties at Abiquiu Lake. (His mother pretends to assume he came home after she went to sleep, and if they cross paths in the morning as he lets himself in, she'll merely comment, "You're up early.") He feels both more and less hopeful about the prospects with Brianna, because she is different from these other women: earnest, self-contained, less likely to be interested in him.

When Brianna drove him home, afterward, the night was dense around the car, the dashboard lights cozy. The road rose and fell, curved in all the familiar ways, but still Amadeo had the wild sense that he could be going anywhere, he and this girl, that they could drive all the way to Denver or even farther—Seattle, Canada. Escape, adventure: Why hasn't he done more of that in his life? Why has he stuck so close to home like a decrepit house pet that no longer brings anyone any joy? There's nothing holding him back. He was suddenly so itchy for adventure he wanted to yell. He pressed an imaginary gas pedal in the floor mat as if to urge the car on into the thrilling night, and, as if they were piloting the car together, they crested a hill and sank with exhilarating speed.

Now his uncle turns slowly into the drive and rolls to a stop in front of the house. "Thanks, Tío." Amadeo slams the door, gathers his shopping bags from the bed, and the truck backs out, rumbles away.

At first Amadeo thinks what he's hearing is an animal howling, except it is coming from inside the house: his daughter, sobbing. Oh god. A mountain lion attack. Or Angel has been beaten up. Raped at gunpoint. He envisions the endless parade of twisted perps whose glowering mug shots crowd the evening news. Or, worse: the baby has fallen, his little teacup head cracked on the linoleum.

He bangs into the house, plunges down the hall past grinning school portraits toward the cries, which are coming from the open bathroom. An image comes to Amadeo of himself bent over the coffin of his infant grandson, a grown man laid waste by grief.

"Angel!" he shouts as he turns into the bathroom.

There she is, on the edge of the tub, her shirt gathered to expose her belly. At her feet, in his bouncer, Connor. Asleep, his head canted, heavy on his weak neck.

He can't be sleeping, not through these sobs. "What happened? What's wrong?" Amadeo drops to his knees, runs his hands over the baby's face, pinching little arms and legs. The baby twitches and erupts into cries of his own.

"What are you *doing*?" Angel yells. Her face is red and rubbery, slick with tears and snot. "I just got him to sleep. Why would you wake him up?" She pushes Amadeo and, still sobbing, leans down, unhooks the fussing baby from the bouncer, lifts him carelessly. The little head falls back on the neck and Amadeo draws a sharp breath.

"Let me." Angel's in no shape for anything. He takes the infant in both hands, holds him against his chest. It's the first time, he realizes, he's questioned Angel's competence. Until now she's seemed like an expert.

It dawns on him that Angel is terrified. It's obvious. How was he so utterly snowed?

He remembers what Brianna said about Angel being at risk for hurting her own child. "What happened?"

"Look at me." Abruptly, Amadeo is afraid, because what if she has divined what transpired between him and her teacher?

But she's pointing at the stretch marks on her abdomen, red and rippling, like an aerial photograph of a delta.

"What? I don't see what you mean."

Angel throws a roll of toilet paper at his head. *"Liar."*

"Hey," he says sternly, turning himself and the baby away. "Careful."

"You do so see. I'll never wear a bikini again!"

Amadeo can get past his prudish discomfort at the thought of his daughter in a bikini. The real problem is that the stretch marks *are* ugly: deep tender-looking tracks streaking her belly, as if the skin might split.

He thinks of a story his grandmother told him long ago, about how, as a child in this village, she used to walk around barefoot all the time, and when they put her in shoes for school she got a blister. She thought nothing of it until her own mother saw the red streaks running up her legs. The whole story was a cautionary tale about why Amadeo should pray. "We didn't have no antibiotics back then. Back then all we could do was soak in salt water and pray to God. God protected me, mi hijito, but not everyone. There was lots of kids in those days who died of blood poisoning." He tamps down the thoughts, as if they might endanger the infant he holds.

He bounces Connor and starts to formulate his prayer: *Our Father, who art in heaven, please clean up Angel's stretch marks. At least the ones that show from a bikini.* It's a stupid prayer; there's no way God wouldn't find it frivolous. Amadeo surges with anger at this God who can't understand a sixteen-year-old girl's anguish about her body.

"They all say they don't regret it. I *do* regret him. I don't want a baby."

She looks at Connor in Amadeo's arms, and her face fills with startling malevolence. "I hate you, Connor Padilla," she hisses, leaning in close to the little face. "Connor Justin Padilla, I hate you."

"Stop it. Stop it right now." He grabs a mostly dry towel off the rack and drapes it over the whimpering baby.

Angel slides to the ground, the damp bath mat rumpled under her haunches. For a time there is only the sound of her sniffles.

Amadeo retrieves the toilet paper roll and tears off a bunch. "Here."

Angel accepts it, but doesn't wipe her nose. She then turns her tear-streaked face toward him. Her expression is shining, miserable. "Dad, what am I going to do?"

He looks around the bathroom, but there's no help to be found. He's nineteen again and it's summer, and he's with Marissa in her parents' backyard. They stretch out by the kiddie pool, beers warming in their hands and in the sun, while Angel plays. Amadeo has a plastic dinosaur in his hand, a purple stegosaurus, and he's making it dance on the surface of the water, while Angel, with her damp black curls, slick red smile, and swollen diaper, slaps the water with fat hands and laughs her throaty laugh. They're talking about Marissa's older sister's new trailer—two bedrooms, full bath, cream carpet—and Marissa says she wouldn't mind a trailer, they could get a trailer, used at first, and beside them Angel splashes, a blade of grass stuck to her chest. Amadeo says, "You won't catch me living in no trailer. Besides, they just lose value," and Marissa says, stubbing out her cigarette emphatically in the grass, "It's not that I wouldn't rather a house, but when? And we gotta be saving if we ever want to have a place of our own—are you even saving *anything*?" This is when the fight starts, escalates. Amadeo accuses Marissa of getting pregnant just so he'd have to take care of her, and he calls her a whore. (She isn't, he knows that, hasn't done any more than he has.) Then they're both on their feet, beers tipped into the grass, and he slaps her across the upper arm, which is exposed in her sleeveless shirt. Marissa staggers back, reaches behind her into the air to steady herself, finds no hold, falls.

Amadeo looks at his hitting hand, horrified. But if he were honest, he might admit that even as he moved to hit her, he knew he could stop himself and knew he was going to do it regardless. The real surprise is the shock on her face, proof that he can act on the world.

Marissa stands. The skin on her arm turns white, then red, where his palm made contact.

"You asshole. Don't you ever hit me again," she screams at him, throwing plastic buckets and toys. Some strike him, some miss and fall to the grass. She keeps yelling, "Don't you ever hit me again!"

And it is that word, *again*, that terrifies him, as if by uttering it she opens up the possibility that he has it in him to do this again—even, somehow, makes it inevitable. From the kiddie pool, Angel watches her parents, eyes wide and black and unwavering.

"Don't you walk away," Marissa yells, and Amadeo turns just long enough to see her grab the baby, too roughly, Angel's head falling back as Marissa swings her onto her hip, water from the baby's sodden diaper spreading dark across her shirt and denim cutoffs, down her short brown legs. She's calling him names, and he's thinking of how loud her voice must be so near Angel's soft pink ear. Even as he starts the truck, Amadeo doesn't think he'll leave. His breath is ragged, he's shaking, and he's on Paseo de Oñate when he realizes he's still gripping the stegosaurus in his hand.

Now he slides down beside his daughter and pulls her to him.

———

ALL AFTERNOON Angel is remote. He holds Connor, and when the baby becomes fussy from hunger, she takes him wordlessly and positions him against her, her movements careful. By evening, though, she is once again narrating to the baby every detail of every moment: "What's Mama cooking? She's cooking chicken breasts. One, two, three." He allows himself to think that whatever mood struck her has passed, and he tells himself that if only she'll be okay, if only Connor will be okay, he'll never speak with Brianna again, except, of course, in the way that a caring father interacts with his daughter's teacher.

Angel coos at Connor. Impossible that his daughter could possibly feel such despair. Yes, she's going through a difficult time, and Connor's not sleeping well, but she's young, she's pretty, she has a new baby in a soft little duck suit.

As the summer wears on, Yolanda's great-grandson grows, good-natured and rashy. His eczema covers his bottom and encircles his little scrotum, red and painful-looking, creeps down the backs of his legs. His thighs are scaly and dry, little white rings of roughness around new pink skin beneath. Angel spends hours on the internet looking for cures, insists on leaving him naked whenever possible.

"You're a little yucky," sings Angel sweetly from the bathroom as she daubs him with cream as thick as oil paint. He kneads his toes. "You're a sticky yucky baby-pie. Let's get that old rash *off* you."

A baby should be the ideal antidote to death. Watching him grow new rolls of fat and learn to laugh and kick should be exactly the thing to distract Yolanda from her own failing body. But for reasons she cannot understand, she is having trouble focusing on him.

Her interests have constricted around her. She no longer cares to watch her telenovelas, no longer feels compelled by the outlandish plots. She no longer cares about work. She doesn't have the energy anymore to even flip through a magazine. She spends the hours she isn't at work or appointments lying on her bed, looking up into the canopy.

Angel doesn't knock, just comes right in, and Yolanda feels a wringing little twinge of annoyance, but she pats the bedspread anyway and says, "Come sit down."

Angel flings herself, limbs flopping every which way, her hair spread on the satin sham. She's not a child; she has a woman's body, but still, she seems to think she can climb into her grandmother's bed and curl up. She thinks she is safe here.

"What's going on, honey?"

"Gramma, do you love him?"

"Connor? Mi hijita, of course I do." But as much as she loves him, she loves him at a remove. She likes to watch him, but doesn't want to hold him.

"I feel like you don't love him, Gramma." Angel's voice is thick, and Yolanda can see how much it costs her to say this. "I mean, I know you love him. I just thought you'd love him more. Like you love me."

"Oh, hijita." How can she explain that the love she feels already is too much to lose? How can she be asked to get to know and then part from someone else? "I love you both more than anything."

Angel smiles through tears. "More than my dad?"

Yolanda chuckles. "All my babies. I love all my babies with my whole heart."

Angel is silent, plucking at the satin of the duvet. Finally she says, "I'm scared, Gramma."

Me, too, Yolanda nearly says. Instead she grips her granddaughter's hand. "Oh, hijita. The baby blues pass."

Amadeo's business model is simple. He drives around the Española Valley—rather, Angel drives, and Amadeo directs, while Connor blows raspberries with merry imperiousness from the backseat—searching for windshields in need of repair. Angel has thrown herself into the endeavor with surprising zeal. She insisted on being made full partner, which isn't exactly fair, since Amadeo is doing all the work and will be getting his license back in four months anyway, but his hands were tied.

"I'm a skilled worker. It takes *skill* to drive." Angel makes a big show of keeping track of her hours on a table she printed out at school and keeps in the glove compartment. Inexplicably, her mood has improved. Angel is a good driver—cautious, yet willing to make up time on long, straight stretches—which pleases Amadeo.

Everywhere they go, sunlight flashes off windshields, catches in the cracks and divots, and from his place in the passenger seat, the cracks seem to Amadeo like scattered diamonds waiting to be gathered. In his rear-facing car seat, Connor, who is so well behaved Amadeo sometimes wonders if there isn't something amiss, babbles and flaps his arms, batting at the plush rattles that dangle before him.

They circle parking lots of shopping centers, supermarkets, casinos, as far north as Taos, as far south as Santa Fe. Whenever he sees a crack or a divot or bull's-eye in a windshield, he slips his card under the wiper, along with his photocopied note—*Hi! I see you have a crack! I can help! Remember: cracks spread and cracks are dangerous. Let me save your life!!!!!!! All cracks fixed, cheap.* This is what is known as targeted marketing. All he has to do is wait for the calls to pour in. They haven't yet, but he has faith. Amadeo is pleased with his flyer—it seems he has struck the perfect balance between friendliness and stern paternalistic care. He imagines it must make his customers feel good, knowing that Amadeo is in the world, looking out for them.

For him, this isn't just a profit thing. Amadeo truly *is* concerned for these would-be customers. He's haunted by images of people for whom he is too late: the woman turning left into an eighteen-wheeler obscured by a crack, or the small child dragged under the wheels of a sedan, tricycle sparking across the blacktop. He pictures himself arriving on the scene, kit in hand, just in time to prevent an accident.

Angel sits as upright as a debutante, gripping the wheel. When a song she likes comes on, her scowl breaks and she sings along, shimmying and bopping intently. Amadeo is reminded of Angel as she was when she was a little kid; she has that same intensity of being. Angel so entirely inhabits her own life. Amadeo can't remember ever feeling that he belonged entirely to his life, not when he was sixteen or six or twenty-six. It seems to him that he's always been hiding out in his mother's living room, waiting for his true existence to find him. Now, though, as his daughter taps her thumbs on the wheel to the music, it occurs to him that life has started. This is it, here.

He has his daughter, and he has a job. And there's another bright spot: Brianna, with whom Amadeo has been texting. They met up again two nights ago, and she fell asleep on his chest, her hair across his shoulder. He cuts a look at Angel again, uneasy.

She grins. "What?"

"Keep your eye on the road."

Today, on their third afternoon out, Amadeo and Angel return to the parking lot of the Golden Mesa Casino, which, at eleven in the morning, is already filled with sedans. Angel allows old people to pass in front of her as they hobble across the blacktop toward the automatic doors and the dim air-conditioning inside. Among the squashed paper soda cups and food wrappers, Amadeo sees his flyers blowing around the parking lot, which might explain why he hasn't gotten any calls yet.

"Hang on here, will you?" he asks, and Angel pulls over to a curb.

Amadeo chases the flyers, stoops to catch them—this early in his business he must be frugal—and places them under the wipers of the parked cars. This time he doesn't just target the cars with dings, because maybe the owners have cracks in the windshields of cars in their driveways at home. Maybe their relatives drive around with their windshields refracting light.

"Hey," calls a security guard, shuffling toward him. "You can't be doing that here." The man's walkie-talkie crackles at his waist.

"I'm just trying to make a living, man," Amadeo says in his most charming tone. "I'm not bothering no one."

The guard shakes his head. He's sweating, the drops sliding beneath his black crew cut. "No soliciting." He puts his hand to his walkie-talkie, ready to call for backup.

"Excuse me, sir," says Angel, who has appeared at Amadeo's side. Behind her, the truck chimes its incessant reminders: *key in the ignition, door open, baby in the backseat.* "I know you're doing your job, but please look the other way? Just to be nice? We're trying to start this business and it's been hard to get customers."

The guard considers Angel, and Amadeo does, too: her green hoodie, her long straight hair pulled into a crooked ponytail, the loose strands framing her round face. She smiles sweetly. Pink cheeks and chapped lips. Her demeanor is genuine, as if she isn't trying to get away with something.

"Sorry," mumbles the man. "Unless you're here to gamble, you gotta go."

Defeated, they get into the truck. She slams her door and clicks her seat belt with emphasis, glaring at the guard's broad retreating back. "Dick."

"Hey now. Don't talk like that." Amadeo pivots in his seat to check the baby. When he reaches back, Connor seizes his grandfather's hand and shakes it, crowing with loopy joy.

The guard, halfway across the lot, seems relieved when Angel starts the engine.

"Screw that guy," she says. "We'll come back at night. We just have to go stealth."

Amadeo looks at her admiringly. "Stealth. I like that."

"We can't take no for an answer. No one's responsible for our happiness but us."

Amadeo is oddly comforted by these corny platitudes that she clearly believes. She believes them because she hears them from Brianna, delivered with the young woman's enthusiasm and seriousness. He thinks of the work Angel is doing for his business, thinks about her admiration for her teacher. It occurs to him that Angel is giving him permission. Briefly he imagines himself and Brianna, married, living in a big house somewhere green and lush, sunlight streaming though large windows. They could have another kid, start a real life, the kind of life recognizable from television commercials, all of them living together in a house with a lawn and a porch with pillars, the kind of life you were supposed to get, not this half-formed humiliating thing he's been living.

He reaches out to touch Angel's wrist. He looks at his hand on her wrist, then drops it back to his lap.

She turns to him with surprise.

"Eyes on the road," he says. "You're right. Let's come back tonight."

The other girls are doing Vocabulary Building when Angel shuts the classroom door and goes down the hall to the nursery. Connor is having his Tummy Time on the blue mat, swimming his arms and legs through the air like a beached sea mammal. His little neck strains to hold his head up, and his face and the parts of his scalp visible through his patchy hair redden with his exertion. Finally he drops his face into the mat, and Angel has to stop herself from rushing to sweep him up. But he doesn't cry. Instead he lifts his head once more, his focus as strained as constipation. He starts paddling again.

Angel loves leaving her classroom to feed Connor. It feels at once wonderfully decadent and justified. Once in third grade, her mother picked her up from school at ten in the morning to take her to a doctor's appointment, and before she went back, they stopped for lunch. It had felt like a marvelous treat, eating her baked potato (extra bacon bits) from its paper boat, chatting with her mother, while back in the school cafeteria, her classmates were lined up at sticky tables that smelled of mop water and bologna. Each time she gets up from her desk to find Connor, Angel misses her mother.

Connor flips over and now squints at a fluorescent panel far above him.

"Hey," Angel says to Lynne and Gail, the women in their fifties who watch the kids. At the sound of her voice he cranes his head toward her and flaps, mouth open in a gummy smile.

Lynne, hunched cross-legged on the mat near him, looks up from her phone. "There's your mom," she tells him mildly.

"Connor's already had two BMs," says Gail, gesturing to the bulletin board covered in Daily Logs. She's eating yogurt at a tiny table, her big bottom engulfing the dinky wooden chair. Across from her, Ysenia's baby, who has the wrinkled, squashed face of a pug, carries Cheerios to her mouth one by one, inspecting each gravely.

Before Connor was born, she admired Gail and Lynne's adept, no-nonsense approach to child care, their easy, unsentimental, and democratically cheerful way with the babies. But now, seeing them handle Connor without any special affection, she finds them suspect. She sweeps Connor into her arms with a sense of rescuing him from their indifference. Her joy at having his little face close to her own is so complete that she can't even be annoyed with them.

"I missed you, I missed you," she chants quietly into his shoulder.

For weeks Angel has waited in dread to be overtaken again by darkness, but, thank heavens, she hasn't. She can't even imagine, now, where that madness came from. Everything in Angel's life seems lighter and more possible. Even the sting of Brianna's rejection has lessened.

The nursery is outfitted with eight cribs. Connor's, with its fleecy yellow blanket and turtle crib sheet, is the second-farthest from the door, which makes him the second-least-likely to be kidnapped, unless the kidnapper is basing his selection on looks, in which case her child is in trouble. The babies are never, of course, left unattended, but disastrous scenarios constantly arise in Angel's imagination.

In the corner is a folding screen painted with Japanese cranes, and behind this is a padded rocking chair, where Angel nurses her baby. She rocks them both into drowsiness, listening to Connor's rhythmic snuffling, to the babbling and cries from the other side of the screen, the squeaking of toys and rattling of blocks. Ysenia's baby whacks her spoon on the table, and Lynne and Gail chatter about the patio furniture Gail is considering buying. Angel cups her son's foot in her hand, gazing down into his little red shell ear and his half-closed, black-lashed eye. His fontanel pulses.

Every once in a while, driving around after school with her dad, she needs to pull over to feed Connor. She circles the truck, gets in the backseat, and pulls him toward her. Each time, her dad gets out of the truck and stands a few feet away. Occasionally he checks his phone, presumably texting Yolanda or one or another of his friends, guys he went to school with or has met at the car races he likes to go to a few times a year, in Albuquerque or Bernalillo, but mostly kicking at the gravel and squinting into the bowl of the sky. Angel feels pleasantly sleepy in the afternoon, the baby kneading her breast, the sun warming the cab, the breeze lifting her hair from the roots.

Occasionally she'll call something out to her dad, but if the wind carries her question away, he'll say "Huh?" without coming closer, afraid, she knows, to see her breast.

He's not so bad, her dad. She can see the effort he's making. In parking lots, while she stays with the baby, he jogs from car to car, moving purposefully, clamping windshield wipers over his flyers. She has her doubts about the viability of this enterprise. It's been three weeks, and they still haven't gotten any calls. She can't get past the fact that this was a kit purchased from the television, that this same kit was presumably sold to hundreds of other lonely men awake and drinking in the middle of the night and hoping for another shot at a career. She wonders if it's generational, this trust in television, and she pities her dad for being taken in. The fact is, she doesn't see a whole lot of pocked windshields. In the whole Family Foundations parking lot, which can have up to twenty cars parked in it—more if the liquor store custom-ers park there—there are only four cars with tiny dings, and though they've left flyers, no one has called. The fact is, dings just aren't that big a deal.

She hopes she's wrong. She hopes Creative Windshield Solutions takes off, and that he makes as much as he says he will. Angel has the uneasy sense that in not truly believing in her father's venture, she's dooming it. So she's all the more determined to help him out. That way, if it doesn't work, then the failure will belong to them both, and he won't have to feel, once again, that he's foundered.

After she burps Connor, she still isn't ready to leave him. He stands on her lap with his wobbly legs, high-stepping his round socked feet on her thighs. He belches again happily, oblivious to the trickle of milk at his mouth, and his damp little hands grasp her cheeks, tangle in her hair.

"Hey," Lizette says, thumping around the screen, Mercedes held casually in her arm. "Ditching Vocabulary Building?" She cocks her hip and boosts Mercedes higher.

"No," says Angel quickly. "I just needed to feed him."

Lizette drags another rocking chair behind the screen and flops into it, legs splayed. Mercedes rests her head sweetly against Lizette's chest and gazes at Angel through clear eyes.

"You missed *bucolic*, *temperate*, and *patronize*. Speaking of *patronize*, personally I'm sick of Brianna. Bitch needs to get laid."

Despite herself, Angel is shocked. She tries for a sardonic tone. "Right, because we both know *that* solves everything."

Lizette gives a half-smile. "I'm sick of this whole damn program."

"I know—me, too," Angel says, though she isn't sick of it at all. "You wouldn't leave, though, right? You wouldn't, like, drop out for reals? We need our GEDs if we're going to make something of ourselves. Plus, Brianna can be pretty great, don't you think?" She can be; she is. Since the Open House, Brianna has, in fact, been remarkably warm toward Angel, and Angel is grateful to have been forgiven for her inappropriate boundary-crossing.

Lizette pushes her thick hair back and laughs at Angel, then kicks off against the floor with her sneaker so her chair rocks dramatically. Mercedes raises her head in alarm, then gives her mother a wet grin. Lizette doesn't smile back. "I forgot she was your best friend. Maybe *you* want to be the one to do her."

"Don't talk like that in front of the babies." Angel stands, reluctant to go. "I guess I better go learn some new words." She angles Connor so he faces Lizette, then makes him wave. "Say bye to Mercedes. Say bye to your little girlfriend."

"Girlfriend." Lizette snorts. "How do you know he's not gay?"

Angel turns Connor again and peers into his face. He grabs hold of a hank of her hair and gives it a friendly shake. "He's not gay. That's gross. Anyways, he doesn't even have an opinion on peas versus carrots yet."

"*Fish* versus carrots, more like. You're the one who said they were dating."

"I said Mercedes was his girlfriend. That could mean anything. Like, we're girlfriends." Angel flushes. "You know, like, *girlfriend*!" She goes for a hammy delivery of this last word, but can't commit, and instead it comes out merely squeaky.

Lizette looks at Angel steadily for a moment from under those thick lashes. "If you say so." Mercedes has begun to protest the delay and now tries to burrow openmouthed through Lizette's Raiders sweatshirt. "So um, if you don't mind, I gotta feed her." Lizette jerks her chin toward the door.

Each afternoon when his daughter gets home from Smart Starts!, she asks, "Any windshield calls?" But each day Amadeo has to shake his head. He double-checks his number on the flyer, checks that his phone is fully charged. Really there was no need to pay the forty dollars extra for expedited shipping.

"It takes time," Angel assures him. "You think Target was always the world's best superstore?" Then, with tact, she changes the subject.

When the first call comes, Angel is at school, which turns out to be a good thing.

"You fix car windows?" the man says.

"Most definitely." Amadeo glances at the clock above the stove. Angel will be home in an hour, so they can head out then. "Where you located?"

"Do you take insurance?"

"No," says Amadeo.

The guy goes on as if Amadeo hasn't said a word. "My window's all busted up. Passenger side. Some asshole smashed it, didn't even take nothing."

"Oh, see, if it's totally broken I can't help you. If you got a crack, then I'm your man."

"You can't replace a window?" The incredulity in the guy's tone is insulting.

"No," says Amadeo deliberately. "I just told you that."

"You kidding me? I got your flyer right here. You said, let me see—" A rustle, then the man comes back on the line. "*Let me save your life!!!!!!!*

236

All cracks fixed, cheap," emphasis on *all.* "I'm gonna call Windshield Doctor. I only called you because you said you were cheap."

"Yeah, well, a pile of shattered glass isn't a crack," Amadeo says, but the line is dead.

————

FOR TWO DAYS, Amadeo refuses to go on his rounds. "There's no point."

"You can't get discouraged." The concern in Angel's expression makes him feel worse.

"It's fine, Angel. Let it be."

"We just got to let the advertising do its work. People will call."

The next morning, he wakes to find that Angel has slipped an article under his door: *Fail Your Way to Success: Lessons in Resilience.* At the top, in Brianna's photocopied handwriting, are reading comprehension questions. The text is covered in pink highlighter. Amadeo snorts, but he's moved by Angel's gesture, and actually the article is pretty inspiring. Apparently seventy percent of start-ups fail. There are some useful tips for instilling resilience in children, too, and he sees where Angel gets some of the things she tells Connor: "You're really trying to lift your head, baby. It's hard work, but keep trying and you'll get it." Amadeo doesn't recall ever having praised Angel for hard work—and certainly not for lifting her head, which seems like a low bar—yet Angel has turned out to be remarkably resilient.

That night Amadeo intercepts his mother as she walks in the door, laden with grocery bags, the plastic handles cutting into her wrists. "Mom, listen. Can you take my flyers to work? Pass them out? I can't believe I didn't think of this before."

His mother's coworkers do this kind of thing, swap favors and support each other's enterprises. For years Yolanda has been bringing home vitamins and health drinks and cosmetics from one or another of "the girls" at work. While the state's dilatory business creeps along, interminable meetings arranged and attended, meaningless press conferences held, bills proposed and drafted that will never see the light of day, other business flourishes in the halls and offices of the Capitol building: turquoise jewelry is haggled over, Super Bowl pools bought into, home-made tamales and tortillas pulled from coolers and tucked snugly into desk drawers until five o'clock. All around the circular halls, money is changing hands, private economies prospering. When Amadeo was a kid, whenever his school held magazine or chocolate fund-raisers, while his friends trudged door to door or sat bored in hot supermarket park-ing lots, Amadeo had only to send his mother to work with the order form and wait for his incentive prizes to roll in.

Yolanda detangles herself from the bags, but shows no sign of put-ting the groceries away. She leans against the counter and rubs her eyes so violently that Amadeo winces. "Oh, honey, I'm not so sure."

"You never believe in me!" Glancing at his daughter feeding the baby in the living room, he lowers his voice. "I need a support system."

Yolanda's lips part, and she seems about to say something, then to change her mind. She holds her hand out for the flyers. "I'll take them."

Yolanda drives herself to her appointment at the Cancer Center, sits tethered to the IV for hours while toxic fluids are pumped into her. Some people sit in recliners, but because she can't bear to make conversation, Yolanda prefers to lie on one of the raised beds with the pink curtain shut around her. Beyond, a man murmurs weakly while his daughter encourages him. A television chatters. Two women—sisters?—with similarly robust voices complain about the parking, the facilities, the care. "I'm getting me an appointment at Mayo in Phoenix." Very close, the pages of a magazine turn. Here you can almost convince yourself that chemotherapy is as routine and harmless as a trip to the hair salon.

She settles against the pillow, arms limp. The sleeves of her sweater are rolled. She's weightless and warm under the cotton blanket. Her last sensation is of the pull of the tape on the back of her hand, and then she's gulped under into a black sleep.

When Yolanda wakes to the clinic's cool light and whir, Anthony is standing at her bedside. Not Anthony as he was when she last saw him, paunchy, face bloated with addiction and unhappiness, but as he was when he was a teenager, when Yolanda was still a kid looking up to him and her cousin Elwin: athletic and slender, his hair a mop.

After Elwin's Rosary, as the old people dabbed at their eyes and sipped coffee in Fidelia's living room, Anthony, in his new suit, found her. Without a word, he drew her to him and did not let go, sobbing into her hair. She'd stroked his back, murmuring, and had felt, beneath her sadness, a swelling sense of herself as a woman, offering comfort. After, her dress had been creased where it was pressed between them.

Anthony's hand rests on the blanket near her shoulder, a crescent of white under each clean nail. He watches her with steady brown eyes. His lips are chapped.

"You're here," she says with surprise.

He tips his head, gravely considering.

The breath stills in her chest. She's afraid of what he will say to her.

He reaches toward her and slowly runs a single nail along the back of her hand, along where the needle pierces her skin. Yolanda wants to flinch, to jerk her arm away, but she only watches, sickened, as his nail scrapes up the crepey skin of her arm. It doesn't hurt, but everything in her shrinks from his touch. He moves slowly, watching her face all the while, until he's reached her elbow. Her heart gives a sick thump. Eyes widening, he pushes his finger under her sleeve, then grins, his stretched lips taut and pale.

Yolanda's eyes are dry and burning. When she blinks, Anthony is gone.

A moment later, the technician comes with a paper cup of water to detach Yolanda from the tubes. "You've got someone to drive you, hon?" Yolanda nods and pushes through the pink curtain and makes for the hallway, not even bothering to fluff her flattened hair.

Without allowing herself to think, Yolanda gets behind the wheel, bilious and shaking, the sweat seeping from her cold skin. Her flesh is tight under the tape and the gauze where the needle was withdrawn.

Anthony was a dream, Yolanda tells herself. No: a hallucination. Dr. Konecky warned her that hallucinations would come. Or he was the son of one of the other patients, or even a patient himself, a creepy young man who slipped behind Yolanda's pink curtain, and Yolanda, in her haze of sickness and exhaustion and emotion, the tumor threatening to smother her clarity, jumped to the wildest possible conclusion. Her husband is dead, and therefore not wandering the halls of the Cancer Center.

But while there isn't a mark from his touch on her skin, she can still feel the prickling shadow of the scratch, the pressure of his nail as it traveled up her arm, the eerie violation of his finger under her sleeve, and she knows that his presence was real.

Anthony, the father of her children, her one love, her one ruinous love. Yolanda sucks in air noisily as a wave of nausea passes over her.

———

ON THE HIGHWAY north toward home, Yolanda speeds, trying to out-run Anthony, but he's there with her, vivid and insistent.

After she made him move out, he came back just once. Yolanda arrived home from work to find him screaming at the children, drunk. Amadeo's lunch box was splayed on the kitchen floor, the plastic cracked. Sticky wrappings scattered, and a juice box leaked onto the linoleum.

"Daddy, stop." Valerie put an arm around her father, and Anthony pushed her off him roughly. Amadeo stood frozen by the door. "It's our fault," Valerie told Yolanda. "We were fighting. Dodo wouldn't put his lunch box away."

"Take your brother to your room," said Yolanda, and dutifully, chin trembling, Valerie led him away.

Anthony slid to the floor against the cabinet, his cries getting qui-eter and quieter.

Yolanda stood over him, still holding her purse. "Did you hurt them?"

"No." His voice was injured, bleary.

"You need to leave."

"Please, Yo. Let me come home." The silence dilated between them, punctuated by his sniffles. Finally he said, "I loved Elwin."

Yolanda was exhausted, wrung. "We all loved Elwin," she said coldly. "That was thirteen years ago."

"I really loved Elwin," he said. When he looked up, his eyes were red and swimming and imploring. "Yolanda, I'm gay."

The words skewered her. "No you're not. You're a selfish, mean drunk."

How she wishes, now, she had responded differently. How she wishes she hadn't been so hurt and afraid and furious. Poor Anthony, a kid crushed under longing he didn't know what to do with, in the claustrophobia of those times and this village, of the church and his parents' home, suffering from the loss of the first boy he'd ever loved. No wonder he sought every escape he could; no wonder he turned his desire from gold into straw, transformed it into an open-mawed chem-ical hunger that devoured them all.

By the time he finally showed himself to Yolanda, it was too late. She didn't know how to tell him, then, that she could, eventually, accept that part of him, but not the rages and drunkenness and certainly not the heroin. At the time, she needed to clear him from her life entirely. It took all her strength to make him leave.

Now, as she drives, she rewrites the scene, says the things she wishes she'd said: I don't mind that you are gay. We are family and you are our children's father and they need you. Maybe that acceptance would have been enough to pull him back from the edge.

Just beyond Pojoaque, her breath still short, Yolanda sees the blue-red flash in her rearview mirror. "Shit," she says, yanked back to the present. She slows, and the car vibrates over the corrugated edge of asphalt.

She watches through the side mirror as the cruiser pulls smoothly behind her.

"License and registration." *Ernie Montoya*, his name tag says. He shows her his badge, which, even though she knows it's part of the procedure, knows it's the law, strikes her as a courteous gesture.

Ernie Montoya is in his early forties, a few silver hairs gleaming in his buzz cut. He has a smooth moon-shaped face, a shadow of whiskers above his upper lip. "That was a forty-five zone," he says, examining her license. "You were going seventy." He nudges his chin back up the road. "Right through town, ma'am. Little kids could be crossing the road there."

She nearly argues that no little kids cross the road there, that it's clearly a highway, and that if little kids *are* crossing the road, then their parents are the ones who should be arrested.

You hear about women getting off for flirting, for crying. Yolanda crafts her defense: I've never had a speeding ticket. Not once since I was sixteen! I follow rules! *I'm* the one always telling people to slow down. She could say, I have cancer.

He taps the inside of her car door through the window. "Wait here."

It takes a long time for him to note her license plate, to type it all into his little laptop, to say whatever he has to say to his partner, whose face is obscured by the light of the setting sun on the cruiser's windshield. With a shock she realizes that her doctors must surely have reported her to the DMV for her faulty brain; he's going to see the note on her record and take her away in handcuffs. While Yolanda waits, caught, oblivious cars crest the rise, slow when they see the cruiser. They whoosh by, sending dry wind over her face.

When Ernie Montoya returns, he rests his hands again on the window, his fingers inches from her shoulder. He looks grave. The jig is up, her secret is out, and the burden of its weight will be lifted from her. Yolanda wants to be seen. She wants her name entered into the computer, anchoring her solidly in the world.

But Ernie Montoya just says regretfully, "I'm going to have to give you a citation."

Tears sting her eyes.

"Don't feel bad," says Ernie Montoya. "Everyone gets tickets. I did myself, just last year, up there in Colorado. Really, it's not that big a deal."

"That's it? Just a ticket?"

He laughs. "What, you want to go to jail?" He smiles kindly and hands her the citation with her driver's license. "Your license expires end of next month. Don't forget to renew it. People forget all the time, and that carries a doozy of a fine."

By the end of next month she might be blind. By the end of next month she might be in a hospital bed, hooked up to machines. She might be gone.

"Hey, don't be too hard on yourself, Ms. Padilla. I mean it. Drive safe." Ernie Montoya taps the edge of her window one last time.

As she watches him pull back onto the highway, she thinks of Anthony, her husband, touching her with that single nail, and she's filled with grief for their broken, damaged love, and for the life they never had together. She's filled with grief for her children, who will have to go on without her.

One afternoon in August, Amadeo practices on a tiny last divot on his truck's windshield, and then decides it's about time to change the oil and filter. He's allowed to work on his truck, after all. The birds are noisy in the trees. Across the road, the leaves of the corn in the Romeros' little plot droop in graceful resignation and the feathery tassels tickle the breeze. He pauses every once in a while to check for texts from Brianna, despite the fact that she's told him she tries not to text at school.

Amadeo has been in good spirits, hasn't had anything to drink since that first date, and doesn't even miss it, or not so much anyway. When he needs to unwind, sink away from himself, or to celebrate, he remembers that he's closest to being the person he wants to be than he has ever been before.

What he's doing isn't necessarily a betrayal of his daughter. After all, things might work out with Brianna. They might get married, and Angel would get her idol for a stepmother. Angel loves her! Still, he's listed Brianna in his phone as *DWI Class Teacher.*

When he's with Brianna, he forgets about his other life completely. The world vibrates with possibility. This morning at dawn, for instance, the air fresh and dry and chilly, making him feel clean despite the sticky aftermath of sex. Riding home beside Brianna along the empty blacktop with a light heart, the quiet easy between them, they watched the mountain's shadow recede as the sun rose behind it, everything painted in the brightening pale wash of morning. He took Brianna's hand, and she smiled as if she understood his elation.

He's draining the old oil into a cut-open milk jug when Angel comes out, stomping across the gravel.

"Hey," he calls to her sneakered feet.

"Dad." She doesn't squat to peer under at him. "Ryan Johnson wants to come meet the baby."

"Who?" Amadeo wriggles out, lifting himself painfully over the gravel, and squints up, wiping sweat from his face with his bicep. His hands are slick with oil.

Angel looks at the sky. "His father."

Fear scissors through him. "Whose father?" Amadeo is aware that he's playing dumb, and playing it badly, because he doesn't want Connor's life to open up to include people he doesn't know and hasn't vetted. Somehow he'd allowed himself to forget that there *is* a father.

Amadeo is curious, too, however. Because who was this guy who managed to get his daughter naked? He pictures a charmer, a thick-lashed handsome boy.

"He's coming in twenty minutes, so could you just be here?"

"You told him where we live?" He sits up. Angel tears the skin edging her thumbnail. She seems almost afraid. "Is he dangerous? Do you think he might—" Hurt her, he means, but not just that. Did this guy force himself on her? At the thought, a queasy fury passes through him, sharpening at the prospect of an actual target. He would kill this guy.

"No," says Angel, catching his expression, and her face screws up in annoyance. "Just be here, okay, Dad? Like, in the room?"

Amadeo scrubs his hands and face. He'd like a shower, but he wants to be in position when this kid shows up. So he waits, smelling of body odor and engine grease, while Angel gets ready.

She looks no less nervous when she emerges in her maternity jeans and a tank top, the fat white straps of her nursing bra digging into her shoulders. She reeks of perfume, Yolanda's Shalimar, a middle-aged lady smell. Across her cheeks the foundation is thick and matte like clay. Her lipstick is shimmery pink and sticky.

"You look good."

"I look like ass," she says bleakly. "Nothing fits."

"Hey, no. You're losing weight already."

"Whatever. I can hide behind Connor." She lifts the baby from his bouncer by his upper arms and swings him over to her lap. "Could you at least change your shirt before he gets here? And don't you dare start drinking."

He doesn't even defend himself, just goes to put on a shirt that won't shame her.

Ryan Johnson shows up in a beat-up dark green minivan. They watch in silence from the window. The kid looks around as if he doesn't understand how he got here. They wait for him to approach the house, hunt for a doorbell, then squeak open the screen to knock.

Angel gestures impatiently for Amadeo to answer the door.

Ryan is not the handsome vato Amadeo pictured, but a skinny curly-haired blond with a yellowing whitehead swelling his nose. It seems like a character flaw that he hasn't popped the pimple. "Hi." The kid flashes an anxious smile at Amadeo and, behind him, Angel, revealing a lot of fleshy, pink gum. His teeth are small and a little thin-looking, as if he didn't get enough calcium during some critical years. But it's a sweet smile, and Amadeo is relieved that this kid is a harmless dork.

"Hey." Angel starts bouncing Connor industriously on her hip as if to quiet him, except that he's limp and asleep.

Amadeo reaches for the baby, but Angel elbows him away. She fiddles with the orange feet on Connor's suit, straightening, smoothing. There's always something to adjust on a baby.

Angel doesn't offer him a seat. Ryan smiles again, this time more of a joyless grimace. He tugs at the misshapen hem of his blue T-shirt. Amadeo imagines that the boy's mother chose it to match his eyes.

Amadeo watches Ryan watch the baby. The kid has the pallor and posture of an egg noodle. "I can't believe it," Ryan says. His eyes are wide with feeling.

"Can't believe what?" Angel's voice is surly, and no one replies.

"I would have come before," he tells Amadeo, "but Angel"—he darts a worried look at her—"I only just found out last night. I swear I would have come before."

"That's great," Amadeo says encouragingly.

Everyone's eyes are on the baby, as everyone's eyes always are, but it's particularly pronounced now, when no one can bear to look at anyone else.

"Want a Coke?" Amadeo is already filling cups with ice, welcoming the grinding clatter of the ice maker. He pours soda over the crackling ice, passes the glasses around.

Angel sips, and Amadeo remembers too late that she no longer drinks soda.

"Oh, here." He reaches for her glass. "I forgot. Let me get milk for you."

Angel waves him off. "It's cool."

"I didn't know you had a dad," says Ryan. "For some reason I thought he was dead."

Amadeo starts. "You thought I was dead?"

"He's not dead. Obviously. I just don't talk about him much."

"Gee, thanks," says Amadeo, ready to joke. See? He's not reading insult into every little thing. He chuckles gamely.

"School's pretty good this year," Ryan says.

Silence.

"You like school, Ryan?" Amadeo has got to quit watching television. The scene he's in now is Father Meets Daughter's Boyfriend, and the role calls for him to be cheerful, hapless, well-meaning. Except that Amadeo is no television father and this kid is not Angel's boyfriend.

"I like it okay. I play basketball."

"JV," says Angel.

"How do you know I haven't moved up?" He clutches his knobby wrists. "You weren't at school for practically all year last year."

"I know you're not on varsity."

Amadeo begins to feel bad for the kid. "Here, sit," he tells them.

Angel obeys, but when Ryan sits next to her on the couch, she scoots away so she's wedged against the armrest.

"Why is his head like that? So bumpy."

Offense flares in Amadeo, but Angel just shrugs. "His skull bones are still moving around."

Ryan extends a long finger, lets it hover over the black curls, but then thinks better of it, and touches Connor's red fist instead. "Hi, little dude." He sits back against the cushions, but his eyes don't stray from the baby.

Amadeo peers at Connor, trying to see a resemblance between him and Ryan. Connor did not get Ryan's long face or weak chin, certainly not his coloring. But there is something in the shape of his mouth.

"Can I hold him?" Ryan asks.

"He's your kid, too." Her tone is bitter, but then she says, more softly, "Sure." She places Connor in Ryan's arms. The maneuver requires her to get near him, but once the baby has been transferred, she retreats to the corner of the couch again. She drags her legs up.

Ryan draws Connor cautiously toward his skinny chest. He seems relieved when Angel takes the baby back.

"So how did you two meet?" Amadeo immediately regrets asking, because the question seems just a hair away from asking how Connor was conceived.

"Geometry," Angel says flatly. "Mrs. Esposito."

"Angel's really good at geometry. Was. I called her Angle. Obtuse Angle. For, like, a joke." Ryan laughs, a dweeby, breathy laugh. Amadeo pictures him powering through a clumsy flirtation, maybe yanking a braid or two. He wouldn't have expected a math joke to work on his daughter, but maybe that just shows how little he knows her.

Angel's face has reddened. "I hated that class."

"It wasn't bad. I have her again, third period."

Angel stares down at the baby angrily. A long silence, before Amadeo asks, "So what are you learning in math now? Maybe you could help fill Angel in."

His daughter flashes him a furious glance.

Ryan stands and wipes his hands on his jeans. "I guess I should go."

Later, Amadeo ventures, "Weird that Connor is half white." Then, when Angel doesn't reply, "He doesn't seem like a bad kid, Ryan."

Yolanda still isn't home. Angel has just changed and fed Connor, and now he's sprawled asleep on the couch. Connor screws up his face, irritated in his sleep, and thrusts his dimpled chin up. The scowl loosens.

"Good for him for coming by. Not all guys would." Amadeo is

thinking of the moment at the very end of Ryan's visit that neither he nor Angel has mentioned. Ryan stepped toward Angel, pressed his lips against the baby's forehead, and didn't remove them for a long time, the seconds ticking by while Amadeo and Angel watched him, aghast. Finally, he looked up and said quietly, "It's crazy, but I love him."

Angel appeared not to have heard Ryan then, and she appears not to hear Amadeo now. She inspects her thumbnail.

A scary thought occurs to Amadeo, the kind of thought that would have occurred months ago to a responsible adult. "Wait, his family, they're not going to try to take him away, are they?"

"He's not going to tell his mom. She'd be pissed. I shouldn't've even told *him* about it. I guess I wanted him to feel like shit, since I did. I think he did, too."

Amadeo is troubled by the implication: that it wasn't obvious to Ryan and everyone else at Angel's school who the father was, that there were other boys in the mix. Amadeo also doesn't believe anyone could keep a secret this big from his own mother, especially not someone as basically sweet as Ryan appears to be.

"I wish I hadn't told him. I don't want him coming around. I don't want him holding him again." She stands with effort and scoops up the baby. "I'm putting him to bed."

Before lunch, Angel stops by the nursery to feed Connor. It takes longer than usual—he is distracted and keeps pulling away to babble at her—so she is last to come out to the patio. On the horizon, purple clouds are mounding. The other girls have already crowded around the first picnic table, spread their sandwiches and string cheese and carrots. The wrappers flap in the wind. Angel looks skeptically at the second picnic table, where Jen sits alone, eating an apple and texting one-handed.

"Scooch," Lizette orders Ysenia. She doesn't look at Angel, but indicates with her thumb where Angel should sit beside her, and takes another bite of her sandwich.

"I was here," Ysenia protests, but she moves down nonetheless, pulling her lunch with her.

Angel squeezes in, puzzled and pleased, because it's the first time since her falling-out with Priscilla last fall that anyone's saved her a place for lunch, and she's forgotten how good it feels to be awaited. "Hey," she says to the table at large, but mostly to Lizette.

Lizette nods in curt acknowledgment. Angel, aware of Lizette and Ysenia pressed on either side of her, their warm thighs and upper arms, opens her lunch bag carefully so as not to bump them.

"Don't get too excited. It's just turkey." Lizette brandishes her own floppy sandwich, the pale wheat bread damp and smooth from the plastic wrap.

After that, at lunch and in the classroom, it's understood that Angel's seat is beside Lizette, and the other girls make way for her, just as they make way for Christy and Trinity.

Angel isn't sure why Lizette picked her, and certainly Lizette never indicates that she has reasons—Lizette's attention is like grace: unasked for, undeserved, and, Angel suspects, sometimes terrible.

———

AT COMMUNITY MEETING on Friday, Brianna announces that, in pairs, they're going to do research projects on the culture and parenting practices in a country of their choice. "So I want you to find a partner and let me know Monday what country you want to research. Think about places you're curious about. You can consult the library or the internet. This is your opportunity to take a kind of trip to a part of the world you've never seen."

Angel thinks about African babies nursing as their mothers pound roots, of South American babies strapped to their mothers' backs with colorful cloths, of fancy English kids singing and dancing along with Mary Poppins.

Lizette raises her hand, a single lazy flap. "Me and Angel are going to do Finland." She says it as though they've discussed it already, as though they knew anything about this project to begin with.

Brianna starts. "Finland. Okay," she says slowly. "Anyone else have ideas?"

Jen looks around the room. "Anyone want to do China with me? My pastor did missionary work in China, so we'd have a head start."

Lizette is hunched over her desk, her chin almost touching the *Cosmo* lying open before her, her sleeves pulled over her hands. She seems intent on Community Meeting. It was nice of her to decide to work with Angel, though it would have been nicer if she'd consulted Angel. And Finland? Angel is aware that Finland is a country, possibly in Siberia or Europe, but has no image at all of Finnish children. She thinks they must be either very blond or very dark and dressed in polar bear skins.

The typed outline is due at the end of next week, full ten-to-twelve-page reports and presentations—with visual aids—a week after that. "You are encouraged but not required to cook a native dish for the class to try." Brianna consults her notes. "Okay. Any other issues that have come up for you this week? Trinity, spit out the gum." She taps *Respect the classroom and equipment.* "You know better."

Trinity spits her gum into her hand. "Sorry, miss." She shakes her hand over the trash until the wad unsticks from her palm.

Angel considers bringing up Ryan Johnson and her quivery feeling that she made a dreadful mistake in telling him about Connor, but she isn't sure she wants her class knowing about him.

She doesn't even know why she told him. "Hi, Angle!" he'd chirped. He'd called out of the blue to see "what's up," without mentioning the baby or her pregnancy, as if it might embarrass her. "You're not missing much at school. I have Mrs. Esposito again, so that's cool." Angel had been furious that Ryan could be so cheerfully oblivious to his part in her exile. Listening to him go on about the basketball team's win against Los Alamos, she'd felt so desolate she had to say something to stop him in his tracks. "The baby's yours, too, so you can quit being so proud of yourself. I'm not the only one who fucked up."

"Wait, are you for serious? It's *mine*?"

"*He* is yours. Don't act so surprised. You know how babies are made, right? You heard why I dropped out and you didn't even wonder?"

"I don't know," he said. "I'm, like, on the honor roll."

She'd hung up on him, but an hour or so later he called back, and didn't quit until she agreed to let him come over. In the last few days, he's texted constantly, just to say hello and to ask about the baby. He hasn't threatened to take Connor away from her, but she still has the sense that with Ryan on the scene things are even more out of her control.

"Hey, miss," says Ysenia. "I pick Paris for my country report. Their kids never sass, and they're all fashionable. I saw that on *Good Morning America*."

"Yes!" says Jen. "And Paris moms never gain weight."

"Paris isn't a country, dumbass," says Lizette.

"Out," Brianna tells Lizette. Her response is so swift and cutting that the breath freezes in Angel's chest, a cold sealed cavity. "Get out now, Lizette. You may not speak to another person that way in my class-room." Brianna jabs the air.

Lizette's eyes flash wide in fear. Then her face smooths, and she flips her hair. "All right." She gathers her purse and magazine. "See y'all," she says to the students, lips pursed sardonically. Angel watches, dismayed. Lizette winks.

"*Now*, Lizette." Brianna is still pointing at the door. She lowers her hand as if it's an alien object and puts it in her pocket. "Wait for me in the hall."

Christy starts giggling, her face turning red and unhappy. "Chris, stop it," Trinity whispers.

"Any other issues for Community Meeting?" Brianna asks. "Well, then. Adjourned. You can spend the last twenty minutes until dismissal reading silently." She follows Lizette to the hallway, and though Angel strains to hear, she can't even pick up murmurs.

Later, on her way out, laden with Connor and her backpack and dia-per bag, Brianna calls to her from the classroom door.

"Could I see you for a moment, please, Angel?"

"Sure." She approaches Brianna's desk with the uneasy feeling that she's done something wrong.

"I noticed that Lizette volunteered you to be her partner for the for-eign country project. Are you okay with that?"

"Yeah," Angel says. "Course."

"I just wanted to check. I remember being your age and getting saddled with partners who didn't pull their weight. I know how frus-trating that can be for a good student." Brianna's forehead creases as if she's very troubled. "I'm glad Lizette has you as a friend. It's good of you. And maybe you can help her. But listen"—Brianna tugs a strand of Angel's hair gently, and Angel flushes and steps back, remembering about boundaries—"unhappy people, they can try to bring you down."

"She won't bring me down." Angel wants Brianna to tug her hair again—the unexpected affection felt so good—but Brianna is scruti-nizing her own nails.

"How are things at home?" Brianna asks. "Your dad doing okay?"

"My dad? Yeah, everyone's good."

"I'm glad. Everyone in good spirits?"

Angel nearly mentions Ryan Johnson. Maybe Brianna has advice. But Angel's scalp prickles. She has the sense that this is an important moment, that her character is being tested. "Listen, I know you don't like Lizette, but—"

"I don't not like Lizette. That's just not the case at all."

"I mean, I know she can seem disrespectful, but she's had a sad life. She's an orphan."

Brianna nods, that professional enamel hardening. "Be that as it may, Angel, everyone is subject to the classroom rules, and I'd be remiss if I didn't hold her to the same high standards as everyone else."

When Yolanda can't sleep, she walks up and down the length of the house. The pain is a ball of clay behind her eyes. Sometimes, by pressing the heels of her hands into her skull, she can push the clay into a manageable shape, and it will stay more or less contained for up to a minute.

Now, after two in the morning, the house, with its cinderblock walls, feels tomb-like, so Yolanda eases the front door open and steps outside into the cool air. But the night is so immense, and the stars scattered sharp and high are so coldly beautiful, that Yolanda flees back inside.

This evening, as they were watching television, Yolanda surprised herself by beginning to cry. The commercial was sad, sure, involving a girl and her old dog and a kindly father, but Yolanda is not usually vulnerable to sentimentality.

"Are you crying, Gramma?" Angel asked.

"No." Yolanda laughed through her tears. Who was she identifying with, anyway: the girl? The father? The dying dog?

"You're crying over an insurance commercial?" Angel jostled her with her elbow.

"Get a grip, Mom," Amadeo said affectionately. "Geez, what a softy."

All at once Yolanda remembered: "Your dad wanted to get you a dog, Dodo. You loved your stuffed dog, and he wanted you to have a real one." Anthony had harped on it for weeks during a manic phase in that last year of their marriage, and Yolanda had argued against it, because the care and feeding would fall to her. Amadeo hadn't even, in the beginning, wanted a real dog, not until Anthony gave him the hard sell, and she'd resented Anthony for putting her in the role of the starchy, mean mother. "Do you remember?"

Amadeo appeared not to have heard her, and even this struck her as funny. The hilarity swept her up and up. She glimpsed herself in the mirrored back of the doll cabinet and was startled by her stretched lips, her face glistening grotesquely in the lamplight. Fear stuttered across Angel's smile, so Yolanda gasped, dragged a sob back into herself.

"Whoa boy." She wiped her eyes. "Don't know what's got into me."

They swiveled their heads back to the television, chuckling. The whole episode ended before the commercial break.

"Mom," Amadeo said, "we need more cheese. Get the sharp cheddar. That Mexican blend don't taste like nothing."

Yolanda wants to prepare her children for her absence, but she can't bear the thought of them imagining the world without her, as if by imagining it, they will push her one step closer to total erasure. Still, she longs to unburden herself. At the supermarket, a girl with bleached hair barely glances at Yolanda as she scans her groceries. I'm dying! Yolanda imagines telling her. I'm dying, she imagines telling Monica Gutierrez-Larsen or Sylvie Archuleta or Bunny Flores. She pictures the compassion that would roll out and surround her like fog. She would fall backward, let her bones and aching head sink into that compassion.

She thinks of this bedroom enduring without her. All her belongings, so carefully chosen, so carefully tended. Who will appreciate her dressing table, her satin lampshade, the lace curtains she hand-washes each year? Valerie, Yolanda knows, thinks it's all tacky. If it's up to her, Valerie will deposit it in the Goodwill parking lot after hours. Maybe, Yolanda thinks hopefully, one of the girls will want her bed.

Why does she spend so much time thinking about sadness? She doesn't have to, she realizes. She doesn't have to grieve what she will never see: Lily in college, maybe with contacts and some cute clothes; Sarah—what?—playing professional soccer?; Angel as an adult, married, perhaps, to a man who will give her the stability she needs to catch up on everything she's missing out on. Connor walking and talking and starting school, becoming a full person. These futures aren't hers anyway, were never promised to her, were never promised to any of them. Yolanda doesn't have to keep banging her head against that terrible, immutable fact. She doesn't even have to see the fact as particularly terrible.

Instead she can enjoy the time she has left. She can gaze up into the pink of her canopy bed. *Allow the body to be a colander*, recommends the *Mindfulness for Pain* CD they gave her. She just has to let the pain pass through her on its way to somewhere else.

Yolanda is aware that this clarity will dart out of sight any moment, that she will, more than likely, wake up tomorrow to a brain cluttered with all the usual preoccupations. But this glimmer, regardless of how brief it may be, surely counts for something. Even when it is lost to her, this glimmer will be like a window open in a distant room of a rambling, stuffy house, stirring the air. She can see the dust motes swirling, golden and mesmerizing.

On Monday, Angel and Lizette meet after school to work on their project.

Lizette's house, where she lives with her older brother and his girlfriend, is on a dead-end in a run-down development. The homes are identical: brown stucco with six ornamental vigas poking out just below the roofline, a small weed yard. At the end of the street, where the asphalt meets a low cinderblock wall, the desert stretches.

"How old's your brother?" Angel asks, slowing her pace to match Lizette's.

"Twenty-one."

"Cool," says Angel. "So he can buy for you." She wants Lizette to think she has a wild side.

Lizette shrugs.

It's a windy afternoon, and the sky is pale and dusty, but with heavy monsoon clouds banked at the horizon. Although Mercedes has been fussing the twenty minutes or so from Smart Starts!, Lizette moves without urgency, with her rolling fat-girl walk. Angel left her father's truck in the lot because they only had the one car seat, and now she is impatient and neck-sore and sweaty, regretting she didn't bring the stroller, antsy to put down Connor and her bags. Also, for some reason, she's tongue-tied and nervous.

"I'm just up here." Lizette lifts two fingers from Mercedes's back to gesture.

Before them is a junkyard of car parts. Engines lurk in the weeds, dark and greasy, and tools and bolts and other choking hazards scatter across the surface of a bent Formica table. The garage gapes, spilling still more automotive bounty, as well as a massive unfurling roll of plastic garbage bags, the end of which flaps taut and threatening in the wind. In the driveway, a rusting motorcycle lists to the side on its frail kickstand.

Angel imagines Connor pinned by the bike, his fragile skull crushed and his face ground into the dirt. Somehow, when she was pregnant, it had never occurred to her that Connor would be born mortal, vulnerable to the forces of the world. It hadn't occurred to her that it was within the realm of possibility that she might outlive him. She squeezes the image from her mind, afraid—as always—that she is inviting the universe to visit upon her son this very brutality. She smiles down at him bravely, and he offers his drool-soaked fist. She can't forget that she told him she hated him. "I'll be good," she murmurs into his scalp. "I promise you I'll be good. I promise so much, baby."

To Angel's relief, Lizette passes the junky house and turns up the walk at the last house, where a prim blue wicker wreath hangs on the door. Here the weeds are almost pretty, high and green, some dotted with tiny yellow flowers. Angel is ashamed that she expected the worst of Lizette. Someone has cleared a small plot, slightly off-center, and planted tomatoes. They droop against their wire cages like adolescents. "That's nice," says Angel. "Your brother's girlfriend do that?"

"My brother. Me and her hate tomatoes." Tilting back so Mercedes rests on her chest and both hands are free, Lizette rummages through her diaper bag. "I can never find my fucking keys."

In the front window is posted a handwritten *Beware of Dog* sign, though there is not, as far as Angel knows, a dog. At least she hopes there isn't. Dogs have always scared her, ever since she was eight and Priscilla's stepdad's Rottweiler lunged at her. Again she tightens her hold on Connor. She heard once about a pit bull that ate a baby right out of its crib.

If the dog shows any sign of aggression, any whatsoever, even just mild exuberance, she'll take Connor and leave, never mind if Lizette thinks she's uncool. Angel carries Connor to the plants, shading his patchy scalp with her palm. "See? Tomatoes." They dangle as shriveled and tender as testicles. Connor humors her, frowning seriously for a moment at her finger, before shifting his gaze to the fascinating chaos next door that threatens to breach the property line.

On the porch, Mercedes starts wailing in earnest. Lizette has set her on the concrete, and she kicks vigorously, her eyes cinched against the sun.

"Are you sure the ground's not hot? I can hold her."

"Found 'em." Lizette swoops down and deposits the squalling infant back on her shoulder. Her upper arms are splotched pink.

"You got a dog?"

"Nah. That's to scare thieves. I told my brother it wouldn't work."

Angel is heartened by the specter of this brother, house-proud and fussy. Surely Mercedes and Lizette are in good hands.

"What we really need is to toss shit all over the yard."

Inside, the drawn curtains glow yellow with the afternoon. The air is mossy from the swamp cooler. Angel steps cautiously after her friend, as if a dog still might leap out at her from the shadows.

Any tidiness seems to have remained outside; as Angel follows Lizette to the back of the house, she gets the general impression of *stuff*: piles of laundry, boxes of Pampers, and loose rolls of toilet paper, bags of chips and shoes and dishes on every surface. It's the result, Angel supposes, of people who are basically kids living together unsupervised. Her real concern, Angel realizes, isn't attacking dogs or falling motorcycles, but the uncle. He served a prison sentence—just a few months, though. She doesn't think he comes by, but still.

"They let him out?" Angel asked, dismayed, when Lizette mentioned this at lunch a couple weeks ago.

"He's on parole. It's not like I see him. Just barely one time at my cousin's." Her brother went with him once to the mud bog races. Lizette didn't even seem upset when she related this. "Joe feels bad for him. His life is shit, which, good. My cousins won't even talk to him, but they barely talk to me either, so."

Angel had wanted to ask why Lizette didn't have an abortion, but suspects that arranging a procedure would have been tantamount to admitting what had happened to her. The logistics were scary and impossible enough for Angel, and Angel wasn't raped. Plus, it feels obscene to ask such a question in front of Mercedes, who is so adorable that to imagine her never existing is sad.

"Do you like your brother's girlfriend?" Angel calls now over Mercedes's cries.

"Selena's cool," Lizette says. Angel strains to hear her, because, as if unwilling to concede anything to anyone, she doesn't raise her voice over the baby's screams. "She's, like, obsessed with Mercedes, always telling Joe she wants one. But I think they're going to break up soon. They don't say it, but they're always fighting. She's gotten into chiva. Not bad or nothing, but it bugs my brother. He won't touch it 'cause that's how our mom died."

"God." Angel wants to offer sympathy, but doesn't know how Lizette will react. She hopes the girlfriend does leave, and soon, taking all her drugs with her.

Lizette pops a finger in Mercedes's mouth, and the baby quiets for a moment, then pushes it away. "I really hope they don't break up." Angel is surprised by the note of vulnerability in her voice.

"Yeah." Angel reminds herself that Lizette is motherless and alone, and that this girlfriend of Lizette's brother is family, some of the only family she has left, and retracts her wish. In her own arms, Connor whimpers, irritable, arches his back.

At the end of a dim hall, Lizette pushes open her door. The room is crowded with furniture: unmade single bed with faded black sheets, torn brocade armchair, heavy wood bureau, and, jutting into the middle of the room, a crib. A black beanbag slouches in the corner. On the walls are Kanye and Jay-Z posters, and, incongruously, given what Angel knows of Lizette's tastes, a quilted pink *L*. Angel thinks of Lizette's dead mother, choosing that pink *L* for her little girl, taking it home and hammering a nail in the wall. She wonders how much later that mother died.

"If they do break up, which one'll stay here in the house?"

Lizette sinks into the sagging armchair and maneuvers under her shirt, exposing a fold of belly. She grabs a pair of sweatpants off the floor to cover herself, and, almost without looking, gets Mercedes positioned. The crying ceases. "I don't ask. The only good thing is they got four more months on the lease, so I'm not homeless yet."

At that word, *homeless*, Angel misses a breath. "But even if your brother leaves, you're going to move with him, right?"

"I don't know. He won't want me hanging around, not if he's single. Plus I'm almost eighteen. I could find my own place."

She doesn't even seem worried. Angel nearly says, You can stay with me, at my grandma's, but then looks away. An embarrassed heat overtakes her, and she pats Connor too rapidly to be soothing.

Connor fusses, mouthing the fabric of her T-shirt. Finally, she steps around the tangle of clothes on the floor, perches on the unmade bed, and begins to feed him, too. She hunches and half turns to cover herself. They sit, the only sound the snork and smack of the babies, and the air feels thick. Angel finds that she can't look at Lizette, and trains her eyes on Connor's head instead. Why isn't Lizette more worried about her future? Angel is almost angry at her.

"So I started doing research," Angel says. "The child care over there in Finland is great. Did you know that? They're number one in the world on education."

"I know."

"You picked Finland on purpose?"

Lizette drops her head back, exasperated. "Uh, *yeah*. I heard a lady in the office talking to some other lady about it. I wanted us to get the best country."

Angel regards Lizette with admiration. "Well, get this. I researched foods. There's lots of crap we can't get, like reindeer, and they got all these crazy berries, like a cloudberry, ever heard of it? But one of their main foods is egg butter, like fourteen hard-boiled eggs mashed up with a whole lot of butter. They smear it on pie."

Lizette repositions a leg of the sweatpants over her shoulder, then swings Mercedes upright and gives her a few firm whacks on the back. "Egg butter? Fucking sick."

"Yeah, but if you think about it, it's basically just egg salad."

"Like I said, fucking sick. Also, who puts egg salad on *pie*? We should cook that for our report and make Brianna eat it."

"Isn't she vegan?"

"You'd know better than me." Lizette gives a crooked, challenging half-smile. Angel's heart starts up a jittery percussion.

The small window is divided into panes by a plastic grid that seems not entirely affixed, and the slanted diamonds of light fall across the floor and a half-full soda bottle. An amber-colored pool of light refracts onto a crumpled white T-shirt, and Angel focuses on this spot.

Her mouth is dry. When did Angel start looking at Lizette like this? Or rather, when did looking at Lizette become so difficult? She is constantly aware of Lizette's movement in the classroom; wherever Lizette is, Angel is oriented toward that place.

Before long, Lizette heaves herself up and deposits Mercedes in the crib. Connor, too, is asleep, his mouth slack.

"So." Angel tugs her shirt down, her movements exaggerated, then stands. She sets Connor beside Mercedes, noting that the crib sheet is none too clean. Good for his immune system, she tells herself. Her back to Lizette, she reattaches her bra, smooths her shirt. Mercedes is not much bigger than Connor, despite being seven months to his three and a half. Her chin is canted up, as if in defiance, but her face is, for once, relaxed. Angel places a flannel blanket over both babies. Then she digs in her backpack for her laptop and notebook. She opens the laptop, a protective barrier.

"There's something I've always wondered," Angel says, though she only wondered it just this minute. "Does all breast milk taste the same?"

Lizette leans against the dresser, sardonic. "Are you asking to suck my titty?"

"No." Angel's cheeks warm. "God! No. I was just wondering. Biologically."

Lizette laughs, an edge of meanness. "You want to suck my fucking titty."

"I don't," Angel says hotly. "You would think that. You think everyone wants to."

"I'll let you if you want to."

Angel trains her burning eyes on the screen, begins clicking randomly. "Shut up."

Lizette kneels before Angel, takes the laptop from her and sets it on the floor. "I'll taste if you taste."

Angel jolts back as Lizette lifts the hem of her shirt. "Jerk," Angel says, without conviction. "Stop making fun of me." She pushes Lizette's head away with her palm, but Lizette's hands are inside Angel's shirt, cupping her breasts, and her mouth is hot on Angel's stomach. Angel's hands drop to her sides. She isn't breathing. She may never breathe again. Lizette unsnaps the front clasp of Angel's bra, and Angel's awful milk-heavy boobs swing free. She puts her arms up protectively, but Lizette nudges her away with her head, as insistent as a dog.

Lizette cups one of Angel's breasts in her hand and squeezes, and Angel gasps at the pang. The pull against her nipple is stronger than Connor's, a little painful, and not erotic. Lizette raises her head, releases the nipple with a little pop. "Yum," she says, and licks her lips. She stands and pushes Angel onto the bed. All the while she holds Angel with those green eyes, and Angel is scooped out with desire. Then she leans in, and Angel raises her head to meet Lizette's mouth with her own.

———

AT HOME THAT NIGHT, Angel can't eat the hamburger her grandmother places before her; she's nauseated and light-headed, her limbs twitchy and unnatural. She thinks of her lips against Lizette's, and her core sloshes.

After Connor's bath, Angel nuzzles him, breathing in his clean milky sweetness. He giggles at her hair and lips on his belly, his red mouth wet and delighted, the gurgle caught in his throat. She covers his head and hands and belly with kisses, both of them laughing. Then, all at once, Angel is troubled by the overlap between this intimacy and the other—the kissing, the nakedness—and she pulls away, bundles him swiftly into his red pajamas. He reaches for her face, but, seeing her expression, the smile fades. When she picks him up, she holds him face-out.

She doesn't *think* kissing him counts as child abuse. But, my god, to think that this afternoon, she did all *that* in front of him, which certainly does count as child abuse. Even if he was asleep, it will at the very least fuck him up severely.

Her worries mutate and multiply: What if Lizette was trying to humiliate her? What if there was a camera, and this time there really are pictures of Angel, naked and compromised, spreading through the internet? Whole videos, even?

By morning, Angel is rigid with tension and sleeplessness. As they mill around before Morning Check-In, Lizette flicks her upper arm. "Hey." Before Angel can respond, Lizette has turned away and is saying something to Christy about a television show.

Could Angel have imagined the events of yesterday? But she's never been especially imaginative: how could she come up with something so outlandish? It seems impossible that she's done the things she's done with the girl at the desk ten feet away, because if they've done those things, how do they manage to be in the same room without setting upon each other?

As Brianna makes announcements—a free résumé workshop at the public library, a used clothing and housewares fair at Sacred Heart of Jesus—a text beeps through on Angel's phone. Angel's heart lurches. She glances at Lizette, who slips her own phone into the purse at her feet.

"Angel," snaps Brianna. "Turn it off and put it away."

"Sorry, miss." She reads it before zipping her phone into her backpack. *Good 2cu xx.*

When she straightens, flushed, Brianna is watching her, stony-faced.

Brianna lies on the brick floor, her head cushioned by the braided rug. Her phone, on speaker, rests on her stomach. It's a Saturday night, and once again Brianna is home in her yoga pants. Later, she will watch several episodes of a BBC mystery about a serial killer in the Outer Hebrides, and she'll fall asleep to the murmur of brogues sifting around her.

She's talking to Sierra in Portland, who is not in for the night, but, rather, getting ready to go out. "Oh, just drinks, then dinner with friends, and then we'll stop by a burlesque show, and then probably a club after." Sierra, it turns out, is sleeping with both a musician and their former human biology professor, who flies up regularly to see her. "I call them 'the Body' and 'the Brain,'" Sierra says. "I can't decide which I like more."

"If you can't pick one, maybe you don't actually like either." Brianna hates her prissiness. But it doesn't seem fair that Sierra bewitches men so casually.

"Maybe. So tell me about the student's dad? That still on?"

Brianna affirms. "I don't know, though. It's fun when it happens, but after I'm like, what am I doing?" She wants to explain how attracted she is to him, how she imagines them together, actually together, sees herself as a young, cool stepmom to Angel, singing together in the kitchen as they make cookies. But she can't tell Sierra this; the fact is that she's ashamed of Amadeo, because he hasn't been to college, doesn't have a job, and that even as she's imagining a future for them, she isn't sure this is the future she wants, but she still wants him.

Sierra is talking to someone else now, her voice muffled as though

266

she's tucked Brianna into her armpit. "Sorry," she says, clear again. "I'm getting wine. Well, I mean, do you have better options?"

Brianna should be offended, but Sierra isn't wrong. She admits that, no, she doesn't. "I spend all day around teenage girls."

"So, go with it. Have fun. It's not like you're going to marry him. In the meantime, there's nothing wrong with getting practice."

Practice. Last time, in bed, he stopped moving above her right in the middle of things. "Can I ask you something? Is it, like, normal, for a girl to say she regrets her baby?"

Brianna had swiped her hair out of her face, pushed herself onto her elbow. "Angel said that? Is she depressed?"

"I don't know," he said, troubled. "Is it bad?"

Brianna had thrilled at his respect for her authority, his trust that she might be able to help them. "I mean, it's definitely normal for her to have mixed feelings. She's had to give up a lot. But, like, is she eating properly? Sleeping? I haven't noticed any changes at school, but I will keep an eye out."

"Can we talk about this later?" he asked, and it was only then that the strangeness of pausing sex to talk about his daughter struck her.

"Well, I'm at the bar," Sierra says now. "Hey!"

"Yeah?"

"No, just saying hi to someone. I should go."

Instead of hanging up, Brianna watches her phone's screen, listening to the joyful sounds of friends meeting up in a distant, exciting city, until the call cuts off. She drops her phone back onto her stomach and it slides onto the brick floor with a clatter. She gazes around the room again: her dimly glowing paper lantern; her wall of art museum postcards; her Klimt poster peeling up in the corner. All the sad artifacts of her careful, small life.

Hi, she texts Amadeo. *What are you up to?*

Each afternoon for the next two weeks, Angel and Lizette arrange study dates after Smart Starts! "Are we going to do our project after school?" Angel will say with studied nonchalance.

Lizette shrugs. "Sure. My house or yours?"

And Angel, as though actually considering bringing Lizette to her grandmother's, where her dad sits in front of the internet all day, mulls it over. "Yours is closer." Neither Lizette's brother nor his girlfriend is ever around.

Angel has already told her father she has to scale back on her work for Creative Windshield Solutions due to a school project, and he doesn't object. Concern for her father flashes to the front of her mind, then dissolves.

Oh, god, Angel thinks, in bed with Lizette. I am a lesbian, and the thought thrills and horrifies her. *Lesbian.* It is a truly gross word, an unwholesome fusion of *lesion* and *alien*. There are, of course, girls at her old school who make out with other girls at parties while guys whoop and holler and try to muscle in, and then there's the small cadre of real lesbians, but they are the weird girls, the determinedly ugly ones with their sports bras and oversized Lobos shirts, baggy jeans and hideous glasses. They have Bieber haircuts or half-buzzed heads. They call themselves artists or are in bands, and they look down on anyone who wants to look like an actual girl. And now Angel is one of them.

Carpet-muncher, lesbo, dyke.

Before, when she considered what lesbians did to each other, it seemed pathetic and desperate. It would be wet and smelly and disgusting. But though she is doing what lesbians do, this doesn't feel disgusting at all. Never did she feel this way with boys. Tenderness, yes. Pity. But not the rich swelling of affection, the unbearable musky love that wells in her. She likes the way they fit together, the safety of it, their bodies neatly matched, the cool slide of skin on skin.

After, Lizette pulls Angel to her, and this is Angel's favorite part, her cheek against Lizette's sweaty chest, their long hair tangled together on the pillow.

Pale hatch marks mar the flesh on Lizette's thighs and left arm, notches scored onto a prison wall. Some are newish, pink and tender; a couple still have a thread of raised scab. Angel counts them like beads on an abacus, each line a record of misery or rage or boredom or whatever it was that made Lizette do this. Angel wants to understand, but knows if she asked, Lizette's wary face would snap shut for good.

———

ON THE AFTERNOON BEFORE their presentation on Finland, they meet at Lizette's to finish their poster and make egg butter.

Lizette clears some dirty dishes and cereal boxes and strewn junk mail from the counter. While the babies play on a blanket on the kitchen floor, Angel sets to peeling the two dozen hard-boiled eggs. The eggs are hot, and Angel's fingers burn as she picks the bits of shell off the slimy whites. The texture puts her in mind of the sheep's eyeball they dissected in biology her first semester of high school.

Lizette, who has refused to peel an egg ("They smell like donkey ass"), presses against her. "Come on."

"Stop it. Help me out." Every time Angel is so grateful when Lizette wants her, so afraid that she won't again.

"You have to let them cool, anyways." Lizette juts her chin at the bedroom. On the floor Mercedes gums an animal cracker, smears the soggy paste all over a pink bear. Beside her, Connor breathes through a snotty nose and pushes himself up on his forearms.

"After we finish. After they fall asleep."

"Fine," Lizette says with a dramatic sigh. "I'll help crack." Taking two eggs in each hand, she whacks them against the counter. The sulfuric funk rises around them.

It's a miracle that the person Angel loves like this should have ended up in her classroom at Smart Starts!, a miracle that she should be able to love like this at all. It's so sudden and astonishing, unthinkable even a week ago. Such a strange progression of chance and error and damage led them to this place.

The project is slow-going, because the shells stick and Angel has to stop to kiss Lizette and to hold Connor, who is under the weather.

"I hope the whole class doesn't catch his cold," Angel says, wiping his nose. "I mean, I'll wash my hands, but still."

"No way anyone's going to eat this shit. Snot would improve it. *Egg butter.*"

———

AFTER, ANGEL PUSHES her lips and nose into the cool curve of Lizette's neck, but Lizette shrugs her off.

"You're squashing me."

"No way. I'm barely touching you." Angel laughs, but not really, and rearranges herself to give Lizette more space. "Are you okay?"

"Shut up."

Lizette's mood is scaring her. She seems to have drifted very far away. It hurts to look at her this close, she's so beautiful: the shape of her lips, the roundness of her cheeks and chin, the dense black lashes around her green eyes, even the two or three tiny pimples on her forehead.

"Lizette?" With her fingers, Angel climbs Lizette's scars like a ladder from forearm to inner elbow to bicep. There are two new marks, tender red gashes.

Why? she wants to ask, but she can't force the word out of her, not with Lizette so distant. What happened since yesterday? Is Angel to blame? She thinks of the blade drawing across skin, the stinging snag of it, and her eyes water. She wants to press that sadness out of Lizette, feel the barrier of skin melt away.

In the crib the babies sprawl, limbs tangled. Connor's damp curls adhere to his temples, Mercedes's straight hair is a sweaty little pelt. Briefly Angel imagines a future for all of them, herself as the mother, Lizette as the tougher man-figure, all four of them in a pretty cottage somewhere green. Oregon, maybe. The babies would grow up together, and she sees them, brother and sister, hand in hand on the playground, looking out for one another. They would create a world without raping uncles or disappointing fathers, without the long parade of men mooching and drinking and yelling and sulking. It would be a safe world for those babies. Lizette would soften and heal, too, would come to love Angel. It might take time, but Angel doesn't mind; Angel is young and can wait.

The egg butter congeals in the refrigerator, the finished poster board waits by the door. After tomorrow, there will be no excuse for Angel to spend every afternoon with Lizette.

"Hey, Lizette. Monday? After Smart Starts!? I thought maybe we could take the babies to the library. To story time."

Lizette opens her eyes, and Angel wills her to train them on her, but she stares at the ceiling. "You wanna hear some lady read kids' books to you?"

"I thought it'd be fun."

"Angel, they don't even talk. They don't care about no story time."

"Well." Angel's face heats. "What about dinner? You know, like a date." She pictures them sharing a bowl of chips and salsa, maybe at Serafina's. No one would know. They'd just be two girls out for a meal. They wouldn't have to stick their tongues down each other's throats. But they'd know, the two of them, and that prospect thrills her. "Lizette?"

She strokes Lizette's arm, feels the goose bumps rise under her fingertips. Her heart pounds as she waits for the answer. Lizette swats her away. "I've created a monster. I never should've let you eat me out."

Stung, Angel drops onto the pillow. Shame buzzes in her head; she feels swallowed by silence.

Lizette kicks the covers off. "Ugh." She gets up and scratches her scalp roughly with both hands, then steps heavily to her bureau. "This is so fucking *boring*." She wrenches a drawer open and digs around. Angel watches her, cheek against her hand, her throat tight in a way that means tears will come if she isn't careful. Lizette's back is evenly pale. She doesn't wear a swimming suit, Angel remembers, won't go swimming at all. Lizette yanks clothing from the drawer, drops it on the ground, searching. It must mean something, right, that Lizette has permitted Angel to see her naked? But perhaps Lizette doesn't even care enough about Angel to be self-conscious in front of her.

"He better not've fucking stole it." Lizette wrenches open another drawer. "I'll fucking kill him."

Angel sits up in alarm—is she looking for heroin? A gun? Mercedes whimpers at her mother's voice but doesn't wake.

"Oh, here it is." Lizette brandishes a joint. "Want some?"

Angel looks at the sleeping babies. "We'd have to do it away from them."

"It's okay."

Angel wants to remind Lizette that she knows better, but doesn't want to scare her away, not now that she's acknowledging Angel again. "Still," she says uneasily.

"*Fine*. We'll blow it out the window if you care. There isn't even that much smoke." She pushes open the window with such aggression Angel fears it might shatter.

Lizette lights the joint and takes a deep drag. A thread of smoke rises, hangs in the air a moment before the draft blows it toward the center of the room. Angel thinks about her milk.

"Ooh," Lizette singsongs as Angel accepts the joint.

She inhales, holding the smoke in, then splutters, spraying saliva.

Lizette takes the joint back and laughs meanly. "I thought you were a bad girl."

"I'm not." Angel squeezes her voice out beyond the deep unbearable tickle, coughs again. "I never said I was. Why are you being like this?" The more she talks, the angrier she gets. "Anyways, I used to smoke all the time, like last summer. Just because I'm not dying to brain-damage my kid doesn't make me a goody-goody."

Angel stands and scoops her shirt and her underpants off the floor, untangles them with shaking hands. She can't put them on fast enough, and her clumsiness angers her still more. Fuck Lizette.

She leans over the crib, and the babies' heads loom. She lifts Connor with extraordinary gentleness.

"Don't leave," says Lizette from the bed, resigned or contrite or maybe just tired. She's on her side, head propped on a hand, stretched out like a pinup. "I'm sorry."

Angel doesn't answer, but sits on the chair with its filthy blue upholstery, her back to Lizette. She closes her eyes and kisses Connor's head, his sweat sticky against her lips. The world blurs around her. In her arms, Connor pulses, dissolves and re-forms, dissolves and re-forms.

"Hey. Come here. Weed always makes me want to fuck." Lizette pulls on her arm, dragging Angel to her feet and to the bed.

"I need to put him down. Hang on."

But Lizette keeps pulling, her fingers in the waistband of Angel's underpants, pushing them down roughly so they're twisted around her thighs, and Angel has to wrench herself away. "Hang *on*," she says.

But after she's put Connor in the crib and reluctantly joined Lizette in bed, Angel isn't mad anymore. She lies back against the flat pillow, marveling at how quickly her anger fades, marveling that she can be at once bodiless and only body. Even Connor's cries, when they start, don't break her concentration.

Angel and Lizette stand at the front of the room, their poster propped on the ledge of the whiteboard. They are last to present, after Russia, China, and Italy.

"Go ahead, girls," Brianna says, and Angel's stomach flips like a chilled fish. Lizette has hardly spoken to her today, but now she turns and smiles warmly, as if there's never been strangeness between them. Instead of her usual sweatshirt, Lizette has dressed up in a green satiny button-down. She tugs at the cuffs.

"Finland is a country in Scandinavia," Angel begins, and then the presentation spills from them in a steady, measured flow.

"Finnish kids are the happiest kids in the world, and they have the least homework but they still succeed on tests and whatnot."

Their presentation and accompanying visuals are good—almost embarrassingly good, compared to those of their classmates, most of whom just slapped printouts from Wikipedia on their boards. Because Angel and Lizette needed this project as a pretext, they've worked hard on it, harder than either of them realized. Angel is soaring.

"Since 1930 every new baby gets a bunch of baby stuff, for free from the government," says Lizette. "Clothes and towels and everything. Like, everything you need for the first year."

"But the really important part is the box it comes in, just a regular cardboard box for the baby to sleep in. Finnish babies sleep in boxes." This is Angel's favorite part. "It was started to cut down on babies dying of SIDS, which they were doing a lot of before the boxes, and now that they sleep in cardboard, the death rate is really low."

Lizette's eyes shine. "It's all totally free. Health care, too. The poor people get the same care as the rich people, except no one's totally poor, not like here. And the moms get *paid* to stay home with their babies because that's an important job, too, and that makes the babies grow up healthier."

"That's communism," says Jen. "Not cool."

"You for real?" cries Ysenia. "Who cares if it's communism if even poor babies get to be healthy?"

"It's not communism," says Angel firmly. "It's called"—she consults her notes—"*democratic socialism*, and every rich country besides us does it and they're all better off."

"Not fair!" says Trinity, and they're all alarmed to see that she has tears in her eyes. "Kristiana deserves that, too. All of our babies do. Instead we got to spend a buttload of money we don't got and no one even cares if McDonald's is the only crap job we can get where we get burned by the fryer and we have to leave our baby with our sister whose boyfriend gets high. That's messed!"

A pall falls over the classroom. Everyone averts their eyes as Trinity stands and leaves, shutting the door quietly behind her. Christy follows.

"Well," says Lizette. "It's not like Finland is paradise one hundred percent. It's cold as junk and they have to eat *that* crap." She gestures to the table where their International Feast is arranged. The bowl of egg butter sits, sulfuric and glistening yellow, on the table with the other national cuisines—boiled potatoes, microwavable egg rolls, cold bow-tie pasta drenched in Ragú.

Brianna steps forward and starts the applause. "Thank you, girls. That was incredibly informative, and you delved into serious policy questions. These are all issues that you can be active in championing, and when you turn eighteen, you can vote for representatives who keep the interests of your children in mind." But the girls are already helping themselves to the feast.

As the others line up, Lizette leans into Angel, unsmiling, raising a wry eyebrow. "Hey," she says, her breath on Angel's ear so that Angel immediately gets wet, right in the middle of everything. "We kicked ass."

The world is wider, more enormous, more filled with possibility than Angel ever suspected. She could visit Finland, move there even. She and Lizette could move together, dress the babies up in little down-filled suits and Nordic sweaters, enroll them in free preschool, feed them sweet braided breads and egg butter and reindeer puree.

"You guys," Jen calls from across the classroom. She holds up her plate of egg butter in one hand, a laden spoon in the other. "This is *awesome*. Good job, you guys!"

Brianna strides over. "That was wonderful, girls." She touches their poster board, with its carefully penned statistics on Finnish education and blue-and-white flag, and Lizette's remarkably lovely drawing of a reindeer in a sauna.

Angel is surprised by Lizette's grin.

Brianna turns her attention to Angel. "You worked really diligently. I'm delighted to see this."

Angel wishes Brianna would include Lizette in that glow of approval. She grabs Lizette's arm. "Yeah, we both worked really diligently."

But it's too late, and Lizette pulls away, her face steely.

Yolanda used to love going out with friends after work, but has done less of it since Cal. She retouches her makeup at her desk, dissatisfied with how papery her skin looks, how deeply set her eyes. She fluffs her hair, but it's thinning and brittle and without any curl at all.

This morning Monica alighted at Yolanda's elbow, the fingertips of one hand tense against the gleaming desktop. "What's going on with you, Yo?"

Yolanda blinked gluey eyes. On her computer, an email from Facilities Operations regarding an upcoming carpet cleaning. She wondered what she'd been doing in the moments leading up to Monica's arrival at her side.

Monica peered at her with an intensity usually reserved for her job, her carefully shaped eyebrows canted. "Are you working too hard?"

Yolanda's throat knotted, because, as busy as Monica is, she noticed.

But Monica didn't wait for an answer. "Tell you what," she said briskly. "Let's go out tonight, yes?" Then Monica pushed off Yolanda's desk, propelling herself into the next task.

Monica has invited Sylvie and Bunny, too. They're waiting in the doorway with their coats and purses. "Cocktail time," Sylvie calls.

"You girls ready?" asks Bunny, her tone, as always, laced with concern. Bunny Flores has a small face with features that crowd inward toward her pointy nose. She is only in her fifties, but suffers a host of physical problems. A bad hip, even after two surgeries, causes her pain. She also has problems with crystals in her ear and about twice a year gets sudden, debilitating vertigo. Once Yolanda came upon her in the women's bathroom, on her hands and knees, clutching the tiles as if the floor were a vertical wall she was trying to climb. Bunny is single, openhearted and generous, considerate of her friends in the way of female saints and sickly Victorian children. If you compliment a necklace, she'll take it off and give it to you. Yolanda always attributed these kindnesses to Bunny's failing body, but now that she herself is ill, must concede that Bunny is simply a good person in a way Yolanda will never be.

"Let's go to the Cowgirl!" Monica says, rushing out of the inner office with her purse and about five totes from various state conferences. Yolanda has nothing against the Cowgirl, but she is uncharacteristically irritated that her boss doesn't leave the choice of restaurant open for discussion. Isn't *Yolanda* the point of this dinner?

A proper dying woman would set aside vanities and desire, would smile at strangers and loved ones alike with wan generosity. But Yolanda is just as easily peeved as she ever was. She still expends her swiftly draining energy on annoyance with Monica Gutierrez-Larsen for bossing their girls' night.

Yolanda massages her eye sockets, trying to will herself into a better mood.

"Let's walk, shall we?" Monica suggests.

"No way," says Sylvie, to Yolanda's relief. "In these shoes? Besides, Bunny's got a handicap placard." So they all pile into Bunny's SUV and she drives them the half mile to Guadalupe Street.

A bluegrass band is playing, the name of which Yolanda forgets the moment she reads it on the poster: a young bearded man in flannel and slim jeans and vintage cowboy boots works a fiddle, his face contorted in concentration, while a big girl in a black slip and vintage boots of her own alternates between guitar and mandolin. They've perfected an old-timey sound punctuated with whoops and thigh-slapping, and when they address the audience between songs, they do so in a breathless, ambiguously rural accent that's probably put on.

"First pitcher of margaritas on me!" Monica's spirits are so high that Yolanda wonders if she's drunk already.

Yolanda herself feels quiet and stiff and strange, and is having trouble attending to the conversation, which consists entirely of work gossip. Leonor Nelson is having an affair with Paul Marcus, who everyone, apparently, thought was gay.

"Oh, come on, Yo," says Sylvie. "How could you *not* think he's gay? He's always been single. He walks with his shoulders back like this!"

"Poor Leonor," says Bunny. "For her sake I hope he's not gay."

The songs are simple and catchy, and Yolanda taps her feet. She's barely touched her margarita, because, side effect of the chemo, the cold hurts her fingertips. When the doctor told her an occasional glass of wine was okay, she'd nearly laughed. She couldn't imagine wanting to pour more poison into her system. Now, though, she pulls the stem toward her and sips from the edge, and as the liquor moves through her, her mood lifts.

When her pulled pork sandwich arrives, she's starving. It's perfect: savory and spicy and sweet, the bread collapsing under the sauce.

"Look at you eating with a fork," says Sylvie.

"A real lady!" Monica cries, then orders another pitcher.

With a start, Yolanda realizes she'll need to give her notice soon. She hates the thought of letting Monica down. Monica will need to start looking into hiring a new assistant. Yolanda herself will probably have to train her replacement.

Between sets, while the boy and girl guzzle beer, bottles dangling with careful casualness from between their fingers as they swipe their sweaty foreheads, the stereo system plays songs Yolanda knows: Johnny Cash, Doc Watson, Guy Clark, Hank Williams.

When "Honky Tonk Blues" comes on, a fat man in worn jeans and cowboy boots gets up and, in the tight space between the stage and the tables, begins to dance a one-man two-step, arms out, inviting an invisible partner. He's acne-scarred with a pitted, bulbous nose. Long, curling eyebrows, full, feminine lips, jowls as dangling and red as wattles on a chicken. He is, Yolanda thinks, the ugliest man she's ever seen.

"He's good," says Monica, and indeed, the man is light on his feet.

The women watch, laughing. He winks and smiles; he is performing, hips swaying, and then he's dancing with easy steps toward their table. His eyes are on Yolanda.

"Dance with me," the man says, extending his hand.

Yolanda waves him away. "Oh, no, I'm not dancing."

"Not yet you aren't, but just wait five seconds. Five, four, three—" He pulls her onto her feet while behind her Monica and the girls call "Go! Go!"

"There's not even a dance floor," Yolanda protests. She is drunk on the few sips of her margarita, laughing. She feels full of meat and tequila. He spins her skillfully, eyes on her all the while, and she realizes, with a shock, that despite her scrawniness, there's still something in her that he's attracted to. He really is very ugly—round and short as a toad, with odd patchy muttonchops and sweat glazing his bald pink head. His eyes, though, are brown and kind and she thinks of the knowing sad eyes of some large gentle creature: a gorilla, a horse, a Saint Bernard. Yolanda must have thought he'd smell bad, because she's surprised by the pleasant muted scent of soap. She moves her face closer. Under her palm, his shoulder in its polo shirt is humid and comforting.

Yolanda isn't a terrific dancer, but tonight she lands on exactly the right foot. She remembers something a man once told her when she was out dancing twenty years ago: "If I make a mistake it's my fault, and if you make a mistake, well, that's my fault, too." This is how she feels in the man's expert arms, like nothing is expected of her but being.

When the music slows for Nanci Griffith's recording of "Speed of the Sound of Loneliness," Yolanda pulls away. "Thank you. That was fun."

But the man's hand remains gently at her waist. "One more."

"Okay." Yolanda isn't even sure she hears herself. He holds her lightly at a respectful distance, his belly just grazing hers, and she feels herself ease against him. *What in the world's come over you?* Nanci sings.

He spins her smoothly, draws her back in, and there, over his shoulder, at a table alone, is Anthony. He watches Yolanda in the arms of this man, tapping one finger on the table, his cuffs short at his wrists. Yolanda falters, but her partner doesn't let her fall behind. Anthony smiles, but his eyes are sad. This time she feels no fear. Come dance, she thinks. He shakes his head.

She closes her eyes and the music moves through her, everything sleepy and slow, and she is clutching the warm cotton of the man's shoulder. Together they are awash in light and sound and a straining, delicate sadness. *Out there running just to be on the run.* As the music trails away, Yolanda grips the back of the man's shirt. She doesn't want to be let go.

Then the man bends his face to the side of her neck and kisses her. The kiss is truly the most erotic kiss she's ever received. The surprise of it sends a wave of sensation down her spine.

"Thank you," the man says, with a funny little bow. Yolanda makes her way back to the table of women. She shakes her head to clear the haze.

"You got kissed," Monica says in a stage whisper, refilling her glass. "By a goblin!"

Not a goblin, Yolanda wants to say, but she can't bring herself to form words. She wants only to focus on the feeling of his lips at her neck.

The band starts up again, and the conversation moves back to work gossip: some other flirtation, the bad attitude of a man down the hall, the arrest of a state representative's teenage son for hosting a raucous party. A couple has been seated at Anthony's table across the room, and Anthony himself is nowhere, bones in a grave in the Las Penas cemetery. A couple times she glances over her shoulder to where the man is sitting with his own cluster of friends. He winks.

Back in the Capitol garage, Yolanda walks Monica to her car. Her boss is more or less steady on her feet.

"Are you okay to drive?" Yolanda asks. The effects of her own sips of margarita have long faded.

"Yeah," says Monica, looking at the time on her phone.

"You're sure?" Yolanda is eager to be alone and on her own way home. She wants to think about the dance, about that kiss. She gives Monica an appraising look, and Monica's car, too, a black BMW with a prism dangling from the rearview mirror. "Hey," she says. "You have a crack in your windshield. My son can fix it. He's an expert."

Monica studies the bull's-eye. "I'd love that. That thing drives me nuts."

Driving, Yolanda scans the radio stations, trying to find those old songs, to find anything that matches her mood, but the country station is playing new songs full of bluster and patriotism, and she turns it off. In the silence of her hour's drive north, she carries the glow of that kiss, holding it as a kind of talisman against seizures.

As she pulls into her driveway, something sharp twists above her heart. It hurts, the knowledge that life can still hold moments like these. Out of nowhere, a dance, a visitation, a kiss. *This* is the world she's leaving.

Perhaps because Lizette hasn't been in touch, and because Angel is feeling overlooked and sad, when Ryan texts asking if he can come by again, she lets him. She could use the distraction, she figures, could use his dumb, dog-like admiration.

It's Saturday afternoon, and her grandmother is running errands in town. Her dad has hitched a ride with her "to hang out with a friend." From his vagueness on the topic, Angel suspects it's a date. What kind of woman would consent to go out with her unemployed, live-at-home, license-suspended father is beyond Angel, but apparently it's the same kind of woman who would be up for a Saturday afternoon date while his mother stops by the Center Market.

Ryan told her he'd be there at two thirty, and, indeed, he pulls up at 2:28 exactly. Only when she lets him into the house does Angel realize they haven't been alone together since that fateful night. She suspects he's thinking the same thing, because he looks even more slouched than usual, standing in the kitchen, biting his dry lip, his pale arms sticking out of his Beatles T-shirt. He picks at his thumbnail. "Where's Connor?"

"He's still napping, so."

"Oh," says Ryan, disappointed, but just then Connor whimpers sleepily from the bedroom.

"I'll get him," she says, relieved, though ordinarily she'd see if he'd fall back asleep.

Ryan trots after Angel as she goes down the hall to retrieve the baby, looking with frank interest at the framed photos on the wall: Valerie grinning at age four, Amadeo scowling at six, a picture of Angel herself as a bald infant in a puffy red dress.

Keep your eyes to yourself, Angel wants to say. "Wait here," she tells him outside her bedroom door. No way does she want him picturing where she sleeps. She slips in and pulls the door shut after her.

"I've been reading books about babies!" Ryan calls.

As unwelcoming as she feels, Angel is glad he's shown up. Not because she likes his company especially—he's such a freak that it's embarrassing—but there's something reassuring about his presence. Alone in this house, she can't help thinking of creepy men peering through the windows at her. She can't help thinking of Mike.

They sit in the living room eating potato chips, Ryan flopped out on the floor with Connor, jangling toys in his face to make him laugh. Angel watches with an eagle eye, and when Ryan picks up the baby, her heart lurches, but Connor jabbers happily.

Ryan has brought dispatches from EVHS. Some of the items of gossip are so dull that she can scarcely imagine she once used to care. The science teacher slipped his nephew, who is also his student, the answer key to a weekly quiz; Janelle Garcia and Charlie Chacon have gotten together.

Other items of gossip, however, smart. "Oh, yeah, your friend Priscilla hangs out with Jasmine Lucero now. I heard Jasmine's grandma is taking them to SeaWorld."

"What? She hates Jasmine Lucero. She said Jasmine smells like old-lady garlic breath."

Ryan's lip curls in distaste. "God. Priscilla's kind of a B-I-T-you-know-what."

"You can just say *bitch*," Angel says, grateful.

"My mom hates that word. I'm never supposed to call a woman that. It's even worse to call a man that because then it's like the insult is that the man is a woman, you know?"

"So don't say it, then."

Ryan sniffs Connor. "Can I try to do his diaper?"

"Whatever." She brings the bag and sets up the changing pad and watches anxiously as he blunders his way through it.

"There you go, little guy. They've got videos online. You can learn anything online."

Connor gazes at the ceiling with glossy eyes. Ryan has strapped him into his clean diaper but has not yet put his legs back into the sleeper. Instead he prods the baby's smooth chest as if checking a nectarine for ripeness.

Angel swats his hands. "What are you poking him for?"

"I was just wondering if he got my sternum thing."

"Your *what*?"

"You know, that weird thing I had." He's nodding at her like she's stupid. "My missing sternum. My chest bone. I told you about it. You know, my scar? I'm self-conscious about it."

Angel strains to remember their conversations before and after geometry, the night she slept with him. "That's not a thing. How can a whole bone be missing?"

Ryan is turning redder. "I don't know. It just was. They gave me a surgery when I was a baby. I kind of wondered if Connor got it, but he didn't." Ryan looks almost disappointed. "I mean, it's pretty rare."

He can't help looking so defeated, Angel thinks. He didn't even get his share of bones. He needs a stand and a metal rod to keep him upright, like one of her grandmother's porcelain dolls.

"Well, Connor got a sternum." Her tone is defensive. "Give him here." She taps around his chest, but everything seems solid enough.

"It was good they fixed it when they did. Because otherwise if I knocked into anything it could go straight through to my heart."

Angel doesn't remember a scar. She should have noticed something like that. But the truth was that she wasn't noticing him at all; her memory of that night is just a vague impression of pale boniness, some grateful muttering that made her despise him, and her own pleasure that made her despise herself. She doesn't remember whether his eyes were open or closed, can't even remember feeling him above her or inside her. She was noticing herself, her own nudity and her sense of power, as if she were a beneficent fairy bestowing a blessing, or a superhero with a cape saving him from his own pathetic life. The Devirginator. She imagines her costume: slimming black leather, a red satin cape.

It must have been his virginity that attracted her to him in the first place, she thinks, eyeing him. Otherwise she can't fathom what induced her to set down her beer at that party and lead him to the filthy back bedroom—some man's surely, a brother or uncle or even the boy throwing the party, unmade bed, the random tangle of video games and electronics, the warm thick animal smell like a ferret's cage. Certainly *she* led *him*. There is no way he would have had the balls to make the move on her. Which is both disturbing and comforting; disturbing because it is Angel's own fault she got pregnant, comforting because it is her own fault, which makes her feel free somehow, defiant, in charge of her own destiny.

What was she thinking? Look at him: skinny, narrow-chested, and apparently skeletally incomplete, less of a person than a regular person. Through his pale hair, his scalp is spotted with scaly barnacles. The thought of sex with Ryan is incomprehensible and also a little gross, particularly when she considers Lizette, with her beauty and presence and swagger. Angel's heart stutters.

"You have all your bones!" Ryan tells Connor. He pushes the baby's kicking legs through the leg holes, does the snaps, one, two, three. Now he lifts him high, their eyes locked on one another's, Connor shrieking with joy and grasping at the air. "Superbaby!"

onday morning, Amadeo leans into the dark upholstery of his mother's car. It's just after dawn, but he is alert and excited, the plastic toolbox stowed carefully in the trunk. He shaved and dressed in a plaid button-down shirt, and drank three cups of coffee for maximum alertness.

On Saturday, when Amadeo wandered into the kitchen, his mother withdrew her head from the oven, steel wool in hand, and announced, "I got you a customer. Monica's got a big crack, size of my fist." She demonstrated, fingers ensconced in yellow rubber gloves.

"Ha," said Angel from the table, bringing a spoonful of rice cereal to Connor's mouth. "A big crack."

"Watch it," says Amadeo, swatting her with the dish towel.

Amadeo kissed his mother. "Well, you *need* to work, honey." As if Amadeo didn't know that. "You know how busy that Monica is; she's very important. She can't just be taking off work to get her car repaired." Yolanda straightened, pleased. But then she looked at Amadeo sternly. "So you need to be ready to go with me Monday morning."

"Hell, I'll *be* ready."

"Dang! I've got school," Angel wailed. "I can't believe I'm missing our first job."

"Also, hijito," his mother said, "I said you'd do it for free, but don't worry, I'll pay you."

"Okay," agreed Amadeo, crestfallen, because he was looking forward to cashing that first check. "I guess word of mouth is the best advertising a business can get."

"*You* can't pay him, Gramma. This is like his training. His internship."

"I see," Yolanda said.

Now, she drives, both tense hands gripping the wheel, her face pinched.

"What's your deal?" Amadeo asks, wounded. "Are you mad at me, Mom?"

She flashes a wan smile, glances without seeing him, and says vaguely, "Oh, no, hijito. I didn't sleep too good."

Amadeo also had trouble sleeping the night before—it's his first job, and though he doesn't like to admit it, he gets nervous, talking to people like this, professionals, people with degrees and paychecks and power.

The rest of the way to Santa Fe, Amadeo sits back, listening to the inane chatter of the morning DJs, uneasiness forming and re-forming behind his rib cage.

Chief Clerk Monica Gutierrez-Larsen meets them in the parking garage under the Capitol. The woman is miniature in a miniature beige suit. Her clicking heels echo as she approaches. "I'm *so* glad to meet you," she says, smiling a glossy, white-toothed smile and shaking his hand with a tiny, powerful grip. "Your mom talks about you all the time. You're so nice to do this."

She is attractive, intimidating, and younger than Amadeo expected, mid- to late thirties; for a moment he's indignant that his mother should have such admiration for someone so much younger than herself, someone, in fact, awfully close to his own age. Amadeo pictures this woman out on the campaign trail, a pocket-sized powerhouse beaming her way into office.

Repair kit in hand, he follows Monica to her car in its reserved spot, a black BMW about six or seven years old, and though the bull's-eye is obvious, she points it out. It's the circumference of a Little Debbie cupcake, webbed with cracks and positioned near the bottom of the windshield on the driver's side.

"Can you fix that, hijito?" Yolanda asks. "You can fix that, right?"

"It wouldn't be a problem for a normal-sized person, but I'm so short"—Monica Gutierrez-Larsen laughs agreeably—"it's always right smack in the middle of the left lane. At night it catches the taillights and the whole thing blazes up like a big red snowflake."

"Huh," muses Amadeo. He sets his kit on the grease-spotted concrete, runs his finger over the crack and flinches. A line of blood spreads on his fingertip. He taps the windshield more gingerly, then bends to look the chief clerk in the eye. "I can repair your windshield so this"— he taps the bull's-eye once more—"is invisible. It will be fixed both aesthetically and structurally. I can guarantee that you'll see better and be safer." A feeling of competence swells in him.

"Great," Monica says, looking at her watch. "I've gotta run. Nine o'clock meeting." She pulls a face at Yolanda. "See you in there, Yo." And then she is off, feet fast and fierce in their tiny shoes.

Yolanda hands him a twenty. "Get yourself some lunch downtown after, and we'll meet back here at five fifteen. I'll pay you a little something later. Good luck, hijito." She kisses Amadeo on the cheek, leaving him beside the BMW.

Cars stream into the garage, doors and trunks slam, alarms beep and squawk as doors are locked. Other people click past him and into the building. Amadeo kneels beside his kit, enjoying this busy feeling of purpose. He wishes someone would stop him, question his presence, so Amadeo can say, "Hell yes, I have business here. See this Beemer I'm fixing? It belongs to Monica Gutierrez-Larsen. The chief clerk? You may have heard of her." Amadeo wishes he had more clients so he could spread this directed, occupied feeling over more of his day.

He imagines Monica's gratitude. She'll come down, eager to see his progress. She'll have taken off her suit jacket and, impressed by his abilities, will look at him more closely. This time she'll see him not just as her secretary's undereducated son, but as a doer, a fixer, a man who's good with his hands, at ease in his body. She won't know why, but she'll find herself attracted to his nonchalance, his smooth sexual energy that's understated yet nonetheless exerting a pull on her.

He winces at this fantasy, but then he's imagining telling Brianna about today. "Oh, the chief clerk's a family friend. We're pretty close." He'll imply a flirtation between them, maybe even a full-blown sexual past, and then he'll get to assuage Brianna's jealousy. "You got nothing to worry about. I'm into *you*," and she'll raise her gaze to meet his, eyes dewy and grateful.

They've continued to meet up, he and Brianna, every week or so, nearly always at her house. Once she made him dinner—quinoa salad, tofu stir-fry—and once they watched a raunchy buddy comedy (his selection—he immediately realized it was a bad choice, but she laughed along) on her laptop. Dinner in Española is out: "Someone might see us," she said.

The gulf between them—educational and aspirational—seems to make her more uncomfortable than it makes Amadeo. Once, lying in bed after sex, she chatted merrily about the Obama administration's new federal grants for social programs in disadvantaged communities.

"I'd love to design something even better and more comprehensive than Smart Starts!, you know, that looks at the health of whole families. I'm applying for MPH programs, either in New Mexico or back in Oregon."

"What are those?" Amadeo asked.

"Master of Public Health?" She reddened. "But it's not like everyone needs to go to grad school."

"I know that."

"I mean, yeah. And it's not a given that I'll get in. It's a total privilege that I even get to consider it. Not everyone has the luxury, and I totally recognize that."

"Okay." The silence lay between them, morphing into a kind of discontent. Amadeo was about to say, "I could have applied to MPH programs, too, I just never wanted to," when, thank god, she stood, clutching her discarded shirt to her chest, and slipped into the bathroom, indicating that this date was over.

The uncertainty between them has allowed Amadeo to dodge the question of whether he should tell Angel. A few times, she's asked, "Where have you *been*? Another hot date?"

He said he was out with a friend, and she asked, "You have friends?"

When he's finished fixing the chief clerk's car, Amadeo decides, he'll walk around the Plaza until noon, then get a good lunch at Tomasita's, in celebration of the Creative Windshield Solutions launch. He imagines a cold beer sweating circles on the tabletop, then catches himself.

He sticks the largest adhesive rubber donut seal he has around the crack. The hole in the rubber isn't big enough to encompass the bull's-eye, but he figures he can repair it in stages. Then he places the clear suction cup over the seal.

He likes pressing the trigger of the syringe, likes watching the liquid resin squirt, its chemical acetone smell. He puts a little extra for good measure.

But he's put too much, and because the seal is too small for the bull's-eye, there is no vacuum. The resin oozes under the seal and pools around it like mercury, a shining, quivering meniscus. Also, his hands are shaking, probably from the coffee. The light in the underground parking structure is flickery and orange. He places the sheet of plastic film over the resin to contain it. The liquid spreads. He swabs at the excess, but it's begun to drip down the clean slope of the windshield, and soon Amadeo's fingertips are tacky.

Also a bit of resin drips on the hood. Amadeo swipes at it with the heel of his hand, but it only smears across the black paint. The quick-dry formula is drying quickly.

He needs paper towels. He tries to get inside the building, but the lock requires an ID, so he bangs on the door until someone pushes it open.

"Yeah?" asks an old guy in no-iron pants and a bolo tie.

Amadeo explains himself, but the guy, bored, waves him through and continues down the circular hall.

Amadeo doesn't know which way to turn to find the nearest men's room, so he jogs, eliciting dirty looks from women in their frumpy office wear.

Apparently the State of New Mexico, in a push to embrace green technologies, has done away with paper towels, opting instead for low-energy hand dryers. Amadeo grabs a wad of toilet paper from the stall, then, pleased with his good thinking, grabs a second, which he runs under the tap.

In the garage, Amadeo leans over the hood of Monica Gutierrez-

Larsen's car and begins to scrub. The toilet paper sticks, leaving fibrous white tracks in the paint. "Fuck," he mutters, and tries to rub them away with his thumb, but they only become grubby and smudged. He tries to wipe up the mess on the windshield, but the resin has already dried. It looks like a jumbo tube of superglue has exploded.

Only now does Amadeo panic, looking around—for what? Help? Witnesses? He makes for the bright daylight at the garage exit, leaving behind the mess and his open toolbox.

In the glare of morning, he hoofs it downtown. The sky is blue and wide, the air cool. He needs a drink, but nothing is open except some breakfast places. Up and down the narrow porticoed streets, people are beginning to unlock their shops.

He's jogging now, up San Francisco Street, through the Plaza, trying to outrun his failure. He pictures Monica Gutierrez-Larsen in her silk blouse, discovering what he's done to her paint job. She squints at the streaks in the dim orange light, irate, disgusted. But no: it's early still—only fifteen minutes have elapsed. The chief clerk won't know what he's done for a long time, and somehow this fact only makes the situation worse; for now he's the only one who knows.

The blunt square towers of the cathedral rise beyond La Fonda. Maybe, just maybe, they'll be hearing confession. He likes the idea of spilling his guts to someone who is required to forgive him. When he pushes open the heavy door, though, he sees that an early and sparsely attended Mass is in progress. One or two old faces turn to look at Amadeo as he hesitates in the doorway, wild-eyed and sweating, and the priest drones on. If he joins them, and closes his eyes to pray, there's a chance God will hear him, but there's a better chance that he'll have to sit with the intolerable, spinning anxiety that's expanding in his skull and chest and throat. Amadeo backs out, and the door shuts with finality.

He cuts over to Alameda, runs, then walks back west through the narrow park along the river, breathing heavily. The light is so dry and bright, it's like grit in his eye. Birds call to each other in the tall, drooping cottonwoods, and the leaves make rocking shadows on the dry grass. The river is just a concrete riverbed with a few puddles here and there reflecting blue. It should be peaceful, but it isn't. It's a pathetic, skinny little park, parched and studded with dog shit. A homeless man with a full blond beard sits on a picnic table in his drab-colored layers.

Whatever is building in Amadeo needs a release. "Fuck, fuck, fuck," he mutters, and he thumps his head with the heel of his hand over and over for the metallic jolt. He winds up and kicks the trunk of a cotton-wood, but his foot bounces off ineffectually. Infuriated, he kicks again and pain shoots up his shin. "Fuck!" he shouts. At the intersection down the street, the man selling newspapers turns.

From behind his facial hair, the homeless man watches Amadeo with intelligent eyes.

"Take a picture, asshole," Amadeo snaps, then feels sicker. The homeless man averts his gaze, as if Amadeo might be dangerous, and Amadeo's eyes smart. He kicks the tree again, and for an instant the punishment is so intense he thinks he might have broken his foot. Feeling marginally better, he limps off.

The pain doesn't last. Up and down streets, he walks, then runs, then walks again, fueled by vibrating self-loathing. In his mind, his crime balloons to fit his shame, and as it does, so does his pity for himself. He ruined a car, his prospects, his entire life. He's a failure, an idiot, a fucking waste, his father's son, and none of it is fair because he *tries*. He can never catch a break, can never dig himself out of this hole he was born into. He tried to do something nice—to fix some bitch's window—for free! And here's the thanks he gets? Monica Gutierrez-Larsen despised him, he could see that. She was patronizing him, the no-good son of her secretary. She didn't even say thank you, just felt entitled to free work on her fucking BMW. She's lucky he didn't smash the entire fucking windshield.

He jabs at the scars on the front and back of both his hands, willing them to hurt, but they don't. His life isn't supposed to be like this. Good Friday was supposed to save Amadeo. He was supposed to be past the shame and failure and the mistakes that hardly seem to be his own and that unravel beyond his control.

Amadeo feels cheated. By Passion Week, by the penitentes, by Jesus himself. The fact is that no one can be crucified every day—not even Jesus could pull off that miracle. Jesus never had to face the long dull aftermath of crucifixion, the daily business of shitting and tooth-cleaning and waking reluctantly to a new day. Jesus never had to watch people return to their own concerns and forget what he did for them.

No, instead Jesus died on the cross, and before the women quit weeping outside his tomb, before all those Marys had to deal with gro-cery shopping and returning to work and paying the bills, Jesus rose from the dead! Oh, he must have felt smug, up there on the cross with that trick up his sleeve. He was spirited away to heaven where he lives in the lap of luxury, looking down on the people with their big endless worshipful party. Because what is Christianity except a never-ending memorial service with people singing his praises and invoking his name until the end of fucking time, just because one day he got three nails and a poke in the ribs?

It's not like Jesus was the only person to ever suffer, Amadeo thinks sourly as he jogs through the Plaza, head down. Hadn't people died before? Haven't they died since? And in worse ways, too. How about all the Jews in the Holocaust? How about that guy down in Arizona who used a two-hundred-year-old saguaro cactus for target practice and it fell on him, pinning his torso to the dirt, and he bled and bled, taking ever-shallower breaths, and they say he wasn't even dead when the vultures and coyotes starting taking away pieces of him. That guy definitely had Jesus beat for suffering. In fact, now that he thinks of it, what Jesus went through barely even *counts* as suffering when he knew all along he had good things coming down the pike. Daddy would bail him out, sweep him up to heaven and seat him at his right hand. Real suffering isn't just about physical pain, but about not knowing when the pain will end, not knowing what the point of it all is.

He failed, Amadeo realizes. Failed deeply, irredeemably. This isn't the surprise, though. The surprise is that for all those weeks of Lent, Amadeo managed to convince himself that failure wasn't inevitable. All along, however, some absolute core in him had known failure was com-ing the second he saw Angel waiting for him on the steps.

Kaune's Market is mercifully open, and Amadeo buys himself a forty of overpriced craft beer. It's nine now. More people are around, and the last thing he needs is a cop hassling him, so he opens it in the alley by the dumpster. The trash smell is thick in the warm September air. He barely tastes the beer, but it's refreshing, and he drinks it down quickly. His burp is big and soft, and in its wake his anxious stomach settles some.

The alcohol does its magic, and Amadeo feels calmer. He walks back toward the park. He'll apologize to the blond guy. "No hard feelings, man. I'm going through some shit. Sorry for—" How to phrase it? He's sorry for calling the guy an asshole, sorry for snapping at him, sorriest for treating the man like someone who deserves Amadeo's venom. How do you say that to a homeless person? But when he gets to the river, the picnic table is empty. Now he has the homeless guy to feel bad about.

Amadeo makes his way to Evangelo's in time for it to open, where he sits drinking and watching ESPN, because at this point it's all shit and who cares if he's off the wagon. He drinks until the sick pounding of his heart slows, and then he keeps drinking.

He can guess what's going on back in the parking garage. At lunch Yolanda probably insisted on going out to the car with Monica, eager to see Amadeo's job well done. Together they would have discovered the disaster Amadeo made of her car. Yolanda would have apologized over and over, humiliated, and she would have offered to pay for the damage, and maybe Monica took her up on it, but maybe, in a gesture of largesse, she didn't, which would have humiliated his mother still further.

On the street, tourists stream past the window, arms full of shopping bags from the trading post, the bookstore, the folk art shop. He rests his head against the cool window.

Yolanda leans into her chair, suffused with an unfamiliar euphoria. In this very building, her son, five months clean, is doing his first repair job, getting his life in order, and all around her the business of the State of New Mexico ticks along.

Since Friday, she has felt changed, as if some scratchy scrim has lifted, leaving her soft and bare to the sky. For the first time, she feels equal to the task of dying.

She's supposed to be printing certificates of commendation for the members of a high school basketball team in Grant County, but the names on the list before her won't stay put. The tumor is an insistent pressure on the top left of her head, and when she ignores it, it nudges her gently, like a blind old cat.

Yolanda sets the list of basketball players aside. Her hands rest quietly in her lap. Above her, the light buzzes and an indistinct conversation down the hall drifts toward her.

She closes her eyes, placing herself again in the bar on Friday. The heavily lacquered tables sticky with spilled beer and barbecue sauce, the red plastic baskets, the yeasty, greasy smell of beer and fries, the man's arms encircling her.

Why does the body continue to yearn? Even now. Friday night she'd thought the magic of that kiss was her own allure, but maybe the magic came from him. Maybe he really *was* a goblin with some uncanny power, maybe he kissed girls in bars all over New Mexico and planted the memory of himself in them like a magic bean.

Girl. She has to laugh. How can Yolanda, terminally ill at age fifty-five, still think of herself as a girl? Surely this is a sign of a failed personality.

That kiss made her feel profoundly sexy, sexier than she has in decades. Maybe sexier than she's ever felt, because even if Anthony pushed her against the refrigerator, the car, the malformed trunk of the globe willow tree in the backyard, even if Yolanda found herself gutted with desire, there was always something missing. She hadn't yet understood that she would never be enough for him.

All the men over the years. Yolanda is so *tired* of the vigilance, the effort: having to be always alert for romantic possibility, seeing herself through other people's eyes, finding after the whole rigmarole of grooming and dating and seduction that she doesn't want the person she's won over. Yolanda won't get what she longed for all those years—love and romance, the grand culmination, the quiet aging companionship—but what she has isn't so bad. Her house, her bedroom, her gleaming dressing table with the pink brocade bench, the smell of Pledge and the dusty burning vacuum smell, her son and granddaughter and the baby in the living room with the television. Maybe all she ever really wanted was to be led around a dance floor and a single kiss on the side of her neck. Except that now she wants another.

At five fifteen Amadeo makes it back to the Capitol and walks down the ramp into the garage. He's calmer now, the drink muffling the world.

He'll sleep on the way home to avoid his mother's disappointment. She is not the type to press him or reproach him; her shoulders will slump, and her face will be drawn, and that will be bad enough. Tonight he can apologize, promise to do better.

His mother is waiting for him, as they planned, but not at her car. As his eyes adjust to the dim, flickering fluorescence, he realizes that his mother is standing by Monica Gutierrez-Larsen's car, and that Monica Gutierrez-Larsen is there, too, sitting on the bumper. His toolbox is on the hood, all packed up.

The two of them aren't talking. Monica scrolls through her phone. Yolanda clutches herself, small and shamed.

For a moment he considers fleeing back up the ramp.

"Oh, mi hijito," his mother says as he approaches, and her voice is so sad he wants to pull her into his chest to comfort her, but she's across the parking garage and the car is between them. Monica Gutierrez-Larsen rises, and the two women watch him.

The chief clerk is now wearing sneakers with her suit. They're lightweight and neon, expensive, and he gets a flash of her in performance gear running on trails. Her face is unsmiling, but she seems to be watching him with curiosity.

"Where have you been?" His mother's voice is strangled. She's shaking.

"We've been trying to call you," says Monica Gutierrez-Larsen.

With one finger—the nail buffed and painted a neat pale pink—she pushes his cell phone across the hood toward him an inch. "Guess you left in a hurry?"

He's about to defend himself, to tell her that her piece-of-shit car was too far gone for him to work with, or, maybe, maybe, to beg forgiveness. His head is fuzzy, the thoughts coming slow and thick.

"You need to pay for this, hijito." In this light, his mother looks unlike herself: the bones of her face protrude, casting deep shadows around her eyes and in the hollows of her cheeks. She is leaning against the hood, fingers splayed, arms tense. She lists to the side and her eyes flutter open and shut.

"We can work something out," Monica says crisply. "A payment plan. It would be best, I think, if we manage this between ourselves, and keep your mother out of it."

"Something's happening," his mother says.

"Everyone makes mistakes, of course. But mistakes have consequences."

Amadeo's entire face is hot with the shame of being reprimanded by this tiny woman his own age. He raises entreating hands to his mother. "Why aren't you helping me?"

"How can I help you?" Her voice is low and oddly staccato, her eyes flicking rapidly. She cuts off. Her lips are pale.

"Yolanda?" Monica Gutierrez-Larsen steps toward his mother but doesn't touch her, and then Yolanda slides to the concrete.

His mother is making a joke, though she does not make jokes, not like this. By the time he circles the car, Monica Gutierrez-Larsen is squatting beside her, and his mother's arms and legs are jerking.

———

YOLANDA IS IN emergency surgery at St. Vincent's. Amadeo walks tight, anxious circles around the waiting area. He's completely sober: his vision clear and dry under the vivid lights, his mouth parched. The set expressions on the faces of the doctors do not inspire confidence, and neither does anything they say, which isn't much, only that Yolanda is undergoing brain surgery and they will update Amadeo as soon as they have news.

Amadeo extends his pacing to the wide halls and calls Valerie, who drives up immediately from Albuquerque with the girls. As she drives, she keeps him on speaker, assailing him with questions he doesn't know the answers to.

"All I know is they're operating on her."

"I can't hear you!" she says. "Hold the phone *higher*, Lily!"

"Is Lily in the front seat? Is she big enough for that?"

"Not technically," Lily says, her calm voice loud in the speaker. "But she needs me to navigate her."

"Oh, shut up," his sister snaps.

"Hey!" protests Lily. "That's child abuse! Verbal-style!" Farther in the background Sarah chimes in, fragments of chirping static.

"I'm not talking to *you*," Valerie says, her voice muddled and desperate.

"Is Gramma going to die?" Lily asks, and Amadeo halts his pacing, his breath still in his chest, waiting for his sister's response. But there's only the distant whir of the car engine. Then he realizes that Lily is asking *him*, waiting for *his* answer, and that not just Lily is waiting.

"I don't know." He clears his throat. "You shouldn't be on the phone," he tells his sister with effort. "It's not safe. Call when you get here."

Amadeo tries to sit in the waiting room with its calming desert colors, but he keeps springing up. You don't know anything, he reminds himself. She might be fine.

Tears rush his eyes. He looks around the corridor to see who might be noticing. Part of him hopes someone *does* notice, that someone will unravel this nightmare. He imagines something out of an old folktale: a saint or a bruja in the guise of a hunched woman, resting a hand on his shoulder, holding Amadeo steady with a clear gray-brown gaze, rearranging fate and circumstance with a quiet, cryptic utterance. Amadeo would blink and she would be gone, and his mother would be walking toward him down the hall, her step firm as she returns to him, a little smile at the corners of her mouth.

But in the corridor, people move with swift, oiled competence. No one looks his way.

As he waits, the thought crosses his mind that he's off the hook for damaging Monica Gutierrez-Larsen's car, and he's immediately ashamed.

He nearly calls Angel, but he doesn't want to scare her, not yet. He thinks about calling Brianna, then puts his phone away.

Half an hour later a pretty woman in scrubs approaches to tell him that his mother is in post-op, still under anesthesia, and that the doctor will be out to speak with him soon.

When his sister arrives, rushing through the automatic doors, Amadeo slackens in relief. She's frantic, whipping her head around to look for him. Sarah and Lily hurry behind, pinched and worried and clutching enough books for a week of waiting.

At the sight of his sister, Amadeo's eyes fill again. He wants to embrace her, but he isn't sure whether this crisis is enough to bring on a détente.

Valerie also seems uncertain, and stops short before him. "Have you heard anything?"

"Hi, Uncle Amadeo," Lily says gravely, glancing at her mother. Valerie is in loose yoga pants and a Lobos T-shirt with a thickly embroidered emblem, her long hair pulled back in a messy ponytail, but her face, though tired-looking and creased with worry, is still made-up. He's not used to seeing her dressed so carelessly. He imagines she must have just changed out of her work clothes when she got his call.

"Mom's in post-op. Post-operation," he clarifies. "Her doctor is going to talk to us soon."

Lily looks around mournfully, blinking behind her glasses. "It's cold in here." She's right. It's freezing. Amadeo hadn't noticed. His nieces' bare arms are goose-bumped.

"Here," he says, unbuttoning his plaid shirt. "I guess you'll have to trade off." He's self-conscious in his undershirt; he feels like a stereotype, like he should be bumping along in a flame-emblazoned lowrider.

Lily hesitates, and doesn't look at him as she takes it and wraps it around herself. "Thanks, Uncle Amadeo."

Just then the pretty woman in scrubs approaches. "Mr. and Mrs. Padilla? Dr. Seth and Dr. Konecky, your mother's neurosurgeon and oncologist, are ready to see you. I'll take you to the private lounge."

Anguish flashes in Valerie's face, and, to Amadeo's surprise, she leaves it to him to clarify their relationship. "She's my sister."

Valerie points the girls to a bank of seats against the wall. "Wait for us here." The girls eye the chairs, but don't sit.

"Can't I go in with you?" Lily asks. "I also want to hear how Gramma is."

"Me, too, I want to go," says Sarah. "You're not the only one who cares about her."

Valerie shakes her head. "Stay there."

Even though the corridor is clear, Amadeo and his sister walk so close together that their arms brush.

He hates how they look: his sister in her shapeless lounging clothes, her ponytail sagging, himself in his wife-beater, tattoos exposed. Sloppy. They are going into battle unprepared, unarmored. Valerie has a master's degree! he wants to shout.

At the door of the lounge, they pause. Beside him, Amadeo can sense Valerie steeling herself. He touches her wrist—to give comfort or to take it, he isn't sure—and then they go in.

In the lounge, a Himalayan salt lamp glows pinkly on a side table. Valerie's demeanor is deferential. She keeps her hands clasped before her like a schoolgirl afraid of punishment, which comes anyway.

"We've removed most of the biggest tumor," Dr. Seth says. "And part of another. But a third is inoperable. Based on its location, getting at it would cause severe damage to the brain tissue." He's what Amadeo might expect from a brain surgeon, if he'd ever bothered to imagine one. He's a small and precise man, long-fingered, with a faint British accent. His bald head is shiny. Easy to sterilize before surgery, Amadeo thinks, which makes him think of vultures; he saw once on a nature program that their baldness is an adaptive trait to cut down on the parasites they're exposed to when they dive headfirst into rotting bodies. This in turn makes him think of his mother as a corpse, a thought so horrible bile rises in his throat. He coughs, gags, but doesn't, thank god, throw up.

She's alive, he tells himself. She's alive, she's herself, she's your mother.

"Your mother suffered a grand mal seizure this afternoon. With every seizure, there's a strong possibility of brain damage," says Dr. Seth, "and the seizures will come more frequently."

"Can stress trigger it?" Amadeo asks. "Like, if something stressful happened?"

"Of course. Our bodies and minds are intrinsically linked, and it wouldn't be surprising if she was under a great deal of pressure."

Amadeo is awash in hot horror. Her eyes had flickered so strangely in the orange light of the parking garage as she waited for him.

"But it could happen without obvious triggers, too. With this condition, it was going to happen."

Both Amadeo and Valerie have trouble absorbing the bewildering news that the hospital already has their mother on file, that apparently she's been in treatment since June.

"She would have told us," Amadeo says lamely, and the doctors press their lips in sympathy.

"Her fall that night," says Valerie, stricken. "Remember?" She turns to Amadeo, her tone less accusing than imploring. "Haven't you noticed symptoms?"

Of course he'd noticed—he just didn't let himself think about the moments of vertigo, the increasingly random things she'd say, or the spacey, panicked look that would come over her, as though she was lost in their own living room. It never occurred to him that anything truly bad could befall his mother, who is the surest force in his life. And Amadeo himself hurried her condition along by making her so unhappy.

"How could she have known and not told us?" Valerie asks the doctors in a drowning voice, searching each of their faces, and Amadeo is surprised by the protectiveness he feels for her. "Didn't she need us?"

Dr. Konecky raises her palms with compassion. "You'll have to talk to her about it. But it's possible your mother wanted to maintain control of the news, given how out-of-control the diagnosis is." She posits this gently, regretfully, as though she risks blowing their feeble little minds with a theory so profound. Amadeo expects Valerie to lash out at the lank-haired doctor, but his sister doesn't seem to take offense.

It's after ten when they're allowed to see their mother. In the waiting room, the girls have fallen asleep. Lily, still wrapped in Amadeo's shirt, is slumped in her chair with her fat novel open in her lap, her neck kinked in a way that makes Amadeo wince. Sarah sprawls on a love seat wearing an oversized purple sweatshirt that Valerie was forced to spend forty-five dollars on in the gift shop. *Santa Fe: Living the Dream!* "Whose bright fucking idea was it to sell these in a fucking hospital?" Valerie said as she handed over her credit card. "I fucking hate this city."

Shoulder to shoulder, brother and sister stand before the figure in the hospital bed. Amadeo tries to ignore the bandage swaddling her head like a turban. He tries instead to look into her drawn, clay-colored face, and to see his mother, but the familiar lines around her mouth only make the full effect more chilling and unfamiliar.

She's sleeping, motionless and small under the light blanket. Oxygen tube in her nostrils, IVs in her arm. She's lost a lot of weight, Amadeo realizes with a shock. Can she have lost all this weight since this morning? Surely not. But how has he not noticed?

Amadeo puts his arm around his sister, and she sags against him. He thinks of those afternoons on the couch when they were kids. But after a moment she steps away and sits heavily in the vinyl chair.

"Mom? Are you awake?" Yolanda's eyes slide back and forth beneath her thin purple lids. Valerie stands abruptly. "She must be cold." She starts opening cupboards, revealing only cleaning products and sterile supplies.

Amadeo's last visit to the hospital, to the Española maternity ward, had been stressful, sure, and scary, too, but exciting. He didn't actually believe that anything truly dire could happen to his daughter. Here, though, the air is leaden. He should call Angel, he thinks, but then Valerie slams a cupboard.

"Why would they give her just one shitty blanket? It's twenty fucking degrees in here."

Were they supposed to buy flowers or something to brighten the place up? "Hey, Val. Should we buy flowers?"

"She's not going to be here that long."

Amadeo jerks his head back.

Valerie turns slowly, pale. "I mean," she says, "she's going home soon. We'll get her flowers at home."

At night, the sounds of the hospital are more pronounced: the whirs and ticks and pulses, the murmurs from the hallway. On the other side of the room, behind the patterned green curtain, there's another patient, a Marcella Tran, according to the whiteboard, but she's so quiet Amadeo doesn't believe she's there until he peers behind the curtain. A heavy Asian woman wearing a satin shower cap gazes at him impassively, and Amadeo retreats. He sits in one of the chairs, and only then does Valerie settle beside him.

From underneath the bandage, a tuft of hair emerges, bristly and dry against the pillowcase. They didn't shave her whole head, the doctors said, just a semicircular line for the incision. They then peeled back their mother's scalp and, with a delicate power saw, cut into bone. They've left the skull open, accessible for more surgeries. Amadeo can't think about it, can't think about it. He only realizes that he's grabbed his sister's forearm when she puts her hand on top of his. She rubs the back of his hand with a thumb. The gesture seems automatic, the kind of comfort she might offer one of her daughters. Again, he flashes to when they were children, clutching each other.

"Val," Amadeo whispers. "Do you remember when Dad died, how every day after school we sat on the couch hugging?"

Valerie looks into his face, startled, then suspicious. She withdraws her hand. "Why?"

"I was just wondering, is all. If you remembered."

"I don't," says Valerie, but her color has risen and her voice doesn't sound as guarded as usual. "Why are you asking me that now?"

Amadeo shrugs. He wants some confirmation that those afternoons happened, that they don't exist in Amadeo's memory alone, wants some reassurance that comfort might still be possible between them.

"I don't remember it," repeats Valerie.

Amadeo must have dozed, because time collapses. Beside him, the chair is empty. Valerie must have gone to check on the girls.

When his mother wakes, a sob escapes him. Her face is calm, her eyes low-lidded and glazed. She gazes around the dim room, barely lingering on her son.

"I'm sorry, Mom! I'm so sorry! When were you going to tell us?" Tears stream down his cheeks. But Yolanda's eyelids drop shut, as if flipping a switch to turn off his voice.

All at once he remembers Angel. His ringer has been off, and he hasn't checked it. Nine missed calls, fifteen escalating texts. *Hey Dad! How'd the job go????? Where RU guys? Where the heck are you? It's after eight! Pick up your phone!!!!!!!! God!!!! Where ARE YOU????? Please call me I'm really really worried.* The last, sent nine minutes ago, 12:35 a.m., reads, *If you don't call back in ten minutes, I'm calling the police.* He dials.

———

AND SO BEGINS the time of the caretaking. She's going to die at home, Yolanda informs them. "No more hospitals, no more surgeries."

"But what if they can save you?"

"They can't save me," Yolanda says, which is more or less what the doctors said.

"I don't like to give prognoses, because they can so often be off," said Dr. Konecky, "and there isn't much evidence that they contribute to quality of life."

Only when Amadeo pushed, did she admit, "I'd say we're looking at two or three months." Valerie gripped his arm.

Amadeo can hardly believe that they discharge his mother. They're going to let them take her home? They're just going to trust her care to Amadeo and Valerie and Angel?

It's dreadful, the inevitability that his mother will hurt herself, knock into things, fall, draw a cup of hot coffee onto her lap, that even worse things are to come.

But they manage, more or less. Once a week someone from hospice checks in on them. Valerie visits on weekends, arms full of lasagnas and plastic containers of mixed greens. She lets the girls watch TV and play with the baby while she sits by Yolanda, dabbing her eyes and talking about the old days. Angel dashes around gathering laundry.

Amadeo begins to change Connor, sometimes even without being asked. Connor kicks his bare brown legs and chuckles at the novelty of his grandfather involving himself with his diaper. Each time, the second the old diaper is peeled away, Connor pees, his face going serious until the stream ebbs.

"Oh, nah!" Amadeo swabs his jeans.

"You got to be ready to cover him with a cloth!" Angel cries, laughing. Angel holds her grandmother's arm as they make their slow, shuffling way to the bathroom. "Amazing. It only took brain cancer to get him to help out."

Yolanda laughs, whole body, clinging to the doorway and to Angel, and Amadeo laughs, too, because he's so grateful that Angel can still make his mother laugh.

"Hey now, that's not fair," he says, but they all know it is, and Connor cracks up, too, like a slightly daft dinner guest dying to get in on the joke.

"What a bunch of lunatics," says Angel, shaking her head.

In a notebook, Angel has introduced a complex record-keeping system to track Yolanda's medications and meals and bowel movements.

"Oh no you don't. Don't you be marking down those things. That's embarrassing."

"Why?" Angel brandishes a second notebook. "I'm in here. And Connor's in this one. I don't see what's so embarrassing about knowing what your body is doing."

"Can we keep track of my craps, too?" Amadeo asks.

"Sick," says Angel, and Connor and Yolanda dissolve into laughter again.

t's just over a week since Yolanda's been released from the hospital, and she can get up and move around, with a walker for balance. She doesn't mind using the walker, and considers this a personal failing. Her grandmother, who, when given a walker at the age of ninety-six and implored by doctors and Yolanda's mother and Yolanda herself to please for the love of God use it, would lift it clear off the floor and lug it around the house.

She never thought she'd say it, but it's a blessing having Amadeo unemployed. He's so unnerved by the fact of her dying that he's started helping around the house. He doesn't vacuum, but she's seen him plucking larger bits of debris off the carpet by hand. He runs the dishwasher. "Where does this go, Mom?" he calls from the kitchen, waving a measuring cup, as if he hasn't lived in this house his entire life.

Yolanda lifts her head carefully from where it is nestled in the wing of the armchair—it's so heavy on its stalk—and focuses on the cup in his hand. "In that bucket." Not bucket. "Carton?" Not carton. She feels the shape of the correct word, the particular thrust and heft, but then, when she opens her mouth, the word will not emerge. "Craze?"

Amadeo watches her, his mouth ajar, lower lip trembling. He sets the measuring cup on the counter, shuts the dishwasher.

Here, in the living room, the blinds are lowered, the afternoon light thick and insinuating against the closed slats. Did they leave them drawn for her sake?

It seems only moments ago that Angel helped Yolanda dress, changed her gauze, then, with a kiss on the forehead, left for school with the baby. Yolanda's mind is keener with Angel around. Possibly because she doesn't want to let the girl down or scare her. It makes her long for Angel's return, though she brings with her a wincing clatter.

Time has become strange: too swift, then gummy. She marvels at how much she used to accomplish in a day: all those hours at work, the grocery shopping, paying bills, cooking, sometimes even getting her nails done. Yolanda examines the chipped pink polish. She chose that color from the gleaming array on the wall, but can't recall when, or whether it was in the salon in Santa Fe or the one in Española. The nail bed is purple where the nails have grown out. The skin around them is fragile, waxy yellow, taut.

"Dodo? When does—that girl come home?" She shakes her head in irritation. "Angel. Angel."

"Soon. Can I get you anything?"

Outside, a car on the gravel. Yolanda turns again to the closed blinds. She's trapped in this dusky, closed house. "Open the shades, would you, hijito?"

He hops to, eager. "Maybe that's Angel, home early." Then: "Oh, shit." Outside, the black BMW comes to a stop behind his truck. Casting a cringing look at his mother, he slinks down the hall to his bedroom and shuts the door. Amadeo was to fix Monica's windshield, she recalls, but the events leading to her seizure are wispy and dreamlike and her head hurts when she tries to concentrate on them. It must have gone well, because Monica is here.

As she pulls herself up, she decides not to care about what she's wearing—faded sweatpants, an old sweatshirt of Amadeo's with frayed cuffs, that disconcerting bandage taped to her head—but when she opens the door, Yolanda registers, in the slow, shocked way Monica takes her in from behind the massive bouquet, just how bad she looks.

"Oh, you sweetheart." Monica makes as if to hand her the giant crayon-colored roses and lilies and plasticky greens, but seems to think better of it, and instead inches around the walker and sets the vase on the breakfast bar. "This is from everyone at the office. We miss you." Technically, Yolanda is on medical leave, but, based on the size of that bouquet, it must be clear to everyone else, too, that she won't be returning.

Monica gives Yolanda a gentle hug over the walker. Yolanda's hands tighten on the rubber grips; she's afraid she'll tip. Over her boss's shoulder, she sees herself in the mirror by the door: the dull clumps of hair emerging from the bandage, her dry, creased face free of makeup.

Monica herself is neat in black, fragrant as always. Yolanda wonders if she considers this visit a professional obligation. She should be able to tell, having worked with her every day for three years, but Monica is so adept at social niceties. "Come sit," Monica says, as if she is the hostess. "Can I get you water? Make you tea?"

Yolanda rolls the wheels over the carpet, back to her armchair, the maroon jacquard puckered from her many hours sitting, and lowers herself. "There's a bucket," she says. "For the flowers." She flaps a frustrated hand at the cupboard above the breakfast bar.

Monica pauses in unwrapping her scarf, a fine, transparent black wool. Her face contorts in a showy effort to understand. "Oh? It came with a vase. See?" She taps the vase. Her voice is high, sunny.

Monica has also brought a card. When Yolanda sets the sealed envelope on the cushion beside her, Monica tears into it herself, handing the open card to Yolanda so she can read the cramped, cheery messages of goodwill. "We all signed it."

"Ah," says Yolanda, setting it down without reading. "That's nice."

Yolanda tries to see her house through her boss's eyes: the gold-framed photos of her kids and grandkids, diapers and wipes stacked on the table, the toys scattered across the floor, half a cold frozen pizza languishing on the coffee table that her son served for lunch. There was a time when Yolanda would have been powerfully moved to have Monica visit her, when she would have cleaned and shopped and cooked in preparation.

Monica sits on the edge of the couch, smiling brightly, doom in her eyes.

"How are you, Yo? Everyone misses you at work."

At the window, a hummingbird visits the feeder, glinting blue and green. The heat kicks on, sending the plastic blinds at the patio doors clacking. The scent of the flowers stirs, syrupy and artificial. She thinks of her dead mother, laid out for the Rosary, that pale little body rigid with embalming fluid in her broad-collared floral dress.

"Well, you haven't missed much. Bunny had one of her vertigo attacks on Thursday. Janice Sena said she stood up from her desk and slammed right down again, clutching her head." She looks sideways at Yolanda, her awareness of what she's just said hitting her, and rushes. "Then she gave her head a good thump, left, right, like she was getting water out of her ear, and just started typing again."

"Oh, that Bucket," says Yolanda, then grimaces. Words are misbehaving today. "Bunket." The word pulses, replicating, making distorted copies of itself. Yolanda grabs one of them, holds it before her in her mind, but cannot for the life of her think what it connotes.

She understands that she's freaking Monica out, that she should muster her old personality, but she's too tired.

"Are you here alone, Yo? Is anyone taking care of you?"

"My son," Yolanda says, dismissing the parade of *bucket*, relieved that these other words, singular and meaningful, click into place. "My Amadeo."

At the sound of his name, Amadeo appears in the doorway. He is barefoot, hangdog.

"Ah," says Monica. "Good."

"Hey." Amadeo avoids Monica's eye, and she avoids his.

"My son can fix your car," Yolanda says. "You can, right?"

Monica hesitates. Amadeo clears his throat. "I'm sorry I . . ." he starts, then trails off.

"Yes?" Monica regards him. "You're sorry for——? Please go on."

Amadeo licks his lips.

"People make mistakes, but to run off like that, that was wrong." Monica is trembling. "You didn't even apologize."

Yolanda looks on with interest.

"Listen, lady, you want work for free, you can——" Amadeo stops, looks wretchedly at Yolanda.

"What am I doing?" says Monica. "I shouldn't have brought it up. I'm sorry, Yolanda."

Just then, Angel crashes through the door with her bags. "Hi, every-one!" Connor is limp in her arms, asleep. Yolanda closes her eyes against the noise, but nonetheless relaxes.

"You must be Angel. Monica."

"Oh, the chief clerk! My grandma really admires you." She shifts the baby and sticks her hand out.

"She has only wonderful things to say about you."

"I'm here," Yolanda reminds them, opening her eyes.

Her son is still in the doorway, as if he doesn't know whether to come into the room or flee to the back of the house. Yolanda pats the arm of her chair as if to invite him over to her, but he doesn't see.

"So my dad fixed your windshield?" Angel squints through the front window. "It looks great, Dad!"

Monica regards Amadeo steadily. What is between them? Could they be attracted to one another, her boss and her son?

"Well," says Amadeo. "Actually."

"It turned out I had to get a new windshield, anyway." Monica stands. "I should let you rest, Yolanda." In a moment, she's rewrapped her scarf, kissed Yolanda, and the BMW is backing down the driveway.

Yolanda didn't even ask who has replaced her, but as soon as she thinks the question, she loses interest.

At school, Angel does not have to think about her grandmother. The ruckus and noise and the sheer inconsequentiality of the daily schedule is a comforting distraction. If Angel is taking GED practice tests (up ten points on Reasoning Through Language Arts!), she's not thinking about her grandmother at home staring at daytime television, her head cocked strangely. Angel isn't thinking about her father making some sad lunch of canned beef stew, or their lurching conversations, her father's attempts to be comforting and upbeat, a performance that can't possibly convince either of them.

Angel has all but quit keeping her emotions journal; she doesn't want to think about the sheer injustice of it all. Just as things were becoming bearable, just as she'd hit a kind of rhythm in her days and Connor started sleeping through the night, just as her father was beginning to be *engaged*, this disaster hits.

Angel hasn't told anyone at school. Instead she applies herself with renewed devotion to counting her sleep hours, Connor's sleep hours, to noting the time and length of his feedings, even color-coding her own meals by food group with her gel pens. In this way the school day passes in manageable, unthinking chunks, until the time comes to zip shut her backpack and to gather Connor's baggie of soiled clothing and to load him into his car seat.

But as she gazes out the classroom window at the stark city, everything she hears and sees and does is filtered through her new understanding that she will lose her grandmother.

Lizette has hardly spoken to Angel since their Finland project. For three weeks—how has it only been three weeks, when so much has happened?—she's sat at the desk nearest the whiteboard, bent over her workbook, but she just seems to be drawing circles in the margins. She hasn't once antagonized Jen—not even when Jen distributed flyers for the day care center at her church—and when Brianna calls on her, her replies are muted.

Angel misses her. She hates that even in the midst of this crisis, she is distracted by longing. She has tried positioning herself in Lizette's way when class is released, but Lizette moves smoothly past her. Lizette no longer saves her a seat at lunch, and she speaks to Angel with the same cool, offhanded ease with which she speaks to anyone else. Angel doesn't understand how it was all shut off so entirely. She is humiliated that she ever allowed herself to be so vulnerable. And there's no one she can talk to about it.

Angel can't shake the feeling that she, Angel, is responsible for the horror that has swamped her family. Not because God hates lesbians and thinks they don't deserve grandmothers—Angel can't believe that, not when God is love and mercy and goodness—but because there must have been something wrong about her joy, about the way the hours fell away in Lizette's presence. That fact is, Angel's attention was completely absorbed by Lizette—by the exhilaration of those afternoons in her bed, yes, but also by the marvelous, singular person of Lizette.

And when her mother asked after her grandmother, Angel hadn't heeded the warning, hadn't even been able to recognize it as a warning, simply because it came from her mother.

So Angel deserves this swollen, hot-faced rejection. She deserves this hurt. Perhaps she even deserves to lose her grandmother.

Lizette rests her head in the crook of one arm and bounces the tip of her pen off her notebook. Her shining hair falls heavily across her cheek. Angel imagines lifting that hair, drawing it behind Lizette's ear to expose the clean curve of jaw, but then turns back to her workbook, biting down on her own pen until her teeth ache. The intensity of Angel's attention must surely reach Lizette, must feel as weighted as a hand pressed against her skin. But Lizette continues to tap her pen.

Angel stands. She palms her phone, slips it in the pocket of her hoodie. She doesn't even peek through the nursery window. In the bathroom, she leans against the wall and checks her phone.

There's no word from home, from her grandmother, from her father. No word from her mother, either, big surprise. As usual, Angel is thinking more about them than any of them are thinking about her. She hasn't told her mother about Yolanda, because she can't stand the thought of Marissa swooping in, too late, all concern and readiness to help and smug pleasure at having seen what Angel did not, when until now she's been so entirely unconcerned about anyone other than herself. She doesn't deserve to know what's going on with them. Unless she calls. If she calls, then Angel will tell her. Why won't her mother call?

Everything OK? she texts her father. To her grandmother she simply writes: *Thinking about you. Love you.* If it's a good day, her grandmother can still read her texts, might even send a bizarre reply, co-authored by autocorrect. *Lemonade constrict.*

Ryan, however, has written. *Hey Angle, what's happening?* As she taps away at her screen, another beeps through. *You busy lately? It would be great to see you guys. I could come see Connor anytime after school!!* He makes liberal use of exclamation points and grinning emojis. He even stopped by last week, sat chatting with Yolanda in the living room. Yolanda loved him, smiling spacily at him from under her crocheted blanket, offering soda that Angel had to get up to pour. Ryan just took Yolanda's interest in him for granted. "You're a good boy," Yolanda said with effort, and Ryan replied, "Thanks!"

Angel pauses with her fingers above the screen. The bathroom door swings open and, fearing it's Brianna, Angel quickly snaps up and turns on the tap.

"Hey," says Lizette, as the door wheezes shut behind her. Lizette holds Angel's gaze in the mirror, unsmiling, and Angel's heart pounds. She swallows and turns off the tap.

Another text chimes through. Angel glances at her phone. *LMK!!!!!*

"Who's that?" Lizette steps behind her.

"No one." Angel silences the phone and slips it in her pocket, glad

Lizette sees that she has other people in her life. She grips the wet edge of the counter to steady herself.

"I bet." Lizette pulls her in and hooks her chin over Angel's shoulder. Angel wants to close her eyes and surrender against that softness at her back, but there's something rigid in her that she doesn't understand. Lizette's chin digs into her shoulder, her arms are tight around her chest; Angel presses her nails against the counter. She forces herself to look at their reflection, to meet those green eyes. Lizette's lips—soft lips, dry lips, pink without gloss or color—are challenging. Her loose hair falls down Angel's throat and sweater, but Angel is immovable. If breath were possible, she knows she would inhale the citrus of Lizette's shampoo, the warm, salt smell of her skin.

It occurs to Angel that love doesn't feel good to her. It's truly love-*sickness*: malarial, systemic. It's left her shaky and unable to eat, unable to sleep, unable to concentrate.

"Who was that?" Lizette's voice is low, almost dangerous, and Angel wonders for a moment if she'll wrest the phone from her pocket and find her out. But somehow, in speaking, Lizette has broken the taut enchantment; whatever was keeping Angel immobile has vanished.

"No one." This time a smile tugs at her mouth. She turns in the embrace to face Lizette, but when Angel moves to kiss her, Lizette pulls away, swats Angel's ass.

"Good." Lizette walks to the door, her Pumas scuffing along with indifference.

Her hand is on the knob when Angel calls out. "My grandma is dying." This is the first time she's said the words, and Angel is surprised by how easy they are to say, how simply the situation can be summed up.

Lizette pauses. Under her gaze Angel backs against the bathroom wall. She slides down the tiles and hugs her knees to her. Her belly is still full against her thighs. She can't look at Lizette, can't bear to be rejected again.

Lizette sits heavily beside her. "That sucks," she says, cold.

"Like, really soon she's dying." Angel can't keep the desperate pitch from her voice. "Really soon." She hates her tone, as if she's pleading, trying to convince. She's using this information as a kind of currency, spending it on sympathy, to get what she wants, which is for Lizette to hold her and care for her and to want to take her out in public. She wants Lizette to be her girlfriend.

"Sucks," Lizette says again. She stares straight ahead, emotionless as wax.

"Yeah." Angel thinks of all the people Lizette has lost: her mother, her father, that network of family that fell away after what her uncle did to her. In the face of all that loss, a dying grandmother is nothing. A dying grandmother is normal, expected, even *right*. It's impossible to explain to Lizette what Yolanda's dying means, how the natural order of her world is about to be upset, how Yolanda is like the keystone of an arch, and without her, everything will collapse to rubble.

"Wait," she says. "How's stuff with you? I mean, like with your brother and his girlfriend? Are they . . ."

"My brother's living with this new chick." Lizette's voice is steady. "She's okay. I don't know her that good."

"Oh my god, Lizette. What are you going to do?"

"Figure it out. Get a job. I'm staying with Selena until the lease runs out in December. He's paying my part until then."

"But where will you go? Do you have family you can stay with?" She doesn't, Angel doesn't think, except those cousins. "Who will you stay with?"

"Will you quit?" Lizette turns on her, almost savage. "I said I don't *know*, Angel."

"Sorry."

They sit for a long time, listening to the pipes and distant voices passing in the hall. Again she thinks of asking Lizette to move in with them, but it's not her house, not her place to ask, and where would Lizette sleep? In Angel's single bed? She almost laughs to think of her father's and grandmother's reactions to that. Soon, of course, there will be room, a whole empty room. Angel can't bear to think of it.

"Hey, sorry 'bout your grandma." Lizette wraps one arm around Angel and pulls her head to her shoulder. It's not comfortable, and the gesture isn't anything more than what a regular friend might do, but

Angel allows her eyes to fall shut. A tap dribbles, and the funk of disinfectant is all around them.

"So," says Lizette, waggling Angel's ear not very gently. Angel catches her breath. She wants, wants, wants. Her breastbone could nearly crack with longing, her nerve endings straining, her very marrow pressing to the edges of her bones toward Lizette. She lifts her lips to meet Lizette's. Lizette places a single finger against Angel's chest and pushes her back. "If you want, we can go to story time."

"Can I go to your house?"

"We'll see."

Lizette kisses her, then hoists herself up and bangs out of the bathroom.

News spreads, and Yolanda receives cards and calls and visits from old friends and second cousins, some of whom she hasn't seen in years. Yolanda feels for them; no one knows how to talk to the dying. She sits for as long as she can force herself to, but she's so tired, and she wonders what, really, she means to them. They laugh, rehashing old stories—the time she leaned against the punch table at the fiesta and the whole thing tipped, the time the cashbox at Willard Romero's grocery was stolen, and the culprit turned out to be someone's seventy-year-old grandma—and that feels good, but there's a seed of resistance rooted in her chest, a little piece that has already said goodbye to these extraneous people.

She assumed that it was only a matter of time before Cal showed up, but as the weeks pass, it becomes less clear how he'd hear the news. They don't have mutual friends—the few times they went out with others, it was with his friends and their wives, not people likely to hear about Yolanda's diagnosis. And he's been so thoroughly respectful of her wishes that he hasn't called.

Still, she waits for him, and is, frankly, surprised to find herself waiting.

When she finally picks up the phone, her hand shakes with nervousness. She sits at her dressing table, back to the mirror because she can't bear to look at the skinny creature with the comical bandage on her head. As she listens to the ringtone, Yolanda pictures him in his kitchen, spare but for a flourishing potted Christmas cactus on the table, gazing at her name on his phone, considering before silencing it. It's what she deserves, leaving him like that, giving him the laziest possible explanation——*I need time*——but she can't help feeling piqued: Cal never screens her calls.

"Yolanda." His voice is gravelly and warm from cigarettes. "It's you."

Hearing him, Yolanda is for a moment no longer sick; for a moment, she's her old, pre-dying self, and they're about to arrange a steak dinner followed by pleasant sex in his dusty bedroom with those beautifully oiled shelves that he's filled with paperback mysteries and power tools and assorted bottles of vitamins. How easy to fall back into that old life——and then the impossibility crashes into her.

"Yolanda?" She pictures him extracting a toothpick from between his teeth, gazing at it blankly a moment before setting it on the table.

Yolanda's voice won't come. In its absence it takes shape: a toad, solid and afraid, backing down her throat with powerful legs.

Cal sighs. She imagines him chewing his thin lip.

"Cal," she finally says, relieved that her mind is clear, her voice still her own. "I need to start by saying I'm sorry." But instead she can't resist self-dramatizing. "I wanted to see you. I have brain cancer. I'm dying." This is the wrong note, the falsest note she can strike while technically still being honest.

But Cal doesn't seem to hold the drama against her, maybe doesn't even notice the performance. Being Cal, he attributes the best possible motives to her.

"I wondered if something bad happened. It had to be bad, for you to leave like that. That wasn't you. I wrecked my brain to come up with what I done." He falters here, hearing, perhaps, his unfortunate phrasing. "I've been worried, Yolanda."

"I know."

The conversation proceeds: Cal is disbelieving, and Yolanda manages to sound stalwart and brave as she confirms that, yes, her time is limited, very limited.

"Oh, no. Are they sure? Can I see you? Now?"

She agrees; they hang up. It's that easy to get Cal to come back to her. She throws the phone onto the bed, but misses and it falls to the floor. Can't Yolanda even *die* with dignity? Now she's simply pushed pain onto Cal; before, at least, he could hate her for leaving, but now she's made him subordinate his suffering to hers.

He's there within the hour.

"Oh, hey," says Amadeo from the couch, surprised, when Cal steps into the kitchen, and beats a retreat to his room. Yolanda knows that Amadeo likes Cal, but he's always been cagey around her boyfriends. Cal is tall and stooped, canvas jacket zipped up. He turns his acrylic stocking cap in his hands.

He's come directly from the job site (she was wrong, after all, to picture him standing in his kitchen; she'd already forgotten that people work on weekdays) and still smells of sawdust; he's covered in it. Yolanda can't help but picture it falling to the floor. Oh, shut *up*, she tells herself. This is a reunion.

"Yo," he says, and pulls her into his arms. She allows herself to relax against him, to remember his old smell beneath the sawdust. The smell is the smell of life before her diagnosis, and breathing him in now brings her back to that old person. He pulls her tighter and arousal quickens in her.

She knows Cal's body so well—long and brown and wiry, the ripples of loose flesh on his back. She's seen pictures of the sandy-haired boy he once was, and can occasionally glimpse that boy's stubborn, jutted jaw. He is a man who for decades worked outside with his shirt off, a man whose neck actually is red from the years of sun, crisscrossed in pale creases. She liked to run her finger along those creases. But she's certain that if she were to lead him to her bedroom at the back of the house, he'd resist. With a shock, Yolanda remembers her current bony state.

"Oh, god," he murmurs into her shoulder. "Why did you keep it from me?"

"You were having fun. You were on—" She sticks on the word. She sees real fear in his eyes, but pushes past, airily. "I didn't want to bring you down." This is disingenuous, and the knowledge flickers across his face, too. That he doesn't call her on it is another sign of his generosity. He asks all the right questions: though it clearly pains him, he asks if they've told her how long she has.

"Months, not years." Yolanda means for her voice to be clipped, but it cracks into self-pity. For a moment she cries into the coarse canvas of his jacket.

Cal pats her, and then gently steps out of her clutching embrace. His eyes are full of compassion and hurt. He unzips his jacket, removes it, and hangs it carefully on the back of a kitchen chair. He's looking at his hands, not her, and Yolanda is afraid. "It's been nearly six months since you've spoken to me, Yo. After over a year together. Why call now?"

Yolanda shrugs. Because I missed you, she might say. Because I'm scared. Because I need to be distracted from what is happening. Because I am alone.

Cal waits for her answer, and when it doesn't come, he lets out a long breath, swipes his calloused hand down his cheek with a sound of sandpaper. He sits. Elbows on thighs, head dropped over limp hands. The knees of his Levi's are worn nearly white. He searches the linoleum between his work boots. She remains standing before him, a child being reprimanded. The shoulders in his sweatshirt are strong.

When he lifts his head, those brown, kind basset-hound eyes are steady. "If you want to go it alone, you can, Yo. But you should be aware that it's hard for me, too."

Oh, I'm sorry, she nearly says, flaring. What can I do to make my terminal cancer easier on you? But it's not what she wants or means, and she knows she couldn't get the sentences out whole anyway.

"I'd like to help you, and it hurts that you don't want me to." He doesn't seem to know what to do with his hands, swipes them down his thighs, then hooks thumbs in pockets, before letting them fall once again. "I'd like to say that I'll always be here for you, but I'm not sure it's an offer that won't expire."

She knows that he has only said what is true, and that it is, further-more, a brave thing to say. She thinks about Cal's marriage, the ex-wife who dropped him once she got her real estate license and whom he has never once, in Yolanda's hearing, bad-mouthed. He's not a man who deserves to be left, and yet he has been, again and again. He's a good man.

"Expire. Well." Yolanda forces a laugh. "I guess the question is which expires first, me or the offer." The words come, assured and correct, as if her brain has gathered its forces for this parting.

Cal shakes his head. "You don't have to be so self-protective, Yolanda." Yolanda senses that if she took his hand now, he would follow her to the bedroom. It would be easy, wonderfully easy, to draw him toward her, to move his hands to her breasts. And god knows Yolanda needs it. She wants him on top of her, crushing the pain out of her.

He's not her true love, and she understands that she won't, after all, find that now. She can appreciate the comfort he gives, the possibility that when it happens she won't be alone. But she doesn't reach for him. Perhaps she simply—even at this stage—needs to prove to him that she doesn't need him. Perhaps, for once, she is thinking of Cal.

"Thank you for coming, Cal," she says gently, focusing hard on each word. "It means so much to me. I appreciate the time we've had together." The words sound scripted, simultaneously too saccharine and too cold, but they are true.

The muscles in Cal's jaw pulse. "Okay," he says finally, breaking eye contact. He stands, pushing up with palms on thighs, then slaps his thighs once with finality. He's not looking at her at all. "Okay," he says, and then he's gone.

Amadeo marvels at his daughter's ease with his uncle. Tío Tíve now delivers groceries to their house, once or twice a week, batting away Amadeo's thanks, setting them before Angel like offerings. At first he brings the same cans of beans and beef stew and packaged tortillas that he buys for himself, until Angel intervenes.

"This is so nice of you, Tío. To help you next time, I made a little list of things that we specially need. Like, vegetables and stuff."

Angel kisses his cheek and starts putting the food away. Outside, Tíve's dog Honey waits patiently by the door, her head on her paws.

"You want some juice, Tío?" Amadeo offers. Tíve seems glad to linger, sitting with Yolanda, if she's up, or with Angel as she cooks and bounces the baby. Amadeo joins in, too, and they all talk while his mother withdraws into some perplexed corner of her mind. Tío Tíve steals looks at her: she, who was always dashing about, is now suffused with stillness. Her face is even thinner, the skin creased around her bruised eyes. She stares at a spot on her lap and works her mouth silently around a word.

One day, when Tíve drops the groceries by, Amadeo's mother is up and lucid and sitting at the kitchen table.

"Please, Tío," she says, drawing her purse to her, "I need to pay. I get . . . debility?"

Amadeo looks away. He can't stand the search for words.

"Disability, Gramma?" Angel asks. She makes furtive eye contact with Tíve. She's at the counter, holding the baby, forming pink hamburger patties on a cutting board with one hand.

"Dizzabilty." She picks slowly through her purse. Tío Tíve watches in alarm as this thin, erratic woman fumbles with her wallet.

"Take," Yolanda says, pulling out bills. Her hair beneath her cap is fine and dull gray except at the still-dyed tips.

"No, Yo. I'm not gonna."

Yolanda shakes her hands, upset. The bills drop to the table. One flutters to the ground. Amadeo retrieves it and places it before her.

"Can you call my mom to get me?"

Tíve opens his mouth but does not speak.

"Gramma," says Angel, "your mom can't come now. But we're here with you." Connor lunges toward the raw beef, open palm swiping, and Angel jolts back, dropping a patty on the floor with a smack.

"Give him here," Tíve says, taking Connor, who objects and then quiets. "Can I take him outside to see Honey? She's gentle."

Angel hesitates. "I guess that's okay. Just keep him above her head. And get his coat." She catches Amadeo's eye. *Go with him.*

"She's losing things every day," Amadeo tells his uncle in a low voice.

Tíve takes the concrete steps one by one, balancing precariously, and it's all Amadeo can do not to grab Connor from his arms. "That idiot Anthony never put a railing out here. For years he said he would. All you kids climbing up and down them on your hands and knees. Your poor mom. The things she put up with." Tíve sighs. "Your dad was a good friend to my Elwin." Tíve eases himself down to sit, and Amadeo sits beside him.

Amadeo thinks of that photo of the two young men. He can't reconcile that smiling young face with his shadowy sense of his father. He remembers navigating cautiously around him, afraid of setting him off.

Honey gets to her feet, grinning her frilled black-edged lips and wagging her tail nub. Her coat gleams auburn. Connor regards the dog sternly and then looks to his grandfather and great-great-great-uncle and breaks into a laugh. "Stay down there," Amadeo tells Honey, and her nub wags more enthusiastically.

"I never knew my boy when he was this age." Tíve says. "In those days the men worked for their families. Most days the baby was asleep by the time I got home for dinner."

"I try to help."

"You gotta do better than your dad."

Amadeo's face heats. The piñons are glazed in the low autumn light.

Honey noses the baby's fat legs in their striped pants, leaving smudges of damp. Connor looks to Tíve in wide-eyed apprehension. He whimpers, but doesn't commit to distress. "Hey, you're okay," the old man says, waving the baby's hand. "She's a nice doggy. You ever meet a doggy-woggy?"

Until his mother said it that night, Amadeo had no idea his father wanted to get him a dog. He doesn't remember at all. For his father to want a dog for him—companionship, affection—he must have cared. Perhaps he knew he wouldn't be around long.

"I should have been there more for your dad. But after Elwin—" His uncle cuts off. "I didn't know how to help nobody."

"I can't think of anything sadder." Losing Angel: the thought is unimaginable.

His uncle doesn't answer for a long moment.

"The night before I left for basic training in 1942, my dad took me out walking, up to the old morada." Tíve nudged his chin in the direction of the town. "My whole life my dad limped—in the war, he got mustard-gassed and his leg never healed. Even back then the morada was just a pile of dirt. He told me, 'My dad held every office at some point: Hermano Mayor, rezador, sangrador.' Told me he wished he'd kept it going."

Amadeo thought of his uncle, so young, standing with his own father in the adobe ruins, plaster-cracked and doorless. Maybe he'd been thinking of the meal his mother and sisters were preparing for him back at the house, or of the inconceivable journey across the ocean that lay ahead of him. Perhaps Tíve's father rolled a cigarette and handed it to Tíve, rolled a second for himself, then dropped the match and scuffed out the red glow.

Tíve shifts Connor's weight. "My dad told me, used to be the morada was the heart of our village. He told me, 'Make sure you come home, son. Las Penas isn't dead yet.' Maybe now it really is."

Amadeo imagines the village as it was in those long-ago days, vibrant with fiestas and matanzas, weddings and bailes. If he strains, he can almost hear the ghostly whoops and accordion and stomping feet from some long-ago dance.

Dog and baby strain toward each other. Connor frowns, reaching, and Honey grins, breathing excitedly. When Connor makes contact, he closes his fingers around her wet nose, gives her whole snout a good shake. Honey submits, but twitches her pale eyebrows with worry at Tío. At the sound of Connor's happy, gurgling shriek, the old man laughs.

Amadeo smiles, but he's troubled. "We're still here, Tío. We're still in this town. Connor's growing up here."

"It's not right. I should go before your mom. I should have gone before all of them."

Amadeo cannot formulate a response because behind them comes the sound of uneven steps, and the screen pushes out. "Dodo."

They turn to see his mother swaying in the doorway above, watching them with a strange intensity. Amadeo thinks she's about to reprimand them for letting the baby play with the dog.

"Yeah, Mom?"

Tío clambers up unsteadily. Alarmed, Amadeo stands, too, his hand hovering under his uncle's elbow. He can almost see gravity claw at the old man, sees in his mind the moment he tips down the concrete steps into the gravel with Connor, but then Tío is on his feet. Connor wriggles to reach down for Honey.

"Can I take him, Tío? Let me take him."

But Tío grips the baby, watching Yolanda. The screen is between them, his uncle on the top step, his mother pushing out.

So Amadeo cups his uncle's elbow and braces the handle of the screen door, because he doesn't want to throw either his mother or his uncle off-balance. "Let's go inside, Mom. Let's all go inside."

"No," she says, and shakes her head fervently like a toddler. The cap has come askew, revealing pale scalp beneath her thin hair. She doesn't budge from the doorway. Her fingers against the doorjamb are tense and gripping, purple. She pushes the screen against them.

"Dodo."

Amadeo wants everyone inside. He wants his uncle to put down Connor's squirming weight. He wants everyone settled on solid ground.

She seems to be struggling to get the words out. "I loved your dad, Dodo." Her lips tremble. "No matter he was gay."

"Gay?" His mother has deteriorated so much. Carefully he says, "Oh, Mom. Dad wasn't gay. He just had a hard time."

Amadeo lifts his grandson from his uncle's arms, and Tíve catches hold of the baby's shirt to steady himself. Amadeo then eases the door open, takes his mother by the upper arm, and guides her backwards into the house.

———

THE HOUSE is submerged in a midmorning quiet, the windows sealed against the birdsong outside. Except for an occasional faintly echoing tick, like a fingernail absently grazing a duct deep in the house, the heating vents are still. It's an empty quiet, although the house is not, in fact, empty.

Amadeo stretches across his rumpled bed with his shirt off while his mother dozes in her own bedroom. Connor was up all night screaming in teething pain. Around one, after Angel fed him again and rubbed his gums with numbing ointment, her face pale, voice drawn and cranky, Amadeo got up from playing Thorscape, took the baby, and sent her to bed. Until four in the morning, he paced the hot living room with his grandson, narrating everything the way Angel taught him—"There's the lamp. See the light? See the light on the window?"—Connor's eyes getting glassier and glassier, his whimpers getting weaker and more widely spaced, until finally he dropped off and Amadeo could deposit him in his crib in Angel's room, where his daughter was a smoothly breathing mound under the blanket.

The thermostat has been set at seventy-seven, but even so his mother is buried under layers of sweaters and quilts, time seeping out of her. He stares at the pebbled stucco on his ceiling, trying to accustom himself to the idea of her absence, but like a plant angling itself imperceptibly toward a sunny window, Amadeo is aware of his mother's pulse across the hall, its quiet determined effort to keep her alive.

His mother is dying—she will die. Why is it so difficult to wrap his head around this simple, immutable fact? He feels the tug of both this inevitable future and of the past, when his mother was in her true form: quick and purposeful and smiling, with warm brown eyes, hair lush and long and evenly dyed.

For now, she is herself and not herself—stick-limbed, gray-skinned, the curiosity in her eyes receding, her voice both high and gravelly—an unwelcome version of herself that he nonetheless clings to. When she slips into light, permeable sleep, he can't stop checking on her, longing for her to jolt awake and reassure him.

His mother, who saved them all from their father, who fed them and buoyed them, who—why does he only now understand this?—was the font of all strength, is withdrawing, becoming small and peevish and disoriented. Amadeo can feel his memories of her being written over by this new, inferior version.

Now he'll never nap. He smashes his face into his sweaty pillow. The sense of quiet has fled, replaced by hot, jittery anxiety.

When his phone chirps, he startles, blinks stinging eyes. Brianna. *How are you??* Then, a moment later: *Would you want to hang out sometime soon?*

From his dresser, beer cans emit their yeasty funk. He must dispose of them before Angel gets home, or be subjected to her tight disapproval. His bedroom is chaotic with strewn clothes. His sheets smell grungy—his mother hasn't, for obvious reasons, been washing them of late.

His thumbs hover over the phone. Amadeo hasn't seen Brianna in weeks, not since before his mother's seizure, and he feels unfairly caught out.

Angel must not have told Brianna about Yolanda's diagnosis, otherwise surely she would have reached out to Amadeo with sympathy. With a pang, he wonders who his daughter is talking to about her troubles. Angel is probably frowning into her social studies book while, fifteen feet away, her teacher taps her phone, setting up an assignation with her father.

Since he met Brianna, everything had been going so well for him, and he'd begun seeing his every move—his interactions with Angel, his grandfathering, Creative Windshield Solutions—through her eyes. Under Brianna's imaginary attention, Amadeo felt more virtuous: patient, selfless, a good father and grandfather. More of the man that other men seem to be effortlessly, more of the man he always imagined he truly was, in his purest state.

But then that double punch of Monica's car and his mother's collapse undid his entire life. Failure upon failure. He couldn't call her.

His phone chimes. *It would be great to see you.* He can sense her anxiety, which makes him anxious, too, and vaguely guilty, and resentful that he's being made to feel guilty, because hasn't he been doing the right thing, caring for his mother?

Things have been crazy, Amadeo types, but instead of sending it, he calls her, not examining his reasons. His pulse throbs in his temple.

"Hey," she says, voice low and cautious. "How have you been?"

"Okay. Busy. Things have been crazy." He's trying to think how to tell her about his mother, but then she breaks in.

"It's just kind of weird that you haven't been in touch. I mean, I'm not saying we're in a relationship or anything, it's just pretty weird. Like, we were seeing each other every week. Texting all the time. We"—and here she drops her voice still lower—"*slept* together."

"You think I don't know that?"

"And then you disappear. Like, what am I supposed to think?"

Amadeo should want to comfort her or explain himself, but instead he's furious. His heart hops, ready for a fight. Who does she think she is, ambushing him like this? He called to tell her about his mother.

"I don't know what you think this is," he starts, then falters.

"Listen. I've taken real professional and ethical risks to be with . . . to spend time with you." She's whispering harshly, and he has the uneasy sense that tears are around the corner. But then she takes a deep breath. "Sorry," she says, voice clearing. "Okay, using my words. I guess I just thought you'd call and was bummed that you didn't."

Her frankness sets Amadeo at a disadvantage. "Well, sometimes you're not the most important thing going on."

A beat. "Okay, then. What *is* going on? Can we at least talk about it? About what's happening with us? It seems like we should talk about it."

Amadeo has the sense of losing ground. "Listen, you're a great girl and all, but there's a lot of shit happening in my life right now." This is a breakup script, he realizes.

"So what, you're ghosting me?"

"No, because if I was ghosting you, I wouldn't be calling, would I. My fucking mother is dying, okay? So get the fuck over yourself."

He hangs up. It was a slam dunk, an absolute, unassailable win, but the rush of vindication doesn't come. *My fucking mother is dying.* Stupid. He should have said, *My mother is fucking dying.* He punches the mattress. It's so damn hot in here. "Argh!" he yells, then stops. He listens for his mother's croaking, plaintive voice, for a breath. But all is quiet.

Angel's life is split in two. The first part is home, where she's always cooking or tending or rushing to do her homework, where, each day, her grandmother and her son display new behaviors, new changes to their bodies.

Connor almost crawls now, rocking back and forth on his hands and knees as if he's about to launch himself across a ravine, before splaying flat and dragging himself army-style across the floor. His bare chest squeaks on the linoleum, but he doesn't seem to mind.

For her part, Yolanda is becoming vague, hesitant in her speech and movements. She's misshapen, too, simultaneously too thin—breasts and belly deflated—and, from the steroids, swollen. Her cheeks have puffed; her skin is the color of dust. Her wrists, which were always narrow and graceful, have thickened, so that the silver bracelet she's worn Angel's entire life is a tight band.

One afternoon Angel comes across her grandmother standing before the bathroom mirror, smoothing the hair at her temple, smoothing, smoothing. Each time, it springs up, wiry and unruly.

"You okay?" Be careful, she wants to tell her grandmother. At the back of her head, the skin is stapled shut, the bone still not closed over.

Her grandmother frowns. "I don't feel like that."

"Like what, Gramma?"

She flaps her hand at the reflection. "Not inside. Inside me I'm cute."

"You're cute," Angel says. "You're still cute."

Her grandmother catches sight of Angel's troubled expression and smiles, skin creased around her mouth, teeth bared. "Can you call my mother?"

At Smart Starts!, every part of the day is designed to support Angel and to keep her mind on other things, and a smile or a stray touch from Lizette can, for up to half an hour at a time, wipe away her sadness.

The trouble starts midmorning one Wednesday in early October, when, twenty minutes into GED workbook time, Jen announces that she is selling raffle tickets to raise funds for her church's trip to Honduras. "It's the last day. I keep forgetting to tell you guys."

"Not the time, Jen," Brianna says, looking up from her laptop.

"They're only five dollars apiece." Jen waves her roll of paper tickets. "The prize is a spa day at Ojo Caliente."

"I'll buy one," says Tabitha, digging her wallet out of her purse. "I could use a spa day. What do they do, like massage you and paint your nails?"

"How're you going to get to Ojo Caliente, Tabitha?" asks Ysenia. "In your pumpkin chariot? You don't got money to waste on no raffle."

"It's not a *waste*," says Jen. "It's to benefit people in need."

"We got people in need right here," says Ysenia. "In this very room. We even got people from Honduras in Española. You want to encourage more to come over here where everyone's all strung out and there's crap for jobs?"

Jen sighs. "I don't know why you're complaining. You get food stamps. Plus you have a free lunch every day and—"

"Every *week*day," cuts in Ysenia.

"I'm just saying you're lucky, because there are churches right here in this town waiting and hoping you'll join." Jen looks like she might cry.

"I'm pretty sure there's churches in Honduras," Christy says.

"You know, you could buy a whole roll of tickets for nothing at Dollarland," says Trinity helpfully. "Then you'd definitely win."

Jen has buried her face in her hands, and only now does Angel notice that she's not wearing her promise ring.

"Hey," Angel whispers. "Are you okay? Are things cool with Jared?"

Jen looks squarely at Angel, stricken. Her eyes gleam with unspilled tears.

Lizette closes her workbook quietly and stands. She announces, "I'd like to call a Community Meeting."

Brianna sits up in surprise. "Uh, okay," she says, then looks as if she regrets it.

The girls scramble their desks into a circle, as if it's totally normal protocol for a student to call Community Meeting. Angel hesitates, then drags her own desk into the circle.

Lizette paces at the front of the classroom while the girls settle. Near the door, Brianna stands uncertainly, arms crossed, weight on one foot. It's a provisional stance, as if she might at any moment turn and bolt. Lizette stops pacing, and now she faces their teacher. "I have an issue I need to raise about favoritism."

Brianna opens her mouth, shuts it.

"And one of your favorites is Angel, which, whatever. And one of them is Jen, who breaks rules all the time, trying to convert our butts during work period. I was in the middle of a math practice test just now when she started running her mouth. Which is not *respecting others* or *supporting each other*." She taps the relevant rules, numbers one and five, on the butcher paper.

Jen clutches her roll of raffle tickets, her nostrils flared and white. Tears roll down her face.

"Lizette," says Angel quietly. "Stop." I don't think Jen's okay, she wants to say, but doesn't want to embarrass Jen.

"Shut up," Lizette tells her, and turns back to Brianna. "Some of us want to do our work and get our GEDs. So my point is, don't have favorites, and make everyone follow the rules the same way. Please." She clears her throat. "That's all." She sits at her desk and stares ahead of her at a spot on the carpet.

The girls swivel toward Brianna. Their teacher inhales shakily, but the breath seems to steady her. "That was way out of line, Lizette." Her voice is rigid. She strides to the front of the classroom and faces them, legs apart, hands on hips, shoulders flung back: her power stance. "I do not have favorites, I absolutely do not. If you have issues you want to bring up about how I run this class, we can schedule a meeting. I am always available."

"Right. You're always so supportive of me."

"Please stop fighting, guys," Jen says.

"You held the classroom hostage with that little 'Community Meeting' stunt. You wanted to humiliate me publicly."

"That's not true! You claim this is a democracy. But you're a dictator!"

"Um, okay. Let's have a little perspective, shall we? Also, I never claimed this was a *democracy*. I claimed that the students should have some input, a limited stake in the running of the classroom. But I *am* the teacher. It is my *job*, a job for which I'm paid very badly, to ensure that this whole ship doesn't sink." Brianna has abandoned the power stance. She's keyed up, hands flying here and there and chopping at the air. As her voice climbs, Angel hunches as if under a barrage. A deep embarrassment is welling in her: for Brianna, who should know better than to let Lizette get to her, and also for Lizette, who should know better than to behave this way. Both of them are being idiots. "I *am* the one with a degree and a shitty little salary and training in parent outreach."

"This is our school!" says Lizette.

"If it weren't for this school, you'd be dropouts."

The girls turn shocked faces on their teacher. "I wouldn't," says Ysenia. I wouldn't either, thinks Angel, but she isn't at all sure that's true. After all, she left EVHS.

Lizette's eyes are a glint of green between thick lashes. "You don't even got a kid. What do you know about what we go through?"

"Yeah, miss," says Christy, as if genuinely curious. "Do you even got a stepkid? A baby brother?"

"Children are raised successfully every day." Brianna enunciates each word.

"Just not by us," says Angel quietly.

Brianna widens her eyes at Angel. Her hands fall to her sides, then she looks around the classroom helplessly. "Excuse me, please." She makes for the door.

"Hey!" yells Lizette. Brianna stops, then turns. "You can't *walk out* of Community Meeting."

Angel is surprised at Lizette's tone: the woundedness, the shock that Brianna would disrespect such an essential, esteemed institution.

"Yeah," says Jen. "Let's just work it out together."

Brianna shakes her head and leaves. Behind her, the door falls quietly shut.

"Are you serious?" Jen demands of the shut door.

"Fucking bitch," says Lizette. Her arms clutch her middle, as if she's been punched.

"Stop, Lizette," says Angel.

"You got the hots for her? You like a white girl? You like tiny little titties?"

Ysenia scrunches up her nose. "*Too* far. That is seriously disgusting, Lizette."

Angel flushes. "You're not being fair."

"What the fuck is fair? *She's* not fair. Just because she thinks you're so great, Angel. What makes you so much better than any of us?"

"I'm not better," Angel says, stung. The argument is moving too swiftly, she can't grasp it. She stands before Lizette, but now Lizette is glaring stubbornly at her lap. Angel longs to touch her, but doesn't know if she's allowed to touch her at this stage of their relationship or whatever it is, and plus they're in public, and she's lost track of the distinction between what's a normal gesture and what could give them away. "We need this program."

Angel is about to put an arm around her, to draw her close, but then Ysenia is kneeling before Lizette on the carpet, both arms encircling her. "It's okay, Liz." Lizette drops her head onto Ysenia's shoulder and shuts her eyes. Her expression releases in a way it never has with Angel.

"She's not a bad person, and when we leave we'll have options." Angel is panicky. "Like, we could go to college. We could move away."

From the knot of Ysenia's arms, Lizette raises her green eyes to Angel as if she's the only one in the room. Between the heavy swaths of hair, her face is open, needing, and the sight of it guts Angel. Lizette is asking her for help.

If only they could be alone. If only everything keeping them apart—school and Brianna and illness and their babies—could be swept aside, and they could be pressed against each other. Then they could talk properly.

She moves toward Lizette, arms out. "Just go along with it, Lizette."

What was open in Lizette's face now snaps shut. She narrows those eyes and Angel freezes. Her mouth—that beautiful mouth—lifts in a sneer. "Go along with it. Right." She seems to come to a decision. "Fuck this." Lizette doesn't even sound mad anymore, just resigned. She extracts herself from Ysenia's clasp and stands, sweeps her belongings from her desk—papers, lip gloss, journal, hand sanitizer, pacifier, pens—dumps them into her purse, swings the purse onto her shoulder, and then she's out the door and down the hall toward the nursery.

"Wait," says Jen, and several of the girls call, too, but only Angel follows her.

"Lizette!"

She wheels around. "Fuck you, Angel."

Angel jerks back. Her face pulses with heat.

Lizette will run into Brianna in the hall, Angel thinks. Brianna will apologize, and they'll make up, and both of them will return to the classroom. The class will push the desks back to how they should be at ten thirty on a Wednesday morning, and they'll all go on with their workbooks. Later, Lizette and Angel will stand together somewhere quiet, and Lizette will pull her in, and this hurt will be worth it.

But no, a few minutes later, as the girls sit in silence, some with their eyes fixed on the classroom door, some fixed on the window, which overlooks the Family Foundations entrance, Lizette steps outside, Mercedes in her arms. The girls cluster at the window, but in a moment she's disappeared around the corner of the building.

Trinity is the first to speak. "You guys, what just happened?"

Amadeo hasn't been to the morada in months, not since Good Friday. He's almost surprised when he finds the key still on his dresser, behind a tissue box and among a clutter of loose vitamins and scratched CDs and the certificate of completion from his DWI class. He didn't expect he'd need to come back here, not after getting the nails.

He doesn't switch on the light. The morada remains largely empty until the next Ash Wednesday. Lemony sun filters weakly through the beige-painted window, illuminating the chaotic brushstrokes. The sealed air is hushed and smells faintly of dirt. Amadeo kneels before the statue of the suffering Christ and bows his head. He didn't bring his Rosary, which is just as well, because he's never prayed it alone and he doesn't know all the Mysteries, doesn't even know whether it's the day or the season or whatever for the Sorrowful or the Glorious or the Luminous. He clamps shut his eyes and tries to focus on the shifting red-black behind his eyelids. *Our Father, who art in heaven*, he begins, then loses track: *Please, God, let my mother be all right.* A stupid prayer, because his mother is most emphatically not going to be *all right*. Almost instantly, he's slipped back into thinking about Brianna, his sadness at how things ended, and then he's running through the conversation again, heart thudding, and then he's crying out in his mind to Brianna or God or to whomever, justifying himself, and before he knows it, he's not praying at all, but ranting.

Once again he trains his eyes on the Christ up there.

"My mother's dying," he tells the statue.

The man on his cross offers nothing. He is gazing at his own bleeding feet.

Jesus also had to take leave of his mother. Amadeo tries to remember this, but the story feels distant and dead.

The story was sadder for Mary, Amadeo realizes, because Jesus never doubted he was the Son of God. Mary, on the other hand—surely *she* had her doubts. Even if she loved her son and was proud of him, and liked the stuff he was saying about love and humility and all that, surely she sometimes wondered if her kid was nothing more than a deluded narcissist, with gifts, not of prophecy or divinity, but mere charisma. At what point did she begin to believe him, this kid whose diapers she changed and spit-up she wiped? Did she ever wonder if the wine and fishes were cheap conjuring tricks? Until they rolled that stone away, was she ever entirely free of doubt?

At what point might he, Amadeo, begin to believe that Connor, with his unhinged joyful garble, his single-minded focus on gumming his copy of *Good Night, Gorilla*, might have something to teach him?

He always assumed there was time, time to grow up, time to quit drinking, time to become the astonishing individual he's surely been on his way to becoming. Now, what's the point? Who is his audience?

The morada is changed. How had he ever believed this place held magic? It's just an old gas station, empty but for some benches. He feels like a fool for ever having trusted in it. He should have known better than to seek comfort here.

This whole enterprise—the hermandad, the ritual—it's all just created by people, feeble, limited people. He thinks of himself hauling the cross up Calvario. His swagger, his exaggerated acting, his humiliating belief that the performance meant something. All the while his mother was losing herself.

"Why?" he asks the man on the cross. "Why do you got to make it all so hard?" But he's entirely alone in this room.

He flexes his hand, pokes the pink knot of scar. He remembers the fact that the injury hurt, but he can't summon an actual memory of the pain, which is something his mother has said about childbirth. "That's why, like an idiot, I went and did it again. But you were worth it, hijito." If he can't remember the pain, how could it have meant anything at all? How could Christ's pain have meant anything over all these centuries?

The knuckles of his thumbs are pressed into his eye sockets, smearing flashes of red and green, when he hears a key grinding in the door. He leans back on his heels, blinks. The door scrapes along the concrete, and daylight leaps in.

"Oh," says Al Martinez. He runs his hands through still-thick hair. "I didn't think anyone was here. The lot was empty." Another younger, smaller man is with him.

"Hey," Amadeo says eagerly, standing.

The two men hover near the door. "Don't let me disturb you," says Al.

"No, no! I'm not disturbed."

"This is my boy, Isaiah. Isaiah, Amadeo." Al flashes a guilty glance at his son.

So this is the addict. "Good to meet you, man." Amadeo shakes his hand.

Isaiah Martinez is thinner and less robust than his father, but takes after him, with a short beard and features that are fine and handsome. When he smiles, the skin around his steady eyes creases.

"I wanted to show him the place," Al says.

Amadeo would like to engage the old guy in conversation, but they've never spoken about anything not directly related to the morada. Maybe they can go get something to eat. "So how're you guys doing?"

But both men have turned away from Amadeo. Isaiah is standing with his arms loose at his sides, staring at the statue of Christ.

For his part, Amadeo sees only Al's expression—the love and worry, the gentle loosening of the older man's features—and he is struck in his solar plexus by something he can't precisely identify, something that isn't quite envy and isn't admiration, but is in the same family. The feeling is aching, and pleasurable, too, and also unbearable in its intensity. He chuckles unconvincingly. "Yeah, whoever made that Jesus didn't hold back, huh."

Isaiah turns and smiles a pained smile at Amadeo, eyes shining. "My girlfriend OD'd last night. Just thirty years old and a hundred pounds and now she's gone." When his father puts a hand on his wrist, Isaiah falters. "I wish I'd been there."

Amadeo hooks his thumbs in his pockets, then removes them. He straightens.

"Listen, son," Al says, swiveling his attention slowly to Amadeo. "Will you pray with us?"

And as if he's a child being led to some place of safety where he's never been, Amadeo nods, and the three of them make their way to their knees. There, with the press of the concrete rooting him to the dirt and the whole spinning planet, Amadeo thinks not of himself, but prays, truly prays, for this lost young woman and this addicted man and for this father who loves him.

Only when she gets home on Friday afternoon, with the whole desolate weekend ahead of her, does Angel understand that the fight on Wednesday was irrevocable. Lizette made her decision, and she will not be going back on it. Angel drops onto her bed, watching from a fetal position as Connor plays with a sealed tube of diaper ointment on the floor.

Angel is sick of irrevocability: of fights, of illness, of death.

How are you? she texts Lizette, then feels stupid. As overtures go, it's too flip. Angel should address the fight, should address the fact that Lizette hasn't been in school. She should address the fact that, without Lizette, Smart Starts! is a different, much worse place. They've all turned against Brianna, even Jen. Brianna has been formal and unsmiling, setting them to work individually in their workbooks.

This afternoon's Community Meeting was a subdued affair, with no mention of Wednesday. "Okay," Brianna said into the silence as the girls looked at their nails. "How about we go around and do Peaches and Pits." And when Ysenia, who went first, gave only a Peach ("We had a birthday for my grandpa and that was fun"), Brianna didn't press her, and no one else offered a Pit either.

When it was Angel's turn, she truly couldn't think of a Peach, but she was surprised by the spite in her voice when she spoke. "I don't have a Peach." Her arms were crossed, a defiant posture that Angel realized was Lizette's.

Brianna startled, seeming to also recognize Lizette. "Okay. Pass, then. Christy?"

Lizette was right; in walking out on Wednesday, Brianna shook the bedrock of the classroom, and then betrayed them all further by letting Lizette walk out. After school, Angel peered into Lizette's desk, hoping to find something of hers, something she could hold, maybe, or something essential she'd need to return to her. But Lizette had cleared out everything.

She hasn't texted back. Angel should probably address the fact that she's been going nuts without any word from her, that she checks her phone a thousand times a day, that her heart hurts from being clenched. She should, probably, address the fact that she's in love with Lizette. So she adds, *Are you okay?* Which is lame, and offensive, too, because she's assuming that Lizette isn't okay, that what happened was terrible, and won't pointing out how terrible it is make Lizette feel worse? *How are you?* she tries—a nice, neutral, open-ended question, one that demonstrates caring—but it's too ordinary. And now the sheer number of texts—six, including three unanswered ones from yesterday—looks so desperate. She should stop—let Lizette answer if she wants, and if she doesn't, well, then, fine. But why should Angel be ashamed of how she feels? *Be true to yourself*, the magnet on her grandmother's fridge implores. *I miss you*, she writes, but rethinks it. *Miss you.*

Then she remembers the glaring fact that the lease is up in less than two months and Lizette is almost homeless. She's been so wrapped up in her grandmother that she hasn't even thought about the urgency of Lizette's situation. *Are you okay?*

Stop, Angel rebukes herself. She jams her phone in her sock drawer.

Just before bed, Angel allows herself to check her phone. Lizette hasn't texted, but there is a missed call from her, fifty-three minutes ago.

Angel sits upright on the edge of her bed and rings back, almost numb with nervousness.

"Hey." Angel can't read her tone from the single word. Depressed? Aggressive?

"Are you okay?" Angel tears her nail too close to the quick. "Where are you at?"

"Home."

"Oh. Good. So when do you move?"

"Just before Christmas."

Angel's heart pounds. "Do you . . . have a place to go?"

"Yeah, my one cousin's friend said I could crash with her for a while."

Angel is jealous of this anonymous friend who is able to offer Lizette such essential, material aid. "Oh. Okay. So you'll be okay?"

"Yes, Angel," Lizette drones. "You're not my mother."

"I'm really relieved. Did you get my texts?"

"Yeah."

"Well, we all miss you."

Silence. In the crib across the room, Connor wakes, sits up with bleary effort, and looks around, his cheek creased from the crib sheet. His face cinches as he works up to a wail, but when he sees his mother he smiles and bucks.

Angel flashes him an automatic smile and inhales. "You're, like, the main part of Smart Starts! It's boring without you. Who's supposed to keep Jen in check?"

Silence. Connor has found a board book in his bed. He turns it in both hands, inspecting it nearsightedly.

"Brianna seemed really sorry," Angel says.

"I don't fucking care." The words come out with startling velocity.

"I mean, she said that. Said, 'I wish Lizette would come back.'"

"She said that?" There's hope in Lizette's voice, hope so naked that Angel is taken aback. "Did she say that?" Lizette repeats with urgency.

"Yeah! Yeah." But her voice wavers. Angel is not a good liar, and this fact enrages her. She should be better, especially now, when the stakes are this high.

"I gotta go. Nice fucking try, Angel."

"Wait. Can't I see you?"

The pause is long enough that Angel wonders if the call has been dropped.

"Lizette?"

Then she says with a sigh, "I don't know. I gotta go."

For a long time Angel sits with her phone in her lap. As close an observer of Lizette as Angel has been all these months, she somehow missed this central, astonishing fact: that for all her bluster and antagonism, Lizette cares what Brianna thinks of her. She wants—desperately—for Brianna to help her.

And why shouldn't she want that? Lizette is a kid, a kid well within her rights to expect help from her teacher. Except that of course she doesn't, because she is also a kid who's been wronged and hurt and abandoned by every adult she's ever known.

Angel must talk to Brianna, must make her see how much Lizette and Mercedes need the program. And Angel needs Lizette. Their teacher can convince Lizette to return—Angel's sure of this—if only Angel can convince Brianna to convince her.

Over and over since Wednesday, Amadeo has picked up his phone to call Brianna. He needs to apologize—sour nausea rises like a fast incoming tide every time he thinks of her. And he thinks of her often—her alert face, the way she tucks her feet under her when they watch a movie, her weight against his chest.

On Sunday, once he's helped his mother with her breakfast, he goes to the morada again to pray, because that's where his priorities should lie, not on earthly concerns about some woman. Once he's there, though, he realizes that he's actually waiting for Al and Isaiah. He wants the reassurance of their steady, male presence. He wants reassurance that, simply by virtue of being on his knees in this building, he's in the right. Also, he wants to pray with them again.

"Where're you working now, son?" Al asked last time, as they locked up the morada.

Amadeo confessed that he isn't working, not exactly, that his business hasn't taken off, but his mom is sick, and he has to be with her, but that also he's worried about money. "You know, with her being sick and all. I just—I don't know why I don't have a job yet."

Isaiah said, "Listen, man. We're hiring at Lowe's. Let me know."

Amadeo was filled with a sense of well-being; here was this stranger, offering help.

"Okay," he said eagerly. "I will."

Now, Amadeo sits on the bench for nearly an hour, looking at his hands, but no one comes by. He wonders how Isaiah is holding up.

What would Jesus do? he asks himself, and the answer is clear: Jesus would follow up with Isaiah and get a job. Jesus would take care of his mother and his daughter. Jesus would call Brianna and apologize. Jesus would make things right, and Jesus would see if there was still any chance for something between them.

So call he does, as he walks home. It goes to voicemail, but then a second later she calls back.

"I wasn't going to pick up, but I changed my mind."

"Oh. Thanks."

"You were really a dick to me. How could I know your mom was sick?"

"I know," Amadeo says. "I'm sorry. Hey, do you want to hang out?"

"Are you calling because you want to hook up?" Her voice is defensive.

"No," Amadeo says, and wonders if she's right. He doesn't think so, but there's a chance she sees him more clearly than he sees himself. "Not that I'd mind. But I thought we could talk."

"God," she says. "Fine. Let's get together."

After school Monday, as the other girls gather their bags, Angel lingers near Brianna's desk, her weight uneven on her feet. "Miss?" she asks, because *Brianna* seems too familiar, given the shift in the classroom atmosphere.

Brianna flicks her eyes from her computer screen. "Yes, Angel. How can I help you?" Her voice isn't cold exactly, more wary.

It wouldn't be accurate to say that Brianna has aged in the last week—she doesn't have new wrinkles or a sudden stoop, she doesn't appear exhausted, nothing so clear as that—but ever since Lizette left, there's been a ragged, unhappy electricity around her that makes Angel think of her mother.

"What, Angel?" Brianna's eyes slide back to her screen.

And because she's thinking of her mother, of her mother's helplessness in the face of authority, and of how she rejected her mother's attempt to draw her back home, and then of her grandmother, Angel loses her nerve.

"Oh, nothing. See you tomorrow."

"You sure?" Brianna asks, and this time the softening in her voice makes Angel's step stutter, but not enough to break her momentum.

"See you tomorrow," she says, almost fleeing to the hall. Immediately, though, Angel regrets leaving—her job, after all, is to help Lizette. Why is she so afraid of Brianna? She clenches her fist in frustration. In the nursery, she recaptures her resolve, but by the time she gathers Connor, the classroom is empty. Brianna is talking to Raquel in the front office.

Angel pauses outside the door, but they're going on and on about quarterly reports, so she gives up. "Come on, baby," she mutters. "We're going home."

In the parking lot, though, she wavers again. She can't stand the thought of going home, of facing the long afternoon and evening with this important thing left undone. So instead of going to her grand-mother's car, she crosses the parking lot to the Jack in the Box. She'll get a milkshake, let Brianna finish up her meeting with Raquel and get some distance from the school day and from the other girls' reproachful silences, then try again. "Please call Lizette," she'll say. "I'm worried about her."

She's thrown away her cup, changed Connor's diaper on the grubby plastic changing table in the bathroom, and is pushing through the glass door to the parking lot outside, when she sees Brianna and her father. They are leaning against Brianna's green car, their heads bent together. Her father's hand is on her shoulder, and whatever they're discussing, it's obviously more intimate than anything they have any business discussing.

Later, Amadeo will scroll through the minutes before Angel approached them, ask himself what exactly they were doing at what point, and whether Angel could have seen them touching. He doesn't think so.

It's true that when he first rushed up to Brianna, he drew her in for a kiss and she responded and then pulled away. For a moment she kept her hand in his, and it felt good and right, but then she pulled her hand away, too. All of this—kiss, hand—lasted for no more than a couple seconds—no time at all, really, given the length of a whole life, say, or even the length of a single day. They stayed leaning against the car, not touching, while many long minutes passed— seven or eight or even nine maybe—long enough for Amadeo to apologize again, and for Brianna to say that he shouldn't have sworn at her and none of this was a good idea, and for Amadeo to ask her to tell him honestly, to seriously just say it, that he doesn't matter to her, and for Amadeo to consider pulling her in for another kiss, then to decide against it because he was afraid of how she stood there, the bridge of her nose white, the wisps of her hair flying around her face in the dry afternoon wind. Long enough for Brianna to repeat that this was all a bad idea, and she never should have slept with a student's father, and for Amadeo to tell her that his mom is doing bad, really bad, and Brianna has to understand just how much he's going through, it's crazy, like, actually the hardest time in his life. They stood there long enough for Amadeo, panic rising, to make argument after argument in favor of a relationship—don't they like each other? Don't they owe it to each other to try?—and she listened to all of this, her throat and face flushed, and he touched her shoulder to make her look at him—

There was time after the kiss for all this to occur before Brianna raised her head and murmured, "Shit."

At the time, however, Amadeo simply registers Brianna's curse and elaborates on it, thinking only, oh shit, oh fucking shit, he's been caught. Also Angel shouldn't even be here—he and Brianna arranged to meet here, now, precisely because Angel should be home—and why isn't she home? Shouldn't she be looking after his mother?

As Angel approaches, Brianna steps away from Amadeo, putting a decorous distance between them.

Angel's expression is still questioning, uncertain. Her eyes flick from one to the other, wary.

Amadeo is struck by how sapped his daughter looks, weighed down by the infant and by all of the infant's accoutrements. Her hair is escaping her ponytail. Connor is also out of sorts; he glances at his grandfather before grabbing a hank of his mother's hair and smashing it against his cheek. He drops his face against her shoulder in a gesture that looks very much like despair.

Amadeo is a father, a grandfather. He's involved in an adult relationship. His terminally ill mother depends on him. All of these things may be true on the surface, but in the face of Angel's exhaustion, whatever is going on between Amadeo and Brianna seems very slight and very juvenile.

Brianna plays it off like a champ; Amadeo is impressed by how swiftly she gathers herself. "Hi, Angel! You're still here? Your dad was just telling me that you've been reading a lot lately. I'm glad to hear it."

"Oh," says Angel.

Amadeo forces a laugh, but doesn't manage a smile. "A real bookworm," he says, though it isn't true. When would she have time to read?

Angel produces the car keys. "I'm going home." Without glancing at them again, she crosses the parking lot to Yolanda's car, which he'd failed to notice.

"See you tomorrow!" Brianna's countenance is shiny, impenetrable, and Amadeo draws inspiration from her demeanor. He wonders if she actually doesn't feel bad or if she's just good at hiding it. But what is there to feel bad about, really? They're adults, and people meet each other where they meet each other. It's not like there's a scandal here. It's not like *he's* Brianna's student.

"I stopped by to see if you were still here!" calls Amadeo to his daughter. Somewhere behind his sternum, a gnarl of dread is accruing mass, a dark pearl.

Angel unlocks the car, snaps Connor into the back, slams first one door, then the other, starts the engine.

"*Go,*" Brianna hisses. "Take care of that."

"Wait!" He looks to Brianna, and mouths, *I'll call you*, but she presses her lips and is already turning away, shaking her head.

When he gets in the car, Amadeo stares out the windshield, his hands folded primly across his knees. Somehow he can't remember how he usually sits. "What's up," he says jovially, but it's not a question. "I can ride home with you, yeah?"

She pulls out of the lot and turns into the stream of traffic.

He doesn't want to give Angel the opportunity to ignore him, so he scrolls through old texts, as if catching up on much-needed news. In the back Connor whimpers. Her stops are easy and smooth, her turns fluid. He can't help but feel proud.

"You're a good driver," he says, but Angel doesn't even spare him a snort.

Of course he was going to get caught. Amadeo never gets away with anything. But then, is it such a crime to be sleeping with Brianna? No one's being hurt, except maybe Angel, who doesn't have any actual claim on her teacher. She has no right to act all betrayed.

He ventures a glance at her righteous posture. He can't even begin to imagine what she's thinking. He should ask, but he can't muster the courage.

"So," says Angel, "you're, what? Sleeping together?"

Amadeo is almost relieved. "It hasn't even been that long, Angel."

"Oh, god. You are?" From the blanched shock in her face, he understands that she didn't, in fact, know this.

"It's a total nothing. Like, if it was something, I'd have told you. Honest. And it's over now."

"Don't even fucking talk to me. Don't even say one word."

Amadeo hadn't realized how venomous Angel could be. His tongue feels fat and scummy. He makes fists so tight his nails dig into his palm.

If only he knew what exactly she was mad about: the fact of their relationship or the fact that it was a secret. "I mean, we *couldn't* really tell you, because Brianna didn't want people thinking she played favorites. You know, like, that you were her favorite because she had a thing for me."

Angel turns flat eyes on him. "Did you hear what I said? I don't want to hear one more word from your mouth."

"Seriously, the best thing we had in common was you."

Angel rolls down the window as if he's made a stink in the car, and the wind blasts around them. She's drowning him out.

He puts up his hands in surrender—*Fine, I'll shut up.* The drive has never felt so long. They've left the dry, dusty valley and have climbed into thick, sheltering trees. It's a beautiful afternoon, the chilly wind whipping up the scent of piñon, the sunlight thick and mild as a benediction.

"Come on, Angel. Don't be like this."

They pull into the driveway. Angel shuts off the engine but doesn't get out. Without looking at him, she says, "Gramma's going to die soon. If you keep treating people so bad, who're you going to have left?" She unsnaps her seat belt. Even after she's gathered Connor, Amadeo doesn't move, gazing unseeing at the house, his eyes scratchy, stunned.

C lass started less than an hour ago. The students are bent over their workbooks. It's so quiet that Brianna can hear the mechanical click as the minute hand advances. Each time she glances at Angel, a geyser of anxiety jets through her, but Angel does not look up from her work.

Last night Brianna didn't sleep; rather, she slept, but woke after half an hour, and then twisted in her sheets, heart hammering, until morning. The one thing she has in her life is her job, this job she is good at, actually good at! And now she's jeopardized it by behaving in the most unprofessional way possible.

This morning she dressed in her red wool suit—blazer, stiff white blouse, skirt—complete with heels and dangling earrings. Her intention was to stride into the classroom girded for battle, professionally put together, impervious. But now that she's here, she keeps tugging on her skirt, buttoning and unbuttoning the blazer. She excuses herself to use the restroom, but can't bear to see her own reflection. Her thin hair pulled into that mingy, marble-sized bun makes her head look oddly small, her temples and forehead scraped and exposed.

"You going somewhere, miss?" Ysenia asks when Brianna returns. "You got a business meeting?" Her tone is merely polite, devoid of the energy and good-natured nosiness with which the girls once approached her.

"A job interview?" asks Jen.

Brianna rolls her eyes, but her face heats. "I don't remark upon your clothes, girls. I expect you to extend me the same courtesy. I should be able to dress however I want without commentary."

"Okay," Ysenia says agreeably. "Well, good luck."

Brianna removes her blazer, then sits back down at her desk. After a moment, the sounds of pencil-scratching and page-turning resume. Brianna presses her palm against her breastbone, trying to relieve the pressure there. All night, beneath her heart's hammering, was a constant low humming ache. Because, why? Is this heartbreak? Was she in *love* with Amadeo?

All at once Ysenia stands, walks over to Lizette's empty desk. She drags it to the wall, the legs leaving tracks in the short pile of the institutional carpet. "It's too sad to look at," she explains.

"She's not dead or nothing, Senia," Christy reminds her, then adds, "but it's still sad."

"Sad as crap," says Trinity.

At her desk, Angel blinks wildly. The girl is just a child, a vulnerable child, and all at once Brianna is furious, because why is Angel blaming Brianna for Lizette's poor choices? Brianna's mouth twitches as if she's working to dissolve some bitter lozenge. "Angel," she says. "Are you chewing gum?"

The girls regard Brianna, then swivel to Angel.

Now Angel meets her eye. Brianna's shoulders hunch within the boxy confines of her power suit.

"Spit out your gum," says Brianna.

In the space Lizette once occupied, there are four divots pressed into the carpet.

Angel holds Brianna's gaze and begins to chew, slow, determined, openmouthed.

"I'm serious. Spit it out." At Brianna's temples and above her upper lip, sweat rises.

"No." The word comes out parched. Angel licks her lips. "No."

Brianna half stands, her skirt rumpled and riding up, then stops in that position. "I am warning you, Angel. We have rules here, and if you want to stay in this community you need to abide by them."

"You kicked Lizette out for nothing."

"Lizette left. She made the decision to leave."

"Because you forced her out! She needed help, more help than any of us, and instead you forced her out! Right now she probably doesn't even have food in the house except maybe cereal. She only has her brother and he moved out, and now where's she going to go? To some stranger she barely knows? With a GED she could've done so many good things, like a job. And what about Mercedes? None of this is Mercedes's fault."

Brianna is miserable; she doesn't want to be doing this, but can't stop herself. "Angel, I am warning you: Get control of yourself. You are pushing boundaries, and that will not be tolerated."

"Boundaries?" cries Angel. "Oh, please, tell me more about boundaries. Tell how sleeping with my dad isn't pushing boundaries!"

Brianna's breath is sharp.

"Wait, what?" asks Trinity. "Are you for serious?"

Angel is crying, her sobs loud and messy. The girls watch—some with eyes on Angel, some with eyes on Brianna, their mouths actually agape.

"Angelica Padilla, spit out your gum now, or there will be serious consequences." It never crossed her mind that Angel would confront her, and like this, in public. She assumed that Angel would turn inward with her suspicions, that she'd second-guess herself—and that if Angel *did* somehow give voice to her suspicions—in private, after school, maybe—that she'd ultimately believe Brianna, might even apologize for thinking her teacher could be so preposterously unprofessional. Brianna had trusted in her power over the girl. Foolish, foolish. And she feels obscurely betrayed by Angel, too, as if she broke a pact—of what? Affection? After all Brianna has done to support her!

The movement of Angel's mouth is robotic. Her face is contorted, anguished, as she chomps. She looks like she is about to be ill.

"Okay, Angel. You've made your decision. Out."

Angel's mouth stills. Her tear-glossed eyes widen in disbelief.

Brianna holds her gaze for a moment, then, feeling very calm and self-contained, sits and turns her attention to the stack of papers on her desk. Ache blooms in her heart. Evenly, without looking up, she says, "You heard me. Don't come back."

Just a couple hours after his daughter leaves for school, she's back, Connor babbling in her arms. Without a word, she tosses the keys on the table, and spends the rest of the morning shut in his mother's room with the baby.

Amadeo gets up several times, beer in hand, pretending that he's on the way to the bathroom, but instead stands listening at his mother's bedroom door. Occasionally he hears murmurs, but mostly silence. Maybe they're napping in there. Or maybe Angel has already told his mother that he slept with her teacher, and they're so united against him they're beyond language.

When Angel helps her grandmother to the bathroom, or changes Connor, Amadeo tries to catch her eye, but she doesn't look down the hall in his direction. Each time the door clicks shut behind her. Amadeo brings lunch—two bowls of canned chicken noodle—but no one answers his knock. He leaves the tray outside the door, and when he comes back, one has been brought inside, the other left untouched.

At dusk, she emerges again, whispering to Connor. She crosses the hall, shutting the bathroom door. Water runs, and she's in there so long he understands that she's bathing the baby. Connor squeals, but his daughter's replies are muted.

Amadeo sits rigidly on the couch, his eye trained on the hall, his tense fingers pressing into the warm can. The beers do nothing to still his agitation.

The living room has darkened. He's lying in wait for his daughter, though he doesn't exactly know what he wants from her. Rather, he does know what he wants from her: attention, forgiveness, love. He wants her to join him in the living room. All things he has no right to.

When she opens the door, Connor rubs his eyes and the top of his head, mussing his damp curls. The smell of baby shampoo reaches Amadeo and fills him with a yearning nostalgia for a simpler, cozier time, a time that has never, for him, existed.

"Hey!" he calls, and she freezes without turning. "Aren't you going to eat? Have you eaten all day?"

"No. Thanks. We're going to bed."

"We need to talk." His voice comes out sounding high. "You can't just ignore me. I'm your dad." He realizes that pulling rank is not the best tactic, given his recent sins against her, and given how much responsibility she has had to shoulder. Her face is in shadow.

"What do you want to talk about?" She hitches the baby higher on her hip.

Amadeo falters. "Nothing, I guess. You go ahead and put him to bed."

Now she turns to him. Her jaw is set. When Connor catches sight of his grandfather, his face splits into a rubbery grin and he grabs at the air to wave. Amadeo doesn't wave back. "We could talk about the fact that you're drinking all the damn time. Or, you know, we could talk about how I'm doing in school. You may be interested to know that I got kicked out. For chewing a piece of gum. Your little girlfriend expelled me."

"What? But you're one of the best in the class. Brianna told me so."

Angel flaps one arm up at the pointlessness of his argument, lets it fall.

"She can't do that to you. I'm going to talk to her. I'll go there now."

"You think that's gonna work? Mr. President of the PTA? And how are you going to get there? Limo?"

"I'll take care of this, Angel."

"Whatever."

Long after, Amadeo contemplates the phone in his hand, then dials. As he listens to the phone ring and ring, his heart sloshes in his chest. He's enraged at this woman for bullying his daughter, but he's nervous, too, and he hates that he's so nervous. And he's also unsure, both of his own rights and of Angel's. He's already composing his voicemail in his head (*It's Amadeo, we need to talk*) when she picks up.

"Before you say anything, I want to be clear that I am speaking to you in an official capacity, as Angel's teacher."

"You're ruining her life over a piece of gum?"

Brianna laughs, one contemptuous honk. "That's a bit of an over-statement, don't you think?"

"You're kicking her out of school over a piece of *gum*. It's not about gum, and you know it."

Amadeo pictures her exactly, her splotchy flushed throat, the anxious blinking. But when she speaks her voice is smooth and collected, brittle. It is the voice of Valerie, of Monica Gutierrez-Larsen, the voice of all these pushy professional women who think they can get the best of him.

"I don't know what you're talking about, Mr. Padilla. The zero-tolerance rule is what keeps the program functioning."

"*Mr. Padilla*? You fucking joking me?"

Brianna presses on. "It's what keeps the classroom a safe space. I would be remiss in my responsibilities if I allowed students to break rules without consequences. Consequences are what teach us—"

"I think my daughter knows about consequences. You can't just kick a kid out for chewing gum."

"I can. Angelica broke the classroom rules. Gum is a choking hazard. Gum destroys classroom equipment."

"Angel spits her gum in the trash. And what kind of fucking equipment you got in there?"

"Smart Starts! is a privilege, not a right, and it is supported by a private foundation. We have a waiting list of girls who will be grateful for Angel's spot and who are more than willing to abide by the rules."

She must have rehearsed this. This Brianna sounds not at all like the awkward girl who was so ashamed of her virginity. He's shivering as if he were cold. Maybe he is cold.

"I hope you're satisfied," Amadeo says. "Taking out your feelings about whatever happened with us on a kid. On *two* kids. You're fucking mental."

"This has nothing to do with my *feelings*, Mr. Padilla. This is about policy."

"Would you quit with that bullshit? We've seen each other naked. I'm sorry it didn't work out with us. What, you wanted to be Angel's stepmother?" Again that imagined future presents itself: the green lawn, the big house with pillars and sunny rooms, Amadeo and Brianna and Angel and Connor, and, in Brianna's arms, a new baby. He's imagined it so clearly it has the quality of a memory. He realizes with a pang that he'd never included his mother in this picture.

"Why would you *tell* her? Do you always talk to your daughter about your sex life?"

"I didn't tell her. She ran into us, remember? She *asked* me."

"So? Then you *lie*."

"I'm not going to lie to my kid. I'm trying to be an honest person that takes responsibility."

"Dandy for you. You have nothing to lose. I jeopardized my whole job for this."

"My daughter! I have my daughter to lose!"

"Thank you for calling, Mr. Padilla. I appreciate your concern, and I know that your concern is very valuable to your daughter. She'll continue to need your support."

"Please," says Amadeo. "Angel loves school. She loves *you*. Her grandmother is dying right now. My mother."

After a silence, Brianna says slowly, "Listen. At this point it's out of my hands. But Angel could talk to the agency president."

"Oh, fuck you," Amadeo says. He throws the phone across the living room. It lands on the kitchen linoleum and skids into the baseboards. "Fucking *bitch*," he says, and then worries that Brianna has heard him. He retrieves the phone and puts his ear to it. But the phone isn't working. It won't work again. Then he worries that he's wakened his mother or daughter or the baby. He steps quietly into the hall, listens, but there's no sound coming from either bedroom.

Now he wants to wake Angel, to let her know he tried, to let her know how truly awful Brianna is. As if Eric Maxwell would listen to a sixteen-year-old girl. He wants Angel to know that he sacrificed his cell phone to her cause. But he checks his impulse to prove to her what a good father he is, because a good father wouldn't tell his daughter about any of this. A good father would protect her.

Amadeo whirls uselessly on one foot. Then he goes to the fridge and helps himself to another beer.

The first early snow comes, a dry flurry that doesn't accumulate and stops by noon, and along with it the spicy smell of piñon smoke rising from neighbors' chimneys. It's late November. In Española, Christmas decorations are up, but Angel rarely goes into town now.

There was talk about moving Yolanda to Valerie's in Albuquerque, where she'd be closer to hospitals, but Yolanda wept. "My house."

So they've pushed Yolanda's canopy bed against the wall, taken out the bureau and dressing table, all to make room for an ugly hospital bed that rises and falls. And a commode with a removable gray plastic pan. Yolanda is now unable to do things that she could manage even a week and a half ago: walk with assistance to the bathroom, for example.

Yolanda drifts, she mumbles, she counts to herself, brow furrowed. She sips most of her food through a straw: apple juice, thick vitamin shakes, chocolate milk made with half-and-half for the calories.

It's beyond Angel's comprehension how something in the brain can cause her grandmother to lose so much weight in just a few short weeks. Nonetheless, it's physical work, helping Yolanda onto the wheelchair or commode. When her grandmother stands—lurching, unsteady—her buttocks and thighs under her nightgown are so emaciated that the elastic on her underpants slips.

When it becomes clear that Yolanda can no longer clean herself, she submits to Angel, her face pinched with humiliation. They buy plastic boxes of baby wipes in bulk. Angel holds each wipe in her hands to warm it, whether she uses it on Connor or on her grandmother.

"Well," Yolanda says, resigned. "I guess I've wiped your button. Batten."

Once, to her eternal shame, Angel grouches, "Why can't *Dad* ever help?"

"No!" cries Yolanda, and Angel is shocked by the look of alarm that crosses her grandmother's face.

"I'm sorry, I'm sorry. I didn't mean that."

The caretaking is all-consuming. Angel doesn't know what they'd have done if she hadn't been expelled. Yet she mourns her time at Smart Starts!, and goes over and over the events of that morning. She wanted to spit the gum out, she really did. The wad was stale, and as she chewed the sour mass, jaw aching, nausea rising, her mouth filled with saliva. Her teacher was unmoved by Angel's sorrow, completely without sympathy or kindness or love, and Angel wasn't so caught up in her sobs that she didn't register the distaste in Brianna's expression.

Driving to school that morning, Angel had thought about how it would be when she and Brianna finally talked about everything— Lizette, her father. She was scared of the conversation, yet also looked forward to it. Angel would explain that her feelings were hurt, and Brianna would apologize. Or if she didn't apologize, she would at least explain to Angel that actually it was fine, totally normal, that she'd slept with Amadeo, that they were adults and it wasn't actually the betrayal Angel felt it was. There was never any question in Angel's mind that she would forgive her teacher. She expected, after all, that people would mistreat her—that people in general mistreat other people— and though she minded, really, really minded, what she wanted was the time after, when they could be closer for it. Even if Brianna and her father had lied outright and told her that nothing had ever happened between them, Angel would have believed them. Even in the face of glaring evidence, Angel would have believed them, because she needs them.

Her whole life, Angel has tiptoed around adults, trying to be good, then all at once this anger poured out of her, all of it directed at this woman Angel loves—*loved*, she realizes now. The crazy thing is that Angel even once dreamed of Brianna being her stepmother. Now, she feels actual hatred toward Brianna, who is not at all the person she pretended to be, the person Angel needed her to be.

Her grandmother is all Angel has left, her grandmother and her son.

———

THANKSGIVING IS SUBDUED, without arguments or the smell of cooking. Valerie brings most of the dishes already prepared in plastic containers, which they reheat, without even putting out platters. Yolanda sits quietly in her wheelchair, eating nothing, gesturing as if punctuating a silent conversation with someone not there. Tíve steals glances at his niece and then looks away, Adam's apple bobbing. Lily's eyes keep welling up, but she swipes the tears away, no-nonsense.

Even Sarah, who can usually be counted on to enliven a gathering, is muted. "This is good chicken, Mom," she says gravely.

"Thanks. I figure no one likes turkey anyhow."

With difficulty, Yolanda lifts her dinner roll from a pool of gravy on her untouched plate and inspects it. She is slouched in her chair, head tilted. For nearly a minute, as she stares at the roll, gravy drips onto her dress, and they all watch in silence. Finally she drops the roll. It tumbles down her front, bounces off her lap to the floor, the stillness broken.

Around the table, exhalations. Yolanda works her lips. When Tíve cuts himself a bite of chicken, the knife squeals against his plate.

Valerie clears her throat. "Angel said you got your license reinstated, brother."

"Yeah."

Ordinarily Angel might point out that he's still on probation, but she doesn't.

"Good." Valerie's voice is loud. "Mom's not able to tell you this anymore, so I have to. She depends on you, Angel depends on you, that baby depends on you."

Angel flashes an alarmed look at her father, but he just pushes his fork into his uneaten potatoes. "You think I don't know that?"

"Mom," says Lily. "Leave him alone. You're just sad."

"Yeah." Valerie's eyes redden. "I'm not wrong, but yeah."

They are all relieved when Yolanda nods off. Angel and Valerie help her into bed, turn the blinds to cut off the sunlight. Soon after, Valerie and the girls leave, and all around, the hugs are long and quiet.

———

THAT EVENING, Ryan shows up in a puffer coat. "Hey!" he calls, cheerful, and then he catches sight of Yolanda listing in the chair, despite the cushions Angel has shoved around her. "Hey," he says, hushed. He's come bearing gifts: a chocolate Advent calendar each for Connor and Angel, with $1.99 stickers still affixed, and a box of Get Well Wellness tea. "For your grandma." He reddens.

Angel doesn't even have the heart to rip into him. "Gramma, remember Ryan, Connor's dad?"

Yolanda brightens; this is more interest than she's shown in weeks.

"Nice to see you, Mrs. Padilla," Ryan says, hand extended. "Happy Thanksgiving." When it's clear that Yolanda won't lift her hand to his, he places the tea on the slope of her lap. "Just a little something."

She's not speaking well today, but she smiles, turns the box of tea in her hands, cellophane crinkling.

"I hope you feel better."

With embarrassment, Angel notes that her grandmother's sweatpants are bunched and puffy at the crotch, and there's yogurt crusted on her chin that Angel failed to wipe away. It's intolerable that Ryan should see them like this, should stand before them, pleased with his meager, useless gifts.

"Thanks for coming," Angel says. "We're kind of busy."

Yolanda gazes at the door long after Angel has shut it behind him. "Nice boy," she says.

———

THE NEXT AFTERNOON, during Connor's nap, Angel lies beside her grandmother on the small hospital bed, careful not to crush her limbs. The bed creaks, but holds them both.

The television is on, some manic game show, with dramatic music and flashing lights and stricken faces. Some days, Angel tries to engage with the television, cracking jokes, making guesses of her own, an energetic performance for her grandmother. But today, she is quiet, her head on the edge of her grandmother's pillow.

As if her body is turning into something else already, Yolanda doesn't smell like herself. The ghost of that old powdery scent is there, but it's morphed into something waxy and sweet that goes to the back of the throat.

Beside her, the baby monitor winks its red light. They've moved the transmitter from next to Connor's crib to Yolanda's bedside table; now it picks up her thin cries as she sleeps. She sleeps almost as much as Connor did right after his birth. "Mama," they sometimes hear. Or, "Wait, please." Mostly it's garble, delivered with conviction: "Forty eighty I says trespasses." Once, horribly, she called, "Stop! You're hurting me!" Her voice through the monitor is somehow both reedy and gravelly, unlike her waking voice, which is unlike her old, healthy voice. Sometimes she just moans.

Now, beginning to retch, Yolanda tries to pull herself up. Angel stands swiftly, helps her lean over the mixing bowl—the same mixing bowl with the dent that Yolanda used when she taught Angel to make tortillas. She holds the back of her grandmother's head in her hand as if she were an infant, careful with her soft spot under the knit cap. Yolanda vomits, a watery, foul-smelling green fluid. It seems impossible that a body so frail can be wracked so violently. Yolanda drops back against the pillow. Her eyes are more dimensional, the closed lids translucent and shiny.

"Here, let's get you cleaned up." Angel uses one of Connor's terry washcloths to wipe her grandmother's trembling chin.

Her grandmother's eyes flutter, but remain shut. "I'm a mess."

Each time her grandmother tries to speak, Angel tenses, praying for lucidity. Today she's been sharp. Angel takes her grandmother's hand. It is warm and smooth, the skin loose over the delicate bones. "Your hands are always so soft. Why are they always so soft?"

Her grandmother's eyes open slightly and she laughs, a low weak chuffing. "I'm not doing dishes no more."

For a time, they lie there, watching the shifting pattern of the sunlight on the ceiling.

Her grandmother pats her hand. "Glad you're here, hijita. Right with me."

"I'm glad you're here. I'm glad we're here together."

"You're good girl."

All at once, tears slide from Angel's eyes. "No I'm not."

"Yes." Her grandmother's lips barely move. "Hijita, promise. Get a kind boyfriend."

Sadness presses like a knuckle against her throat. "Yeah," she says. "Okay."

Her grandmother takes a deep breath that Angel can feel all along the length of her body.

The room is quiet, a night-light glowing in the corner. Yolanda wakes in a panic. She's forgotten something. She cannot sit up, but she searches the shadowy room, gasping, oppressed, terrified. She has no memory of the faces that had crowded close to assure her of their love, no settled feeling of reconciliation or resolution. Just pure disorientation, immense and intolerable, untethered from reason or cause. There is a shape there in the dark beside her. Anthony? she asks, but the word means nothing to her, and she's not sure she spoke it.

"Mom? I'm right here." Amadeo touches her hand, and, just like that, the terror is gone. Yolanda sinks back against the pillow. She is aware of being awash in love, love flowing from the world toward her, and she is afloat on it. She is in the bottom of a boat rocking on a serene ocean, gazing up into the depths of stars, anchored safely to the dock by her son's hand. Somewhere she can hear the water lap against pilings.

And then Yolanda is dancing in the arms of a very ugly man. The room is light and Gram Parsons and Emmylou Harris are singing about highways. It's an incredible song, she realizes now, and wonders why she never noticed before. Her body is filled with the music, and the man's arms around her are steady and pliant, guiding her across the floor. Tang of barbecue and beer, the easy give of the boards under her feet, the clean scent of his shaving cream and soap. She feels sated, afloat on the music, steady on her feet. The man says something to her, and though she doesn't hear, she laughs and nods. *Out with the truckers and the kickers and the cowboy angels.*

He pulls her close as he guides her smoothly through a turn. The spin is easy and graceful, and he takes her around the dance floor again.

She is weightless, and when she leans into him, it's as if his heat alone holds her aloft.

The song is on its last refrain, and Yolanda isn't ready for it to end, but there is still time. *Twenty thousand roads I went down, down, down*. The man bends toward her, and Yolanda is poised for the kiss she knows will come. She is waiting for it. Goose bumps rise on her arms as she anticipates the delicious mild scratch of his stubble, the press of his lips against her neck, the electric rush that will pass through her like absolution.

Yolanda is still waiting when time stutters and blinks out.

This is death, then: a brief spot of light on earth extinguished, a rippling point of energy swept clear. A kiss, a song, the warm circle of a stranger's arms—these things and others—the whole crush of memory and hope, the constant babble of the mind, everything that composes a person—gone.

The baby is seven months old. He still needs his diapers changed, still demands milk and love and Nurturing Touch. Angel isn't even sure he notices that Yolanda is gone. He has developed a bizarrely intense attention span, and exhibits a particular interest in junk mail, turning promotional postcards from department stores inexpertly in his hands, studying them with no less wonderment than if they'd been dispatches from Jupiter.

When he bends over his postcard, the sight of the chaotic duckling fuzz and that bare, vulnerable little channel at the base of his skull leaves Angel weak. After many minutes have passed, Connor will lower the postcard, blink, swivel his head in search of his mother, and then, when he finds her, erupt in emphatic babble.

Will Connor remember Yolanda at all? As a shadow or a sensation, as a vague feeling from those long, early days of his infancy? The thought that he won't is unbearable. Connor pumps his arms, whacking his own face with the postcard, startling himself quiet before emitting a peal of laughter at the joke of it all.

Angel had sort of believed that death—the death of someone essential and life-defining—meant the end of everything, but here she is, mashing banana with a fork, loading the dishwasher. Here she is (having placed Connor in his pen), doing something as mundane and necessary as choosing from among the bottles lined up along the edge of the bathtub and shampooing her hair.

This heartache is so much larger than anything she's felt. It's agony—she can't sit still, it hurts so much—and also enlivening. Angel had no idea that the world could hold ache like this, just as, before Connor was born, she had no idea it could hold such love.

But she can't cry. Right after Connor was born, Angel cried so often that sometimes she didn't even notice. Sometimes she'd be moving through the house, breasts leaking, Connor fussy in her arms, and would only become aware of her own sobs when she realized she had to blow her nose. But since her grandmother's death, apart from some dry convulsions the night of, all those once-plentiful free-flowing tears have dried up. If only she could cry, she might find some relief.

Yolanda's death has meant tasks—now, instead of spooning thin oatmeal into her grandmother's mouth, she deals with the men who come to collect the hospital bed and the wheelchair and all the other equipment on loan. There are copies of the death certificate to order, thank-yous to be written to all those faceless friends of Yolanda's who sent flowers and notes. The bills are piling up—phone, utilities, cable—and she sorts them and sets them aside for her father.

She's glad to be busy. But still, somehow, the days feel slack and empty, Angel rattling around in them. She who'd once felt so overwhelmed by the needs of her son, who'd longed for his naps just so she could think for one stinking second, now lingers at his crib, listening to his near-silent breath, waiting for him to wake up and keep her company.

Here's what she doesn't want to think about: her grandmother's death has brought—horribly, undeniably—relief. She'd been warned that this would be the case, by the hospice aide and the doctor, but the warnings don't make her feel any less shitty.

What also feels shitty is her inability to make herself comfort her father, who seems to be having no trouble at all accessing *his* tears. He's spent the last two weeks sobbing and casting plaintive looks at her from across various rooms.

"I feel so bad," he whimpers, his red eyes imploring.

"Yeah," she says, and returns to wiping mashed peas from Connor's chin. His face is chapped. The house is hot and dry, and outside the air is cold and dry, snow bunched like squeaking dirty Styrofoam. Angel's knuckles crack and bleed.

Yolanda's death should have drawn them closer, but it hasn't. Instead of compassion for her father, she feels resentment, because he made her do so many punishing jobs, jobs no kid should have to do, and now he wants her to *comfort* him? Worse, he stays up late every night, drinking, tears running down his cheeks, as if he's the only one who lost anything. In the morning, she gathers the bottles—and not just beer now, vodka, too—and puts them in the recycling. He doesn't keep the beer in the fridge anymore, not after she poured them all down the sink two days after the funeral, so he's stashing them somewhere else, out back or in his room (is she supposed to search for them?), drinking them warm, which is all the more pathetic. Just looking at him slumped at the table, eyes red and lips trembling, makes her so mad she wants to spit or smash a window or stomp a hole right through the kitchen linoleum.

Hard little bitch.

To her credit, Marissa has been by every couple days, bringing lentil soup and Angel's favorite homemade tortillas from the lady with the cooler in the Superette parking lot and a double batch of green chile mac and cheese.

"Thanks," Angel says, pulling away from her mother's tight embrace too soon.

"God," Marissa says, turning in a slow circle around the living room while Angel scrubs at a baking sheet from the entire frozen pizza she ate for lunch. Angel has been starving since her grandmother died, a sucking black nothingness. She's been gorging on the food neighbors bring; just last night she ate an entire Frito pie casserole, standing joylessly over the dish with her fork at the counter, then, after, lay in bed, heavy and sick and sleepless.

"I can't believe Yolanda is gone. Like, really gone."

"I know," Amadeo says from the couch, his plate heaped with Marissa's food.

"Well, believe it." Angel's voice is as dry as her eyes.

"I mean, she was, like, my mother-in-law," Marissa says, turning her tear-glossed gaze on Angel.

"No she wasn't."

"Well, closest thing to." A note of stubbornness has come into her voice.

"She liked you," Amadeo says, and both Angel and Marissa turn to him in surprise.

"Really?" Marissa sits beside him on the couch.

"Yeah, of course. She thought I was an idiot for breaking up with you."

Marissa laughs. "You didn't break up with me. That would've been the mature path to take. You were just a dick and then quit calling until I got the message."

Angel puts down her scouring pad and listens in amazement. She's never heard her mother and father talking to each other like this, with kind directness, has so rarely ever even seen them in the same room.

"Well, yeah. That was my mom's point, too."

There was a time, when Angel was seven or eight, when her dearest wish was for her mother and father to get back together. "Never gonna happen," her mother said brusquely the one time Angel brought it up. "That's a mistake you don't make twice."

Now Marissa's voice softens. "Remember when we were in high school and Yolanda used to buy us those frozen hash brown patties and after school we'd make green chile and bacon sandwiches, with them as the bread? Still when I have hash browns I think of being pregnant and hanging out at your house. Remember how Val would be so mad about all our dishes in the sink, but she'd do them anyway before your mom got home?"

"Ah, shit, yeah. Poor Val."

"What jerks we were. How's Val doing? Is she pretty shook up? She was always real protective of your mom."

"Yeah," Amadeo says, and, eyes filling, he excuses himself.

As she's leaving, Marissa hesitates at the door. "Anytime you want to come home, Ange, you know you can. We could set up the crib in the laundry room, turn the whole thing into a nursery. When you were a baby you loved the sound of the washing machine. It put you right to sleep."

"Thanks," Angel says, exhausted. "We're fine."

———

FOR WEEKS NOW, Angel has been sending Lizette a text a day. *Hey*, she says. *What's up?* Or *Call me!* Or *I got expelled, too.* Even, *I miss you.* But Lizette never replies.

Therefore when Ryan asks if he can come over after school, Angel says sure. *He* is reliable in his texts, so over the past weeks, she's told him about getting kicked out, and about her grandmother dying. On the subject of Smart Starts!, he was gratifyingly outraged. "Dang, that's so wrong!" On the subject of her grandmother, his mournful sympathy comforted her. Once the conversation continued until Angel told him she had to go to bed. Always, he sends the last text, and the first the next day. Angel's role in these conversations is harsh, mocking, reluctant, but she enjoys them in a grim sort of way, enjoys his devotion, and figures she deserves it, given how her life is going.

Angel watches from the window as he jog-skips to the door, his backpack bumping up and down with him, but once he's out of her sight line, a long moment passes before he knocks. Angel can't see him, but imagines him adjusting his nards in his pants in that disgusting way boys do.

Connor is out of sorts, rubbing his face clumsily. He was up in the night, screaming and arching his back in discomfort from the new tooth perforating his top gum.

Her father is god knows where with the truck, probably draining the last of Yolanda's savings account at the liquor store. Angel pushes that thought from her mind.

"Hey," Ryan says as she opens the door. He bends over for a hug, but she has Connor in front of her like a shield, and he ends up patting her on the arm. "I'm really sorry about your grandma."

"Thanks."

He keeps looking at her steadily, and Angel winces under his attention. "I didn't know her that well, but she was nice to me."

"I know."

"Hiya, little dude," Ryan coos, and Connor's face scrunches into a lopsided, drooly grin. Ryan leans his face close to Connor's, which means his face is also close to Angel's, and she can see a yellow-tipped zit on his cheek. She shifts Connor away.

Ryan moves, too, though, and keeps talking gibberish an inch from the baby's face, and Connor's delight rises into squeals. "Little doodarooni, little doodaroonikiss."

"Careful. You'll make him puke. He just had yams." She gestures to the orange-streaked surface of Connor's high chair.

Connor's laugh turns to whimpers. He thrusts his arms down, as if trying to push everything away, and his fist gets tangled in a fold in his pants, triggering another wail. She jiggles him. "Hush now."

"What's wrong with him?" Ryan asks in alarm.

"He's getting another tooth. It's normal." She holds the writhing baby close, not wanting to let him go. "I guess I should put him down. I hoped he'd stay up for your visit."

In his adult voice, Ryan says, "Oh dang. I miss this guy."

"Say night-night," Angel instructs Connor, who screams in response.

"Okay," says Ryan, disappointed. "Night-night, little feller."

As Angel carries Connor off to her room, Ryan drops his backpack onto the floor with a thump. The thought of those algebra and life sciences textbooks fills Angel with hot, yearning anxiety, because she must be falling so far behind. She probably can't even fathom how far behind she is.

After Connor has been put down, Angel expects Ryan to go, but when she emerges, reattaching her bra under her shirt, she finds that he's cleaned up the yammy high chair, done the stray dishes on the counter, taken out the kitchen trash, and is in the midst of wiping down the counters, too. Angel sits on the couch, tucks her feet under her, watching.

"What are you doing? Why are you being so nice?"

He rinses the sponge, places it beside the sink, and comes to sit beside her. "So how are you? Really?" His Adam's apple bobs nervously.

Angel shakes her head. Her throat is tight, and, now of all times, she can feel the tears coming. And because she can't bear to cry in front of Ryan, she pulls him toward her and kisses him.

His mouth is muggy and tastes faintly of a cherry cough drop. After she pulls away, he keeps his eyes shut and chin canted toward her for a beat too long.

When he opens his eyes, they're gleaming, and he says, "I really, really like you."

"I didn't mean to do that." Angel thinks with anguish about Lizette, the taunting quirk of her mouth when she's about to kiss Angel. The unfairness is staggering—that *he's* the one here, that she loves Lizette in the first place. Again, the tears threaten to come. She swallows and leans in again, but because she doesn't want to kiss him, she pushes her hand up his T-shirt. Needing no encouragement, he pulls the shirt over his head, dropping it to the ground.

Ryan tucks his elbows close to his skinny torso. "Your dad's out?"

"Yeah. We'll hear him if he gets home."

She traces her finger down his chest, and, in fact, there's a narrow thrumming trench, and alongside it, an even paler scar. He's nearly hairless—another thing she doesn't remember from that first time—and his skin is a little sticky to the touch. He watches her, eyes hazy, lips parted, his chest rising and falling rapidly. He's so trusting—though why he would trust her, she who has been so mean to him—is beyond her. It makes her hate him, and love him a little, too. If she could only be into him, it would make such clear, easy sense. She imagines pushing through his chest as though he were a too-ripe tomato, which makes her think of the sad tomato plants tended by Lizette's brother, and then of Lizette. She imagines Lizette watching her here with Ryan, imagines the hot twist of envy Lizette would surely feel, so she leans into Ryan. She runs her hands down the smooth skin of his back, slides a finger into his waistband. See? she imagines telling Lizette.

Ryan murmurs. He lifts her shirt, then takes it off, and she allows this, allows him also to unhook her bra, still with the sense that she is performing for Lizette. She turns her back to him and peels the nursing bra off, sweaty and sour. She tucks it under her shirt on the cushion, then turns back, supporting her heavy breasts with her forearm. Her nipples are alarming: eager, wrinkled things, and she covers them, embarrassed.

But when his hand is in her underwear, his crooked finger digging around, she tenses. Angel lies against the couch, watching the light shift on the pebbled plaster ceiling. She wonders if she can feel any pleasure from this, and then, when she decides not, takes his bony wrist and removes his hand.

"You don't want it?" he asks, disappointed.

"No." She arches her back to zip up her jeans, then pushes herself up and away from him. "Sorry." She puts on her shirt, balls up her bra to deal with later, and crosses her arms.

"I want you so bad," he says, but not wheedling, just a statement of fact.

"Oh." Angel tries to think of the kind thing to say.

Ryan sits up, too, and smooths his hair. The skin at his throat and chest pulses. He looks straight ahead. They both do, at Yolanda's doll cabinet: the big-headed little blondes in their dirndls, the porcelain Princess Di with the satin wedding dress and gruesomely painted teeth, the dead-eyed Victorian girl with her elaborate velvet hat. Angel realizes she has no idea what those dolls meant to her grandmother, doesn't know which were Yolanda's when she was a girl, which were Valerie's, why Yolanda bought the rest. And now, of course, it's too late to ask.

"Is this going to be weird?" Ryan asks bleakly.

"How much weirder can it be?"

Ryan untangles his shirt, pale shoulders hunched for modesty. After he puts it on, they sit, side by side.

"Should we check on Connor?" Ryan asks.

"I don't want to wake him." But after a moment, as if the baby knows his services are required, from down the hall and behind the closed door comes a string of babble.

She's happy to see him sitting up in the room's dimness, turning toward her, eyes bright as he raises his arms. Out in the living room, he torques his body, reaches for Ryan.

"Oh, he loves me!" Ryan takes him onto his lap. Baby and boy regard each other with broad grins, and though she knows it's absurd, knows that when it comes down to it, Connor prefers her to anyone else on the planet, she still feels a stab of betrayal. He's never been like this with Lizette, and Lizette has never shown much interest in him.

She needs to see her. "Listen, why don't we go into town?" She makes her voice light and flirty. A plan is forming in her mind. They'll go to Lizette's—she isn't due to move for another couple days—just friends casually stopping by to say hello. Angel's mistake was being too available, and Angel needs to demonstrate that she is desired. Lizette will glean what has transpired between Angel and Ryan, and if she doesn't, Angel will tell her, and when Lizette truly understands what she is about to lose, she'll come back to her.

"Hey, yeah!" says Ryan, his normal voice restored, the awkwardness behind them. "I'll take you guys to dinner." He flushes. "Not, like, a date. Unless . . . ?" He trails off. "Have you even left the house, since, you know, your grandma?"

"No," she admits, aware that, although this is the truth, she is making use of it. "Sure, okay. Can we go to Lotaburger?" Lotaburger is quick, and it's right around the corner from Lizette's. Angel feels empty and light, as if she is shaping her own life, and she feels powerful, too, because somehow Ryan thinks this is his idea.

"Yes! It'll be so fun!"

"And then I want you to meet my friend."

"Really?" Ryan's eyes are shining.

Angel dismisses the pang of guilt. "You guys will like each other."

She buttons Connor into his puffy winter jacket and checks the supplies in the diaper bag, which Ryan takes from her hands. Outside, he cranes to watch as Angel straps the car seat into the back of his minivan. "Oh, I get it, you put the belt through that thing?"

While Ryan drives, Angel texts Lizette. *You home? Can we stop by to say hi?* It's just another in the long series of unanswered texts.

At the restaurant, Ryan wets napkins under the water spigot on the soda machine, then scrubs dried ketchup from the table like an old lady. When they call his number, he retrieves the tray and arranges the table with warm paper-wrapped packages and baskets of fries and sweating cups of soda.

Lizette still hasn't answered. The smell of fries and cooked meat is delicious, and the inside of the restaurant is cheery, strung with limp Christmas garlands, but Angel doesn't think she can eat a bite. "I'm really not hungry." She's nervous now, afraid her plan won't work. She's afraid to see Lizette.

"Well." He nudges a burger closer to her. "In case you change your mind." Pointing at a cheeseburger, he says, "This one is for Connor. The green chile is on the side."

On her lap, Connor strains toward it, but she pushes it out of his reach. "You got him a hamburger? He's seven months old. He eats, like, a pinch of bread, maybe. An arrowroot cookie. I brought his pears in the bag."

"Oh." Ryan bites his lip.

She unwraps her burger and takes a bite, then sets it down again. Outside, the concrete tables are abandoned in the cold. The early-evening light is a crisp blue; Angel wonders if it might snow.

She thinks she can sense Lizette nearby, across the road, the street obscured by the big sign for Selmo's Muffler Services, but the distance might as well be a thousand miles. The buildings of Española are low under the darkening sky, and everything is suffused with a sad, wintry desolation. Ache spreads behind Angel's breastbone.

What if Lizette just sees Ryan as a loser and isn't jealous at all? What if, after all, Lizette is completely indifferent? What if Ryan is the best she can ever do?

She hands Connor a fry, which he gums into oblivion before flinging it away. Ryan hands him another.

"Don't give him no more. I don't want him getting a taste for fat and salt."

Angel takes another bite of her hamburger. Connor reaches up and bats it, and she swivels out of his reach. His dimpled chin shines with drool.

"Here, let me hold him." Ryan places his burger on the wrapper and lifts Connor from her arms. "So you can eat."

He bounces his leg and Connor laughs, and reaches up to grab a handful of Ryan's patchy facial hair. Ryan laughs and gently pries away the hand. "You slimed me with French fry, little guy."

Swallowing the last bite of her burger, Angel sees them as a stranger might: a family sitting together over a meal, a beautiful laughing baby and his two young parents. Too-young parents. Despair floods her. So as to crowd out the quivering nervousness in her stomach, she finishes her fries, then Connor's, then starts in on his burger.

"So, what're you going to do now?" Ryan asks. "When are you going back to your school?"

Angel doesn't answer. With difficulty, she swallows. She's beginning to feel sick.

"Seriously," Ryan says, animated. "Did you ask if you can go back? Did you ever talk to the principal?"

"There's no principal. It's not that kind of school. There's just the president. Eric Maxwell."

"Well, talk to that guy, then. You have to. Get your mom and dad to. Like, when I skipped a grade, it wouldn't have happened if my mom hadn't driven the principal nuts. They want to keep parents happy."

"You skipped a grade? So wait, *how* old are you?"

Ryan flushes. "I just turned fifteen."

"God," says Angel.

"Don't worry, I'm legal to drive you guys on my learner's, because he's my immediate family." Connor clenches Ryan's nose and squeals. "You got me!" cries Ryan. To Angel: "He got me!"

Angel doesn't even fake a smile. The fact that it didn't occur to her to challenge her expulsion—didn't occur to her mother or her father, either—is galling.

"Why don't you just say you're sorry you were chewing gum?" Ryan asks. "If it'll get you back into the program. You don't have to mean it. People say crap they don't mean all the dang time. Like, on my application for media camp I said I had leadership qualities. I don't actually have too many leadership qualities."

Angel folds the burger wrapper carefully, matching up the corners, pressing the crease flat. "But then Brianna will think it's okay to push people around. She'll think it's okay to sleep with my dad and the dads of all the other girls and to be mean to this one girl who's got the hardest life of anyone. It's messed up." Ryan's gaze is steady; he's really listening. The intensity of his attention is making her talk more, and with this awareness, she falters. "I don't want her to win."

He keeps looking at her, though, with kind eyes, like those of some understanding, wise animal. "Win what, though? It's not a war. It's not a game. It's your life."

Angel's eyes well, and her left one overflows. The tear runs fat and hot down her cheek, and she swipes it away. Yes. It's her *life*, her one life, to be treasured and tended and protected. How has she never seen it like this? How has it taken Ryan, this pale, zitty teenager, to show her this?

But then Ryan says, "You gotta just ask for what you want."

Angel looks at him in disbelief. *Just ask for what you want.* Of course *he* thinks he can just ask for what he wants. He's a guy, white, the precious only child of a mother focused entirely on him. He's got a minivan and a college fund. He's every bit as culpable for Connor's creation, yet being a parent hasn't cramped *his* style any. He's still in school, acing English and kissing up to teachers. He goes to fucking *media camp.* What even is that? Where he learns to be a newscaster? Angel would like to do that, why not? She thinks of how in geometry, he always raised his hand, regardless of whether he knew the right answer. At the time, she thought his willingness to be so publicly wrong stemmed from a kind of misplaced, witless courage, and she'd been almost touched, but now she sees it for what it is: pure entitlement. She thinks of her own grandmother, greeting him with such obvious pleasure, praising him for stopping by. Oh, what a good boy! As if, for the simple gesture of not completely ignoring his own infant son, he's in the running for a Nobel.

"I mean it," he says earnestly, bouncing Connor. "The future is yours." He's proud of himself, she realizes, truly thinks he's helping someone less fortunate, buying her a hamburger dinner out of his allowance and giving her an inspiring little heart-to-heart. He thinks he's doing his part to *encourage* her. He'll probably put it on his college application: *mentored a teen mother.*

Now he's staring at her, puzzled. He can't even guess at how little he understands.

A rage rises in Angel so vicious she can't stand it. She wants to leap up, but holds herself motionless. "He's not yours, you know," she says.

Ryan's knee stills, and the smile drops from his face. Connor's shrieks last a beat longer, and he rocks on his butt, trying to get Ryan's knee to bounce again.

Ryan's mouth actually drops. "What do you mean?" The words sound as if they've been squeezed from him.

Satisfaction washes through Angel. She half thought he'd be relieved, then realizes, no, of course she knew he'd be hurt, and that's why she said it. "I lied to you." Her voice is airy, as if it's coming from some other person. "Look at him. He doesn't look nothing like you. You were just too stupid to figure it out." She despises him for taking her at her word, for his kindness to her and to Connor. Doesn't he know she's a slut? Didn't he ever think to wonder if the kid was his? She hates his awful uneven facial hair, his pale skin, his lank curls, the frankness of his vulnerability.

"You're not the only guy I've fucked," she says kindly, cruelly, and is pleased when he flinches at the word. "You're not special."

"I don't think I'm special." On Ryan's lap, Connor leans forward at the waist, grabbing at a napkin and giving it a thrashing.. Ryan holds onto Connor's other hand. "Can I still hang out with him?"

Angel looks at him, astonished. "No," she says, afraid of herself. "I can't trust you with him." She is Connor's mother, and if she doesn't want someone to see her child, they can't see him. Who knew she had it in her, this authority?

"I keep forgetting that you don't like me. I don't know why I keep forgetting that."

Angel is abashed, but why? She *doesn't* like him. And then she's angry again, because it isn't Angel he's sorry to lose, anyway, but Connor.

She stands. She thinks about plucking Connor from Ryan's arms, detaching Connor's clinging fist from Ryan's finger.

"You know what? You want to be his father? Fine. *Be* his father. You can take care of him for once." She swings her purse onto her shoulder.

As she pushes through the glass door, she looks back at them. Connor isn't even watching as his mother strides away: he's riveted by Ryan's stricken face. He stands unsteadily on Ryan's thighs, bucking, his greasy fist tight on Ryan's collar.

Pain is jagged in her chest, and she crosses the parking lot and then the street. The sky is low and deep blue with the cold dusk.

————

ANGEL MANAGES TO make it all the way to Lizette's street, her phone shoved deep in her pocket, fingers clenched around it, before she checks her messages. Ryan hasn't texted. Fuck him, she thinks, each word punctuating a step. Fuck him fuck him. But already, through her jumpy anger, her worry for Connor reasserts itself. Remorse descends like a sodden woolen cloak, itchy and claustrophobic and intolerable.

Her mother, Priscilla, Brianna, and now Ryan. It is so easy to cut people out, to make permanent rifts. She hadn't known this. She'd always thought there was room for fights, for cruelty, that things would work themselves out, given enough time, given enough honest conversation. She hadn't ever really wanted to push any of them away—she was only asking them to draw her close again, testing to see whether they'd let her go. And always, always, they've let her go. The only person who wouldn't let her go is her grandmother, but her grandmother is dead.

Ten minutes from home. Amadeo has spent the day out driving, making up errands in Española to be out of that empty house: gas station, Walmart for diapers, Dollarland for zipping sandwich baggies that don't seal too well, but are fine for crackers. Thank god he can drive again. The stores are frantic with Christmas cheer, tinsel and cardboard cutouts shiver above the aisles. Now it's dusk, and he's climbed out of the flat sea bottom of Española, the lights smeared in his peripheral vision, into the safety of the trees.

He's on the tight road that will lead to his door, and the closer he gets, the higher his anxiety creeps, until he's actually quaking.

It's Angel who does it to him, snapping, putting him in his place, withholding. She's been angry since his mother died, since before, since forever. Just occupying the same room with her is torture, waiting for her to turn on him with righteous condemnation.

Amadeo pulls onto the shoulder, fishes a mini of vodka from the plastic bag on the passenger mat. The metal top comes off with a pleasing little crack, and just the sound calms him, even before the vodka washes over his tongue and down his throat, clean and hot. He needs to still that incessant jitter.

He's not stupid. He's not flouting the law, not really, not endangering anyone. There are no cops up here on the twisting mountain road, especially not now, early on a Tuesday evening, hardly any cars at all, and certainly no pedestrians. It's okay to drive on one drink. Plus, it takes time for the alcohol to enter his bloodstream, won't even hit him until he's home. He knows this from his DWI class, the PowerPoint slides on Blood Alcohol Concentrations and Impairment Over Time.

He's relieved to find his mother's car—Angel's car, now—safe in the drive, the light in the living room. He'll lift the baby from Angel's arms, give her a break, and even if she doesn't show it, she'll be grateful. Amadeo will be grateful, too, for the wriggling, forceful heat of the baby. They can play on the carpet, build a tower with blocks that the baby will demolish, or Amadeo can read to him, holding that sleepy, trusting weight against his heart.

He grabs the plastic bag, bottles clinking, tucks it into his jacket. He's doing nothing wrong, but he doesn't need Angel's disapproval. The liquor is working already. He takes a deep breath, holds the cold purple air in his lungs. One click to lock the truck, that comforting beep, up the steps, screen door pressing against his backside as he puts the key in the lock.

The light shines on an empty house: table clear, Connor's toys in the basket, the clock with flowers instead of numbers ticking.

"Hello?" he calls, but terror grips him, outsized and certain, because he knows that what he's feared has finally come to pass: he's been abandoned.

He drops the bag with a clatter and lurches down the hall, pushing doors, flicking on lights. Angel's room, his own, the bathroom, and— terrible, terrible—his mother's room, the mattress bare on her canopy bed, still pushed against the wall, the blank space where the hospital bed was.

The smell of her sickness is gone; her old smell remains, the mild scent of perfume caught in a scarf, as if the room she inhabited for nearly forty years is not yet ready to give her up.

Amadeo spent so little time in here when his mother was alive. He always felt uneasy in her bedroom: the close, feminine intimacy of this space where his mother dressed and undressed, where, sleeping, she breathed undefended into the dark. Yet he was here, beside her, when her soul unmoored itself from her body. He held her bony hand as she breathed those last breaths: each slow and gasping, with that long suspended pause in between, until finally all that was left was pause.

The room is stark under the bulb. He pulls the door shut behind him.

He returns to the doorway of Angel's room, steps inside. With the crib and changing table, it's crowded, but Angel has made it her own, cleared out Valerie's old books and Garfield figurines. She doesn't have a lot of belongings, his daughter. Her schoolbooks are in the shelf, looking like they haven't been touched since Angel left Smart Starts! The room is even tidier since his mother died, pajamas folded at the foot of the bed, Connor's diapers stacked neatly on the changing table.

His mother's bottle of Shalimar stands on Angel's cream-painted dresser. He takes off the blue top, sniffs, and tears spark in his eyes.

Angel has left him. Taken the baby and gone home to Marissa when he needs her the most, just as he always knew she would. And with the fear, that old anger comes up, familiar and almost comfortable. The little bitch, he thinks. Not just her, but Brianna, too, and Valerie, and Marissa. And especially his mother. *Bitch*, he thinks savagely, the word satisfying and horrible in his head. His vision blurs, the back of his throat thickens.

Rage like a flash flood, a wall of water as solid and sinewy as muscle sweeping down an arroyo, lifting him. He can ride its current until it gives out, leaving him tossed up, exhausted, on its banks. With relief, he sinks into the swirling, dirty force of it, lets it fill his lungs.

He sits on the couch, his bag crinkling against his thigh. One after another, the seals of the metal tops crack. His body loosens. This is how he'll get through the next hours, the next years, drifting in that whirling, obliterating tide, the loop of curses slowing in his head.

The TV is on, the jingles and murmurs and swelling dramatic music on the edges of his awareness. His eyes are barely open. He should just go to sleep. He's adrift on the drunkenness, but each time his eyes shut completely, the world rocks and spins around him.

Neither the rage nor the anesthesia is quite obliterating, though. Amadeo is still here, unable to snuff out that last glimmer of himself. He keeps jolting to awareness, thinking he needs to check on his mother, but then remembers that she's dead, deep in the churchyard's cold, dry dirt.

Still, something nags at him, something he forgot.

Lizette's house in the dark has an abandoned aspect to it. Next door, the front windows are blazing, shades up, Christmas lights illuminating the mounds of junk in the yard. A man passes before the window, head angled over a bowl of something. At Lizette's, the tomato plants are dead stalks. Angel steps almost soundlessly up the walk, and knocks on the door between the security bars, a timid little tap she can barely hear over her heart's sloshing. She knocks again, bolder.

What if Lizette is gone, already moved in with her cousin's friend? What if Selena answers the door? Or someone else entirely? Maybe they've both moved, and the house is now occupied by lurking, threatening men waiting for a teenage girl to present herself at their threshold.

Angel checks her phone again. Ryan still hasn't texted, the dick, and neither has Lizette. He's teaching her a lesson, she gets that, but still, nightmare scenarios present themselves: Ryan leaving Connor at Blake's Lotaburger, Ryan dropping Connor at the police station or on the cold steps of the church.

Finally, approaching footsteps, then a long pause. Angel can feel herself being watched from behind the dark windows. She swallows.

Lizette opens the door, regards Angel through the security screen, then unlocks that, too. "Hey," she says, her tone flat and unsurprised, as if they'd planned this, then turns into the dark of the house without saying anything, leaving Angel to shut the door against the night. Lizette is in sweatpants and an oversized T-shirt. At the end of the hall, the light is on in her room. In the unlit living room, the couch is gone, and the table, too. As Angel follows Lizette through the house, she steps around piles on the floor—papers and clothing, cardboard moving boxes, a wadded blanket. Mercedes's crib has been moved out here, and Angel sees a dark hump inside.

In Lizette's room, the quilted *L* is still on the wall, but the place looks pillaged. Full black garbage bags are everywhere. One already has holes in it where hangers poke through.

"Wow," Angel says lamely. "You're almost packed."

"Yeah," says Lizette, looking around. In the light, Lizette's skin is clay-like, her beautiful eyes heavy. Messy strands have loosened from her ponytail, which looks unwashed.

"Oh, Lizette." Angel steps toward her.

Without preamble or small talk, they're in each other's arms. It's not what Angel has been longing for all these weeks: slow and close and gentle. Lizette is rough with her—the biting kisses make Angel catch her breath—and in response Angel is rough with Lizette. It all takes place under the blazing overhead light.

After, they doze, until, from the crumple of Angel's jeans, her phone blares. *We are fam-i-ly!* Angel detangles herself and lunges for the phone, but misses her dad's call.

"Hang on." She pulls her shirt on, slips out the door to the bathroom. She's about to call back when the texts come through, one, two, three, four. *Where RU? Ur boy Ryan dropped C off. Where RU?????? WHERE U AT DAMMIT???????*

Thank you, God, thank you, thank you. Angel leans against the cold mirror on the back of the door. *Watch him tonight, k? Home in the morning.*

Clearly Lizette's brother was in charge of the cleaning, because the bathroom is wrecked: the toilet paper roll empty, toothpaste and cosmetics smeared in the sink, the trash can smelly and overflowing. A dry, browned maxi pad is stuck to the tile. Pinching the edges, Angel peels it off and balances it atop the trash. She tries to scrub out the sink, but there's no hot water, and she gives up.

Angel steps back down the dark hall. She moves quietly, so as not to wake Mercedes in her crib, or Selena, if she's home. Lizette rouses. "There you are," she says, blinking under the light. She scoots to make room for Angel, lifts the sheet to welcome her.

Angel shudders against Lizette. "I'm cold." She pushes her face into Lizette's smooth shoulder.

Lizette pulls her closer. "Mmm," she says, and just this sound is so affectionate that Angel is comforted.

Angel touches the clean skin beside a new red cut on Lizette's arm. It's ragged and ugly. "When did you do this?" she asks faintly. "Why?"

Lizette shakes Angel off. "None of your business."

Again, Angel imagines a scenario in which Lizette and Mercedes come to live with them. She might be able to convince her dad, she really thinks she could. They have an extra room now. With this thought, a hot pain spreads in her. In their house, Lizette will be locked down, safe. They can help each other with child care, with GED prep. They don't need Smart Starts! Together they can move forward.

"But why are you hurting yourself?" Lizette is receding, and Angel is suddenly furious. "Why haven't you called me back? Why have you been ignoring me?"

Lizette flops onto her back, yanks the sheet over her breasts. "Leave it, Angel."

Angel stares into the light until she sees black daubs. She doesn't think she can speak, but she forces herself. "My grandmother died, and I know you know, because I texted. You haven't even said anything."

A long silence, through which Angel hears only her own heartbeat. She turns her head to study Lizette's profile. Tears leak from the corner of her eye.

"Do you, like, feel bad about this?" Angel gestures at the space between them. "About us?"

"*Us.*" Lizette gives a scraped, mirthless laugh. "Not everything is about you, Angel. You can be so fucking selfish."

"You don't have anywhere to go, do you?" Angel doesn't know why she didn't see this before, but of course it's true.

"It's none of your damn business."

"Listen. Lizette. Why don't you and Mercedes move in with my dad and me? You can." Angel can convince her dad. She'll do what it takes. If Lizette moves in, she pledges, Angel won't kiss her ever again, won't try anything. She'll be satisfied. She won't even think a sexual thought, if only Lizette can be near her and safe. Even as she thinks it, she knows she's lying to herself.

Lizette sits up, exhales loudly. "I'm not ever gonna be your girlfriend."

Angel ignores the pain in her chest. "That's okay. You can still stay with us."

"I'm not bringing that gay shit into my baby's life. That could fuck a kid up."

"No," says Angel. She tries to remember the arguments she's heard. "Babies just need to see loving relationships. Like, people respecting each other."

"Is that what you think this is? A *loving relationship*? You think I *respect* you? We're hooking up, Angel. That's all this is." Lizette holds her gaze, but something in her mouth twitches.

"I don't believe you."

Lizette raises an insolent eyebrow.

"I love you," Angel says. Her voice is hushed and she wonders if she said it or just thought it.

Lizette's laugh is a short rasp. "No you don't."

"I do," says Angel, pushing herself up, and she says it with conviction now. She wants to hold Lizette down, to say it again and again until Lizette believes her, until Lizette knows she is loved and lets the love soften her. But Lizette swipes hair out of her face and turns her back to Angel.

"You're pathetic," says Lizette flatly. "Stupid and pathetic. Just get out."

"But it's the middle of the night."

"You think I give a shit? I told you to leave." Her full lips tremble. Angel reaches for her, but Lizette pushes her away. Now Lizette's eyes are thick-glazed with tears.

"What's wrong? Why are you doing this?"

The tears overflow and spill down her cheek. Very slowly and very clearly, she says, "Get the fuck out of my house."

"Fine." Angel stands and dresses. She's quivering with anger and humiliation, a hot, dry pressure building behind her eyes. She grabs her jacket and purse, holding them tight to her, passes through the dark living room and the shadowed mound in the crib, fumbles with the deadbolt.

Outside, the half-moon is bright over the stucco and asphalt of the neighborhood. The house next door is dark now, but the trash and engine parts gleam like mercury. Dirty rinds of snow fill the gutters.

She can't find her cell phone. Panic mounts in her, that she'll have to go back inside, once again face Lizette. She crouches and digs in her purse. Baby wipes, her notebook and keys and Kleenexes, a squeeze pouch of apple-spinach baby food, her lipstick: it all spills on the driveway. Finally she finds her phone, tangled in a spare onesie.

She's startled to discover that it's after midnight. Her fingers shake as she dials her father. Four rings, then voicemail. She redials. Tries the landline, but it's been disconnected, apparently a bill her father opted not to pay. "Fuck you," she's muttering, "pick up the fucking phone." Her anger doesn't mask her panic. He is home drinking, she knows. Connor's probably choking on the stuffed rabbit her idiot father left in his crib. Which would be her fault, in the end, after abandoning her baby in a fast-food restaurant.

She can't bear to think of Lizette, but her face rises in Angel's mind: eyes wet, expression shuttered and impassive. *Get the fuck out of my house.*

At the end of the road, music blares. A lowrider pauses at a stop sign, rear bouncing. Terror slices through her. The car crosses the intersection, moves on, and the music fades.

She's a fool to be alone on this deserted street. She needs to be somewhere more populated. She makes it as far as the next block when a truck pulls alongside her.

"Hey, baby girl." The man at the wheel is big and pulpy-looking, his sandy hair clipped short. The heat spills from his open window, and classical music plays on the stereo. "You okay?"

Angel runs. Back down Lizette's dark street, shoes clacking on the cold sidewalk, purse banging at her hip. She ducks along the side of the chaotic house, pressing against the stucco. Heart pounding, she peers around. The truck idles there for a long moment more, its brake lights glowing, and then they flash off and the truck drives away.

Shaking, Angel jabs at her phone and dials again. Please Daddy please pick up.

Of course he's going to get her. His daughter is alone on the streets of Española, after midnight, with creeps and tecatos and rapists on the prowl. He almost couldn't understand her through the tears, but managed to get the address out of her.

Amadeo splashes water on his face, runs his whole scalp under the tap. He blinks at his reflection: bleary, red-eyed, puffy. His armpits are damp with the alcohol oozing out of him. If only he hadn't had the last drink. Or the ones before.

Ten minutes ago, he was sitting on the couch, TV going, the sensation of falling, falling, into blessed, swirling nothingness.

Connor is sleeping soundly in Angel's room, where he's been since Ryan brought him by around eight. Amadeo had masked his surprise that the baby was with Ryan, because a good father would keep tabs on his daughter's plans. The kid stood on the step, holding the sleeping baby in the car seat. As Amadeo explained that, no, Angel wasn't here, Ryan regarded him suspiciously, and kept craning over Amadeo's shoulder, as if searching for someone more trustworthy lurking in the house.

"Oh. I thought for sure she'd gotten a ride home." He still didn't hand over the baby. "He'll be okay here? Staying with you?"

By that point in the evening, Amadeo was already too wiped and too drunk to react with anger. "I'm his grandpa. One of his primary caregivers. I stay with him all the time." The words were only a little slurred.

Ryan shifted his weight, uncertain. "Because I could take him home to my house, I guess. To my mom."

Amadeo tamped down his anger. Mildly, he said, "You fucking joking me?"

Ryan seemed to make a decision. "Okay," he said, handing over the seat, "he's asleep, anyway." But his steps were reluctant as he walked back to his car.

Now Amadeo leans over the toilet and reaches down his throat. He wants to empty his stomach of any additional alcohol before it makes it to his bloodstream. He tries to remember the details from his class. *An average-sized man processes one drink per hour.* A quantity of corrosive vomit comes up, along with some scrambled egg and soggy tortilla bits from his dinner. "Please hurry," Angel said on the phone, her voice thick.

"I'm coming," he told her.

In her room, some light from the porch leaks through the blinds. He pauses a moment over the crib. The baby is on his back in his sleep suit, arms flung wide, breath nearly inaudible. Connor sleeps through the night now, and for half a second Amadeo considers leaving him.

Instead he takes up the baby, holding him with deliberate gentleness. He grabs the blanket, too, and the car seat, which Ryan left by the door. It's freezing outside, Amadeo's breath white and thick as he makes his way to the truck. He opens the door, sets the car seat in the back under the dome light, sets Connor, who rubs his closed eyes with his fists, in the car seat. And as he does, one hand under the baby's bottom, he feels the firm warm weight of the diaper, which means it probably ought to have been changed an hour ago. He should bring the diaper bag.

See? He's remembering things, thinking things through. He jogs back to the house, searches for the diaper bag with mounting anxiety—hurry, hurry, picturing Angel standing on the street, Angel approached by strange men—before he sees it by the door where Ryan left it. He rifles in the bag to check for fresh diapers, swings it over his shoulder, and at the last minute he grabs the binky off the table, congratulating himself.

On the way back to the truck, he drops the binky, feels for it, plucks it up and pops it into his mouth to clean the grit off, spits.

In the car, Connor is awake now, staring up at the dome light.

He turns wide eyes on his grandfather, starts babbling, then fussing. Amadeo pushes the binky past his lips, fumbles the straps of the car seat, and snaps him in. Connor begins sucking industriously, returning his attention to the light.

Door shut, dome light off. Behind the wheel, Amadeo rubs his face with both hands. His face is numb. Angel. Hands shaking, he starts the car, backs down the drive, straightens out.

He peers into the dark over the steering wheel. He's fine, going fast, but not too fast. He knows these roads, has driven them his entire life. But something is wrong. He can't see.

He blinks, furious. Why can't he see the road? He thumps the wheel hard with his fist, and the shot of pain enflames his rage. Because why is he out in the middle of the night? Why has he been put in this position?

Angel is alone. He pictures a car slowing beside her, a shadowy man calling her close. Pictures that man grabbing her, pulling her into the car, the squeal of tires.

And then he thinks of Mike. Something happened there, of that he's sure. And where was Amadeo then? In a burst, Amadeo accelerates, the dark piñon flying by, the road lit by the sharp-cornered moon.

All at once he realizes he hasn't turned on his headlights. He snaps them on, and there, stock-still in the middle of the road, eyes blazing, is the coyote.

———

WHEN AMADEO COMES TO, there is no moment of confusion, no where-am-I-what-happened described by people on the news after accidents, no benevolent derangement of time and place. Amadeo lies with his cheek pressed into the cold asphalt, his eyes squeezed shut.

All his anger has fled, the anger that gives him focus and shape and power, leaving him with bottomless, hollow horror. Just this clarity: There is nothing left for him on this earth. Whether he lives or dies, his life has ended on this road.

He keeps his eyes shut, prolonging this moment between his old life that was filled—*filled*, he understands now—with light and love and family, and the new life that will begin when he sees his grandson's motionless, bloodied body. Because he knows, even without looking, that as assiduously as he strapped Connor into his seat, snapping each little clasp with fingers thick with liquor, he hadn't buckled the car seat itself into the truck.

That this child should die—this child who was unplanned and unwanted, dreaded and bemoaned, and now loved, loved so deeply by all of them—is cruel. Connor, with his effortful grunts of concentration, Connor, with his abrupt, joyous laugh, Connor, turning the junk mail delicately in his hands. No child has ever been as needed, as necessary and beloved, and tears leak onto the asphalt.

Amadeo prays to die, and he's never prayed so vehemently in his life. *Take me, take me, take me.* But nothing even hurts. Finally, he can put it off no longer. Amadeo opens his eyes onto a scene of peace, a night as still and bright as that first Christmas.

The moon is barely over half full, but it is huge and flat in the sky above the piñon. Along the edge of the road, the gravel and dust shine silver. There is no sign of the coyote. Blue light pools among the chamisa and clumps of scrub grass, as cold and clear as water. Amadeo has the sense that if he reaches out with his fingers into that blue light, they will find clean, icy depth.

Connor. Amadeo scrambles onto his hands and knees. His jeans are torn clear away from his left leg, his knee and shin scraped bloody. The truck's tail is in the ditch, the windshield is dark and gaping, and the engine ticks. The fender, which has been ripped free against a tree trunk, gleams.

Connor's seat has indeed been flung through the windshield and landed in the middle of the road, somehow upright, facing down the road away from Amadeo.

Amadeo crawls toward his grandson, his vision blurred. For a second, a fraction of a second, Amadeo imagines himself in that future, alone with his bottles, having squandered every good thing.

When Amadeo reaches the seat, he's afraid to touch it, so he crawls to face the child. The baby isn't moving, and his face is round and shining in the moonlight. Shards of safety glass are strewn across his still body, like stars fallen from the black sky all around.

Connor's eyes are open, his head canted up, as though he's mesmerized by the moon. Blank eyes. Amadeo thinks of his own mother, and the cooling stillness of her as he clutched her hand.

Amadeo is making a strange honking animal sound, and he's just realized that they are sobs when Connor turns from the moon. He looks his grandfather full in the face, and then his expression crumples and he sends up a long angry howl, gorgeous and rich and miraculous and slicing through the night.

t's truly cold now, and Angel's denim jacket, chosen hours ago for the quick early-evening outing with Ryan, is unequal to the task. Though the sky is clear, the air has that dry, metallic tang of snow. Her eyes are trained tensely on the street, willing her father's truck to appear. In the distance a coyote yelps in a quick series. Somewhere else, an answering wail, unsettlingly human.

The cry makes Angel think of Connor, and then of La Llorona, the sad haunted woman who drowned her children for her selfish love of a man. She thinks of herself, leaving her child behind for her own self-ish love.

Her cheeks burn with the cold. She wonders if she'll be found tomorrow, features glazed with ice.

Where *is* he?

The night is enormous, the stars icy points. There are no streetlights on Lizette's block. At the distant reaches of the road stands one, its dirty orange light cutting a single circle in the dark.

"Don't worry, I'm coming," her father said, and she could hear, even in those four words, that he was drunk.

"Please hurry," she said.

Angel has the sense of herself as a spark, a lone spark in the vast des-ert, easily extinguished.

Finally, headlights come swiftly toward her, swinging up and down with the bumps in the road. With relief, Angel steps into the road and waves with her whole arm, as if her life depends on it. When the car is almost on her, though, she realizes with terror that it's not her father's truck: it's a dark sedan. Angel backs onto the curb and considers running. Could she make it out to Riverside Drive?

The car slows. Angel's fear is a fist around her throat, and then she understands, all at once, that it's her mother. Her mother, in her old Aladdin sweatshirt, hair in a messy ponytail. Angel can't step forward, so frozen with relief is she, but she bursts into tears.

"Honey."

Her mother gets out of the car, envelops Angel in her arms. She's warm from the car's heater, from the warmth that is always hers. Angel clings to her as if to a buoy in the rocking, infinite ocean. She's heaving, her face drenched. Angel tries to speak, but her voice is clotted with tears.

Her mother holds her close, cupping the back of Angel's head with a palm as though she's an infant. "Listen," her mother says. "There's been an accident. But everyone's okay, sweetie. Everyone's safe."

Part III

LENT

On Ash Wednesday, Amadeo meets with the rest of the hermanos in the morada after five o'clock Mass. As the men, foreheads smudged with ash, clap each other on the back, catching up on news, Tío Tíve stands, small and nervous, gripping his trembling hands. "Okay," he says brusquely. "Sit down."

Frankie Zocal and John Trujillo exchange tolerant, bemused glances. Al Martinez gives Amadeo's shoulder a friendly squeeze, then lowers himself to the bench. Shelby Morales rewraps his gray ponytail in the purple elastic, smoothing the length of it, and looks up at Tíve expectantly, like a student.

The old man is dressed in his best clothes: stiff jeans, pearl-snap shirt. He wears his silver-dollar belt buckle and turquoise bolo tie. Amadeo feels affection for his uncle. He isn't, for a moment, sure why the guy ever seemed so intimidating. The other evening, he stopped by the house, bringing groceries, and stayed for dinner, just a smiling old man clutching a squirming Connor on his skinny lap.

Tíve stands before the men, palms raised like a priest. "I'm retiring. Al Martinez is taking over as Hermano Mayor." Tío Tíve looks oddly ecstatic as he stands before them, light gleaming in his hazy eyes. "This year his son Isaiah is our Jesus. You explain it all to him, Al, and make him pray regular."

From the surprise on Al's face, it is evident that Tío Tíve didn't run any of this by him. With a nod, Al clears his throat. "Brother," he says. "Thank you." He stands, and makes as if to embrace Tíve, but Tíve walks past him, mouth serious, and takes his place on the bench.

"All right," Al says, turning slowly, as if seeing the morada for the first time. "All right. Let us pray."

As Amadeo speaks the words along with the other men, he pities his old self, the self that once believed there was a single, big thing he could do to make up for all his failings. He missed the point. The procession isn't about punishment or shame. It is about needing to take on the pain of loved ones. To take on that pain, first you have to see it. And see how you inflict it.

That December night, as Marissa drove them all down into the valley to get Connor checked out in the ER, Amadeo neither explained nor excused himself. He told Angel everything: the drinking, the coyote, the baby's cry. It was the fullest confession he'd ever made. Amadeo and Angel sat in the back, leaning over Connor's car seat as he babbled. He expected his daughter to lash out, but she was silent, her eyes wide and afraid. "The thing everyone warned me about, that's what I did," Amadeo whispered.

After a scan, their second miracle: Connor was fine. He didn't have even a single cut from the shattered windshield. He'd been thrown clear and had somehow landed upright.

"This accident," the admitting nurse said as she flicked a penlight in and out of Connor's eyes. "Were drugs or alcohol involved?"

"No," Angel said. When the nurse narrowed her eyes at them, Marissa looked to Angel, asking, and then chimed in, in that authoritative office voice that always so impressed Amadeo. "No, none. I was driving." And perhaps because it was a busy night in the ER, the nurse appeared to believe them. She offered to examine Amadeo's leg, but he just shook his head, and she did not press it.

This thing Amadeo did is too terrible and too large for them to deal with. He understands that it will remain with him—and with Angel and Marissa, too—forever. Trotting along his life will run a ghost life, a life in which Connor is killed on this night.

At home, the three of them crouched around Connor's crib as he slept, disbelieving that his chest rose and fell. Amadeo reached through the bars, placed his hand close to the child's muzzle to feel the faint stirring. "I don't know why you lied for me. Both of you."

Amadeo's ears buzzed in the silence.

Then, in a voice that was low and steely, Angel said, "He's okay. And we need you at home. And you'll never drink again." It's true. Each time he wants to, he remembers that night, and when he doesn't drink, it's like a stone, one after another, building a bridge back to her.

Mostly things are good between them now, but occasionally she snaps, and he feels the dart of her anger. Amadeo understands that her forgiveness won't come easily, that for all her sweetness, she holds something back, and he recognizes that this is a sign of her maturity. He's proud of Angel for her anger, proud she sees that his behavior is something to be angry about. He pledges, once again, that he will earn her forgiveness.

All of Lent, Amadeo attends AA meetings, then prays in the morada, alone and with the others. He's lost his faith in processions, though. He knows now that for someone with his particular weaknesses, performance is a distraction. But he enjoys the quiet of the building, with his eyes shut among these murmuring men, his voice folded in with theirs. He is aware of their heat and thrumming thoughts, and as the prayer flows around him, he falls into the current.

Meanwhile, at home, Connor cruises around the house, pulling himself along furniture, delighted by his new perspective. He has five words now: *mama, ball, hat, hot, no.* His daughter turns the pages of her GED study book. Occasionally a whole day passes without them mentioning Yolanda.

Connor sleeps well now, and Angel sleeps better, too. Lately, she has been thinking about returning to her old high school in the fall. The prospect is scary: there would be so much to catch up on, that whole complicated social world to navigate. Would Priscilla speak to her? Would anyone?

The main obstacle is child care. Her father has been helping more, now that he has a full-time job at Lowe's, but it doesn't pay much, and means he can't watch Connor. Her mother has offered to help with day care, and so has Tío Tíve, from his meager Social Security check, but even so there will be a shortfall. Child care is so expensive, and now that she's seen the quality of the nursery at Smart Starts!, she can't imagine leaving him at the grubby KidKorral, even if she could afford it.

But still, Angel thinks about school: the concrete hallways, the din of passing period, the airy openness of the library upstairs. She longs to be back in a regular life of classes and assignments, each day broken into manageable blocks. She longs to be learning.

She thinks about Brianna, too, less with anger now than with sadness. But more frequently, she thinks about the things Brianna taught her—about encouraging Connor's early literacy, about giving him loving boundaries, and mostly about valuing herself. In spite of what happened after, Brianna put the best of herself into these lessons, and for that Angel is grateful.

One Saturday in March, Angel meets Trinity and Christy at the playground next to the library. It's the first time she's seen anyone from Smart Starts!, and, driving, Angel was nervous. But now, sitting under the spring sun, two scrub jays going nuts in the cottonwoods, her spirits rise, because here are her old friends Trinity and Christy, happy to see her.

Angel plops Connor in the sandbox next to two-year-old Kristiana, who regards him levelly. Around her pacifier, Kristiana comments, "Baby."

Connor pushes a handful of sand into his mouth.

Angel sweeps her finger through his wet maw, swiping at his struggling tongue. "Not for eating, hijito."

Sandy spittle drips down his chin. "No no no," he says, beating his arms and gnashing. He takes up another handful, conveying it to his mouth with mercifully spread fingers and poor aim.

"Fine," says Angel, sitting back. "You want to eat it, eat it."

"You can't stop them," Trinity says with authority.

"So," ventures Angel. "How's Smart Starts!?"

Trinity shrugs. "It got crappy after you left."

Angel understands that this isn't exactly the truth, that Trinity is saying this to spare her feelings.

"I mean, the new girls are cool," says Trinity. "But I don't know, it's like Brianna's checked out. She's leaving in June for grad school. Ysenia and Tabitha got their GEDs. I'll be glad to be done."

"I'm passing all my practice tests, but I'm waiting for Trinity so we can leave together," says Christy.

"She got a 180 in science!"

"That's awesome," Angel says, muted.

"McDonald's is giving hiring bonuses. We'll schedule it so one of us can watch the kids while the other works, which is sad, 'cause when are we gonna see each other? Anyways, I'm good on all the subjects but language arts."

"You just gotta try harder," Christy says. "You'll get it."

Carefully, Angel asks, "Are you in touch with everyone?"

"Ysenia wants to get her associate's as a medical assistant, but she's working until April starts school. Tabitha and the kids moved in with her sister in Albuquerque."

From the stroller, Ricky fusses. Christy ties back her hair and gets up to release him. "Jen's taking the test next month. She got a job working at her church's day care center, which is awesome because she'll be with Nathan all day."

"Precious Lambs of Heaven?"

Christy laughs. "She can actually be pretty cool. Jared tried to get back with her, but she told him to get out of her face, which, good."

"You ever hear from Lizette? How's she doing?" Angel keeps her voice even, but fears they'll hear the whole history in her question. Maybe Lizette has told them everything, and they've been laughing at her behind her back.

"Wait, are you for serious? You don't know?" Christy says. "I thought you two were best friends." Her surprise shades to sorrow, and she and Trinity exchange a look.

"What?" asks Angel. Christy seems about to speak and then stops. *"What?"*

"You really didn't hear?" Trinity asks gently. "Mercedes got taken. I guess Lizette started using."

"No," says Angel.

Christy regards her sadly. "I know."

"We saw her at FoodMart," says Trinity.

"She's *all* skinny now."

"I almost wouldn't've recognized her but she came up and was like, 'Hi, guys,' all smiling, but not herself, you know? When she told us about Mercedes, she's like, 'Shit happens, but guess I'm free now.' I was like, 'Do you even feel? I'd kill myself if Kristiana got taken.'" She touches her daughter's back.

"She didn't mean it, Trinity. You could tell she was fronting."

"But I just saw her in December," says Angel. That clear cold night comes back to Angel again, as it does many times each day. But instead of thinking about the accident and Connor and how much she nearly lost, or about Lizette's meanness, she thinks about something she hasn't remembered until now: the crib in Lizette's dark living room, the shadowed hump that Angel assumed was Mercedes. How she wishes she'd checked on her, laid a palm against the sleeping back. She wonders if

Mercedes was already gone or if that night was one of the baby's last with her mother.

"Why didn't she just let me love her?" The question comes out as a croak.

"We all love her," says Christy. "But chiva—it's, like, impossible to fight."

Trinity shakes her head. "Things were never going to go right for Lizette, with the crap she went through."

"No," Angel says. "That's not true." What she means is that there were a million moments when events might have unfolded differently for Lizette, when a word, a gesture, a smile from a caring adult might have changed her course, might still.

"She's right, Trin," says Christy. "There's always hope."

———

RYAN HAS CONTINUED to come by a few days a week. One evening, as the three of them sit on the carpet, building block towers for Connor to knock down, he tugs at the cuffs of his sweater and asks quietly, "That was a lie, right? About me not being his dad?"

Angel nods. "I'm sorry."

"I knew it." A smile twitches his thin lips.

Ryan has, to Angel's surprise, become a good friend. She doesn't confide in him, and they still have little in common, but he is the only person as interested as Angel in the details of Connor's growth, and he seems to be doing a lot of research on early-childhood milestones.

"Come here, doodarooni!" As Connor crawls toward him, slapping the carpet at great speed, Ryan spreads his arms. "Hey there. Come to Dada." He shoots a fearful glance at Angel, as if to gauge her response.

Alarm frills through her, then fades—not entirely, but enough to allow her to feel a kind of warmth, like an open palm against her heart. Ryan wraps Connor in his arms and tips him back. Connor's eyes flutter, and he retracts his arms and neck, chortling in maniacal delight.

Part of Angel, therefore, is not surprised when, one afternoon, her phone chimes, Ryan's messages coming fast upon each other.

Um, I'm sorry, but U should know I told my mom.

She's freaking.

She wants to come by tonight. To meet you guys.

Is that okay?

"Dad?" Angel calls outside.

He pokes his head into the kitchen, gulping from a glass of lemonade. "What's up?"

Her father smells like sweat and sawdust. Recently he has begun messing around with carpentry projects out back—a mini table and a short bookshelf for Connor—using wood purchased with his employee discount and his own father's tools.

She shows him the texts. "What if she tries to take him? Can she do that?"

Her dad bites his lip. "I don't think so." He looks uncertain, though, and rubs his scalp. "What do you know about this lady? Has Ryan said what she's like?"

Angel shrugs. "I don't know. She's a nurse in Los Alamos. And she's, like, a feminist, maybe? She hates the word *bitch*."

"Aw, shit. You think I should call Valerie?"

On the floor, Connor tries to jam the sheep into the wooden frame of his farm puzzle.

Angel hesitates. "No. My mom. I want my mom here."

"Good. We'll deal with it together." He pats Angel's hand. "Hey. It'll be fine. No one's gonna take that baby from us."

That night, Angel, Amadeo, and Marissa await the arrival of Ryan and his mother. They sit in the living room, showered and dressed. Earlier, Angel and her father made an insanely detailed list of chores— *bleach the grout in the shower, scrub cupboard doors, sweep cobweb from hall ceiling*—then divvied them up and set to. Cushions are plumped, baseboards dusted, the crocheted afghan folded neatly over the arm of the couch. Her mother brought a selection of Easter-rabbit sugar cookies, which she arranged on a platter.

"Wish my mom could see this." Her dad reaches to brush a piece of lint from the glass on the doll cabinet. "She once told me her dream was to have every dish clean and put away, but there was always someone there to dirty a glass. Me, usually."

"Well," says Angel. "It's not gonna be perfect for long. That fool will make sure of it." She jerks her thumb at Connor.

Connor is in his nicest polo shirt and pants, but then at the last minute takes a giant dump, so has to be changed into his second-best outfit, which is just denim overalls.

"Why'm I trying to make you maximum cute, anyway?" Angel asks as she buttons him in. "I should make you *less* cute, so they leave us alone. I should leave you in your stinky diaper so they run away. No way, they'll say, get that baby away from me!" Connor's eyes are huge and dark and sparkling. "I'm not going to let no one take you. If they come after you, we'll hit the road, baby. You can support us with your modeling." She smooths a black curl and he laughs at her, showing off his teeth.

Her dad leans over Angel's shoulder, peering at Connor, frowning, and gently touches a thin scratch on his cheek from when he swiped at himself with a stick. "I hope they don't think that's child abuse."

Angel whips around. "Are you for serious?"

"Nah, course not."

"She's raised a baby, Amadeo," says Marissa. "Plus she's a nurse. She'll know babies scratch themselves all the time."

But her dad's expression remains troubled. They're all thinking of the accident, thinking of the horrible thing they can't bear to think about.

The second Amadeo lets them in, Ryan's mother hugs Angel. "Angel? You're Angel. Oh my god, the baby! Oh, what a beauty! I can't believe you've been doing this all alone. I've never been so mad at Ryan in my whole life."

Ryan stands behind her, pulling at his sideburn, his forehead splotched red. "It's true. She was so mad she cried."

Ryan's mother laughs and sticks her hand out to Angel. "I'm Mary Ann, Ryan's mom." She turns to Marissa. "Your daughter is lovely," she says, then flushes.

Marissa hugs Angel to her awkwardly. "Inside and out."

Mary Ann wears jeans and a baggy black sweater. Her hair is pulled back in a gray-blond bun stabbed through with a painted wooden stick. Ryan looms over his mother.

She's brought a gift bag full of toys and outfits sized for a much smaller baby, as if she can't believe it's possible that Connor, this grandchild of hers, has been around for nearly eleven months without her knowing. "Oh god," she says, realizing her mistake as soon as Angel pulls the first miniature blue sweater from the gift bag. "I can exchange it all."

Angel holds the sweater against Connor's round belly. "Hard to believe he ever fit into stuff this tiny. But you did, baby. You did, before you grew so big."

"He's beautiful! He looks just like Ryan." She swats her son. "You idiot. How could you be such an idiot? Oh, what a little darling!"

Angel examines Connor's face skeptically. How odd that this is the face she knows best in the world, and yet she has so little perspective on it. She doesn't see Ryan in him, and she doesn't see herself, either. From the first moment she laid eyes on Connor, he's only ever been himself.

"I'm just so sorry," Mary Ann tells Marissa. "I mean, he *knows* about protection. He's a smart kid—who knew he could be such an idiot? Oh, please can I hold him?"

Ryan sits pinching his big red knuckles, but it's a pleased embarrassment.

Angel hands Connor over. He grabs a hank of Mary Ann's hair, which has come loose from the bun, and delivers it to his mouth.

"He likes you, Mom," says Ryan.

Mary Ann feels around Connor's chest, her brows canted in concern. "Have you been taking him for regular checkups? Did they say if he's inherited Ryan's sternum thing?"

"He's fine."

"Whew. I wouldn't wish that on any mother. Imagine if your baby had nothing but skin between the world and his heart! Do you like your pediatrician? I know someone I can recommend."

Ryan puts a hand on her arm. "Angel's got him a doctor, Mom."

Mary Ann turns on her son, admiration lighting her eyes. "You thought to ask?"

Angel can't stop watching mother and son: Mary Ann's bullying affection, Ryan's acceptance of it. Her mother is watching them, too. When their eyes meet, Angel smiles at her mother bravely, and Marissa's eyes fill, her own smile pained. "Of course I'll come," she told Angel when she called earlier that evening. "I'll be right there."

"So, how's the basketball team, Ryan?" her dad asks. He seems ill at ease, but he's trying to make conversation, for which Angel is grateful.

"We had a pretty decent season." And then he's off, talking about the coach and layups and team captains. Three mothers, two fathers, all of them arranged around Connor, who flaps the gift bag around his head. Angel is still tense—her chest aches with tension—but she breathes deeply and counts, the way Brianna taught them. Her own beating heart feels vulnerable and very close to the surface.

As they're leaving, Mary Ann nudges her son. "Go on. Give it to her."

Ryan produces an envelope and hands it to Angel. "It's money. Like, child support."

"We're fine," Amadeo says, his voice hard. "We don't need your money."

Mary Ann laughs. "Of course you do. Human beings are expensive to raise. I told Ryan I'd help him out until he graduates from college, but that he has to have a job starting pronto."

"Right." Her father nods slowly, wary. "Lowe's is hiring. I just started there."

"Really?" says Ryan. "Cool."

Angel turns the envelope in her hand, flushing. "Well, thanks."

"I'm not sure *thanks* is quite right. It's the least you should expect. This is just the beginning. We'll talk more about what you guys need. We're all family now." Mary Ann hands the baby back to Angel. "Bye, little sweetie. Well, we'll let you have your evening." As they head out to the car, Mary Ann reaches up to tousle Ryan's hair.

"Mary Ann?" Angel calls through the screen door.

She turns. "Yeah, hon?"

"Good to meet you."

"Oh, hon. I'm so happy to meet you."

Before Angel shuts the door, Ryan jogs back across the gravel. They regard each other through the screen.

"Thanks for being nicer to me," he says.

"It's okay."

"Well, bye, Angle. Obtuse Angle."

The moment the door is shut, as if aware of the tension draining from the room, Connor sets to wailing. Angel bounces him quiet.

"Well," says Amadeo. "That wasn't too bad, was it?"

"I like them," Marissa says. "They seem like good people."

"Maybe you and Ryan will, you know . . ." Her dad waggles his head to indicate the range of possibilities.

"Yeah, no. Never gonna happen, Dad."

"Still."

Angel kisses Connor's hair, then sets him down. She hoists the platter. "They didn't even take a cookie. We forgot to offer them something to drink."

"Right. Well, that Mary Ann couldn't stop talking long enough to drink anything. We got through it. You did great, Angel."

"Really great," her mom says. She steps closer and says in a low voice, "Listen, Angel, about Mike. I should have listened to you. I'm sorry."

Angel can't look at her mother, because her eyes have filled.

Connor is grasping the edge of the couch. He looks up at his family, grinning crazily, swinging his belly to and fro, swaying on his wobbly legs like a drunk. Delighted by their eyes on him, he pushes off and takes a step and another, emits a screech, and then, startled by his own sound, falls on his bottom. His face is blank for a moment, then cracks into a lopsided smile.

"Whoa!" cries Angel. "Keep trying, baby. You're working hard."

The hermanos are already making their journey up Calvario in their white pants. Amadeo and his daughter and grandson are late, and they stand at the base, watching Isaiah struggle up the dirt path with his cross. The hermanos form a neat line behind Isaiah, swatting their bare backs, and behind them, a cluster of women bend over their clasped hands. In all, there's a dozen or so figures. The wind carries the pito's distant whistle and scraps of the alabados, but they cannot make out the words.

The cool air lifts around them, and the sun is a light shawl across their shoulders. Somewhere down the road, someone starts up a motor. Closer, a family of quail emerges from the chamisa. The parents catch sight of Amadeo and his daughter and stop, and the babies—four identical walnuts—halt, too, bunching up. They swivel their heads back and forth, plumes waving like antennae, then dart back into the brush, feet too fast to see. Everything is alive, going about its business, indifferent to the drama taking place above them on the dusty slope.

"Do you feel left out?" Angel asks. In her arms, Connor shakes his fist, sending out a stream of commanding jabber.

Amadeo considers. He doesn't. Looking back on his own crucifixion the year before, Amadeo remembers a pureness of feeling that he can't recapture.

Watching Isaiah's body bent under the weight of the cross, Amadeo holds in his mind the suffering of that man two thousand years ago, suffering that was new and astonishing, but also just like the suffering of the men crucified beside him, just like the suffering of every person before and after. The tiny form of Isaiah pauses, then continues up the hill.

At their feet, a shiny beetle trundles over the dirt, bottom high. Connor squawks, straining toward the ground. "Here, let me hold him," Amadeo says.

"Anytime." Angel hands the baby over and stretches. Connor puts his fat arm around Amadeo's neck and pats him casually.

"Think he'll ask for the nails?"

"Nah. Isaiah knows better."

To feel a little of what Christ felt, Tío Tíve said over a year ago. And what Christ felt was love. Amadeo doesn't know how he lost track of this. Love: both gift and challenge.

Standing there, the spring air high and dry, the sky a distilled, wincing blue, he wants to explain this to Angel. She pulls her heavy hair back, twirls the length of it until it twists upon itself, then secures the whole thing in a messy bun on her head. It is a simple gesture, assured and graceful. He holds Connor tighter.

"Are there things you wish you'd told Gramma?" Angel asks.

Amadeo is quiet a long moment. "Yeah. I wish I'd thanked her. Hey. You okay?"

"They made it to the top." She shakes Connor's foot, nodding toward Calvario. "See those people, baby? See that man up there? He died for our sins. Yours, too. Like your diaper this morning. That was the stinkiest sin I've ever seen."

The hermanos are tiny at this distance, like toys, like distant figures in a painting. The cross rises, tips one way, then another, settles upright. The figures cluster around it.

"Look, baby." Connor does not follow his mother's finger. He is transfixed by her expression, his own face awash in wonder.

ACKNOWLEDGMENTS

My deepest gratitude is due to my marvelous agent, Denise Shannon, and to my brilliant, insightful editor, Jill Bialosky, who, all those years ago, first asked me if I'd ever considered extending my short story into a novel. Also at Norton, I'm so grateful to Erin Sinesky Lovett, Steve Colca, Drew Weitman, Don Rifkin, Lauren Abbate, and everyone else who helped shepherd this book into being. Many thanks to my copyeditor, Amy Robbins.

My gratitude to Willing Davidson, who edited the story that this book grew out of for the pages of *The New Yorker*.

Thank you to the individuals who spoke with me about their work: Marie Leyba at Española Valley High School; Eric Gallant at the City of Española Police Department; Judy Goldbogen at the office of the Chief Clerk of the New Mexico House of Representatives. Many thanks to Eric Schindler, Lydia Medina, and Joy Leveen at Child and Family Resources for allowing me to visit the classroom at the Maricopa Center for Adolescent Parents. Thank you to my former colleagues at United Way of Tucson and Southern Arizona for their commitment to quality early childhood education, and especially to LaVonne Douville, whose work and mentorship continue to inspire me.

For their medical expertise and friendship, my thanks to Megan Mickley and Margaret Allen.

Tíve's hermandad is a fictional hermandad in a fictional town. There exists, as far as I know, no morada that was once a filling station. Nonetheless, my fictional version is informed by the work of several scholars of the history of penitentes in northern New Mexico and southern Colorado. I'm particularly grateful to the following books: Marta Weigle's *Brothers of Light, Brothers of Blood: The Penitentes of the Southwest* and *The Penitentes of the Southwest*; *Alabados of New Mexico*, edited by Thomas J. Steele, S.J.; Ray John de Aragón's *Hermanos de la Luz, Brothers of the Light*; and Alice Corbin Henderson's *Brothers of Light: The Penitentes of the Southwest*. The text of Amadeo's entrada is from a translation by Bill Tate, included in *Penitente Self-Government: Brotherhoods and Councils, 1797–1947*, by Thomas J. Steele, S.J., and Rowena A. Rivera.

Angela Garcia's *The Pastoral Clinic: Addiction and Dispossession along the Rio Grande* is a beautifully observed study of the painful effects of the region's history of violence and dispossession.

For the time and space to work, I am beyond grateful to the following institutions and their staff who welcomed me so warmly: Yaddo, Willapa Bay AiR, the Virginia Center for the Creative Arts, Hedgebrook, Civitella Ranieri, the American Academy in Rome, the James Merrill House, and the Sitka Center for Art and Ecology. I am especially grateful to MacDowell, where I started this novel, and the Hermitage Artist Retreat, where I finished it. For opening their homes to me to write, I am grateful to Diana Lett and Susan Rosenberg (and George the tortoise). Thanks also to the Bread Loaf Writers' Conference and the gems at Grace Paley Palooza.

For the support and faith, thank you to the Rona Jaffe Foundation and the Elizabeth George Foundation.

To my students and colleagues at Princeton University, the University of Michigan, Stanford University, and Warren Wilson: how very lucky I am to work among you.

For guidance over the years, many thanks to Deb Allbery, Michael Byers, Peter Ho Davies, Jane Hamilton, A. M. Homes, Jhumpa Lahiri, Yiyun Li, Maureen N. McLane, Jim Richardson, Tracy K. Smith, Elizabeth Tallent, Susan Wheeler, and Tobias Wolff. I am forever indebted to three dear mentors who have recently passed away: Eavan Boland, Ehud Havazelet, and John L'Heureux.

Thank you to my beloved readers, who made this book infinitely better. Jennifer duBois, Lara Vapynar, and Sarah Frisch were beyond generous with their critiques. My mother, Barbra Quade, accompanied me on a research trip and gave invaluable feedback on the manuscript. Mary South read this *twice* and plucked me from despair in those dark, early days of the pandemic. I am eternally grateful to Brittany Perham for the You-Are-Not-Alone chant. And thank you especially to Lydia Conklin, whom I've been so lucky to get to write alongside, who reads every word I write, and whose work I am so fortunate to read. I'm grateful for the years.

To the teachers, social workers, activists, nonprofit workers, and community organizers who devote their lives to improving outcomes for vulnerable children, youth, and families: thank you. To those children and youth who fight so hard for their futures and ours: you give me hope.